"[Walker] delivers an outstanding story fraught with sexual tension and a spine-tingling mystery. *The Departed* will keep readers turning pages faster than they think, trying to put the pieces of the puzzle together."
　　　　　　　　　　　　　　　　　　　　—*Fresh Fiction*

"Walker fans will be captivated by this fast-paced story with passionate characters and a suspenseful plot that will leave their emotions bare. A well-crafted combination of paranormal, romance, and suspense, this book has everything."
　　　　　　　　　　　　　　　　　　　　—*RT Book Reviews*

"An entertaining romantic urban fantasy police procedural."
　　　　　　　　　　　　　　　　　　　　—*Genre Go Round Reviews*

"Chilling [and] heart-wrenching . . . A richly emotional and wildly imaginative story that grips the reader with genuine, vivacious characters and a sinuous, flowing plot."
　　　　　　　　　　　　　　　　　　　　—*Fallen Angel Reviews*

THE MISSING

"Suspense that can rip your heart open and leave you raw . . . The characters are absolutely fantastic, from the leads to the side characters."
　　　　　　　　　　　　　　　　　　　　—*Errant Dreams Reviews*

"Walker pulls it off brilliantly . . . [She] certainly has a future in paranormal and/or romantic suspense."　　　　—*The Romance Reader*

"Great romantic suspense that grips the audience."
　　　　　　　　　　　　　　　　　　　　—*Midwest Book Review*

continued . . .

CHAINS

"This book is a double page-turner. The story is thrilling, and the sex just makes it better—two great reasons not to put it down until the end!"
—*RT Book Reviews*

"Breathtakingly wonderful . . . Smoothly erotic . . . Utterly amazing . . . Will definitely keep your pulse racing!"
—*Errant Dreams Reviews*

"Exciting erotic romantic suspense."
—*Midwest Book Review*

FRAGILE

"[A] flawlessly sexy suspense novel . . . Exhilarating."
—*RT Book Reviews*

"An excellently crafted mystery and romance!"
—*Errant Dreams Reviews*

"Suspense, romance, and an ending that I can't say anything about—because that would be a spoiler . . . I recommend reading this one."
—*The Best Reviews*

"Intense, sexy . . . Ms. Walker has created another unforgettable . . . fast-paced, edgy tale."
—*Fallen Angel Reviews*

HUNTER'S FALL

"Shiloh's books are sinfully good, wickedly sexy, and wildly imaginative!"
—Larissa Ione, *New York Times* bestselling author

HUNTER'S NEED

"A perfect ten! . . . [A] riveting tale that I couldn't put down and wanted to read again as soon as I finished."
—*Romance Reviews Today*

HUNTER'S SALVATION

"One of the best tales in a series that always achieves high marks . . . An excellent thriller."　　　　　*—Midwest Book Review*

HUNTERS: HEART AND SOUL

"Some of the best erotic romantic fantasies on the market. Walker's world is vibrantly alive with this pair."　　　*—The Best Reviews*

HUNTING THE HUNTER

"Action, sex, savvy writing, and characters with larger-than-life personalities that you will not soon forget are where Ms. Walker's talents lie, and she delivered all that and more."

—A Romance Review

"An exhilarating romantic fantasy filled with suspense and . . . star-crossed love . . . Action packed."　　　*—Midwest Book Review*

"Fast paced and very readable . . . Titillating."

—The Romance Reader

"Action packed, with intriguing characters and a very erotic punch, *Hunting the Hunter* had me from page one. Thoroughly enjoyable with a great hero and a story line you can sink your teeth into, this book is a winner."　　　　　*—Fresh Fiction*

"Another promising voice is joining the paranormal genre by bringing her own take on the ever-evolving vampire myth. Walker has set up the bones of an interesting world and populated it with some intriguing characters."　　　　*—RT Book Reviews*

THE
REUNITED

SHILOH WALKER

BERKLEY SENSATION, NEW YORK

THE BERKLEY PUBLISHING GROUP
Published by the Penguin Group
Penguin Group (USA) Inc.
375 Hudson Street, New York, New York 10014, USA
Penguin Group (Canada), 90 Eglinton Avenue East, Suite 700, Toronto, Ontario M4P 2Y3, Canada
(a division of Pearson Penguin Canada Inc.) • Penguin Books Ltd., 80 Strand, London WC2R 0RL,
England • Penguin Ireland, 25 St. Stephen's Green, Dublin 2, Ireland (a division of Penguin
Books Ltd.) • Penguin Group (Australia), 707 Collins Street, Melbourne, Victoria 3008, Australia
(a division of Pearson Australia Group Pty. Ltd.) • Penguin Books India Pvt. Ltd., 11 Community
Centre, Panchsheel Park, New Delhi—110 017, India • Penguin Group (NZ), 67 Apollo Drive, Rosedale,
Auckland 0632, New Zealand (a division of Pearson New Zealand Ltd.) • Penguin Books (South Africa),
Rosebank Office Park, 181 Jan Smuts Avenue, Parktown North 2193, South Africa • Penguin China, B7
Jiaming Center, 27 East Third Ring Road North, Chaoyang District, Beijing 100020, China

Penguin Books Ltd., Registered Offices: 80 Strand, London WC2R 0RL, England

This book is an original publication of The Berkley Publishing Group.

THE REUNITED

PUBLISHING HISTORY
Berkley Sensation trade paperback edition / February 2013

Berkley Sensation trade paperback edition ISBN: 978-0-425-24697-9

An application to register this book for cataloging has been submitted to the Library of Congress.

PRINTED IN THE UNITED STATES OF AMERICA

10 9 8 7 6 5 4 3 2 1

Thanks to all the readers who kept asking for
more of these books ...

Ilona, thanks for letting me use your cat.

And a special thanks to Carrie Ann Ryan ... I needed
the physics help.

Thank God, always, for my family. I love you guys!

ONE

HE knew her face.

Joss Crawford wasn't prone to melodrama, he wasn't prone to wishful thinking, and he didn't much believe in fairy tales. He didn't buy into those crazy stories of love at first sight.

But he knew there was a woman for him—he'd been searching for her his entire life, had dreamed about her always. He looked for her in every face he saw, waited for the moment he'd find her again.

And here she was, striding down the pavement, her face grim, her eyes dark . . . the sight of her was a punch, straight to his heart. She didn't *look* like she should, part of his brain insisted. The rest of him didn't care. He knew her, in his gut, in his heart, in his soul.

Standing rigid, barely able to breathe, much less move, he waited for her to look at him, to see him . . . to *know* him. But it didn't happen.

In fact, she was so busy staring at the pavement and making a concentrated effort to ignore everything around her, she didn't even seem to notice him. She went to go around him and he just couldn't stop himself—he stepped right into her path so that she crashed straight into his chest, all lean limbs and long muscles and golden, sun-kissed skin, a nice, solid weight that he figured would fit his body just about perfectly. She stumbled and he reached up, closed his hands around her upper arms, where the cotton of her shirt kept him from touching bare flesh.

He wanted to touch bare flesh . . . after all this time, he figured he just about *needed* to. But not now.

Right now, she was watching him with dazed, distrustful eyes— wariness flashed through her gaze and he felt her tense.

"You . . ." He didn't even know what to say. A total stranger, and that's what he'd seem like to her, he knew. How could he tell her he'd been dreaming of her for always? Waiting. Searching. Absently, without realizing it, he stroked his thumb across her arm, and it rubbed across the bare skin just below the sleeve of her shirt.

As bare skin touched bare skin, he felt something . . . a buzz in his brain.

And more . . . he felt the echo of it in *her* brain. Followed by a blinding rush of knowledge.

Her pupils flared. She sucked in a breath. "*You . . .*"

"*. . . three . . . !*"

* * *

I am too late, *she thought, running even as she heard the gunshots echo. She ran. She ran so hard. So fast. This could not be happening.*

She burst through the cover of the trees just in time to see him stagger. See him fall.

"No!" She lunged for him.

But hard, cruel hands caught her arms.

Whirling around, she swung out, her hand striking that perfect, chiseled face.

She was on the ground a moment later, her eyes tearing from the blow. Her cheek didn't hurt, not yet. It was numb, but already the numbness was starting to fade.

"You would dare strike me?"

Blinking the tears away, she stared up at the man she had once thought she could love. Such a mistake . . . such a horrid, awful mistake. "I know what you did." She tasted blood now, and realized she'd cut the inside of her mouth when he'd struck her.

He smiled down at her. "Do you?"

"Yes." She turned her head, staring at the fallen man. She lifted her hand. "Please . . ."

T W O

Three weeks earlier

"Now...IF you'll just put your hand ... right about *there* ..."
Special Agent Joss Crawford stood to the back of the
group, his craggy face stoic, mouth unsmiling, eyes unblinking. It
took all of his willpower not to laugh. Keeping a straight face
through this joke was a rough gig, but he did it.

He wasn't sure why he kept coming back here. He could get
where he needed to go without this moron's help.

There was a reason he kept doing the tour, though. He'd figure it out sooner or later. For the sake of his sanity and his
patience, he kind of hoped it would be sooner. The idiot irritated
the hell out of him.

"Do you feel it ..."

Bored, he stared at the area the tour guide had indicated.
Nope. He didn't feel a damn thing.

"Yes, you feel it, don't you? Most of you can just *sense* it ..."
the guide murmured, his skinny, ratlike face animated, dark eyes

glinting in the lights of the flashlights. "That *burst* of cold, feel how it radiates. All around. Almost like a cold wind."

It was *a cold wind*, Joss thought, bored. A cold front was projected to move through, and he had a feeling that had something to do with the sudden cool wind.

But he couldn't blame everything on the weather.

Plenty of weird, though, could be laid at the feet of the guide. If anybody with eyes had bothered to look, they would have seen the clues all over the place. At least, he had.

He'd seen where the dry ice had been used.

He'd caught it when the guide had signaled one of his coworkers, too, and not a second later, there had been *mysterious* banging sounds when they'd stopped in the middle of an open field where supposedly hundreds of Seminoles had been slaughtered four hundred years earlier.

You can almost hear their cries, can't you . . .

If the guide hadn't had the timing wrong, Joss might not have been so skeptical.

All in all, he'd definitely gotten his money's worth, he supposed. Joss took his amusements where he could, and they weren't even at the highlight of the tour.

The Oglesby Cemetery.

Every step pulled him closer. Closer. Closer. If he closed his eyes, he could almost imagine he heard the echo of her laugh. But then it was followed by the harsh, broken sound of her screaming. Pain. Darkness . . . torn away from her . . .

You're going crazy, he thought wearily.

And if anybody knew *why* he was here, they just might try to get him committed. He certainly sounded crazy, he knew. Here to keep watch over the grave of a woman who'd died more than a century earlier.

Keep watch—just as he'd done dozens of times over the years.

* * *

"*You*, sir, have the aura of a man in need."

Joss looked down to see the psychic-wanna-be standing in front of him, an anxious look on that skinny face, his hands clasped in front of his chest, his eyes hopeful, shining.

Aw, shit. He wasn't the target for the night, was he?

Then the man lifted a hand . . .

Yes. He was the target.

Each time he'd done this tour, the guy had picked somebody out of his group to focus on. He seemed to think it added something to the show, Joss figured. Hell, Joss could *really* add something to the show. But he wasn't in the mood to have some fake playing tricks on him, and he damn sure wasn't going to go along with the gag, either.

Instead of responding, he just stared at him.

"And you're so closed *off*," Larry "Cap" Rawlings said, his voice heavy and mournful as he peered up at Joss.

Joss stood six-feet-five. Most people had to peer up at him. Normally, people kept some distance, but this guy was practically standing on his toes, so close that Joss could smell the garlic he'd eaten. It wasn't a pleasant experience. Cap had his head tipped so far back, one push against his chest and he'd be off balance enough to end up on his ass.

Joss amused himself with that image but didn't let it show on his face as he continued to stare at the con artist. "What is it?" Cap asked again. "Why are you here? What draws you here? What do you seek?"

Oh, that's a good guess . . . not. Most of these people here were seeking *something*. Either they wanted some sort of proof of life after death, or they wanted a thrill, or they just wanted something to do. A million other excuses, and a person didn't have to be psychic to figure out the people here were *seeking* anything.

If this guy was a psychic, Joss was a prima ballerina.

"Don't know what you're talking about," Joss said, keeping his voice flat, his face blank, and his eyes shuttered. He also deliberately crossed his arms over his chest and looked away—*keep out, keep out, keep out*—the body movements said it all. Assuming the guy knew how to read body language and had half a brain, maybe he'd just walk away and call it quits.

The guy didn't have half a brain. Joss was guessing he was running on about a third.

"Oh, yes. Yes, you do. You seek answers, but you don't even know if you believe in what you see before you. You don't believe in the . . ." He paused dramatically and looked all around. *"Gift."*

Joss had to bite back a laugh.

The . . . *Gift?* The moron probably didn't even *believe* in psychic talent. It was real. Very real. He had a bona fide psychic standing before him, and Joss came with the freak gift of all freak gifts.

He was a mirror—he mirrored the gift of whoever he'd last connected with—partnered with.

And the last person he'd partnered with had been one of the telepaths on the special task force. Eyes slitted, Joss stared hard at Cap and caught a rush of thought. Current thoughts, recent thoughts, all of them coming together—organized chaos settling inside his mind, like they were just as much a part of Joss's brain as Cap's.

"Motherfuck. I should have picked the old broad. She just wants to hear the same garbage old bitches always want to hear, but I get so tired of that tripe. This guy looked like he'd be more fun, but he's not going to do a damn thing . . .

"If tips are good tonight, I'm gonna call Candise—she's going to blow me so hard to make up for shortchanging me last time.

"Damn it, we need to get moving. If it starts to rain, half of these idiots will whine about a refund . . .

"Why in the fuck couldn't there have been any decent girls on this one . . ."

The wind grew sharper, colder. Lifting his face to it, Joss breathed it in. "Do we really need to stand around here while you try to play armchair psychologist, Cap?" Joss said. "I came out here to see the cemetery—I wanted to do the night walk through, and the only way to do it is with you. If it rains before we get through it because you wanted to chatter, I'm going to ask for my money back."

Something ugly flickered in the man's eyes.

Joss stared him down, and as the guide turned away, he smiled.

* * *

HE couldn't get inside.

But he didn't need to.

Just standing out in front of the little family mausoleum filled him with the strangest sense of peace, even as it flooded him with urgency.

When Joss was here, he didn't hear her screams.

But he needed to find her . . . because until he found her, he was only half of who he needed to be.

He didn't hear her screams, but he could remember the echo of her laughter.

The soft murmur of her voice, even if he couldn't follow the words.

Here, he felt like he was closer to her.

Amelie . . .

Sighing, he sat on the single, small stoop and ran a hand

down his face. Lost in the shadows, he rested his head against the
column behind him and looked toward the door. It was dark and
he couldn't read the little plaques over the door, but he knew
them.

Amelie had died first.

A few years later, her parents had passed on.

There was no other family. Just the parents, their daughter.

His Amelie.

He could keep watch over her all night. Seated there on the
stoop in front of a mausoleum of a family long gone, he felt more
complete than he did at any other time in his life.

And he could have stayed there, happily, for hours. Forever,
even. But his phone intruded, vibrating in his pocket.

Joss ignored it, pulling to mind the memory of her face. He
knew her face, had dreamed of her for so long. Longer than he
could remember.

He'd had her face in his dreams for far longer than he'd known
her name, but he knew her face, knew her name . . . knew that
she'd cried over him. Once . . .

Eyes closed, he thought of the plaque that bore her name.

AMELIE CARRINGTON
BORN APRIL 1, 1870
DIED APRIL 1, 1890

Died on her birthday, twenty years . . . to the day.

Amelie.

The name was a song in his mind.

It whispered to him, called to him. And it had ever since the
first time he'd seen it, back when he'd just been a kid, his first
year in college, stumbling through here on a dare with his friends.

It had been pure chance that he'd found this place. He'd

stumbled onto the porch, ended up much like he was now. And he'd looked up. Seen her name . . .

And it hit him.

Chance.

And fate.

Because he'd found the woman he'd dreamed of for so long. The dreams hadn't started here. He'd always had those, but seeing her resting place had ripped open a hole inside him, like tearing open a floodgate.

He dreamed about a woman who'd died. And when he finally found her, it wasn't *her* . . . she'd been gone for years. More than a century.

After he'd seen this place, everything got so much more intense, almost painful sometimes. Dreams that haunted him even when he was awake, the echo of her laughter chasing him at the oddest times.

He couldn't go a week without the dreams. Couldn't go a day without thinking of her.

All the while, he waited.

Obsessed.

Where are you? Am I going to find you?

Questions he'd asked himself for years. Questions that still had no answers.

Off to the left, he could hear the rest of the tour group—they were all walking around carrying coat hangers. *Dousing rods,* that's what good ol' Cap had called them.

Joss could have told all of them that Cap was wasting their time in this part. There weren't any ghosts waiting for them. If there were any ghosts to be found, they were up in the newer part. Not here. Not that he could really see any ghosts, but that remnant energy was a buzz that a lot of psychics were sensitive to, and he wasn't feeling it here.

His phone vibrated again. And again, indicating that whoever was calling was *not* giving up. Scowling, he pulled it out, thinking he should have left the damn thing in his car. But old habits died hard.

It wasn't a surprise to see the name *Taylor Jones* pop up on the screen. But why in the hell was the boss calling him? He had a few days off. Not that the SAC would let a minor detail like that get in the way. The Special Agent In Charge didn't let little details stop him.

Instead of answering it, Joss hit ignore and went to text him. *Busy. What's up?* Once he'd sent the message, he brushed a few leaves off the stoop, some debris. Once he'd almost brought flowers.

But he hadn't. Because something—not a memory exactly—but something . . .

I would rather see the flowers growing than to have somebody cut them so they wither and die . . .

He didn't want to leave her something that would have made her sad.

He thought about bringing something he could plant. Would that be okay? He'd have to check with the people who took care of the cemetery. They'd ask questions—a hassle, but he had some idea that she'd like something that bloomed. Yeah. He could almost see her smile over that.

His phone buzzed again. Aggravated, he glanced at the screen. *You're needed. And my wife wants to know why you're standing in a graveyard.*

Joss scowled and lifted his head, emerging from the shadowed sanctuary of the crypt and studying the area just beyond the fence line.

Well, hell. He'd just been spotted by the rat-faced tour guide. Cap came scurrying his way, a tight frown on his face as he spied the phone. "You need to put that away. Those are very disruptive to the deceased. Spirits don't like technology."

"Really?" Out of pure curiosity, he texted Taylor back. *Ask Dez if the dead care about technology.*

The answer was almost immediate. *Why in the hell should they? It doesn't affect them, and the older ones aren't even aware of it.*

Glancing up at Cap, he smirked. "I have it on good authority that the dead don't care about technology." Resuming his perusal of the cemetery, he eyed the dim shapes of cars, shadows he couldn't quite make out. Then he saw one car, idling a few dozen yards away, and he knew. When he saw it, he sighed and then looked back at Amelie's crypt. He wanted to linger, say something, but he wasn't about to give this guy any sign of his thoughts. He knew better than that.

I'll be back, baby.

* * *

"You're into ghost tours now?" Dez asked as Joss came striding toward them. Up until three months ago, it had been Desiree Lincoln, but then she'd somehow lost her common sense and she'd married Taylor Jones. She was Desiree Jones now.

Joss tried not to hold that against her.

"Yeah. I wanted to do the real thing, but I figured Taylor would punch my lights out if I asked you out on a date to show me the real ghosts," Joss said, flashing a grin at her.

Dez chuckled. "Nah. He's not the violent type. I might punch out a woman for flirting with him, but he's more collected than that."

Under most circumstances, Joss would have agreed with her. Taylor was a cold bastard and nothing affected him—violence usually came because people got worked up over something. Jones didn't do *worked up*, not really.

Dez was a different story.

Jones had hidden that pretty well from most people and that wasn't particularly easy, considering how he was surrounded by psychics on a daily basis. If anybody could block out their thoughts, it would be Taylor. He had that control thing down pat. Were somebody to look up the word *contained*, they just might see Taylor's picture next to the definition.

But Joss was around Taylor more than most of the others, and if the boss had anybody he'd call a friend, it was Joss. The two of them had spent many a long night together, and usually, Joss had his head jacked up with somebody else's talent, a skill that let him read the heart, the mind, or both. Taylor wasn't the easiest person to read, but eventually Joss figured out that the boss had feelings for Dez that were anything but cool and collected.

Speaking of the boss, he looked over at the car and saw the man of the hour. "You know, I'm supposed to be off. For like the next five days straight. I haven't had many of those mythical off days lately, and I specifically requested a few days of personal time."

"Yes, you did." Taylor shrugged. "Sorry, Crawford. This just got dumped in my lap rather unexpectedly and it can't wait. Your particular talents are needed."

Joss snorted. "My particular talents are nonexistent. I'm a fucking myna bird. I mimic everybody else. Find whoever I mimic and stick them in."

"I can't . . ." He shifted a look at Dez.

It was just a bare glance—a quick flick—and then his eyes were back on Joss's face. But it was enough. Okay . . . so Jones wasn't willing—or able—to send his woman into this? Was that it?

Dez sighed and ran her fingers through her hair. It was a little longer than she usually wore, falling almost to her chin. "He needs more than a ghost talker on this gig, Joss. But if he sends in more than one person, we'll be made. And besides, I'm not exactly the . . . ideal . . . person to do this. And I'm assuming the other person isn't going to work any better than I will."

Joss had heard her. He had. But the one thing his mind focused on was *"more than a ghost talker."*

A sinking sensation settled in Joss's gut.

Without even look at the man, without opening his mind, he knew. "You're going to mind-fuck me again, aren't you?"

Silence stretched out between them.

Finally, Taylor sighed. "Joss, I don't have much choice. You're the only man I've got who can do this. You're the only agent I've got who can pick up any given ability at any given time; I need multiple abilities and I need them now."

"Where?" He didn't bother trying to talk his way out of it. There was no point. He was in this line of work because he had to be. He wasn't in it for fun, for kicks, or for the money. If he was needed, then so be it. He was needed. After one last glance at the garden of stone, he looked toward Taylor. The pull had been stronger this time . . . so much stronger . . .

"Just an hour south. In Orlando."

THREE

"*J*UST . . . GET *away.*" *Blood trickled from his mouth as he spoke.* "*Get away from him, Amelie. Don't let him . . .*"

"*Shhh. Hush, now. Do not fret about me. You need to save your strength,*" *she told him as the blood burned out of him to stain the ground beneath him red. This was her fault. Hers. If she had just left with him as he'd asked . . .* "*Just rest, love. Will you do that for me?*"

He squeezed her hand. "*You have to get away from him. Promise me . . .*"

He pushed something into her hand. Whispered it again. "*Promise . . .*"

* * *

FROM the penthouse, she could see the bright lights of the amusement park . . . and the castle. A bit of whimsy hit her, and she remembered how she'd once stood at the base of that castle as a child, gazing up at it in rapt wonder.

She was glad that girl no longer existed, glad that girl had had the wool ripped away from her eyes a good long time ago, so she couldn't see what was happening to her now.

Glad the girl she'd been wasn't still sitting around waiting for her Cinderella moment. If Drucella Chapman had a Prince Charming in her future, she'd yet to find him. And if he was lurking around, well . . . he'd have to get in line. She had a job to do.

Resting her hands on the balustrade, she thought of the so-called *prince* who was currently in her life. He was more like a snake.

He was the villain of the piece, in truth. And she was trapped with him. For now.

Two years . . . bloody hell. How had she lost two years to this?

Sighing, she lowered her gaze, stared at her hand. It wasn't supposed to be this damned complicated. Patrick Whitmore wasn't supposed to be part of her life, not like this.

Yet here she was, wearing his ring. And in a few short weeks, she was supposed to marry him. It wasn't supposed to happen this way. She should have been done by now, well before this travesty of a wedding. But if she didn't find some way to end this, find some way to pull off a bloody miracle, she was going to be Mrs. Patrick Whitmore very shortly.

Backing out just wasn't an option.

Too much was at stake.

If she had to marry the devil himself to fix things, then she'd do it.

Of course, that wasn't too far off from what she was doing.

It made the bitter pill she had to swallow even more distasteful. The practical, cynical part of her knew she had to do it. So she pulled that practical bitch to the forefront as she turned from the window and made herself ignore what should have been a magical sight.

Patrick Whitmore was just another mark. A job. Nothing more. Nothing less. It was taking a little longer than normal to get that job done, but she'd get it done and then she'd move on . . . forget about the evil that was Patrick Whitmore.

If she *could* . . .

Finish the job first. Then she could worry about getting away . . .

You have to get away from him . . .

Scowling, she shoved that bit of memory back to her mind. Ever since meeting Whitmore, she'd been plagued by nightmares, nasty ones. Her dreams had never been particularly pleasant. So much worse than the typical dream, one where she'd be naked in front of a class, weirder than dreams of talking animals or nightmares where she ran endlessly . . .

There was no understanding her dreams, no understanding why they'd gotten so much worse lately.

And she'd rather not think about them if she didn't have to. She always died in them. Why would *anybody* want to think about that?

The dreams got worse until she'd resorted to taking sleeping pills and hoping they'd helped. The dreams couldn't interfere with the job. With the blasted wedding.

Dru sighed and pushed a hand through her hair. "My bloody wedding."

At least she didn't have to feign the interest in planning it. That was all being done for her, and all she had to do was fake interest in what *they* were doing. Pretend to be excited, pretend to be nervous.

And it wasn't a far stretch for her. She *was* excited. Several years' worth of work were coming down to the finish line. She *was* nervous, and she had every right to be so. After all, if he found her out, he'd very likely kill her. She was on her own and nobody would stop him. Nobody would care.

I could kill you . . .

She jerked her mind back to the matter at hand as those insubstantial bits of thought tried to settle inside her head once more.

He *could* kill her. And she knew it wouldn't be a first for him. He could kill. He had. So she had to be careful.

The knock at the door caught her off guard.

Closing her eyes, she blew out a breath. *It's bloody well past time he let me sleep*, she thought, scowling at her toes. Then she smoothed away the scowl, checked her reflection. She had a part to play. A job to do.

A job she was damn good at.

When Dru opened the door, she did it with a smile on her face.

"Hello, darling," Patrick said, dipping his head to brush his lips against hers.

Her instinct was to flinch away. Dru had long since learned to control those instinctive little tells and she held still under the cool, dry brush of his mouth, smiling at him. "Patrick, what a pleasant surprise. I wasn't expecting to see you so late."

"I just wanted to see you, see how you were settling in, Ella. It's an odd place you wanted to stay." He made no attempt to hide his distaste.

"If this is too much, Patrick, I can find someplace else," she said, folding her hands together, her eyes on the pale cream of the carpet. Taking a stab at his wallet was the best way to get what she wanted. He'd told her she wouldn't be moving in until after the wedding, and although part of her was thankful for that, the other part was frustrated. What if the answers she needed were on the estate?

There were ways around that part, though, and she'd do better if she was someplace more . . . public. Not to mention that she didn't want to be anyplace remotely private, not if she could avoid it.

It had been easy enough, giving him a convincing reason why she wanted to stay here close to the park. Although why she was so certain she had to be *here*, she didn't know. "I just . . . well, I have happy memories of this place. The park, you see," she hedged, glancing out the window at the brightly lit castle. It wasn't a lie. Back in that other life, her parents had brought her to this place, back when she'd still had some bit of innocence to her, back when some part of her had believed in magic.

Back before her life was overrun by monsters.

Like the one standing before her. "Would you like me to stay elsewhere, darling?" she asked, giving him a demure smile.

He waved a hand. "Don't be silly, Ella. I just fail to see the appeal." He glanced around, eyeing the remains of her meal, her laptop. "Are you settling in well?"

"Of course." For the past eighteen months, she'd commuted back and forth between London and Orlando—or rather, that was *Ella's* story. She'd had a lovely apartment here in the States, a lovely flat back home in London. And then three weeks ago, her "employer" let her go . . . oh, the tragedy.

Patrick had been quite happy to step in and take over her life. He'd been ready to do that for quite a while anyway.

The employer was a contact of hers and the job had been real enough, another way to solidify her life as "Ella."

She'd done this sort of deep cover work, but never for so long. Never with the risks so high. For the most part, she was on her own. She'd been treading water, though, and unable to get close enough to him to find more information. So she "lost" her job as a courier, damn all the downsizing companies do these days, although the boss had been quite nice about it and explained that they'd decided to let her go first since she'd be leaving the company shortly—she was getting married, right?

Naturally, Patrick was there to take her life over.

She wondered how he'd ever react if she told him that *he* was the *real* job.

"Ella . . . you're distracted."

Forcing herself to smile, she said, "I'm sorry, Patrick. I was thinking of how wonderful you've been, finding me this place to stay, taking care of me."

He brushed a kiss across her cheek. "You still look tired. You should get more rest, Ella."

Ella . . . yes. The part she played. Along with the lovely rooms, the lovely clothes. The elegant demeanor and the doormat exterior she presented him with. With him, she was *Ella* and she settled seamlessly into that part, smiling at him. "Of course." *Of course I look tired. You have me followed everywhere I go, and although I can bloody damn well lose them, if I do that too often, you'll wonder how I'm able to do it.*

Tired. *Tired* didn't even touch how she felt. Living a lie all this time, hoping against hope . . . losing herself. It had been two years since she had first waded into this job, twelve months since it had completely sucked her in, and every day she felt like she'd died a little more inside. Bloody hell, *yes*, she was tired.

Stop it. Not now, she told herself. Keeping her smile plastered firmly on her face, she moved to sit on the sofa, waiting for him to join her, but he didn't.

He chose to remain standing, looming over her, silent. Watchful. Controlling, egotistical bastard.

She didn't react as he continued his probing stare. After nearly a minute, a faint smile curved his lips and he looked away, moving to the bar to fix himself a drink.

She let herself take a slow breath, wishing her racing heart would slow down. What in the hell was that about? No telling, really. She was terrified of the son of a bitch, but she couldn't let him see that. It would only make him worse. Looking down, she stared at the sophisticated, elegant ring she wore.

It should be getting easier. She was getting closer. She *knew* she was—and her contact had even managed to show her proof. It was sealed up, tight and safe for now. But they needed more. More solid info . . . and an exact location would be nice. Something more than the few incriminating photos. That would be even better.

Could they find it soon enough, though?

Find it, she thought tiredly. She'd thought she'd find something *soon* two years ago, when she'd first stumbled onto this. It had been tangled threads that had led her here, and the more she'd unraveled those threads, the deeper she'd fallen into this mess.

And she was so deep now, she started to worry if she'd ever get out. If she'd survive.

Sometimes, like now, those fears got to be too much, and the weight of what she was doing crashed down so heavily. When that happened, she made herself remember *why* she was doing this. She thought of a girl. A poor, lost girl . . . So much time had passed that sometimes the girl's face would start to fade. Then something would bring it back. Something . . . like Patrick's cruelty. A touch from him . . .

She let herself think about the girl, gave herself a minute to shore up her strength, all the while projecting an outer image of calm. It was worth it, no matter what. In the end, Patrick would go down and he'd never hurt another young woman. She had to remind herself of that, even at times like this when she felt so completely stuck.

"I've been thinking about taking a day away at a spa," she said abruptly, turning around and smiling at him. "I heard about a lovely one that I'd like to try."

"I'll have my assistant set a day up for you here. We've got wonderful facilities, as I'm sure you already know."

Yes . . . someplace just under your nose. What she wanted was to be someplace completely away from his influence. Where he'd have no way of watching over her, spying . . .

Except she had to be close to him for her to get her job done.

He lifted a hand, laid it on her shoulder. The touch was light. "You're not getting . . . nervous . . . are you, Ella?"

Nervous. *Bugger all.* Just his touch made a rush of cold snake through her—water, black and icy, closing over her . . . sucking her under. Brutal hands. Hard laughter.

Did you really think I'd let you leave . . .

Shaken, she forced those dark, odd *terrifying* thoughts aside. *Have to get a grip.* Suppressing the urge to shudder, she eased away from him and went to the bar under the pretense of pouring herself a glass of wine. "A bit, perhaps. A wedding is a rather important event for any bride."

Even an unwilling one . . .

"Just think of it more as a business arrangement," he advised, following her. Once more, he cupped his hands over her shoulders. Squeezed. A little too tight, a little cruel, until his fingers ground into her bones, but it lasted only a second. She swallowed the gasp before it could escape, knowing that any reaction would only make it worse the next time he tried to do it.

She'd learned her lesson well over the past few months.

Through her lashes, she watched as he moved deeper into the

room, like he owned the place. Just as he *thought* he owned her. "A business arrangement," he said again, turning to smile at her. "Thinking about it that way makes it so much easier to ignore any nervous inclinations, don't you think?"

"Of course." She inclined her head, smiling at him as her shoulders throbbed. *One of these days, you icy piece of work, I'll bloody you*. It was a promise she'd made herself months ago.

After the first time he'd hit her.

It was a promise she intended to keep. She'd do it for herself, and for every woman he'd hurt. And there had been so many . . .

"Of course, I shouldn't worry," she murmured as he crossed the floor and settled on the couch, smiling at her, satisfaction glinting in his eyes. He'd hurt her . . . frightened her, even if she refused to show it. He still knew.

Hell, she suspected he *liked* that she didn't show her fear. Made her that much more useful as a showpiece. That's why he wanted to get married anyway.

It was a business arrangement, and that had never been in any doubt.

It's time I found a wife. I believe we suit each other. Neither of us are looking for emotional entanglements, after all.

No. She wasn't looking for an emotional entanglement. She was looking for a way to ruin his life, but that wasn't emotional. Or it hadn't started out that way, at least.

"So, enough with the nerves, right, Ella?" he said, eyeing her narrowly.

"Of course." She smiled at him over the rim of her glass. "It's a business arrangement, naturally. But a wedding is an important thing for a woman. Easier said than done, trying to not be nervous. I'll do better about it, I promise."

"Glad to hear." He studied her critically. "Worrying does you no good. It will give you wrinkles."

Wrinkles—

It was almost laughable. If only that were the worst of her problems.

She had much bigger things to worry about . . . staying alive. Staying two steps ahead of him. Actually, ten would be ideal.

FOUR

"WE'RE closing in on what I think may be the core group for a large human trafficking operation." Special Agent in Charge Taylor Jones sat across from Joss, still wearing a perfectly pressed three-piece suit.

Joss knew enough about clothes to realize it probably cost more than Joss usually spent on clothes in six months. He also knew that the guy had probably been wearing the damn thing all day, but Jones looked like he'd just stepped off the front of a magazine—polished and smooth. That suit might fool a lot of people, just like the impassive face.

Taylor Jones projected the image of a cool, uncaring son of a bitch.

And very often, he was a cool son of a bitch.

Some of the others in the unit thought he had auspicious, lofty desires—maybe political aspirations.

They were wrong, Joss knew.

Taylor's aspirations were simple and not particularly lofty at all. He wanted to put away the monsters. As many of them as he could. The men and women in his unit were the weapons he used to fight the monsters.

It was something he and Joss had in common; it was one of the reasons they got along well enough. They understood each other.

Normally. Right now, Joss was still pissed off. He'd been looking forward to that downtime. More important, he really hated it when Taylor had him get mind-fucked. It was a brutal, awful experience he'd had to do more than once, and each time, he hoped it was done, even though he knew better.

"Just how large an op?" he asked, snagging a French fry from Dez and popping it into his mouth. He'd polished off his Big Mac and fries on the drive over. He was still hungry.

Dez scowled at him. "Leave my fries alone."

He winked at her.

"Children, please," Jones said. He reached down and grabbed a bag, placed it on the table, and pushed it over to Joss. "You'll end up dead of a coronary, the way you eat, Crawford."

"Yeah, well, if it happens, just don't let anybody send flowers . . . I don't want flowers at my funeral." He opened the bag and glanced inside. It was another order of fries. "Man, it's like you read my mind . . . oh, wait, that's my thing."

"You're so juvenile." Dez glanced at him. "Who did you sync him to for the mind reading? Will it hold?"

"No."

Joss and Jones spoke at once.

Dez arched a brow.

Jones gestured and remained silent.

"I'll get overridden. Whoever you want to put in my head, it has to be at the same time. The previous gift will get wiped out—

think of me as a computer, sort of. Each time I sync with some-body, whatever gift I had before gets erased. I get rebooted."

For a second, Dez stared at him, her dark eyes unreadable, and then finally, she shook her head. "Man, that's gotta really suck. How do you control it, taking it in like that?"

"Well, that's the cool part." He grinned at her. "As long as our brave and fearless leader syncs me to somebody with some modicum of control, I take in what they have—again, it's like my brain is a computer and I just copy the data. If you give me bad data? I'm screwed and I've gotta go through the bad data and clean things up before I'm any good, but if you give me solid, good data to work with? Then I'm fine."

"You mean, as long as you're hooking up to somebody who's trained, you're picking up on their training, too?" She glared at him.

"That's it in a nutshell." He shrugged and dragged a French fry through the remaining ketchup, popping it in his mouth. "Before you glare at me, remember . . . if he sticks me with some-body who's screwed up, I'm screwed up until I get a handle on it."

Dark memories rolled through him—he'd dealt with that more often than he cared to remember, but rarely had it been at Jones's hands. It had happened before he realized just what was going on in his head. Jones had been the one to help him get a handle on things.

But he'd been a mess for a while there. A nightmare that he'd rather not have to go through again.

* * *

It was nearly eleven before Patrick finally left.

Dru locked the door and stood there, her head pressed against the cool, smooth surface, and took a deep breath in, blew it out.

Her mouth hurt from the kiss he'd just given her. Although it hadn't really been a kiss.

The son of a bitch had bitten her.

One more mental mark. One more thing he would eventually pay for, Dru told herself.

And if she didn't *need* to finish this job . . . well, she might have put a bullet in his brain before he even made it to the elevator.

But there was the job.

Of course, she'd gotten a good, solid reminder of that right when he'd sunk his teeth into her lip, hard enough to draw blood, hard enough to hurt. She'd felt his pleasure in it—not sexual, precisely. Just a pleasure for causing pain, and then . . . *flash, flash, flash* . . . she was there. It was like a brilliant whirl of light as the memory transfer took place, all happening in the blink of an eye—too fast for her to process, as the memories burned from his mind into hers.

It lasted microseconds for him—he never even seemed to notice. But for her, it was slow, insidious torture, being trapped in the filth of his mind as her awful gift connected them.

Trapped inside his mind was even worse than suffering his touch; it was an ugly place. Filled with memories and thoughts she'd rather never know.

The chunk of memory had lodged inside her head, rather like a bit of food she hadn't properly chewed. It sat there, trapped in her mind, choking her and waiting for her to either get it down or die.

She'd deal with it. He wouldn't do her in as easily as that, the wanker.

First things first, though . . . she dumped the dry red wine she'd poured herself earlier. She hated that fucking shite. Give her a mixed drink, give her a beer, or give her a decent wine that didn't leave her feeling like her mouth was full of sand and she was fine, but those dry reds that Patrick loved . . . she hated them.

After she'd dumped it down the drain, she rinsed out the sink and the glass then mixed herself a rum and diet, heavy on the rum. As she took a sip, she headed over to the wall, dimmed the light.

Once she'd done that, she made her way back to the door. It wasn't the most comfortable spot, but if he came back, she'd rather have a warning and all it took was a physical nudge to pull her back. Having the door open at her back would do it.

Stretching out her legs, she grabbed the book she kept on the table nearby. She'd done this more than once. Being prepared just might save her life.

After she'd downed a third of her drink in one swallow, she closed her eyes. And then she opened her mind . . . fell into his, into that little chunk of memory she'd lifted from him. Fell into a nightmare.

*   *   *

"*. . . THAT one should suit him.*"

"*Awful fucking skinny,*" *somebody muttered.* "*Be like boning a damn chicken.*"

The girl hovered on the floor, clutching her knees to her chest, as though she could just disappear into the hard slab of concrete under her naked butt. But she couldn't disappear, and try as she might, she couldn't shake their notice, either.

Patrick hauled her up, eyeing her critically. "*She's his type. Clean her up. A red dress. It should suit her coloring. We want classy, not one of those whore's dresses you like.*" *He tossed the words over his shoulder before looking back at the woman.* "*You need a shower. You'll bathe. You'll wash your hair. You'll wear the dress.*"

And she just nodded.

He smiled at her. Two weeks ago, one of his girls had tried to argue, tried to fight. And all of them had been witness to what happened after. He'd turned her over to his men. By the time they were done, she'd been bleeding. They'd hauled her bleeding, argumentative ass out into the swamps.

She'd made a nice meal for one of the alligators once his men had broken her legs, her hands. She'd been left just outside the fencing, gagged and crippled. He'd watched her struggle for a while, watched as she tried to crawl. She had even managed to drag herself a few dozen yards.

He'd sat in his security room and watched, recording it. It wasn't that he'd enjoyed watching the woman die, her screams muffled by the gag as the gator tore into her flesh. But they all had to understand how things were done. They were done his way. And only his way.

He'd recorded it, and the women had watched it the next day. A useful training tool for those who'd try to fight.

Rule with an iron fist. It might cost the lives of a few in the end, but most of them got the point early on.

This had been a lesson none here would forget.

Certainly not this lovely piece. He could still see the fear, the lurking horror in her eyes.

Her dark, dazed eyes just stared into his.

"Am I understood?" he asked softly, touching her cheek.

Again, she nodded.

"You'll have to speak tonight. My buyer likes a woman who can talk. Speak up."

"Yes." Tears rolled down her face. "I understand, sir."

His buyer . . .

The flash of memory ended there.

But it was something. A compound. That was a new thing— Dru hadn't ever picked up that much from him before. He didn't own anything in *his* name that could be considered a compound.

At least not that she'd been able to unearth. She'd unearthed plenty, too, but that had been a while back, before she went so deep into this lie she lived.

Who knows what he'd obtained in the months since then?

Her contact was always watching, always digging up more, but they had to keep their discussions brief. Until one of them had solid proof, he didn't tell her anything she didn't need to know.

A compound. Would have to be big, she knew. Gators. Her belly rebelled as that memory rolled through her. She'd watched . . . aw, hell. Tears stung her eyes. Nausea churned in her belly and horror left her numb. Lifting her hands to her face, she gave herself a minute. Just a minute to mourn, to shudder and cringe. The need to vomit churned through her and she breathed shallowly, waiting for the urge to pass.

This was why she was here.

Why she had to do this.

Even if that was a memory she'd rather never, ever have in her mind, it served to remind her.

Somebody, damn it, somebody had to stop him.

And so far, it seemed that somebody was her.

With trembling hands, she reached for her drink, drained the glass. It didn't do a damn thing to numb the horror, so she shoved herself upright and lurched her way back over to the bar. More alcohol. That was what she needed, just to think through this.

He'd let that girl get eaten . . . had crippled her. Just so it would happen.

"*Fuck.*" She groaned, closing her eyes. This was way more than she was capable of handling. She was so far in over her head . . .

I could kill you . . .

Sensation swamped her—

Awful cold closing over her head. Sucking her under. Stealing her away . . . and she welcomed it.

"Not now," she whispered, pressing a fisted hand to her temple. Mental breakdowns later. Much later.

* * *

Two drinks later, Dru stumbled to bed.

She was so bloody tired of all this, her head aching from the stress, body sore, eyes gritty. It wasn't just the memory flashing, although it hit her hard. It was everything. The constant fear, her anger, the knowledge that it was just a matter of time before she was trapped into marrying that arse . . . it was a no-win situation. She would either find the evidence she needed *before* she married him, or she did it after.

Well, not that it would be a real marriage. After all, she couldn't exactly enter into a binding contract if she was lying through her teeth about who she was, could she?

Yet another fear she carried. That Patrick would find out who she was . . . really. Oh, the false persona she was operating under was solid. It had been crafted by the best in the business. But all it would take was one person who knew her. One mistake. Anything.

"Anything," she mumbled. *And I could be the next alligator meal.*

Sinking down on the bed, she curled into a ball and hugged her legs to her chest, still wearing her pants and tank top. Lying there in the dark, she closed her eyes and tried not to think. Tried not to think about all the ways this could go wrong. Just one slip-up. One mistake . . .

Sometimes the urge to cry was overwhelming, but she never let the tears break free. The monster who was her *fiancé* had her room bugged. She'd found them all the first day she'd been in there. She was careful to ignore them, but she'd be damned if she showed her weakness in front of them. Snagging a pillow, she buried her face against it and fought to battle back the tears of weariness and frustration.

Soon, she told herself. It was the mantra that had gotten her through all of this. *Soon.*

Because it was better to sleep angry than scared, she pulled the image of that girl to her mind and let herself think about her. Sarah.

A runaway.

A girl who had been dead for well over a year, and who, *somehow*, was connected to Patrick.

Just thinking of her, concentrating on the girl's face was enough to let it happen, and one of the memory connections flared to life . . .

*   *   *

FLASH, flash flash . . .

"Please . . . just let me go!"

She huddled in the corner. He ignored the tears on her face as he studied her features. She was younger than some of the women he usually took, but she was too pretty for him not to take. "Are you a virgin?"

Her porcelain-pale complexion flushed and she flinched as though he'd struck her, shaking even harder. "Let me go, please," she pleaded. "My mom, my dad . . . they'll pay. They have lots of money."

Patrick laughed. "They don't have enough." Then he nodded at his men. "Check her . . . and be careful." He doubted she'd have a hymen intact, but if she did, the amount of money he'd get for her would double. She was extremely attractive and very young. Some men would pay a ridiculous amount of money for those traits alone. Throw virginity into the mix, and he could be looking at a very sizeable sum of money. Something about the horror in her eyes made him think it was entirely possible.

As his men started toward her, she screamed and shot him a desperate look. "Please don't let them touch me," she begged. "I'll . . . I'll tell you anything. Just . . . just don't . . ."

He arched a brow. "Then answer my question. Are you a virgin?"

She dunked her head. "Yes."

"Wonderful." He smiled and jerked his head, calling his men away. She'd still have to be checked. But he'd have somebody inspect her who would know how to be cautious. "What is your name?"

She swallowed and darted a look at him. "Sarah."

* * *

Two weeks after that, Sarah was dead in a ditch.

Dru lay on the bed, dry-eyed and filled with the anger that had carried her through this job. Sarah had definitely been a virgin. Patrick had been very happy with that and he had a buyer on the East Coast who had wanted her personally delivered.

Patrick had actually *told* the girl what was going to happen to her.

And the girl had done something both incredibly brave . . . and incredibly foolish. More and more girls were aware of their bodies these days. Since the so-called buy had wanted a virgin with an intact hymen, the girl had decided not to *have* an intact hymen. Somewhere during the trip to meet her would-be owner, she'd done what she thought would set her free, or at least Dru assumed that was what she'd done.

Nobody would ever know just *what* she'd done, because when Patrick's men found her in the bathroom of the hotel and dragged her out to Patrick, she had blood on her thighs. And that prized hymen was no more.

Patrick hadn't handled it well.

By the time his men were done with her, even her own father wouldn't have recognized her.

They left her, discarded on the street like so much garbage.

And Dru had made it her mission in life to stop the monster responsible.

* * *

DREAMS awaited her . . . they rose up the second she fell asleep and pulled her under.

Screaming.

Just the screaming. That was all she heard at first. But then, slowly, she began to hear the whispers.

Help us . . .

We're trapped . . .

The voices of girls.

Beyond that, another voice . . . a man's voice . . . *You've got to get away from him. Promise . . .*

Such a low, urgent plea.

He'll kill you . . . a woman's voice. It was a different voice from the other voices . . . calm and controlled, where the others were panicked and terrified. Sad, though, like Dru's death was a foregone conclusion.

He'll kill you if you're not careful.

Dru was trying to be careful. But she had a feeling she was dead anyway.

He'll kill you . . .

In the dream, she saw the blood. She could smell it—thick and sickly sweet—hovering around her. She could taste the pain in the air, heavy with horror and despair.

She wanted to run.

He'll just find you . . . he finds all of them.

But he couldn't find her. Not if she ran hard enough. She knew how—

He finds them all . . .

In her dream, she struggled to breathe while the sheets wrapped around her like chains.

Gasping for air, she tried to break free of the dream, but all it did was shift . . . re-form. She was no longer running, but sinking. Struggling against the icy waters that sucked her under as the oxygen bled away.

Through the murky dark waters, she saw a pair of eyes, staring down at her. Patrick. And he was smiling. She saw the empty void of his soul reflected in his eyes as he watched her.

Did you really think I'd just let you leave . . .

She hadn't come here to *leave*—she'd come to die.

Die . . . yes. She'd wanted to die. Hadn't she? Water rushed into her mouth and she choked. But if she'd wanted to die, why was she fighting this?

As her life trickled away, as she struggled to surface, her heart ached. Wept. *Just let go . . . he's already gone . . . you can go to him. Be with him.*

He . . . ? Who? She didn't know, but she felt like she should.

It doesn't matter. Just let go. Then that monster can't hurt you anymore.

But she didn't want to die.

She wasn't ready. *Yes, you are . . . isn't that why you came back here?*

"No!"

* * *

I'M not ready, he thought dimly, watching her even as the darkness closed in around him. He wanted to hold her. One more time.

"You must save your strength . . ."

No. That wasn't what he had to do. He had to find a way to make her understand. She had to get away—had to get away now, before it was too late . . .

"You have to get away from him. Promise me."

She watched him, her lovely green eyes misted by tears. They were darker, it seemed . . .

"Promise," he demanded as he realized her eyes weren't darker. Everything had gotten dark. He could hardly see. Fuck all. He couldn't see. So weak, he couldn't move. Desperately, he reached down and pulled the knife from his belt, shoved it into her hands. It was a workingman's knife, too big for her hands, but it was something. He squeezed her hand. "Amelie, you must run. Now . . ."

He wasn't ready. He'd promised he'd see her safe. But he could not do that now . . .

Her only chance was to run—

FIVE

R^{*UN—*}
    Even as he came awake, that word echoed through his mind. Joss jackknifed up off the bed, one hand pressed against his gut, where he would have sworn he could feel the brutal, horrifying agony of a bullet lodged inside.

Except he'd come awake like this a hundred times, a thousand. More. Ever since he was nineteen, and he'd stumbled across that mausoleum. Before that, he'd just dreamed about her.

After that, he'd dreamed about his death. The bullet tearing into him. His knowledge that he'd leave her alone. That she'd be vulnerable, that he wouldn't be able to protect her.

So much worse. So very vivid.

And anytime he was close to where he'd found her, close to the cemetery, the dreams were even more powerful.

Apparently, Orlando was close enough to jack him up.

Somehow, Joss didn't think he'd be getting many restful nights. He was stuck here for a while.

* * *

"THERE'S nothing in these damn reports," Joss growled, throwing down a thick stack of paper.

Hours after he'd climbed out of bed, he was ready to fall straight back into it, but he didn't know if he'd get that wish anytime soon. Taylor had kept his ass trapped inside this hotel all damned day, and he was about ready to go out of his ever-loving mind.

And they hadn't even done the thing that was going to *really* drive him up a wall. Joss had to assume they were still awaiting the arrival of whatever agent they needed to sync him with, but he wished they could get it the hell over with.

Taylor eyed him from across the sleek, gleaming wood of the dining room table, one blond brow cocked. The boss had been doing the same thing Joss had—studying reports, photographs, websites—things that had Joss's brains about to bleed out of his ears, but he looked unperturbed and collected, just like he had looked eleven hours earlier.

Joss felt like strangling himself with his shoelaces at this point.

"Is there a problem?"

Shoving back from the table, Joss stood up and started to pace. The understated luxury of the hotel room felt like it was closing in on him. It was a nice hotel—*nice* with a capital *N*, meaning Jones was probably paying for it out of his own pocket. The Bureau wouldn't spring for places like the Peabody.

Jones normally didn't, to Joss's recollection, but maybe it had something to do with his new wife. Dez was stretched out on the couch, doing the same thing they'd been doing. Reading reports. Well, right now, she was *pretending*, but Joss wasn't fooled.

She was running on the same, maxed-out level of stress that he was, but he suspected she had reason. There were shadows in her eyes, sadness in her face. A ghost tugging at her, he could tell. Maybe more than one.

He hadn't done a damn thing yet and he was already going nuts. He didn't even know why.

Joss felt like his skin had shrunk down about two sizes, and he couldn't stay there and keep twiddling his thumbs . . . *waiting*. Eyeing the neatly organized mountains of paperwork, Joss shook his head. "There's nothing *here* for me, boss."

He lifted up a photograph, staring at the girl's picture and wishing it would bump something loose inside his brain, but all he felt was a stir of pity, a rush of anger.

She had been thirteen years old when she went missing.

Yaeli was found three years later, thanks to an anonymous tip. The tip led them to an unmarked grave in Rhode Island. Her father was still in Mexico. Her mother lived in New York. They hadn't gone to the police when she disappeared because her mother was in the States illegally . . . a common story. One that would have no happy ending, and possibly no justice, either.

Joss stroked his finger down the picture. *I'm sorry, sweetheart.*

If he was going to find any justice for her, it would be after they synced him with his next gift set, because he felt absolutely nothing now . . . except that pity, and the rage.

Unable to stare into those dark eyes anymore, he set the picture aside and looked up at Taylor. "There's nothing here for me. Call me when there's either new information or you're ready to do the mind-fuck on me."

He was done.

He couldn't keep reading about all those lost souls . . . disappearance after disappearance.

Not when he kept hearing the sad echo of a woman's soft cry in his mind.

* * *

"Wow. He's as charming as ever," Dez murmured as Joss stalked out. He didn't exactly *slam* the door, but he definitely closed it with a lot of emphatic firmness, she decided. Slanting her husband a look, she added, "No wonder you two get along. You're like birds of a fricking feather. Only he's not as diplomatic as you are."

Jones shrugged. "Crawford can use diplomacy when he has to. Right now, he doesn't have to and he's pissed off. I've run him into the ground lately. There's just no . . ." Sighing, he dropped his pen onto the table and rubbed his eyes.

"No choice," Dez finished for him. Absently, she rubbed her arms and then reached for a blanket. She was cold to the bone, something she might as well get used to, because she couldn't do her part on this job until Jones had done *his* part. She was the cleanup crew, and the cleanup didn't start until everybody else had finished.

Morosely, she stared at the door, still feeling the heavy weight of Joss's presence. "Can he do this?"

"Yeah." Joss was right about one thing. Going through the files, photos, and reports wasn't anything he needed to be here for. It was busy work, something Taylor had hoped would keep the guy occupied while they waited.

Obviously it hadn't worked. Joss was keyed up over something, and Taylor didn't think it was just the mind-fuck. And that mind-fuck was going to be brutal. Worse than normal, because the more complex the gift, the longer it took Joss to acclimate.

The psychic he was planning on using had the most complex set of gifts Taylor had ever seen . . . even more complex than Joss's ability to mirror anybody's gift set.

Still staring at the closed door, he blew out a breath. He wished he could act like he wasn't worried, but this sort of thing was harder on Joss than the man liked to show, and the word *mind-fuck* didn't exactly bring up images of hugs and kittens.

Right now, he was probably heading straight to his room to psych himself up for what was to come. Knowing Joss, his form of psyching himself up involved getting himself good and pissed at Taylor. There may or may not be copious amounts of liquor.

That was fine. It wasn't anything personal toward him, Taylor figured.

"You don't sound too certain there, baby," Dez said.

He slanted a look at her and shrugged. "Oh, I'm certain. Hell, he's the only one we've got who *can* do this."

"This has gotta be the craziest gift out of any of them," she murmured. "And it's not like any of us have *normal* ones."

"Joss is . . . unique," Taylor said after a moment. He pushed away from the desk. Scowling, he thought back to the past night and Joss's wisecrack about asking Dez on a date. "He's also a moron if he thinks I wouldn't deck him if he tried to ask you out on a date."

Dez slid him a sidelong look. Something about the smile on her lips sent his blood straight to the boiling level. Of course, everything about her had that power. "Oh, I think he knows that. Somehow, I think he's known that all along. He was just jerking your chain . . . funny, that. He actually realizes you have a chain to jerk. Most people don't."

"Sure I've got a chain . . . and a ball." He gave her a smile. "And it's got your name on it."

"You calling me a ball and chain there, Jones?"

He bent his head back over the pages spread out before him. "Why, yes, Jones. I think I am."

She snorted and adjusted the blanket she had draped over her, shivering a little. He could see her from the corner of his eye and he watched as she stretched out, wished he could say she was relaxing, but he knew better. She hadn't slept well ever since they'd wandered through a dark, supposedly abandoned warehouse. He'd gotten the address from Jillian. Everything else had come from Dez.

It had been full of ghosts. New ones . . . mostly female, mostly young . . . and all of them had screamed. They wouldn't rest for her, not until they were laid to rest, but Dez couldn't do this job and they couldn't afford to let her work it until they had the men responsible in custody.

That was what was really getting to her, knowing she couldn't help. The tension in her eyes, the rage in her soul, all of it would eat at her until they'd laid those souls to rest.

Something they couldn't do without Joss.

And they couldn't do that just yet, either.

"Who else are you going to have him sync with?"

Tapping his pen on his desk, he pondered just how he was going to make this happen.

Taige was going to have his ass. Cullen would go for his throat.

But he couldn't damn well help it that they'd brought their daughter to Disney World and she'd picked up on a slave ring, could he?

"Uh-oh."

He looked up and saw that Dez had shifted on the couch and was studying him, chin propped in her hand. "That look on your face spells trouble, Taylor."

"Tell me about it." Pinching the bridge of his nose, he leaned back in his chair and closed his eyes. It was bizarre, how easily she could read him now. And to think, a year ago, she hadn't even been in his life . . . because he'd pushed her away.

What in the hell had he been thinking?

A soft sound caught his attention and he lowered his hand, opened his eyes. Dez stood at his side. She lightly pushed on his shoulder and he obliged, turning away from the table. As she straddled him, he loosely wrapped his arms around her waist and stared up at her face. "You're so beautiful," he murmured, reaching up and cupping her cheek, his tanned skin pale against the dark, smooth brown of hers. She felt like satin under his hand . . . soft, warm . . .

"You're trying to distract me."

"No. I'm just telling you that you're beautiful." He slid a hand under her shirt, went to flick her bra open, only to discover it had a front clasp. Improvising, he eased her back and pushed her shirt up, burying his face between her breasts. "If I wanted to distract you, I'd do this."

"And it would work." She combed a hand through his hair. "But you need to tell me what's up . . . what's the deal, Jones?"

"I'm going to have to call Taige." He closed his eyes and rested his head on her shoulder.

Dez stroked the back of his neck, her fingers soothing, gentle. "Okay. That doesn't usually have you so glum. Besides, I know her . . . if you tell her what's at stake, she'll help out."

"It's not Taige's help I need." Lifting his head, he traced his finger over the bow of her lip. "Last month, they took Jillian to Disney. She started having nightmares almost right away, but she didn't tell them."

She nipped his finger and then caught his wrist, tugged his hand away. "That's odd. Wouldn't Taige feel it if Jillian's nightmares were that bad? Both of them have the same kind of gift.

Living together as long as they have, you'd think they'd be a little more in tune than that."

"Nobody is in tune with Jillian anymore, I don't think. They don't have the same gifts. Not anymore. Jillian has the same sort of telepathy that Taige does, but . . ." Taylor rested his head against Dez's chest again, eyes closed, breathing her in, letting the warmth of her soothe him. "She's far surpassed anything Taige will ever be able to do. And she's fourteen. Fourteen years old, Dez. How can she handle it?"

Dez was quiet. Her fingers stroked through his hair, and he concentrated on that simple gesture for a minute before he made himself continue. A kid. Jillian was just a kid. And she had to live with all that darkness in her head. Everything she saw, everything she knew . . . it was hard enough for him to live with, and he did it because it was the job, because he knew he made a difference.

"She ended up calling me. Last month when I had to leave for a few days? It was to come down here. I met her in the park."

"Jillian . . . you met Jillian in Disney World. Taige *let* you?"

"Taige didn't know," Taylor said grimly. "She took off for a few minutes—the kid didn't bother to tell me that part until after we'd met up. She pushed a notebook into my hands and then disappeared. I never saw Taige or Cullen."

"She *disappeared*? *After* what happened to her?"

Taylor shook his head. "I tried to tell her that—the girl has a mind of her own. I think I feel sorry for her parents."

When Jillian Morgan had been younger, she'd been kidnapped. Taylor's unit had been put on the task, and he'd learned some interesting facts about the young girl—namely that she'd actually *known* she would be kidnapped . . . she'd seen it. So far, Taylor had narrowed her gifts down to precognition, psychometry, and telepathy.

He only *hoped* that was all she had inside that brain of hers. But she'd gotten stronger over the years, and it was entirely possible new gifts had emerged as she'd gotten older.

Many of his psychics hadn't even developed any of their gifts until puberty. By the time Jillian had hit that age, she'd already hit a level of control that made some of his people look like rank amateurs.

Now the teenager was living another nightmare . . . somebody else's nightmare. He knew that didn't always make it any easier. Trapped inside somebody else's misery, somebody else's pain. And when she wasn't able to do much more than watch from the sidelines . . .

Except Jillian hadn't watched. There were missing kids. Missing women.

Some of them, Jillian had said, were already gone. *The missing . . .* For Jillian, that meant they'd been killed. And she had decided she'd stop it.

Frustration chewed at him; he'd told Taige this would happen. He'd seen it, even when Jillian had just been a child, just like he'd seen in Taige. His people were *his* for a reason . . . they were warriors. Jillian was already walking down that road.

He hated it. Taige, Cullen, they had no idea how much he hated it.

He'd never track her down, but in the end, it wouldn't matter, because she'd come to him.

His phone started to ring, cutting through the dark, heavy cloud of his thoughts.

He wasn't the least bit amused, or surprised, when Evanescence's "Haunted" came blaring from it. Dez had programmed the ring. He didn't do ringtones—exactly what he needed, to have a ringtone like that go off in the middle of a meeting. But his wife wasn't part of his unit . . . not anymore . . . and she had a sense of humor that was, at best, strange.

It was the ringtone she'd programmed for Taige. Thankfully, he could count on his hands the number of times Taige had called him.

Sighing, he accepted the call, already bracing himself. *Jilly, kid, what have you done now . . .*

"What is your damned room number?"

SIX

"*E*LLA... *I'd like you to meet Patrick Whitmore.*"

Finally. Dru had damn near had to bend over backward just to get a damned invite to the party, and then she'd spent most of the night working the crowd just to get this close to Whitmore.

Just as she'd done three other times, all unsuccessfully.

Whitmore wasn't exactly the easiest man to get up close and personal with, something she'd discovered the hard way. She'd used the time to learn everything she could about him. The type of woman who seemed to catch his eye, their style, their looks . . . she'd made them her own and it was finally paying off.

As Whitmore gave her a casual glance, then a longer second look, Dru smiled, pretending to be just a little nervous as she held out a hand.

Mentally, she braced herself. It wasn't always pleasant, that first touch of bared skin on bared skin, leaving an impression for her to study, for her to learn and understand . . . her ability *might be labeled as psychometry. She didn't know. It worked best on people rather than things and it didn't work on everybody. But sometimes when she touched a person, she took in chunks of memory—good things, bad things, she never knew which it would be.*

The second Whitmore's fingers closed over her hand, she wanted to jerk away.

Flash, flash, flash.

Screams, terror, pain . . . and it made him smile. She pushed it all down inside and locked it down tight.

As his hand tightened, ever so intimately, on hers, she gave him a demure smile.

As he leaned in closer to her, she resisted the urge to pull away.

"Ella . . . a lovely name." He lifted her hand to his lips.

She wanted to back away and put as much distance between her and the monster as she could—that wasn't an option, so she would have been happy to grab something big and heavy—like a sledgehammer—and pound him across the head with it.

In reality, she did none of that.

She pretended to be pleased with his attention, letting her hand linger in his . . . even as the screams continued to rage.

Nobody else heard it, of course. It was just in his mind, buried in his memories. But that was where she excelled . . . peering into those dark places. Unraveling sticky threads . . .

Dru sat at the table across from Patrick and fought the urge to scream. Her head pounded. Her gut was a quesy, roiling mess. Nothing like a hangover and her murderous, slaving fiancé to make for a lovely breakfast.

He'd shown up while she was still in the shower, and when she'd come out to find him in her bedroom, she hadn't had time to brace herself, *shield* herself, before he touched her.

And the memory flash was just . . . a blow.

Heavy, solid, almost completely formed. He'd looked at her as she came out of the bathroom, and something had made him think of the first time he'd seen her.

Now she had *that* in her head, and it had triggered her own memories.

"Are you all right?"

Looking up, she met Patrick's gaze and smiled. "Yes, I'm quite lovely . . . I was just thinking of the time we first met, actually."

"Hmmm." He continued to study her, that critical, dark look on his face, like he was measuring everything about her. Measuring and something about her was lacking today. "Did you sleep well?"

Dru reached for her tea and took a sip. "Yes. It took a while to fall asleep . . . the fireworks." She gave a deprecating smile. "I'd forgotten about the fireworks."

"If you need other accommodations, let me know. You need to have your rest."

"Not necessary, Patrick." She set her cup down and said, "I'll just see about buying some earplugs or perhaps one of those little machines that make white noise. I used to have one, but it broke and I never got around to purchasing a new one."

"I'll take care of it." He rose from the table and came around to stand beside her.

She lifted her head to gaze up at him, pasting that fake as hell, demure smile on her face. *I hate you, you sodding bastard.* He cupped her chin and stroked his thumb across her lower lip. "Will you be running today?" he asked.

"I'm not sure. I might just take a lazy day or call your assistant about setting up the spa day. I haven't decided."

He nodded. "The fitting is coming up. Don't forget about it," he reminded her as he dipped his head.

And as his mouth brushed hers, her breath locked up in her throat and her heart slammed hard against her ribs.

Flash, flash, flash.

"The disposal is complete?"

"Yes, Mr. Whitmore."

She felt his satisfaction. Not *pleasure*. He wasn't *pleased*, Dru knew. He was irritated over the loss of money. There . . . an image floated through his mind, a woman, as she'd been before she died.

Dru locked on it, froze it in her mind.

He was satisfied that his point had been made, even as he was disgusted by the loss of merchandise. But he was willing to admit sometimes a loss was needed to make a point.

A point—as she tried to puzzle that through, the memories she'd taken from him were revealed to her.

"Make sure the others see the recording. This should make sure everybody understands what happens when they cause trouble." Patrick, again. Recording . . .

And just like that, the connection severed.

Dru couldn't hold it any longer, because she was fighting the urge to puke her guts out, fighting not to let him see as he pulled away and then said something else. Through the rush of blood, she heard his voice, but the words didn't connect.

All that mattered was that he was leaving.

Once the door clicked, she wiped her lips on a napkin and rose.

Even though her knees were shaking, even though she wanted to scream, she walked carefully, slowly, sedately into the bathroom. Once there, she went to her knees in front of the toilet. If the cameras or audio devices outside the bathroom caught the sound of her puking, so what? She'd lie and say she had a stomach virus.

Maybe it would get her out of Patrick's tender charms for a few days.

*   *   *

"CAN you describe her any better than that?"

Dru glanced around, keeping it subtle.

She'd swiped the phone. It was one of her best tactics for making untraceable phone calls. But she still had to get off the phone before one of her babysitters showed up—they'd follow her into the loo if she took too long, public or not.

"Not much. They'd worked her over rather bad," she said. "Young, early twenties, I would think. Brown and brown, hair was straight and short, looked like that style where it was longer in the front, shorter in the back. Highlights. Biracial. Early twenties, max. Light-skinned. Can't speak to height, so her weight would be hard to guess, but I can say she was slender, verging on skinny. Had an almost muscular look, like she was really into fitness. Maybe an instructor or something." The muscles she'd seen on that woman didn't come from hitting the gym three or four times a week, she knew that much. "If I could sit down with a sketch artist, I could do better, but I don't see me getting access to one just yet."

On the other end of the phone, her contact sighed. "I'll do what I can, honey, but that's not much to work with."

"I know . . . I'll try to get more info." *Go back into the memory. Look for more.*

"Be careful."

She grimaced as she finished the phone call. She went into the phone's memory and deleted it. It would show on the phone bill, but that would be some time from now and the call had been short. Hopefully, nobody would think to look twice. Carefully, she wiped it down and left it sitting in one of the stalls before she slid out of the bathroom.

She had a *spa day* ahead of her. What a bloody joke.

* * *

BIG blue eyes stared up at hers.

Taige Morgan stared right back at her stepdaughter, not the least bit swayed by that projected air of innocence.

She might have been, once. But she was no longer a newbie at the mom game, and Jillian was going to have to try just a little bit harder and do more than bat her eyes to get out of this mess. The girl was fourteen years old and bordering on genius, too. She should know better than to think batting her lashes was going to do the trick.

Jillian would drive her crazy, Taige thought. Fear, frustration, and love tangled in her gut. She was a mess. And it wasn't going to get any better anytime soon, she knew.

"You can't let him go up there first," Jillian said again.

"Yes." Taige smiled. "I can. I just did."

She'd already given Cullen, her husband, and Jillian's very protective father, Taylor's room number. He'd disappeared into the elevator. She was giving him a five-minute head start. Much longer than that and she might have to bail his fine ass out of jail.

Of course, it might be worth it.

And if Cullen didn't pop Taylor one, Taige was going to. That son of a bitch had pulled her baby into his world . . . she'd warned him about doing that. She'd warned him. He hadn't listened.

Over the past few hours, Jillian had explained just *why* she hadn't been sleeping. Just *why* she hadn't been eating. Just *why* she'd been having nightmares. And just *why* they'd caught her slipping out of the house. Taige sometimes wished she hadn't trained the girl so well.

But that wouldn't have been a blessing. As strong as Jillian was, she needed to be trained. Unfortunately, Taige now stood in Jillian's shadow—the girl's abilities far eclipsed her own, and it had been sheer dumb luck that she'd sensed something . . . off earlier in the day.

If Taige hadn't picked up on that strange little vibe, they wouldn't have realized Jillian was planning anything until the kid had already disappeared.

"Look, Mom . . ." Jillian shuffled her feet, acting like the teenager she was, for once. Sheepish, nervous, embarrassed at being caught in the act. "It's not Taylor's fault I was trying to sneak out. *I* was doing it. It was my idea. I just knew . . . well, I knew he needed me. It's not like he told me to do it or anything."

Taige just stared at her. "Not impressed, darling. You see . . . *Taylor* knows how you are. And he should have called me the second he knew something was going on with you."

"If he'd done that, you and Dad wouldn't have let me *help*." She crossed her arms across her chest, glaring at Taige. Sullen temper sparked in those pretty eyes now.

It made Taige smile inwardly. Too often, this kid didn't act anything like the kid she still was. Even when she was completely in the wrong, it was nice to see Jillian *act* like a teenager. Hell, it was even kind of nice to see her screw up, see her rebel.

Although Taige wished it had been over almost anything but this.

Not this world, she thought, her heart aching. *Not my world.*

"There's no other world I belong in, Mom."

Sighing, Taige closed her eyes. "Shut the door, Jilly."

"I can't always do it." They'd trained Jillian to keep out unwanted thoughts by envisioning other people's minds as rooms . . . and she kept those thoughts out of her head by shutting the door. It usually worked. Not always.

There was a muffled noise and Taige opened her eyes to see the girl coming across the heavily carpeted floor. They were waiting in a little alcove of the hotel, waiting while Cullen and Taylor had a "chat."

Jillian stopped in front of Taige, her eyes solemn and sad.

The look on the child's face was far too adult, far too wise. It just about broke Taige's heart.

"Mom . . . this is what I'm meant for."

"It doesn't have to be." She brushed back the dark, spiraling curls from Jillian's face. Man, she was growing up so fast. It seemed like just yesterday . . .

Unable to think about that . . . about all the yesterdays, while the very pressing reality of *today* was right *here*, Taige pushed it aside. "You're a bright girl, Jilly. You've got so much more you can do, but you've always been so focused on this, sometimes I wonder if you've ever let yourself look at the other options you have."

"Other options." Jillian shook her head and held out a hand. "Can I show you?"

Taige's gut clenched. She didn't ask what. It wasn't like Jillian often asked to do this. How could she say no . . . even when everything inside her rebelled. Jillian saw things so much clearer than Taige ever had, felt things so much more acutely. If Jillian could live with that in her head, then Taige would accept what Jillian had to show her. Even if some part of her would rather hide from it.

Screw being a coward . . . this was her child.

Laying her hand in her daughter's, she glanced around and then back at Jillian. They were alone, or as alone as they were going to be.

"You do things that matter," Jillian whispered. "You always have."

And with that, Taige fell into that bright, shining void that was her daughter's mind.

It wasn't bright for long.

In seconds, they were in darkness. Surrounded by screams. And pain. And death.

* * *

PATRICK *eyed the skinny mess of bones Dontrez had pulled out of the holding cell.*

She'd been a lot prettier than this when they'd grabbed her.

But she'd stopped eating.

A lot of them did that.

She'd start eating again.

All it would take was the right incentive.

He knew all about finding the right incentive.

He gestured to Lydia and said, "Clean her up."

Lydia beckoned for Dontrez to bring the girl. There were screams and tears and struggles. Moments later, there was a slap. Patrick smiled. Lydia dealt with things efficiently. It was why he kept her around.

"Are you certain he'll be satisfied with her?"

Glancing over at the man next to him, he shrugged. "She'll do. He just wants a warm body for the most part. I've got my hands full with other matters. If he wants to be picky, the price will go up."

A soft, warm little head butted his ankle and he smiled, knelt down, and scooped up Demeter. The cat snuggled into his arms as he scratched it under the chin. It was odd, how attached he'd gotten to the little thing. He'd originally gotten her for his last fiancée. He'd thought perhaps having a kitten to mother would

make her stop her constant blathering about a family. It hadn't.
It had just made her that much more moon-eyed and tiresome.

He wondered what she thought of her new life now. He'd
warned her more than once to stop it with the ceaseless prat-
tling, but she hadn't. He'd let his dick do the thinking with her.
Grace had been lovely, there was no doubt about that, but she
hadn't been smart.

Ella was much more suitable.

He'd been considering discarding Grace anyway, but when
he saw Ella, he'd simply known. It was like she'd been waiting
for him.

So Grace was done away with. She was the property of one
of his associates over in Dubai. She'd mentioned wanting to
visit . . . well, she had that wish. And she'd never leave.

He kept the cat, of course.

Maybe he'd give Demeter to Ella.

As a wedding present.

Something to consider.

* * *

IT took all of Taige's control not to react when Jillian broke contact. All of her control not to cry.

"I saw him, Mom," Jillian whispered. There were tears in her
blue eyes. Tears of horror . . . but behind the horror, there was
rage. "I looked at him and I saw inside his mind and it's . . . it's
awful. He buys and sells girls like they were books or shoes. He
was going to marry one of them, but he got bored with her and
he sold her. I could see inside his head and now all of that is
trapped inside me and I can't just . . . I can't . . . I can't . . . ."

Her voice broke and Taige reached out, pulled Jillian against
her. "Hush." She rubbed her cheek against Jillian's soft curls.
"Hush now, baby. I understand. It will be okay, got me?"

"He won't stop." Jillian clutched at Taige desperately. "Even now, I can see him. He's petting a cat and thinking about that girl he was gonna marry and he thinks it's *funny* that she couldn't take her cat when he sold her."

Taige closed her eyes.

"It's like they are just toys to him. He's in my head all the time, and I can't make him stop, because I can't see him all the way . . . And even if I *could*, I'm . . ."

Jillian's voice broke and she started to sob.

But Taige understood.

Just a kid.

She'd been there before.

She knew what it was like to have something awful trapped inside her mind, a knowledge that something bad was happening. Something terrible. Sometimes she'd tried to help. But even then she'd been a little older than Jillian was now. And none of it had ever been anything like this.

"It will be okay, baby," Taige said quietly, easing back and gently forcing the girl's face up. "Look at me . . . we got this. We can handle this, I promise."

Jillian dashed away the tears and stared at her. "I'm just a kid. I know that. I'm just a kid. I don't know what to do. But Taylor can fix this. You could fix it. Dez . . . all of you. You all can make things like this right."

Tipping her head back, Taige stared at the ceiling, wanting to rage. This wasn't fair . . . this was too much of a burden to place on a child. Too much of a burden to place on *her* child, who'd already suffered so much.

"Taylor can make it stop," Jillian said, her voice soft and steady. "That's why I wanted to come here. He knows the way to make it work. All of you know what to do. And I can do one thing that will help. One thing . . . I can do something that matters, too."

The girl eased back, staring at Taige with eyes that burned.

And the courage in her young eyes was enough to lay Taige low.

* * *

IT was a good thing Cullen Morgan knew how to look before he swung, because the door opened to reveal Desiree . . . not Taylor. He smiled.

She didn't smile back.

Maybe she saw something of what he felt on his face. Wouldn't have surprised him. Keeping his smile firmly in place, he asked casually, "Can I come in?"

"Well, I'd say no, but then Taylor would just change my mind for me," she drawled, stepping aside. "I don't see any point in delaying the inevitable anyway."

He arched a brow as he came through the doorway. Taylor was coming out of a sitting area to the right. Cullen stopped, still smiling his pleasant little *Hey, I mean no harm* smile.

Taylor didn't look fooled. "I take it you and Jillian finally talked."

"Oh. For hours." Cullen watched from the corner of his eye as Dez disappeared through a door. "Speaking of talks . . . you had one with my wife . . . at our wedding. Recall *that* talk?"

Taylor grimaced, touched his throat. Cullen had found out after the talk quite some time later . . . the *talk* had mostly been on Taige's part—she'd used her gift to all but choke Taylor after the man had been poking at Jillian too much. With a telepathic child, all it took was *loud* thinking. And Jillian was very, very receptive. "I recall something along those lines, yes."

"You were told you weren't recruiting her, as well. Recall that?"

"Yes." Taylor inclined his head.

"Good."

Five seconds later, Cullen was standing over the cocky, arrogant son of a bitch, his hand hurting like hell, and there was blood trickling from a cut on Taylor's mouth.

To Cullen's mind, it wasn't enough blood. And Taylor didn't look anywhere near scared as he got to his feet. His gaze was still blank, his face was still blank—the way he looked, he could have been out playing golf. He sure as hell didn't look like somebody had just popped him one.

"You son of a bitch, you didn't even try to move," Cullen snarled.

"No." Taylor stared at him, those cool blue eyes level and flat. "If I had a daughter, I'm pretty sure I'd feel the same as you."

"You fucking bastard. You have no *idea* how I feel, how I *would* feel."

"Cullen."

"You know how I *feel*? You fucking robot, you *don't* feel, that's the problem," he roared, ignoring the quiet voice coming from his left.

Taylor just stood there, hands at his sides, face blank. Cullen closed the distance between them, furious. Grabbing the man's suit, he hauled him closer. "You too much of a pussy to fight me? You'll drag kids into your world but you won't face a man? Cowardly piece of shit."

"Oh, now that's it." Two strong, slim hands pushed between them. Cullen wasn't about to let go that easily.

"Back off," he snarled.

And those cool, unfeeling blue eyes blazed with heat. Gently, Taylor nudged Dez off to the side. Not that she was in any mood to be nudged, but the man somehow managed it.

In a quiet, controlled voice, Taylor said, "You're going to watch how you speak to my wife, or I'll break you into so many pieces, they won't have anything left to bury, you hear me?"

"Oh, now that's all nice and sexy, Jones, but the wife can

speak for herself." Dez shoved between them once more. Her eyes hot with fury, she looked from Cullen to her husband. "And you better think again before you try to nudge me aside, buddy, because if you do it? You and me are going to box, you hear me?"

Taylor apparently didn't. "You aren't going to speak to her that way, Morgan."

"Jones . . . you worry about him punching you. I'll worry about how he speaks to me." She wedged herself between and elbowed her husband in the gut until he moved back. Then she shoved against Cullen until he, too, fell back a step.

"Back off, Dez."

"Don't you go telling me to back off, Morgan. Not unless you want me to rearrange that pretty-boy face of yours, and trust me, right now I really want to do it," she said, taking a step in his direction, her chin jerking up. "Oh, you're an idiot, you know that? A first-class moron. He didn't drag Jillian into shit, and if you know a damn thing about that daughter of yours, you could probably figure that out. She called *him*. He didn't call her."

"He's using a *child*."

"She's not a child," Dez said, shaking her head. "I know that hurts you and I'm sorry, but she hasn't really been a *child* since the day she was kidnapped, and if you could let yourself admit it, you'd see the truth of it. You blind fool, what is she supposed to do—ignore the fact that she knows there are women out there . . . some of them as young as she is, being held prisoner? Girls that are going to be sold off to the highest bidder? Girls she can *help*? She's got a nightmare trapped in her head. You want her to go crazy or something?"

"That's enough, Dez." Behind her, Taylor sighed heavily.

She swung her head around, glaring at her husband. "The hell it is. He wants to call you a coward, call you out for using his daughter, when that's not what this is. She was brave enough to come to you, Jones. She's got more courage than he does, for fuck's sake."

"It's got nothing to do with courage," Cullen growled. "And everything to do with protecting my *child*."

"And how can you protect her from what's haunting her?" Dez asked quietly. "Because I've got a good idea what she has trapped inside her head. You can't chase those ghosts away. It's not like it's a monster hiding under her bed, for crying out loud. And it *sucks*, but you can't fix this. You can't. Neither can Taige. Hell, if you'd taken five seconds to ask Taige, she probably would have *told* you that."

"Leave Taige out of this," Cullen rasped.

Spinning away, he covered his face with his hands. *Some of them as young as she is . . . being held prisoner . . .*

Daddy . . . I can't ignore this . . .

She'd whispered that to him. On the plane, as they flew in from Alabama. He'd come, mostly because he'd wanted to hit Taylor and convince the son of a bitch to stay away from his daughter. From his little girl. Because he'd thought he could protect her . . .

They need me, Daddy . . .

"What exactly are you expecting her to do?" he demanded. "Jilly's just a kid."

SEVEN

No, there hadn't been any information in that forest of paper and file folders and pictures, but he'd picked up a few stray images from Dez's brain.

A warehouse.

So Joss had left and was driving around.

Following his gut, he found himself in an area of town he doubted many tourists ever went. It was on the outskirts and he suspected it had seen better days. The warehouse had a For Sale sign on the side, but it had so much graffiti covering it, the only letters he could really make out were part of the *F* and the *L and E.*

Nothing back at the hotel had jumped out at him . . . except the images Dez had tried to keep trapped inside her brain.

They'd made his skin burn.

Made it hurt.

And it was even worse now.

There was death here.

He didn't know how long ago it had happened, but people had died here and it tarnished the air, a vicious black stain that would never fully fade.

It was fucking cold, too. The lingering echo of those trapped here. Which was why the place was so heavily imprinted on Dez's brain, why he'd followed the trail to it so easily. Probably all but infested with ghosts.

He couldn't see them but he felt that eerie echo . . . heard it. Like somebody was whispering just behind him, but it went silent every time he turned around.

Circling around the warehouse, he came to a stop when he caught a glimpse of the moon glinting off the water somewhere in the distance.

It was one of the numerous lakes. No telling which one . . . He'd have to dig out a map just to figure it out. But for some reason, standing there and staring at it hit him like a fist.

A pang of deep, gripping sorrow. Joss could feel his damn throat closing up on him as the wave of grief struck him.

Cold danced along his skin. It was almost the way it hit him when he was picking up a ghost—except he had to have the right gift for that. He didn't have the ability to see them right now. Sense them, maybe, but this . . . this was different.

Pain swelled inside him, stealing away the ability to breathe, to see, to think.

And still, Joss didn't know what this was. What he was feeling. Under the weight of the grief, his shields trembled, shuddered.

The grief pressed closer. Weighed in heavier.

And he thought he heard the faintest echo of a sob. A woman's sob—

Amelie—

Just thinking her name was like a crushing weight had been

dropped on his heart, and he slumped, almost went to the ground. The sound of crying grew louder and louder . . .

And then, the loud, raucous blast of his phone sliced through the night, shattering whatever it was that gripped him.

* * *

THE drive back to the hotel, thanks to traffic, took a good forty minutes, and Joss relished every single second of it. It had been Jones on the phone. The other psychic had arrived.

It was time for Joss to get his mind-fuck on.

Yippie ki-yay. Now if he could have stalled for another two hours. Gotten smashed. Yeah, shit-faced drunk might make this easier to get through, he thought as he stepped off the elevator.

The tension slammed into him, a brutal, double-fisted punch. All around, he could pick up on other thoughts and they were *everywhere*, but none were as chaotic as those coming from Taylor Jones's room.

It wasn't *thoughts*, either.

Wasn't just tension . . . anger. Chaos. Fear. Worry. Regret. An ugly miasma that he didn't even want to step into, but he had no choice.

Who in the hell had Taylor found to . . .

The door opened and he found himself face-to-face with a child.

"What the fuc . . ."

He bit his tongue to try and hold the cuss word back, tasted blood.

She smiled at him. Black curls fell in crazy corkscrews and spirals all over the place. Her eyes, a bright and vivid blue, practically glowed as she smiled at him.

She was a pretty kid. A memorable one, especially considering the wallop of the power he could feel coming from her.

"Hi, Joss!" She grinned at him, a smile that displayed a set of braces with purple rubber bands that matched the purple sweater she wore.

He'd never met that kid before in his life.

* * *

"YOU'RE fu . . . shi . . ." Joss almost choked to keep from swearing in front of her—*again*. Judging by the look on the kid's face, she knew exactly what he was thinking . . . she knew. She was amused. She wanted to laugh.

Ha, ha, kid. So glad I amuse you, he thought sourly, looking away from her and glaring at Jones. "You've got to be kidding me," he said.

Jones just stared back at him.

"You're kidding," Joss said, his voice getting rougher. Shoving back from the table, he stood up and stared at the girl, unable to believe he had to sync his mind to a *child's*.

"You ever known me to have that much of a sense of humor, Crawford?"

Joss wanted to swear. No, what he really wanted to do was hit something, and then head out of there, find a bar, and have a few drinks. Instead, he continued to stare at the girl.

She was strong. He could feel the buzz of her in his mind, even through his shields. Strong, hell. That was kind of like calling a Category 5 hurricane *strong*. The power he sensed in her was devastating. But was she *controlled*? They hadn't even started scraping at the surface of what he was supposed to be getting into, but anything that involved human trafficking was dangerous. He didn't really want to get involved in that sort of shit when he had an uncontrolled gift—

"I've got more control than *you* do," she said, wrinkling her nose at him.

Crossing his arms over his chest, he cocked a brow at her. "Yeah? Then you oughta know you shouldn't go poking your fingers into my brain without asking me."

"I can't help that you think *loud*."

"I *don't* think loud," he said, narrowing his eyes.

"You aren't thinking quiet enough for me." She didn't look bothered by the glare.

It was a glare that normally made people back up about ten paces. She was either too young to have developed that common sense or she'd already figured out the basics of Joss Crawford— he was a mean-ass bastard, but certain groups were safe from him. Namely animals and small kids. They were about the only groups that were off his list.

"Jilly."

The girl looked away and Joss felt a pressure he hadn't even been aware of lift off his mind. Then, the girl looked sheepish, a red flush creeping up her neck as she stared at whoever had said her name.

Turning his head, Joss found himself staring at a ghost.

Taige . . .

"I'll be a motherfucker."

She slanted a narrow look at him, rueful humor glinting in her gray eyes. He grimaced and looked at the kid. "Um, sorry."

The girl giggled.

Taige sighed and shook her head. "Long time, no see, huh, Crawford?" Then she looked back at the girl. "Jilly, sweets, you know that *everybody* sounds loud for you at first. Give him a break and work a little harder at blocking him out, okay?"

Jillian—

Taige—

Pieces of the puzzle started to click together, and he glanced around. Taige was married. Had a stepdaughter. Weird job a few years back—the kid had been gifted . . . shit, he hadn't realized the girl was *that* gifted. The kid's dad was a rich son of a bitch, if Joss recalled correctly.

Absently, he glanced around the room, although he didn't really expect to see anybody. He would have felt another person . . . except, he hadn't. There was a sixth person in the room. A man, about his age.

Joss hadn't sensed him at all.

Instinctively, he tensed, because the guy was almost a void. A blank.

"Not many people can read him," Jillian said.

He looked at the kid. She smiled at him, and there was something smug, yet . . . oddly endearing . . . about that smile. "He's my dad."

Sighing, he looked at Taige. They'd worked together a few times, and he knew she'd hear him. Hoping the *kid* wouldn't, he pushed his thoughts to her. *Just how strong is she?*

Taige stared at him. *Stronger than everybody in here, combined.*

Something that just might have been apprehension settled in Joss's gut as he looked back at the girl. A Category 5 storm, indeed. "How good is your control? Really?"

She glanced at the table, then at Dez for a long minute before looking at him. "Well, there's really only one way to find out, right?"

* * *

"CULLEN, come on." Taige laid a hand on his arm, ignoring everybody else. Taylor had already left. Joss was sitting at the table, slumped in a chair, looking half-asleep. Dez was sitting next to him, and Jilly was in the chair across from hers, sketching.

"Why can't we be in here?"

Taige sighed. "If I'm in here, it's going to interfere with what they are doing. And if you're in here, it's going to be a distraction— one they don't need. Joss knows what he's doing."

"*I* don't." He stared at the table, where his daughter sat with her head bent over the sketchpad. "Taige, what in the hell is going on?"

"This is how she helps." Taige held out a hand. "Do you trust me?"

Eyes the color of the ocean stared into hers. Then he looked back at their daughter.

"Baby . . . I love her. She's my heart, and you know it. Would I *ever* do anything to hurt her?" Taige asked. If he didn't know the answer to that, she thought it just might shatter something inside her. But then, the ache that had been starting to settle eased as he placed his hand in hers. God. Thank God.

As he followed her out into the hallway, Jillian looked up from her sketchbook, a sad look in her eyes.

"What's going on?" Cullen asked once the door shut.

Taige sighed. She'd known he wasn't just operating on blind faith. She didn't blame him. She was a parent. She hadn't given birth to Jillian, but that didn't matter. She was that girl's mother. If she had been in Cullen's shoes, not knowing a damn thing about Joss, or what would happen . . .

"Joss is what Jones has classified as a mirror," she said, glancing over to see the head of the FBI's psychic task force—one that *technically* didn't exist—leaning against the wall, his iPhone in hand, looking like he wasn't aware of anything going on but what he was staring at on the screen.

She knew better.

"A mirror."

"Yeah." She reached up to gather her hair into a tail, smoothing the riotous curls back until they were somewhat manageable.

It had been a crazy, tiring day. If she'd known this shit was coming, she'd have had the mess put into braids or something a few days ago. "His gift is . . . well. Weird. He doesn't *have* a set one; what he does is mirror ours. They call it synching. He syncs to another psychic—or in this case, two—and he can pick up on their gifts. When he's done in there, he'll have all of Dez's abilities and all of Jilly's as well."

It boggled her mind even thinking about it. Jillian, alone, had too much in her head. Taige didn't know how the girl handled it and stayed *sane*. How was he going to handle Dez's ghosts on top of that?

"All?" Cullen said, his lids flickering. That was the only reaction he gave.

"All."

"And how long does it last?"

"Until he hooks up with another psychic—does another sync. It . . ." She frowned, glanced at Jones.

"Reboots. It's a reboot. Wipes the previous gift, or gifts, from his system and he's imprinted with the next gift." Jones looked up, his eyes unreadable.

"Wow. He sounds like a fucking useful workhorse," Cullen said, curling his lip.

"Indeed." Taylor inclined his head, his face impassive.

Asshole. He should have pummeled him a little harder. So what if he wasn't fighting back?

"And what effect will this have on Jillian?"

Taige lifted a brow, a cool look entering her eyes. "Absolutely none."

He stared at her.

She turned away. "I've worked with Crawford before. It was years ago when he was still newer at what he does, but he takes a gift in, and although it does a number on him, I didn't feel a blessed thing. You should know better than to think I'd let her do anything that would hurt her. In any way."

Cullen went to touch her shoulder, but she was already striding down the hall.

As she passed by Taylor, he touched her arm.

Cullen bit back a snarl as Taylor and Taige shared a long look before she pulled away and continued down the hall.

"Taige," Cullen said.

"I'll be back before they are done," she said over her shoulder. "I need a few minutes."

"Damn it, Taige."

But she just kept on walking.

* * *

DEZ's gift, Joss had dealt with before. He'd been imprinted with it and he'd done just fine. Didn't like it, but the good news was, once he synced with somebody else, all her ghosts went away. He might pick up on those faint echoes, the way he had at the cemetery, the way he had at the warehouse, nothing major.

It was nothing like what Dez had to live with, though.

But he thought he'd rather have Dez's gift, any day of the week, than live with what this kid had inside her all the time.

Endless whispers. Echoes of forgotten pain. Glimpses of forgotten pasts and yet-to-be-seen futures. All of it, she had all of that inside her head.

Where in the hell did she have room for her own thoughts?

As the weight of it all slammed into him, stretching his brain to the very limit, *he* was stretched as well; he fought to control his breathing, fought to control his heart rate, his fear.

And *her* fear.

Her terror was a living, breathing beast in his belly, a dragon growing in size that threatened to swallow him whole.

Meditation got him through these things, always, but it wasn't doing him much good right now and he was clinging to consciousness by the skin of his teeth and it *still* wasn't done.

Their faces—*aw, fuck* . . . their faces.

Got to help . . .

Jillian's thoughts, her fears, they were a desperate cry in the back of his mind as face after face circled through his mind.

There was a woman. Head bowed. Dark hair streaming around her shoulders. *He's killing them . . . killing me . . . we can't stop it* . . .

We'll stop it, Joss wanted to tell her. *Look at me . . . let me see your face* . . .

But then she was gone, as ephemeral as mist as, try as he might, he couldn't bring her back.

Jillian's voice continued to whisper, incomprehensible . . . what was she saying . . . *names?* It was almost a rhyme, he thought. But not quite.

Abruptly, the chaos in her mind came to a slamming halt and there was a man.

Everything stopped. And it was like time and space fell away. He and Jillian were no longer in that room, no longer in that hotel. They were somewhere else. He could hear laughter, screams. Smell the heat of the summer sun baking on the sidewalks. Cotton candy and cookies and ice cream . . .

"*What is this?*" *he muttered.*

"*It was here,*" *Jillian said.*

He flinched and looked over at the girl.

She stared straight ahead.

Automatically, he followed the line of her sight, startled to realize he could actually do it—it was so fucking real. Nothing like this had ever happened before when he'd synched to any-

body. *Blips of memory, yeah, but this wasn't a blip. This was like a 3-D flashback from hell.*

"It was here when I saw him. That was when it all started," Jillian said. She shivered and crossed her arms over her chest. Thin arms, skinny, narrow body, hovering just at the verge of womanhood. *She looked so young,* Joss realized. *So afraid.*

It was instinct that made him turn his head and look down at her, wrap his own arm around those narrow shoulders. "Who is he?"

"The one who takes them." She swallowed, staring at the back of the man's head. It was a bright, cheerful place . . . and yet all Jillian could hear were screams. All she could feel was pain. It was like the man had an imprint of his own, and Jillian was keyed into it. And because she was, now Joss was as well. "He takes them. He sells them. He buys them. He gives them away. It's like we're nothing but toys to him. And I can't see him well enough to stop him."

A harsh sob ripped through her, and she covered her face with her hands. "All I had to do was run up there and look at him, but I was too afraid."

Joss rubbed his hand down Jillian's narrow back. "Does he sound like that when you look at him? Feel like that?"

"Yes," she whispered. "It's awful."

"Then you did the right thing. There's no way I'd go running up to somebody like that, if I were in your shoes. You called for the big guns." He hugged her tight.

"I could have found Mom. Said something to her. She could have tried to find him . . ."

"Hey, I said you called in the big guns. Your mom is a tough cookie, but when you've got a big monster, you go for the biggest weapon you have. That's Jones." He continued to stare at the man, committing everything he could to memory, although he knew this was just a memory—a child's memory—and it was entirely possible, and likely, that Jillian wasn't recalling things clearly.

White male. Blond. Possibly around six feet, but hard to say from a distance. Lean build. Suit.

"A monster," Jillian whispered again. And the chaos of her mind returned, and the crystalline clarity of the memory started to fracture. It hazed, covered by a wash of blood.

He'll kill them . . .

That whisper echoed through him, growing in volume until it was a roar. And then, just like that, it was done. Over and done.

It was one thing he couldn't quite define, knowing the sync had completed, that he'd been fully imprinted with the needed gift. Maybe it was just an instinctive thing, but as Jillian's voice continued to echo through his mind, he tore away from her, shoving away from the table. He stumbled exactly three steps before he went to his knees.

Then his hands came out, just barely catching himself before he would have smashed his face into the ground.

He'll kill them, Joss . . .

For long moments, he hovered there, the neurons in his brain all but shrieking from the overload. Too much, too much, too much—

Cold whispers danced down his spine, and he shoved a wall up. No time to deal with the ghosts just yet, and fortunately, that was one mess he knew how to handle. He could shut it off better than Dez could, too, maybe because he was a callous son of a bitch who wouldn't have to handle having a ghost haunt him for the rest of his life.

Groaning, he eased into a sitting position and buried his face in his hands while the voices continued to shriek in his mind. Too many. Coming from everywhere.

Even Jillian's carefully soft voice was too loud.

Dez was at the table, staring at him, and through her eyes, he was treated to a visual of how he looked—*Damn, he's white as a ghost himself now. What in the hell . . .*

Her mental voice was just too loud, though. Too loud, too much. Had to shut it down. Carefully, he eased up thicker shields, although it just barely managed to muffle the louder voices coming from Dez and people out in the hallway and surrounding rooms.

"How do you block them out?" Closing his eyes, he tried to focus on that one minor thing. Had to do that first or he'd go crazy. Everybody worked differently and he needed to know what worked for her.

"Doors," Jillian said simply.

He nodded and pictured one giant, motherfucking door, slamming shut. The cacophonic noise inside his head faded to a dull roar.

"Thank God." He swiped shaking hands down his sweating face. It wasn't enough, nowhere near enough, but it was a start. The second he closed his eyes, he saw that flash again, that man. And he wondered if Jillian could sleep without nightmares about him.

"Where were you?" he asked, his voice hoarse.

She closed her eyes and lowered her head, resting it on the table. "Disney World. Mom and Dad took me to Disney World. We were by the castle when I saw him."

He wanted to puke.

The memory of her terror, as she stood in a place that should have just held joy.

Just a kid.

But he realized she was right. She had more control than he did, because she'd been living with that horror in her mind. Somehow. And it hadn't broken her.

The weight of her gift was a pressure inside his skull, stretching and moving inside him like a leviathan, and he didn't know if he could contain it. Even with the presence of that door in his mind, he could feel everybody, and it was too much.

Dez, Taige, Jones. An odd blank spot that he recognized as Jillian's father, only because he'd inherited that recognition from Jilly. Spread out, all around him, like stars in the night sky, were others.

"Show me how you shut your door," he said gruffly. He'd work on the technique until he had one that suited him, but for now, he'd take the cues from her.

Jillian's mind opened for him. Welcomed him. And he saw the door . . . it was like a stone gate, massive and immense, one that moved easily at her command. And when it was in place, the presence of others settled into the background.

Carefully, he climbed to his feet, still staring at Jillian.

Before she opened her mouth, he knew she would ask.

And even as the words formed in her mind, he knew the question.

"Can you stop him?" she was asking . . .

Even as he was answering, "I don't know. But I'll do it or die trying."

She nodded.

Dez, unaffected, rose from the table.

There was a heavy, strained silence as she moved to open the door for him. As she turned to give him a sympathetic look, he kept his focus on his feet. On the floor. Just one step, then another. *That's it . . . one step, then another . . .*

All the way down the hall, to the elevator.

He kept that right up until he was in his room, right up until he hit the nicely stocked minibar.

There, he hit the alcohol and did it without feeling any shred of guilt at all. With a normal sync, it could take a good twelve to twenty-four hours to adjust, sometimes more. This wasn't normal. This wasn't even in left field. It shot clear past left field, hurtling into unknown territory. For all he knew, he'd be a wreck for the next week.

No. Not acceptable, he thought dully. Not with all these screams. Not with all this pain. Not with the whispers of the dead dancing across his skin.

But he could damn well take a few hours and get shit-faced drunk as he struggled to deal with this, while he tried to process the horror that the little girl had been living with . . . combined with the cries of the ghosts that haunted Desiree Jones.

If he got through this without losing his mind, or without turning into a bona fide alcoholic, it would be a fucking miracle.

EIGHT

"**Y**ou going to talk to me?"

It was hours later.

Jillian had fallen asleep, and Taige had stayed by her side until she knew the girl was sleeping.

Even now, she was having a hard time not going into the teen's room to check on her. *Should have stayed in there*, she thought sourly as Cullen cut her off just outside their daughter's room.

Chicken. Damn straight.

Sometimes it wasn't always a bad thing to back away from an ugly fight. Especially when she knew she might say things that would leave bruises. Or when she'd hear things that would bruise *her*.

But he wouldn't leave it be, so fine.

They'd have their fight.

Carefully, she closed the door, reaching out once more with

her mind to check on Jillian. The girl was asleep, sound asleep, probably for the first time in months. A lash of guilt hit Taige, full across the heart. It wasn't unusual for Jillian to have problems sleeping. Between her gifts and her nightmares, she'd have spells when the restlessness got bad, when she'd sleep for only a few hours. So they'd take her to her therapist, do whatever they could to help get her through whatever was bothering her.

And they'd done that.

But it hadn't been enough because Taige hadn't seen just how much worse it was this time. Over the past few years, Jilly's gift had grown so much and her shielding . . . hell. She left Taige in the dirt and she'd been hiding so much of this. What Taige didn't understand was *why* she'd been hiding. Although considering how Cullen had reacted to today's events? Yeah. Maybe she did understand why.

Worry about this later, she told herself as she made her way into the sitting room. It was on the far side of the suite, and hopefully they could be quiet enough to keep from waking the girl.

Taige layered her shields down tight, knowing that was the only way to keep from leaking over on the girl. Cullen wasn't an issue. She could pick up odd and random thoughts, but she almost always had to be touching him and *looking* for those thoughts. It wasn't much different with Jillian. He was practically a psychic null.

Made it easier to have it out with him—that was for certain.

Flinging herself into a chair, she crossed her legs and stared up at him. Anger and frustration chewed a hole inside her. Underneath all of that there was hurt. He actually thought she'd do anything that would let Jilly get hurt.

"So, get it out," she drawled, smiling at him.

"Get what out?" Cullen crossed his arms over his chest, staring at her like he wasn't exactly sure which way to go from here.

"You want to lay into me over what's going on, I'm sure. Have at it." She pretended to study her nails. A few days ago, she'd decided to have a "girl's day" with Jillian, hoping to cheer the kid up. She'd been bored out of her mind, and Jillian had figured that out about halfway through the manicure, but they'd finished up. Then they'd gone to the beach instead of getting a pedicure. The pale, silvery bluish-green was starting to chip a little. A waste of money, Taige thought. Pretty. But a waste of money.

"I . . . shit. Taige, are you going to look at me or admire your manicure?"

She studied him from under her lashes. "Cullen, I'm tired. It's been a lousy few days, and I want to go to bed. So if you have something to say, please say it. Otherwise . . ."

His mouth opened. Closed. His lids drooped, shielding the lovely blue-green of his eyes. "You ever feel like making things easy, Taige?"

"Sure. I'll make this easy." She got up off the couch and sauntered past him. "Good night. Let me know when you decide to stop being an ass."

She was five inches past him when he caught her arm.

As he whirled her around to face him, she blanked her expression. "Come on, Taige, would you cut me some slack? The last time that bastard was near my daughter, I'd just gotten her back. I'd almost lost you. He'd been pushing and probing at her head and . . ."

* * *

THE warm, smooth gold of her skin had gone pale.

After all these years together, Cullen knew when he'd hurt her, but he didn't quite realize what he'd done.

Snapping his mouth shut, he tugged her close. "What now,

baby?" Stroking her hair back from her face, he dipped his head, nuzzling her neck.

Taige stood woodenly, her body rigid. Unyielding.

Groaning, Cullen dropped his head and rested it on her shoulder. "Taige, darlin', you need to remember, I can't read your mind. I don't know what you're thinking unless you tell me."

Without saying a word, she extricated herself from his arms.

Unable to do anything but let go, Cullen stood. Frustrated, he opened his hands, closed them.

What in the hell had he done now . . .

"She's my daughter, too," Taige said quietly. "I know I didn't give birth to her, but she's my baby, and sometimes I think you forget how much I love her. Sometimes . . ." Her voice trembled, shuddered. Then she took a deep breath and said again, her voice steady once more, "Sometimes I think you forget that we both agreed to do this together. I'd die before I'd do anything that would harm her. But you don't seem to think that. You lump me in the same class you've placed Taylor in."

Then she sighed and shoved her hair back from her face. "But here's the thing . . . I know you hate him. God knows I've had my differences with him. But he understands something about people like me and Jillian. What he's doing right now will probably keep her from going insane—she saw too much this time, Cullen. And it almost broke her." She slanted a look at him, her gray eyes as cold as ice. "So think about that the next time you decide to demonize him. He's an icy piece of work, but he understands what this shit can do to people like me, like Jillian. I don't like his methods, and heaven help him if he seeks her out. But he understand how it haunts us . . . he knows it's a hell we live with. He could have worked this solo, figured out another way to go forward. But he knew she needed to be a part of it. This was the only *safe* way she could do it."

While his mind whirled, tried to process that, she shut the door.

She saw too much.

Almost broke her.

By the time he could even think of anything to say, his legs were numb, his heart too heavy.

"Taige . . ."

But when he went to his wife, she wasn't there.

She'd settled down in the bedroom where their daughter slept.

Leaving him out there.

Alone.

* * *

SHE stood on the bridge, gazing down into the lake.

It was her birthday, and she was spending it in the only place she could imagine being.

Here . . . where she'd spent so many days with him.

The agony was so great, Amelie just didn't think she could take it anymore. Each day, she thought maybe, just maybe it would be the day she decided she was done. But she was almost certain today was the day. She'd even dressed for it, wearing a walking suit of black. The jet beads on it caught what little light managed to filter through the clouds, but she barely noticed.

Her mother had asked her how much longer she'd insist on wearing mourning colors. Amelie had answered, "When I no longer feel as though I'm in mourning."

That time would never come, although she knew she'd have to stop soon. Her parents indulged her, and secretly, she suspected her mother and father were pleased to see her small defiance of Richard. They cared for him as little as she did.

She hoped they'd forgive her if she . . .

No. She wasn't going to think about it yet.

Lydia—Dru didn't care for Lydia, tried to avoid her at all costs. That woman was a piece of work. She suspected Lydia had some pretty deep insights into Patrick's character, but there was no way Dru was going to try for *that* connection.

No until she had to.

But now she had to deal with this . . . and the icy cold anger she could still feel coming from him. She took her cues from it, just as she'd always done. "It's not exactly that I've been dieting," she hedged, giving him a vague smile. "I just have a habit of eating when I'm nervous and I've been careful not to do that. I guess I've been too careful."

He studied her.

Even though she saw it coming, Dru didn't move.

The blow was a light, stinging slap—not hard enough to bruise, not even hard enough to leave a mark. Still, the shock of it knocked the breath out of her and she stumbled back against the wall, her head falling forward until her chin rested against her chest.

If she looked at him, he'd see the hatred she felt for him. If she looked at him, he'd see how much she wanted to kill him. So she didn't dare look at him. Keeping her head low, hair shielding her face, she stood there, shuddering. Shaking.

It wasn't the first time he'd hit her.

It wouldn't be the last.

Tears blinded her and she had to bite her tongue to keep from screaming as he came closer. Not in terror . . . but in rage.

When he reached out to cup her chin, she closed her hands into fists, made herself blank her features. She wanted to beat him bloody. She wanted to spit in his face.

Instead, she stared at him as he critically turned her face this way, then that. "You need to stop pushing me, Ella. We've discussed this. You're a good girl, a good match for me, but sometimes, it's like you enjoy testing me. Like you enjoy pushing me."

While the blood roared in her ears, a strange, swimming
sensation came over her—voices rising up to clamor in her brain.

*"I could kill you. As easy as that and not a soul would say a
word . . ."*

Water . . . cold and black . . . closing around her—

Not now, she thought desperately. She couldn't do this around
him. Shoring up her shields, she swallowed back the bile, swallowed back all the angry, furious words that rose to her lips, begging to be free.

Go fuck yourself—

That was what she wanted to tell him. What she wanted to
say to him. So badly.

One thing silenced her, and it wasn't her fear of him. It was
the death that followed him like a shroud and the knowledge that
it wouldn't stop until *he* was stopped.

"I'm sorry, Patrick. I'll be more aware of things in the future."

It wasn't a lie. She'd be far more aware of things.

N I N E

THE adjustment period sucked. Usually, though, by the end of the first twenty-four hours, he could cope. Thirty-six max.

Joss was moving on seventy-two hours now, and he still felt like he was in a tailspin.

Somewhere near late dawn the third day, though, he finally reached the point he'd been shooting for—that point of control, where he could walk around and not feel like the voices were going to crush him. Where the ghosts weren't going to drive him mad.

Of course, he'd gone nearly twenty hours without sleep. It was weird how sometimes that genius hit right when one was about ready to die or drop. Then, right when he was certain he couldn't fumble and shift those two brain-frying gifts around inside his skull anymore, he found a way to make them fit.

It wasn't comfortable, damn it, but they fit.

Finally able to sleep without hearing the wailing of the dead or the whispers of the living, he collapsed on his bed in the hotel room and slept.

As though they'd been waiting for him to collapse, the dreams attacked. Sucking him under and grabbing on tight, they pulled him down and he was trapped. Locked in a maze of horror where the screams were an endless melody in his mind and the blood colored the air and hung in the back of his mouth, choking him.

He heard their cries. He smelled the blood. He tasted their horror. They were trapped, someplace dark and stinking with their own waste. Hopelessness, helplessness flooded their very souls, and Joss had to fight to keep himself separated from it.

If he didn't, it would overwhelm him and he needed answers.

Dark. Windowless. He ticked off the measurements as best as he could, thinking he was in a room about twenty by twenty. A basement, maybe? He didn't know if houses typically had them around here—something for Jones to check out—

Focus, he told himself as the dream tried to splinter, shattering his train of thought and making him nothing but a creature of fear and pain, drawing him back into that web of terror.

No. He wasn't getting trapped in there.

Mildew. Mold. The place smelled old, and the stink of human excrement was everywhere. Dark, a black void that made him search for windows, doors . . . he saw nothing.

Saw nothing. But he felt them, heard them. They surrounded him. As a girl sobbed, he knelt down, tried to touch her, but his hand passed right through. The same basic response when he tried to speak to her . . . she didn't hear a word. Okay, so Jillian's gifts weren't that mind-numbingly powerful, although damn, it sure as hell would have made this easier.

He'd have to rely on good old investigative shit for now. He searched for details, clues, committing everything he could find to memory. There wasn't much, though. As he swam through the morass of Jillian's memories and visions, he searched for the one thing he *really* needed.

The man Jillian had seen. He needed to see him again—without Jillian's fear to color what he saw.

He searched, he waited, he trolled through all the images and thoughts and dreams she'd pushed into his mind . . . but never did he catch another glimpse of that man.

Her thoughts grew vague, indistinct, and he knew he wouldn't find the answers he needed there. So he gave up. Stopped trying to control the dreams, and even as he let them slide away, the dream shifted, re-formed.

And he was elsewhere.

The stink of body waste and filth melted away, replaced by the soft, delicate scent of woman. He saw her back, narrow and slim. Standing at a balcony, rigid, her shoulders a taut line while her hands rested on the railing. He scowled as he looked around, trying to process what he was seeing.

A hotel. Okay. The woman . . . okay. His gaze lowered and he found himself eyeing her ass for a moment before he forced himself back to the matter at hand—although he couldn't help noticing it was a very, very nice ass. Fancy room. Lights off. Plenty of sun shining in.

And the woman was standing outside, hands on the railing as she stared toward . . . what the hell . . . was that . . . *Focus, Joss.*

"Hello?"

But just as before, she didn't hear him.

Great. Unsure just what he'd dreamed himself into, Joss moved forward, looking around and trying to connect this place to the nightmares he'd picked up from Jillian. Trying to understand who the woman was. Why he was here.

Rich. That's what this was. The place practically bled money. Even the smells were pricey.

The woman lifted a hand—her left hand—tucked her hair back behind her ear, and then paused, lowered it to stare at the ring sparkling there.

Something about her called to him . . . He wanted her to turn around. Look at him. Talk to him.

But she remained blissfully unaware of him, even when he said, "Nice rock."

Of course, he hadn't really *expected* her to hear him . . . nobody else had.

He scowled when she abruptly started to claw at her hand, tearing the ring off with something too close to desperation. Once she had it off, she whirled around and hurled it. He flinched, but it passed right through him.

And then he staggered, went to his knees.

Her face . . .

Her *eyes* . . . so grim, so sad.

And her face . . .

Like a knife, the sight of her ripped something open inside him and he felt himself falling. Desperately, trying to get himself back on balance, he reached for the strands of the dream and tried to weave them back together.

But it was too late.

The dream was gone.

He jackknifed upright in bed, staring around in the dim room. Scrubbing his hand over his face, he groaned.

"What the fuck . . ." he muttered. "What the fuck . . ."

* * *

FOR three days, Patrick ignored her.

If he thought that would bother her, then he didn't know her very well. Well, actually, he *didn't* know her, and that was a good thing.

A tray of food had been sent to her three times a day, and Dru was okay with that. The food was decent, and as long as Patrick wasn't there, she could actually manage to eat. She'd kind of been dreading Friday. Fridays and Saturdays usually entailed elaborate, fancy dinner dates where she had to dress up and pretend to be his little Barbie doll. This Friday, though, there was a tray delivered at dinnertime.

Along with a note:

Ella

You should stay in and eat, rest for a few more days. Relax.

Patrick

Simple. To the point. Anybody who didn't know him would think he was just concerned for her welfare.

After all, there was nothing overly threatening about the note. Or even obliquely threatening about it.

When she touched it, though, her belly cramped with fear.

She could all but taste the need to hurt on him—it was imprinted on the note. It carried his cool fury and his disgust. He might as well have marked her with it. *I'm a sadist and I love to hurt things. Cross me and you'll be next.*

Except he wouldn't go after her . . . not directly at first.

He'd find other ways to undermine her. Ways that would involve seeing those around her suffer. Like the wedding designer . . . Dru had initially wanted to work with a new girl who'd been practically just out of school. It was the one thing she'd tried to do. Not that it mattered so much about the stupid *dress*—she wasn't looking at this as a damned wedding, but if the dickwad was going to shell out the money, it might as well go to somebody who'd need it more than a some bloke who already had clients coming out of his ears, she figured.

But that one thing that she'd wanted to do, he'd smashed it. Right in front of her, the day after she'd refused to have sex with him for the first time.

He'd fired the girl right in front of Dru, told her the work was inept, barely suited to the travesty of a Vegas wedding, much less *his* standards. And as he was paying the bill, he figured he should be pleased with the work, naturally.

That hadn't been the only thing he'd done, though.

Dru shuddered as a memory flash rolled through her mind. When he'd come to her the following night, she'd seen something else in his mind—the events of the night. He'd left her . . . and gone to his little slave shop. He'd been in the mood to hurt somebody. He was still taking care with her, though. Hurting *her* would have to wait. Couldn't leave bruises or anything until after the wedding. So he'd taken his anger out on somebody else.

He hurt her, without even knowing it, by taking his rage out on another.

Sick monster.

Twisted, sick monster, and she was trapped. For now. But damned if she wouldn't try to find a way to get out.

Staring at the note, she read it one more time . . .

Stay in and eat, she thought. *Rest.*

Absently, she reached up and touched her cheek. It hadn't even bruised—she'd watched it for the first two days, wondering if a mark would show, but it hadn't happened. Patrick had a lot of practice in striking women. It sickened her to the very core, knowing that.

"Stay in." She stared off at nothing. "I quite think I've had enough of staying in, actually."

She ignored the food. She wasn't in the mood to eat any

damned thing he'd sent to her. Three days were enough of acting like a kicked puppy. Outside on the balcony, she stared toward the park, her gut in knots, her head pounding. And all the while, rage burned inside her.

Stay in.

She was letting her fear cow her. The one thing she'd told herself she couldn't do and what was she doing?

The rage burned inside, and to her disgust, she realized she was just a step away from crying. She was furious, she was scared, she was angry . . . and trapped. But damned if she'd cry about it.

The headache behind her eyes raged and she went to rub her brow but the ring flashed, caught her attention. Unaware that she was snarling, she stared at the ring for a long, long moment and then, desperately, she grabbed the ring, tore it off her hand. For a second, she was tempted to hurl it off the balcony, but at the last moment, self-preservation stopped her and she whirled around.

As she hurled it across the room, something hazy danced in front of her eyes.

She froze, staring at the spot just a few feet in front of her door.

A man—

But she blinked and when she looked again, whatever she'd seen was gone.

"I'm going crazy," she whispered. And it was entirely possible.

Across the room, her ring lay by the door, glinting. Mocking her. She ignored it. Unable to stay inside another moment, she grabbed her purse. She'd be damned if she remained locked away in this sodding prison. He thought he had her cowed, damn him. And when he realized she'd left, he damn well might make her suffer for it.

But screw it. She couldn't let her fear of him control her. The day she started letting him stop her in *any* way, she was done. She was so utterly filled with fury, she was tempted to flash her middle finger in the direction of the nearest camera.

But she wasn't that far gone. Yet.

She'd come here with a purpose, and she'd see it through. It couldn't happen if she lost her nerve, though, and she had to remember that.

* * *

IT was hot and humid, typical for Orlando, even though it was close to nine.

She didn't care. Just getting out of the hotel *alone* felt wonderful. She'd swung by one of the gift shops, buying a slouchy little cap and stuffing it in her purse. In a bit, she'd don the cap, a pair of sunglasses. She also had a different shirt tucked inside her bag and she'd put that on as well.

It wasn't a real disguise, but it would be enough, she thought, to help her evade being seen by Patrick's men. They were used to seeing her in all the lovely *"Ella"* clothes, not just regular old T-shirts, jeans, and shit.

It would be enough to do the job.

She didn't dare use the charge cards Patrick had given her— she had to give him credit, he didn't slouch on the expenses once they'd gotten engaged. He didn't want a wife, she knew. He just wanted a high-class whore, but he was willing to pay well.

But if he was suspicious enough to check—and he likely was—all it would take was a text from an account watch and plenty of credit cards were equipped with those. Fortunately for her, Dru had resources Patrick couldn't even begin to guess at, and she used cash to pay her way into the park.

Once inside, she hit the restroom, braiding her long hair, pulling on that slouchy cap, and trading her elegant blouse for a close-fitting T-shirt with three-quarter-length sleeves. It clung like a second skin and was thin enough that she could see the outline of her bra. After slipping on the sunglasses, she studied her reflection and decided it would work. It was enough of a one-eighty from her normal appearance that unless somebody was actually *looking* for her, they likely wouldn't notice her.

It wasn't like she actually spent any time in here with her fiancé anyway. Curling her lip, she shoved her belongings into her bag and headed back out into the park, breathing in the scents of sunscreen, food . . . life. It smelled like summer. It smelled like . . . happiness, she decided.

Something about it tugged at memories deep inside.

It was a sad thing, actually, coming in here. She remembered this place, vaguely, from fleeting memories of her childhood, before everything with her parents had gone to hell—first, Mum had died, then her father.

Before that, she'd traveled to the States with them several times as a child and she'd been to Disney World a few times . . . it held happy memories. It shouldn't make her sad.

Maybe it was because back then she'd still had hope. Still believed in magic, and lately, she was trapped in a hell where there was no hope. And he hid himself *here* . . .

It made her ill.

It made her hurt.

Longing to lose herself for just a while, she watched the children, the little girls dressed in their princess finery, listened to the music drifting from carefully hidden speakers.

But she couldn't find the elusive happiness, the escape she'd come here seeking.

Her mind was too focused on *him*.

Rest. He'd told her to rest.

Why? What was he about? she wondered. There had to be something. He'd been careful to keep her under close watch, almost like he was guarding her. It was obsessive how often he seemed to spend the evenings with her. If he wasn't with her, he was out doing things that made her long to kill him.

The days she didn't see him at all were the bad ones, even when she relished not having to deal with him. Because when she faced him again, she knew there would be more evil in his head. He used those evenings away from her to see to his . . . business. That was how he thought of those girls.

His business.

Bastard. Soulless, evil bastard.

Making his money by selling flesh—death was just too good for him.

That was why she had to see this through . . . end it. Make sure he couldn't ever do it again . . . couldn't ever take anybody's daughter. Anybody's sister. Anybody's girlfriend or wife. She had to find out where they were. She'd gotten into this job for *one* reason—a missing runaway. A pretty teenaged girl, her name had been Sarah Hale . . . and she'd disappeared more than two years ago.

Swaying out of the way of a family posing in front of the castle, she veered off to the left, unsure exactly where she was going as she thought back. She really had given more than two years of her life to this.

The girl's father had come to her. His name was David Hale. Sarah had run away after an argument, determined to go live with her mother in New Jersey.

The body had been found in Pennsylvania eight months after Dru had agreed to take the case. She'd returned the retainer he paid her. Wrapped up the odds and ends of all other jobs she'd been working on. And started following the threads of this one.

It hadn't been anything **directly** connected to Sarah that had led her to Florida. It had been a tangled web, and one of those threads had led to Orlando. A source had hinted at something rather twisted that took place among some of the jet set, and she'd made her way through a short list of those people until she'd found the right thread to pull on. All it took was the right memory, the right connection . . . and one of those men had a memory, a connection to Patrick.

Like everything else, it had come to her in a flash, a solid chunk of memory—he'd bought a young woman, a pretty woman in her twenties who'd come to America from Cuba, thinking she'd get citizenship and a new life. She'd ended up some man's slave, courtesy of Patrick and his . . . *associates.*

Ever since then, Dru had been in a state of hyperawareness as she tugged at those strands, pulling those threads. Her mind made connections that didn't seem possible, but sure enough, all the pieces fell into place.

Except the past few months she'd just been . . . stuck.

Waiting. Digging, slowly, patiently. Patient as a bloody saint, in her opinion, but it was taking too long.

There was darkness here. All tied in to money and lust and greed, and it went deep, very deep. Still following her leads, working the case on her own, she'd placed herself in Patrick's way.

He had a thing for long, leggy brunettes, and that's one thing she had working for her. The other thing—she could get a glimmer of what he wanted with just a touch. It wasn't anything she'd consider true mind reading. She knew she had psychic skill, but her strongest ability lay in picking up things already past, those memory flashes that haunted her so.

But that weaker gift was still enough for her to pick up on his needs, his wants, his likes . . . his perversions . . . and she used it. Manipulated herself until she was the very image of the type of woman he was looking for. And she got deeper, and deeper, into this mess until there was no way she could get out, not unless she saw it through.

Seeing it through . . . that would require one simple thing.

Hard evidence.

It wasn't like she could go to the police and say, *Pardon me, sir, but the man who wants to marry me is a slaver. Yes, yes, I know slavery is illegal, but it still happens and I think you should investigate him.*

That would go over rather well, she was sure.

Proof. Had to have proof. And she had to be careful, too. He already had plans in place for what he'd do if he suspected he was being watched. Those girls would die, and they'd die horribly, in a way that was unlikely their bodies would ever be found.

She needed *proof.* She needed to protect the women, the girls he still had tucked away somewhere on a compound. And she had to do it all without him realizing what she was up to. No big deal, right? If she had to take more of his abuse, if she had to tolerate his touch . . . her skin crawled just thinking about it, but she could handle it.

Whatever it took to see this through, to make sure there were no more screams once she walked away from here.

Exhaustion pulled at her. Weary, she sank down on a bench and covered her face with her hands. Out here, under the fading summer sun, it was easier to pretend she wasn't afraid. But she was. She could pretend she wasn't running on the very edge of her wits, even though she knew she lied.

"You can do this." She rubbed her temples. "Just see it through. A little bit longer."

Exhaustion pushed closer and she welcomed it. A few minutes, maybe. Just a few minutes to relax . . . But even as some of the tension started to drain away, one of those fragmented nightmares snaked in, tried to pull her under. The blackness tried to surround her, grabbing at her—gasping for air, she threw it off and stumbled upright.

"Not now," she whispered.

Water . . . closing over her head . . .

You have to get away from him—

That memory flash, the one that made no sense, danced through her head, the man's voice getting louder, louder with each refrain until it was a shriek inside her head. Groaning, she squeezed her eyes closed, tried to block it out.

Couldn't breathe . . .

Get away—

"I'm going mad," she said. "Stark, raving mad."

Here she was, dealing with a psychotic son of a bitch, and instead of thinking that through, she was dealing with dreams and flashes of drowning, while her mind played back warnings of that voice. *You have to get away from him—*

Him? Him, *who?* Patrick? Oh, she *knew* that.

Yes. The logical thing was to get the hell away from him—she was more and more afraid that he was going to kill her. She knew he *would* if he found out what she was up to. Is that what the nightmares were? Some new manifestation of her ability or something? A warning?

Bugger all. She didn't *need* a warning.

"What am I supposed to do? Just walk away?"

Not an option.

She owed those girls. Their screams.

They haunted her. Every time he touched her, she heard those screams. And it got worse. He'd hurt so many people, ruined so many lives.

If she walked, they'd haunt her, every moment for the rest of her life. It wasn't going to happen.

So if the nightmares were some nebulous warning, they could just shut their nebulous ass up.

Looking up at the sky, she mentally squared her shoulders. And *damn* if she'd sit here, feeling sorry for herself. She'd come here to get away from him, to try and breathe away from the stifling presence of his ever-watchful eyes, those bloody cameras. She'd damn well try to enjoy herself while she was at it.

She'd have herself a slice or two of pizza.

She'd ride some rides.

It was Disney World, for pity's sake.

She could find a way to have a bit of fun.

TEN

"THE happiest place on earth." Joss stood in the middle of Main Street USA, looking all around and trying to figure out just what he'd gotten himself into.

The one good thing—Jillian hadn't lied to him when she'd said she had control.

She had it in spades. Once he'd adjusted to the sync, gotten that badly needed sleep and a solid meal, he'd acclimated enough to imagine that door she used. He shut it down tight, and then he went the extra step . . . every damn body had a door, one that led to their mind, and he shut those doors as well, leaving him in the blissful silence of his own mind.

Granted, it didn't do anything for the occasional icy chill of a ghost's touch, their calls, but he could deal with those. People died, and when they died before their time, they left echoes. He didn't like it, but he had to concern himself with saving the ones who were still alive, so he moved the ghosts down on his list. He was good at compartmentalizing.

Now . . . if he could just figure out what in the hell he was doing in Disney World.

What had led him here . . . well, there was that dream. A mere figment, a blind hope.

And instinct.

Actually, instinct wasn't a bad thing to rely on, he told himself, forcing himself to take a step after he saw one of the photographers flash a smile in his direction.

Oh, no. Did he *really* look like he wanted to pose in front of that stupid castle?

Hands jammed in his pockets, he headed down the strip, no particular destination in mind. As a tiny little girl—dressed in a wide-skirted dress of sunny yellow—cut in front of him, he almost tripped over his feet to keep from tripping over *her*. Geez, what did she have on her feet, rockets?

Her mother came running out of a store after her, and automatically, Joss took a step to cut the child off. The little girl stopped in her tracks and smiled up at him, her mouth smeared with chocolate, a rather marked contrast with the glittery stuff on her eyes, her hair.

"I think somebody's looking for you," he said, nodding to the frazzled woman just before she could catch the girl's arm.

The woman gave him a thankful look, and as they melted back into the crowd, Joss did the same, moving with the flow.

Nothing here, he thought, distracted, *nothing* . . .

The road veered in a path off to the left. It wasn't a conscious decision to follow it, but he did so, following it around the curve, passing behind a shop to a small alcove.

And he came up short, freezing in his tracks.

There she was . . . it was the woman he'd glimpsed earlier, in that figment of a vision, just before the dream had fallen apart, but that gut-deep recognition . . . he *knew* her.

He knew her face.

Joss Crawford wasn't prone to melodrama, he wasn't prone to wishful thinking, and he didn't much believe in fairy tales. He didn't buy into those crazy stories of love at first sight.

But he knew there was a woman for him—he'd been searching for her his entire life, had dreamed about her always. He looked for her in every face he saw, waited for the moment he'd find her again.

And here she was, striding down the pavement, her face grim, her eyes dark . . . the sight of her was a punch, straight to his heart. She didn't *look* like she should, part of his brain insisted. The rest of him didn't care. He knew her, in his gut, in his heart, in his soul.

Standing rigid, barely able to breathe, much less move, he waited for her to look at him, to see him . . . to *know* him. But it didn't happen.

In fact, she was so busy staring at the pavement and making a concentrated effort to ignore everything around her, she didn't even seem to notice him. She went to go around him and he just couldn't stop himself—he stepped right into her path so that she crashed straight into his chest, all lean limbs and long muscles and golden, sun-kissed skin, a nice, solid weight that he figured would fit his body just about perfectly. She stumbled and he reached up, closed his hands around her upper arms, where the cotton of her shirt kept him from touching bare flesh.

He wanted to touch bare flesh . . . after all this time, he figured he just about *needed* to. But not now.

Right now, she was watching him with dazed, distrustful eyes—wariness flashed through her gaze and he felt her tense.

"You . . ." He didn't even know what to say. A total stranger, and that's what he'd seem like to her, he knew. How could he tell her he'd been dreaming of her for always? Waiting. Searching. Absently, without realizing it, he stroked his thumb across her arm, and it rubbed across the bare skin just below the sleeve of her shirt.

As bare skin touched bare skin, he felt something . . . a buzz in his brain.

And more . . . he felt the echo of it in *her* brain. Followed by a blinding rush of knowledge.

Her pupils flared. She sucked in a breath. "*You* . .

Her eyes widened.

And a rush of images slammed into them both as that gift he'd absorbed from Jillian faltered under his grasp.

"*You'll come away with me, won't you, Amelie?*"

"*And how are we to live, Thom? Hmmm? I do not think there's room for me on the boat where you work.*"

Pushing her golden hair back from her face, he tipped her chin back, kissed her gently. "We'll be together. And we'll find a way. I'll find other work. Just say you'll come away with me."

His head was spinning, blood roaring, as he jerked his mind and those hazed memories from another life back under his grasp, shoving his shields up. Her eyes, wide and dazed, stared into his.

"You . . ."

Her pupils spiked, flared, and she sucked in a desperate breath.

She swayed closer, and logically, Joss knew it wasn't because she was suddenly overcome, like he was. She didn't *know* him—he would have known it if she had. But she was closer, and she was there, and he could feel the warmth of her, feel *her*, and fuck it, he was just too weak.

Groaning, he dipped his head and pressed his lips to hers.

He was fully prepared for the fact that she was going to haul off and belt him.

He was fully prepared for her to jerk away and scream.

What he wasn't prepared for was for her to sigh against his lips, then open her mouth for him.

What he wasn't prepared for was for her hands to come up, curl into the front of his shirt, tugging him closer.

But that was what she did, and the top of his head almost came off as he caught the first hint of her taste.

The tip of her tongue stroked along his lower lip before pushing into his mouth. He nipped it gently and returned the favor, stroking her tongue with his, tracing the outline of her mouth. She moved closer, her hands moving down to his waist, tugging him closer still, and Joss figured maybe it might be okay to touch her, too.

Fisting one hand in the back of her shirt, he used the other hand on her braid and tugged, angled her head farther back. She was long, and lean, fitting so perfectly against him, and he fucking loved it.

Long and lean, but soft, too, cradling him so perfectly. He could feel the curve of her belly, her breasts, all of her and it was fan-fucking-tastic. Under her shirt, he could feel the silken warmth of her back, and he wanted to drag the shirt away, learn all the curves and hollows and sweet delights of her body.

More . . . he needed more. Couldn't wait to peel her out of those clothes and get her naked—

"Mommy, look, they're kissing!"

The high-pitched laughter managed to penetrate the drunken fog of need that wrapped around his head, and Joss lifted his head, staring into those pale green eyes for an endless moment. By the time he'd slanted a look over, the little girl was being herded away by a grinning set of parents.

In the two seconds it took to check out their potential audience, his potential partner decided to extricate herself from his hands and Joss wanted to howl.

He felt empty—needed to haul her back against him, but how could he explain that?

"Ah . . ." She stared at him, a rosy blush staining her cheeks.

He figured he could say something to help with the embarrassment he knew she was feeling, but he wasn't exactly sure what he should say. If he lied and apologized, she'd know. He wasn't so far gone he'd forgotten about that buzz he'd felt in her brain.

He'd have to be careful here. Very careful.

She continued to stare at him, her head half lowered so that she watched him through her lashes.

"If you're waiting for me to apologize, we're probably going to have a problem," he finally said. "If I said it, I'd be lying. You'd know it."

She lifted a brow. Simple. Eloquent.

"Have dinner with me." Screw the case. He was still trying to wrap his head around the mess that Jillian had thrown into his brain, and he could take a few more hours to adjust, right?

"That's not possible, Mr. . . ."

Shit, what name was he using . . . hell, hopefully if she picked up on any nervousness, she'd relate it to the kiss and the awkwardness of the situation, and *not* realize he'd given her a false name. "Baldwin," he said, grabbing one of his aliases out of the air. "Why not?"

"I'm spoken for." She lifted a hand and glanced down at it, scowling at the pale strip on her finger.

He reached out and caught her hand, rubbing his thumb over the area where the ring had rested. He remembered now . . . that odd dream. The vision. Seeing her staring at the ring, snarling like a caged beast as she tore the bit of jewelry from her hand and threw it. Seeing the rage on her face. "He doesn't make you happy."

Tugging her closer, he slid his free hand up her arm, cupped her cheek. "He doesn't even know much about you, does he?" He brushed his thumb across the satin of her skin and thought about kissing her again.

"No. And that's probably for the best." She tipped her head back to meet his gaze. "Look, this is all terribly . . . well. It's quite intriguing, and I wish I'd met you a few years ago, but I'm engaged and that's all there is to it."

Joss grinned at her. "Is it?" Dipping his head, he pressed his mouth to hers. "Will you do one thing?"

"What?"

He shuddered as he felt her lips moving against his. "Tell me your name."

"It's Dru." She eased her head back and glanced around, a quick, subtle look. Then she looked back at him, and those pretty green eyes held something of sadness. A flash of something he couldn't quite read lingered there. "You feel odd to my head . . . it's almost like you burn. I haven't met too many who did that."

She eased back and reached up, touched his cheek. "I really do wish you'd found me before this."

"I'll find you again, Dru."

"No." She shook her head. "It's best if you don't."

He said nothing. He wasn't going to argue with her, and he already knew it didn't matter . . . he could already see it happening.

They'd see each other again, and soon.

As she turned away, he murmured her name to himself. *Dru.* He supposed he hadn't exactly expected her to be called the same name.

And Dru suited her now.

Simple. Efficient. And if the look in her eyes was any indicator, she was a lot more equipped at taking care of herself than she had been.

He kept his eyes on her narrow back until she was lost among the crowd of people and then he blew out a breath, tipped his head back.

Damn.

"Maybe there's something to be said for this Magic Kingdom shit, after all."

* * *

SHE was on adrenaline overload by the time she made it back to her room.

The flood of memories swimming through her mind weren't *hers*, but they sure as hell felt like it.

"You'll come away with me, won't you?"

A man's face. Familiar in a way she just couldn't place. But she knew she knew him.

"Why didn't I get his name?"

Better off not having it, she tried to tell herself, tried to console herself. But it wasn't working. Already, she missed him, already she wished she hadn't told him no. Although wouldn't *that* have been a lark, having dinner with another man and then having to explain it to Patrick? And he *would* find out. That was just how he was.

Swallowing, she swiped her key card and let herself in, groaning and falling back against the door, sinking down. Her legs felt like Jell-O as she drew them upward, buried her face against them. What had she been thinking, letting him kiss her like that?

Kissing him *back*?

Those eyes of his . . . damn those eyes, they'd all but gutted her. Left her low.

And when he kissed her, she had the strangest sensation he'd kissed her before. Had the strangest sensation he'd touched her before. She didn't usually like kissing. But his kiss, she could get addicted to it. She could come to crave it.

Sex, yes, she usually liked sex, but she was rather good at using her own body to get what she needed from a man, and her hands, if she had to. Kisses were a different story. Too many men were either too bloody hesitant, or they acted like they were trying to ram their tongues down her throat and choke her. Or they acted like they were a damn vacuum and went about sucking her tongue off.

This man, though . . . he kissed like he was made to do just that.

Sighing, she let herself remember it. A wonderful kiss. She had almost lost herself in it.

Then there were his hands, the way he'd stroked them down her back, how he'd pulled her against him as though he had every right to do so—and it *felt* like he had every right.

Dru had lost her mind. It was as simple as that.

No other reason to explain why she'd risk something so utterly dangerous.

Why she was willing to risk it again. Why she was already craving another touch.

Her sex drive had withered away and died the past year, and it was no wonder, considering what she had plunged herself into, and what she had to live with, but now, it had flared to burning, sultry life.

All because of a few light touches and a stolen kiss.

But he'd done it so right. Tugging on her hair like that. Tangling his hand in her shirt. Waiting until she'd moved in on him before he'd really done much of anything, but then he'd taken over in just the right way . . .

Why didn't I get his name?

Now she just had the rest of her life to remember what it was like to have a total stranger kiss the daylights out of her . . . and she had nothing to call him. Maybe she should just make up a name to call him—

The phone on the small table next to her rang.

An icy chill raced down her spine.

Blowing out a breath, she rose. If her knees had been left weak by those kisses, it was something else that weakened them now. It just wasn't acceptable, though. She was tired of being afraid of this monster. Just telling herself to stop being afraid wasn't exactly doing the trick, but damn if it didn't piss her off.

*   *   *

THE sudden bolt of fear that shot through him wasn't his.

All-consuming and breath-stealing, it took Joss a minute to figure that out, though. Hands wrapped around the metal railing, eyes squeezed tightly closed, he slammed up layer after layer of shields, trying to focus past that fear, think beyond it.

It was like trying to move through quicksand.

Finally, though, he managed to get it all under control, and he had that fear separated from his own mind.

Locking in on the source wasn't hard.

He'd been vaguely aware of Dru ever since he'd laid eyes on her. He'd felt a rippling awareness course through her when she looked at him. He'd felt her dazed arousal as they kissed. He'd felt the same gut-deep recognition, even if she didn't know *why* she seemed to know him.

It wasn't hard to trace this back to her.

The hard thing was understanding just why she was suddenly so full of terror.

And then, just like that, it was gone—like she'd turned off a faucet, the fear was abruptly cut off, and once more, all he could feel was that vague sense of awareness.

Closing his eyes, he tried to strengthen that connection, but he couldn't. This screwed-up gift was just too new. Too new, and too much. And the connection to Dru was definitely too new.

Sighing, he lifted his hands, ground the heels of his palms against his eyes, sucked in a deep breath. He needed to think about the job.

He was here for that. He wasn't waiting until it was done to focus on Dru—he could multitask pretty damn well—but he had to focus on the job for now.

The job.

The fucking job—

"*. . . a good one there. Too bad I can't get merchandise while I'm here.*"

That train of thought snaked in through the layers of shielding Joss had slammed into place, and slowly, he lowered his hands, turned his head. Tracking thoughts to their owner wasn't quite the same as following a voice—they didn't exactly leave the easiest sort of trail.

But thankfully, Joss was used to working with telepathic gifts. Considering how damn young Jillian was, she was a virtual artist with hers. It wasn't too hard to home in as those erratic thoughts kept coming.

"*Look at the ass, damn. Down here with some friends, too . . . would be so fucking easy. Maybe I could figure out where she's from . . .*"

Big bastard. Almost as tall as Joss was. Dark-haired. A friendly-looking sort. Managed to move, unnoticed, through the crowds as he trailed along behind a cute little coed. Joss shifted his position, tracking him, following the man's train of thoughts, as they all fell into the line for one of the rides. It was in front of a big, old-looking house. One of the many themed rides here. Joss had already figured out there were nothing *but* theme rides here as he walked around, hoping to find her again.

He had known he wouldn't.

But something wouldn't let him leave.

Guess he knew what it was now.

He shot a cursory glance at the sign and pulled out his phone, pretended to glance around.

Don't pay me any attention . . . I'm just looking for my girl-friend . . . sending her a text, he thought absently, watching the group, watching the guy who was watching the girl.

Even though he was a big, rough-looking piece of work, Joss was good at fading into the woodwork.

So was the guy in front of him.

If Joss hadn't been trained to notice shit, if he hadn't been on the lookout for something off . . . and if he hadn't had that insane gift crammed into his head, he probably wouldn't have looked twice at this guy.

Nobody else seemed to think anything was off with him.

He chatted with the group next to him. Even chatted with the group of college kids. Although not with the pretty girl who'd caught his eye.

"Name is Alyssa. Pretty. Twenty years old. No boyfriend. Lives in Tulsa. Goes to college in Atlanta . . ."

A cool, efficient sort of monster, Joss noticed.

But not efficient enough.

Joss managed to get a few pictures of him. Sent them to Jones, along with a text. *See if anything pops on this guy.*

As the line continued to wind closer to the house, Joss watched, doing his own thing to blend. Chatting. Grumbling about his nonexistent girlfriend. An image of Dru flashed through his mind, and he tried yet again to strengthen that connection.

Just thinking of her made him more aware—she was angry now, angry and frustrated.

It was enough to distract him, and he couldn't afford that right now.

It took a hell of a lot of control, but he had to break that connection. For now.

Until he knew just what he was dealing with, he had to focus on the man standing about fifteen feet away. The man watching a pretty college girl with well-hidden greed.

*   *   *

HE used the name *Mike*. Mike Sellers. It was one of fifteen different aliases.

Mike was bored as hell, and wasn't expecting that to lessen anytime soon. He was being strung along by the arrogant son of a bitch who'd "requested" his services. The request had come from another arrogant son of a bitch, but it was somebody whom Mike just didn't like saying no to.

When certain people asked for favors, it was wise to just say yes. The favors came with a lot of money, and it made those people more inclined to be friendly with you . . . and it also made them less inclined to want you dead.

Mike knew how the game was played.

So he was playing it, even though this current potential customer was being an asshole of the highest order, bringing him in and then ignoring him for days on end.

It was a power play and he knew it. Mike could play that game very well, and he'd done it more than once. He'd play it, because playing it, and winning, just meant he'd get what he wanted in the end.

It wasn't money. Or rather . . . it wasn't *just* the money.

It was the hunt.

Finding a pretty girl . . . like Alyssa. Stalking her. Learning her ways, her pattern. Then catching her. Once he turned her over, he didn't know what happened, nor did he care. Sometimes he took his turn with his prey; sometimes he didn't. If he decided to take Alyssa, he'd take a turn. She was his sort of lady—a beautiful, petite little blonde with big tits, a tight little ass, and when she glanced at him, it was a nervous, blushing sort of smile that made his dick swell up.

A piece like her would be fun to keep around for a while.

Going to the Art Institute in Atlanta. Amazing how easily people tossed out information.

They didn't realize how easily they dropped it.

He'd heard her mention a few of her teachers' names. He could figure out her schedule. Follow her. See if she had a roommate—she probably did. Her clothes were nice, but not quite high-end enough for her to be rich, so she'd probably have a roommate. Another challenge. When to grab her.

It would take some planning . . .

It was also a good way to occupy his mind. That was why he was here, after all. Bored as hell and killing time. It was one of his favorite pastimes, surrounding himself with people, looking for potential merchandise, even if he wasn't actively hunting for a piece. Sometimes, he took a girl just to do it. Just for himself.

He could do that with her. He thought he just might.

A smile curled his lips as she glanced up at him, that hesitant, shy little grin on her face. Oh, yes. He was going to start planning. It would be a while. He'd been told this current job would keep him busy for a few weeks to a few months, and it would likely be an ongoing project if things turned out well.

But it wasn't a problem to wait awhile before moving on Alyssa. A few months down the road, and he could start laying the groundwork as soon as he had an idea what he was doing here.

And he could fantasize even now.

Man, she was going to be fun. He could already see her, tied up and facedown in the workshop he rarely got to use. Screaming behind a gag. He'd take care not to leave a mark on that soft skin . . . it would bring down the price once he was tired of her and sold her.

He never kept them for too long anyway, and it was better to sell them off when he was bored.

An acquaintance of his had told him it was just as much fun to kill them, but that was a waste. Plenty of his buyers liked taking a woman after she'd been broken, and Mike enjoyed that part almost as much as he enjoyed the hunt.

No point in killing them, after all.

* * *

BRING *down the price . . . yeah, you start thinking along those lines*, Joss thought. It was a struggle not to grab the son of a bitch and snap his neck then and there.

As the man who called himself Mike continued his hellish little fantasy, Joss sent another text to Jones. *Check out the name Mike Sellers. I suspect he's one of the connections here. He's new, though—I get the feeling he doesn't know his contact here. Can't pick up a name yet. I'll get one, though.*

Mike didn't know his connection here. This was good. Joss already had a vague idea about just how to proceed from here.

It would be a risky gamble, but instinct was telling him it was the right gamble. Which meant all he needed to do was confirm his suspicions.

And keep from killing that monster in the meantime.

Hard, that, considering he was getting a mental play-by-play of the sick fuck raping that college girl.

He snapped a picture of her as well, sent that one to Jones. *He's got a thing for this girl. I'm in the park. Her name is Alyssa—*

Joss focused his mind on the girl, probed a bit, and then swore as he saw her sway, flinching. She pressed a hand to her head, and he realized he'd pushed inside her head too hard.

He needed to get a better grip on this gift before he did shit like that. He told her *sorry* silently, not that it would do much good. *Her name is Alyssa Brascum. Goes to the Art Institute in Atlanta. This Sellers guy has this idea to grab her later down the road. I plan on interfering with said plan tonight, in a big way, and once I'm done, I doubt his brain will be good for anything, but just in case, we need to figure out what to do about her.*

It wasn't even a minute before Jones's text popped up. *Do you like making my life difficult?*

Consider it payback. I'm supposed to be off. Remember?

ELEVEN

"I thought we'd agreed you would stay in the room for a few more days. Rest. Eat."

Dru stared at her reflection.

Her eyes looked weirdly bright, she thought. "Did we?" she murmured, reaching up to touch her lips with her free hand.

The other hand gripped the phone so hard, it was a wonder the plastic didn't crack.

"Yes. We did." There was no mistaking the anger lurking under Patrick's voice.

"I've been resting for several days, Patrick. Eating rather well, too." She lowered her hand and turned away from the mirror. *Careful*, she thought. She needed to be careful here. "And I appreciate the concern. But I was just ravenous for something different. I'd . . . well. It's Friday and I'd hoped we could go out. I wanted to ask you to take me to eat at one of the Italian places in the park. I wanted to go to *Il Mulino*, but after you sent the tray,

I figured you must have one of your meetings, so I just went into the park for pizza." She paused and then added, "After all, I thought the best way to put the weight back on was by eating the foods that appeal to me."

The long, tense silence on the other end of the line made it pretty damn clear she hadn't done a damn thing to assuage his anger, but she hadn't really expected to.

"And did you eat?"

"Yes." She had. She'd actually eaten three damn pieces of pizza. Right before she'd met . . . *No. Don't think of him. If you think of him, you'll think about that kiss. And you can't do that—oh, that* kiss. *Cool it, Dru. Don't let on like anything is up.*

Bloody fuck, if Patrick had any inkling that she'd been snogging a total stranger . . . *he doesn't feel like a stranger, though . . .*

She needed to have her head examined.

"What else did you do?"

She laughed a little. "Oh, I walked around. Went into the stores, rode some rides. It's been years since I went into the park."

"Hmm. Did you use the credit cards I gave you?"

"Oh, no. I used some cash I had. I . . . well, silly of me perhaps, but I'm still not used to having you pay for things for me," she said glibly. *Looking to trip me up on something, are you, you prick?*

"The reason I gave you the credit cards was so you would use them, Ella. Please keep that in mind. You'll be my wife and I'll be the one providing for you."

She curled her lip, staring at her toes so none of the cameras he had in the room would catch the sneer that crept over her face. "Of course, Patrick. As I said, silly of me. I'm just so used to doing for myself and all that."

"Something you need to get over." He spoke to somebody else, his voice muffled. "I'll be up to see you shortly. I'm glad your appetite is returning. Perhaps you'll be a little less tiresome."

Tiresome. She gripped the phone, clenched her jaw. Oh, she could show him tiresome.

"I can't wait to see you," she murmured.

But he'd already hung up the phone.

Hanging the receiver up, she lifted her head to stare into the mirror.

Tiresome . . . that was his code.

There was one thing she hadn't been prepared for when she started this job. A job she was sacrificing everything for. Even her sense of pride, her self-worth.

She'd never planned on sleeping with him.

Nor would she have if she hadn't realized just how messed up things were. At least she liked to think that. But after he'd raped her, things changed. It hadn't been cruel, not compared to the way he'd treated many of the girls he sold—she knew that in brutal, stark clarity—but the son of a bitch had still ignored her when she said no. She hadn't been able to fight him and make him stop the way she *could* have . . . not without making him question too many things.

It had come to down to two choices . . . lie there and just *take* it, or make him stop. But if she'd done that, it would have shattered everything. All the things she'd done would have been in vain.

She still had the shame, the anger tugging inside her. Even knowing she'd done the right thing, it had taken her weeks to be able to look herself in the eye. Now, she lived with that memory in her head. The next day, he'd informed her, "Hopefully you won't always be so tiresome in bed, Ella."

From then on out, even as the nausea twisted through her later, she made it her mission—she'd damn well *not* have the choice taken out of her hands. If she was going to have sex with the twat, she'd do it on *her* terms.

If that made her less in the eyes of some, so be it. But she'd rather have sex with the monster and be in control than be another one of his victims.

It wouldn't last forever, either.

Sooner or later, it had to end, she told herself.

Sooner or later.

Sooner or later . . . but how much longer was that going to be?

* * *

HE was staying on the property.

Joss figured that little detail out about two hours later, after Mike had finally stopped trailing along after Alyssa Brascum.

Mike had managed to get her full name out of her, had flirted with all the girls in the group, had made buddies with the guys, and then disappeared, a nice, friendly sort of guy who had been killing time in between jobs.

That was the line he'd used.

Contract work. He did contract work and he was between jobs.

Nice way to describe stealing girls, Joss thought as he settled himself down in the shadows, staring toward the little cabin. All around him there were trees, and it was the best camouflage he could ask for. It wasn't bad security there, and Sellers wasn't exactly unaware. Still, neither the security nor Sellers was prepared for somebody like Joss.

As he shifted on the ground, back against a tree, he pulled out his phone, checked his e-mail. So far, no information back from Jones about this scumbag. Not promising, that. Could be somebody they didn't know about.

Could be—

Heat . . .

Joss hissed out a breath as lust hit him square in the gut, hot and hard, like somebody had just shot him full of some seriously powerful aphrodisiacs. Blood drained straight down and his cock grew achingly full, hard, and his blood pounded hot in his veins.

And when he closed his eyes, concentrated, he could feel *her.* All but inside his head. The sensations were so intense, he could practically feel the slide of her skin against his . . . like she was there, and they were both stretched out, naked flesh on naked flesh.

"What the hell . . ."

But even as he muttered that question into the silent night, he knew.

She was thinking of him. Thinking hard and heavy. Thinking hot, dirty little thoughts and getting hotter, dirtier by the second.

When he closed his eyes, he could almost see her spread out beneath him. All night, he'd worked to keep that connection tenuously thin, all but ready to break, but now . . . *now* he threw everything he had into it and he could feel her. All but taste her arousal. All but hear the moans vibrating in her throat as she moved.

Could all but feel his own dick, plunging inside her . . .

Damn.

The woman had one killer imagination.

If he didn't know better, he'd almost swear they were having sex . . .

* * *

It was the only way to get through it.

Lying naked in the bed beside Patrick, eyes closed and her heart racing, she kept her face pressed against the pillow and hoped he'd just keep his bloody mouth shut until she managed to get her mind back together.

That had been . . .

Whoa.

It had almost been like he'd been inside her mind.

As long as she hadn't opened her eyes and looked at Patrick. As long as she hadn't opened her mouth and tried to kiss him. As long as she hadn't breathed in his scent. Just keeping her focus on *him* . . . on Mr. Tall, Dark, and Sexy, a man she'd seen for all of thirty seconds before they decided to go and put their hands all over each other.

Tall, Dark, and Sexy, who felt like she'd known him all of her life. Tall, Dark, and Sexy, who had a mind that felt like . . . *home* . . .

All she'd done was think of him and those fantasies had flared to hot and vibrant life. It had made shagging Patrick much more tolerable, that was for certain, although it was definitely best that she hadn't known Tall, Dark, and Sexy's name.

Dru was quite certain she would have called her fiancé the *wrong* name. Not that she ever cried out his name during sex. He wasn't much more than a vibrator she forced herself to use. But if she'd known Tall, Dark, and Sexy's name . . . Well, that would be trouble, wouldn't it? Patrick would have taken that rather personally.

If he really decided to unload on her . . . shit, what would she do then? Just sit there and take it? Break her cover and risk those girls?

Her heart rate slowly leveled out, but her mind continued to buzz and hum and she could still feel *him*, vibrating inside her head, and she was almost certain she could feel him pushing at her shields, like he was trying to come inside her head. Talk to her, or something. No. *Can't do that*, she thought almost desperately.

Can't have that at all.

Although it felt like she was cutting off her arm, she forced herself to break that connection with him. Floundering, cut adrift in a lake of her own misery, she couldn't keep from shuddering.

Patrick stroked a hand down her back. "Are you cold?"

"Yes," she lied, keeping her voice quiet.

He reached down and flicked a blanket over her, patting her ass. "That was rather nice. I'm almost tempted to stay the night so we can do it again."

Get the fuck out of here, Dru thought. She had to get her head back together. Soothe the ragged bits and pieces of her heart.

He rolled closer and pressed his lips to her shoulder. "You should have told me you wanted to go into the park so much. It's a silly wish, but if you had that much fun, we'll do it occasionally. When you're good."

This time, when he swatted her ass, it wasn't gentle or playful. She bit the inside of her cheek to keep from making a sound. "But don't sneak around on me again, Ella. You'll tell me the next time you wish to go and you'll be escorted. Is that clear?"

"Of course." *You twat.* She was going to bloody him. She really, really was.

"Wonderful. Now, I have to go. I have business yet to see to. I'll use your shower before I go." He kissed her shoulder again and then rolled out of bed, going to the bathroom to flush the condom he'd used.

She had a few precious minutes to herself. A few minutes to calm her breathing, to think about how much she hated him. A few minutes to get her anger under control.

When he came back out, she was sitting on the side of the bed, wearing a robe and waiting for him with one of Ella's little smiles. Polite, demure, and empty.

Patrick looked pleased as he bent over to kiss her forehead.

When his lips touched her forehead, she had to fight the urge not
to recoil . . .

Flash, flash, flash.

New buyer . . .

Meeting . . .

She saw a place in his mind.

She knew *that* place.

It was one of the resorts. She'd been to all of them by now,
having dinner at various restaurants, accompanying him on tours
when he was showing business associates around.

This place was the one done up like a hunting lodge.

Dipping her chin, Dru swallowed the bile churning its way up
her throat.

New buyer.

What the hell did that mean?

And she counted the seconds for him to leave. She had to get
a message out. If her contact could get in there . . . damn it, was
there even any time?

* * *

IT was a harsh shock when Dru ended the contact.

But it was needed.

Especially considering he had his hand wrapped around his
dick and was more focused on jacking off than paying attention
to his target. Hell. He hadn't even realized he'd stood up. He'd
been sitting with his back braced against a tree, staring at the
little cabin.

Now he was standing there with his fly open.

He couldn't think when his head was that full of her, and he
looked down in a daze, realized almost ten minutes had passed
without him even realizing it. Ten minutes while she'd fantasy-
fucked him.

He could all but taste her again. He was that tuned into her. Feel her body sliding against his. Her hands tangling in his hair—

Wait. That wasn't right. He reached up, skimmed a hand back over his short hair. Not enough there to tangle a hand in. What the . . .

Squeezing his eyes closed, Joss tried to reestablish that connection, but all he managed was a surface connection. Faint, just enough to let him pick up on anger. She was pissed about something. Still dazed. And trying hard to keep him out . . . which made him realize she was very aware of him.

Closing his eyes, he readjusted himself, zipping his jeans back up and groaning as his aching cock twitched against the heavy confines of the denim. This was seriously fucked up. He had a job to do. He hadn't *ever* had anything interfere with a job before, and he couldn't afford to let it start happening now.

Just thinking about the job served as a bucket of ice water. Setting his jaw, he stared at the little cabin visible through the trees. He needed to get inside. He was going to have a chat with that son of a bitch.

Nothing like thinking about a serial rapist to get his mind where it needed to be.

Time to get to work.

TWELVE

THE bathroom was the one place he hadn't bugged, and she'd searched damn well. Apparently he was too fastidious to want to watch her as she took a piss, and she was grateful for that much.

Of course, it was the one place she could send a private text.

She took a disposable phone, one she'd activated weeks ago but hadn't yet used. She'd have to toss it after tonight. Sending a text, she included the password along with her message.

Can you get there?

A few seconds passed before the reply came. *Damn, timing is tight. I'll try. But may not happen.*

Good enough.

She deleted the message. Dismantled the phone and flushed the SIM card. Tucking the bits and pieces in the pocket of her robe, she left the bathroom.

Please. Let him find something.

* * *

THE meeting was tonight.

About time. Mike was tired of being Mike. Tired of playing the nice guy. He wanted this part of the job done so he could go back to doing what he did best. Scoring with the girls. Back on the hunt. But first he had to prove to this new client that he could get the girls needed for the first job. Nobody was better at this than he was.

He'd just finished his beer when the knock came.

Tossing the bottle in the trash, he checked his gun. Keeping a loose grip on the Beretta 92FS, he headed to the door. He didn't plan on needing the gun. But Mike was a big believer in being prepared. It was sort of his motto . . . be prepared for everything to go wrong.

With that motto in mind, he kept the Beretta in one hand and the other hand on the doorknob, standing off to the side. He didn't unlock it right away.

Through the door, he called out, "Yes?"

"Interested in a job?"

Smiling a little, he said, "Jobs are always nice. Especially in the current economy."

"Having the right kind of work is nice, too. It doesn't matter what the economy is, if you're not the right man for the work, it just leads to trouble."

"Trouble is never good." Pleased that he had the right person, he slid the Beretta into the sheath under his jacket and opened the door.

The man on the other side of the door looked rough. He looked like trouble. He was big and dark, and looked nothing like the rich fuck Mike had expected. Wary, Mike stepped aside and let the man enter, eyeing him narrowly. He shut the door behind him and turned, keeping the man in his sight at all times.

Instinct started to whisper as the man turned toward him.

He never even had a chance to draw the gun.

A blinding pain practically ripped his mind in two and he collapsed to the ground, unable to draw breath even to scream.

* * *

THIS time, Joss didn't feel bad about unleashing the power of that gift into this son of a bitch's mind. As he took what he needed from him, he stood over Mike Sellers with his hands jammed into his pockets. It was that, or haul the fucker up and pummel him bloody.

Seeing as how the man was almost catatonic at the moment, it wouldn't really be rewarding to beat him up just yet.

There were so many . . .

The faces just kept rolling through his mind. One right after the other—

Cutting off those images, Joss said, "Why are you here?"

Mike Sellers, or whoever he really was, didn't speak, but the mind had the info Joss needed. As it yielded those answers, he braced himself to get even sicker.

He wasn't disappointed.

A job. Yeah, it had been about a job.

There was a saying that Joss liked, by a cartoonist, Frank Tyger. Tyger had once said, "*Doing what you like is freedom. Liking what you do is happiness.*"

Ol' Mike must have felt like a really free, happy man. One who believed in his work and took a hell of a lot of pride in it.

Once Joss had finished, he took a step away and looked around the neat little cabin. He needed a fucking drink. He needed a fucking shower. He *really* needed a fucking vacation— and now sounded like a good time to take one, but just like the monster lying catatonic on the floor behind him, Joss also believed in what he did. He also took a lot of pride in it.

So no vacation. Yet. But he'd have a fucking drink and if the boss didn't like it . . . well. Who said he had to know? Spying a bar, he stormed over to it. Stocked. Excellent. He grabbed the whiskey and eyed the label. What in the hell ever happened to good ol' Jack? He liked Jack Daniels. But just then, he didn't care. Splashing some into a glass, he tossed it back, relishing the hot burn of it down his throat before he turned back to the man lying on the floor.

He was whimpering a little now. Deep in his throat, the way a wounded animal might if it was afraid and hurt.

Savagely, Joss wondered if he could make the perverted freak hurt just a little more.

Except he was expecting company.

That knowledge thrummed inside his head, a head that felt too damn full. He'd felt like he'd found a decent middle ground, but meeting Dru had pushed him off center and he was back to floundering. After another drink, he slammed the glass down and went over to the man. Grabbing him by the front of the shirt, he stared into glassy eyes. There was awareness in there now. Barely.

It took everything he had not to snarl. Not to pound him bloody. Instead, he pushed deeper . . . looked for more. Found it.

"Okay, Bryan."

Lids flickered at the sound of the man's real name. "Yeah," Joss said, smiling. "I know who you are. Bryan Hennegan. Scum-sucking pervert. Rapist. Monster. Kidnapper. Thief. Killer. There are other crimes, but those are the ones I really want to bury you for."

Bryan started to struggle and Joss narrowed his eyes, flexing that insane power inside his head. It rushed to the forefront and he could all but *feel* it as the air molded under his tutelage, wrapped around Bryan, pinned him. *Damn. That's some scary shit there*, he thought, a little dazed as the man's struggles abruptly stopped. "You can't get away from me. You can't escape. And you'll be lucky if you survive long enough for me to turn you over to my boss. Mark my words, I've never wanted a man dead so much as I want you dead."

Bryan whined. It was the most he could manage.

The sound made Joss smile wider. "Feels like a bitch, don't it? Being helpless." Fisting his hand in the front of the man's designer shirt, he dragged his motionless body through the cabin. Needed to hide him. Just get him out of sight for now, before he gave in to temptation and crossed a line.

There weren't a lot of options, so he shoved Hennegan's worthless ass into the minuscule closet in the bedroom. He'd have to improvise, and fast, if the upcoming meeting involved the bedroom, but for now, this would work. He cuffed the man's hands behind his back, used a cable tie on his feet.

Then, because he couldn't risk the guy screwing this up, he did a mental job that sent Hennegan careening into unconsciousness. Hopefully, he'd stay out for a good long while. Hopefully.

Once that was done, Joss headed back into the main part of the cabin and did a quick look around, searching for any sign that might set off an alarm. He and Hennegan were damned close in height, even in body type, so that was good, in case his visitor was looking for a six-feet-five white guy with dark hair. He saw a cell phone, a set of keys. Touching the phone was a bit of a shock, although he'd already figured out that Jillian had psychometry crammed into her crafty psychic bag of tricks. Just touching an object was enough to let her pick up images, impressions. And that was now inside his head, too, and he didn't want that trip into Hennegan's brain.

Shoring up the shields, he steadied himself as he turned off the ringer. *I can do this. I can do it . . .*

After he'd set the phone to silent, he scrolled through the recent numbers, texts, committing them to memory. Useful ability in his line of work, a photographic memory—and that skill was all his.

One set of messages made his mind buzz. There was a series of them. Just the number had set his teeth on edge and he knew, just *knew*, this was the guy—Jillian's monster.

Meeting set for tonight. Looking forward to discussing the new venture. So mild and unassuming. But even reading it made Joss's gut churn. Made screams echo through his mind.

Meeting . . .

As his rage spiraled out of control, he found himself lost in the torrent of Jillian's nightmares. The walls of his control started to crumble. And icy tendrils wrapped around him.

Dez's ghosts. Creeping out to play. That gift was easier for him to control, but once that wall crumbled . . . their whispers were like a cloak of ice, wrapping around him.

Help me . . . please . . . find me. I don't want to stay lost . . . What happened . . . ? I just want to go home—

"Fuck!" He threw the phone down and buried his face in his hands. In his mind, he visualized that stone wall. Jillian's shield. Then his own series of doors, shutting everything out.

To the ghosts who had crept in, he said, *I'll help. I'll find you. But first, I have to find a way inside.*

They didn't listen.

Chances were the ghosts weren't even cognizant. Many of Dez's ghosts weren't. They were just echoes of who they had been in life, and it would take a deeper connection before he could communicate with them. Easing them back into the compartment he'd created in his mind, he slammed the door shut there, too.

Mind-fucked. He was well and completely mind-fucked, and

he was also absolutely *insane* for thinking he was ready to jump into this. He should have taken another day, at least.

Gone back to the hotel, dreamed about Dru. Solidified his shields. Dreamed about Dru . . .

Except if he'd done that, he wouldn't have seen Sellers. Hennegan. Whatever the bastard wanted to call himself. This was his best chance.

"Maybe the only chance." He rubbed the heels of his hands into his eye sockets. Only chance to do it this way, and this way was the best way. He knew that in his gut.

Taking a deep breath, he went through one of the mental exercises he'd learned years ago. It wasn't doing much, but it edged back the fury a little bit. Not a whole lot, but a little. Once he had the fury under control, it was easier to shore up his shields more.

As strange a life as he led, as bizarre a gift as he had, control was vital. It was vital to psychics in general, but most of them—hell, ninety-eight percent of the people Joss worked with—could establish a working rhythm and that led to a natural control.

Joss's gift didn't allow for a rhythm because he never had the same gift type. It was constantly being readjusted, and even if he synced to the same person, their gifts changed and grew over time and he wasn't using those gifts as they changed, which meant he didn't have that built-in adjustment period.

He managed through rock-hard control, and it was never more crucial than when he was pissed.

And damn, shit, and fuck, was he pissed.

It ate at his brain like hungry, bloodthirsty little ants.

But the fury couldn't be in control. Down that road lay madness. Down that road lay failure.

Failure wasn't an option.

He knew how he had to play this, knew he could. It had been

an inkling in his brain from the time Jillian had first placed her small hands in his. Because she'd seen this coming. Then he'd seen Hennegan/Sellers and the idea had bloomed just a bit.

Now it was slowly solidifying, and he knew what he was going to do.

He had to be careful, though, or he was fucked, and so were those girls.

So . . . control.

A good thirty minutes passed before he thought he could function the way he needed to. He took a minute to go to the bedroom and check on his "guest." Still out of it. A hand on the guy's head took him a little deeper into a screwed-up psyche than he wanted to go, but it also told him the guy wasn't going to emerge anytime soon. That psychic jab had a little too much power, especially on top of Joss's less-than-gentle probe. He'd be out for hours.

Back in the main part of the cabin, he had another drink, started dissecting bits and pieces of that screwed-up psyche.

A taker. A user. Entitled son of a bitch. He wanted, so he took. He liked *things* . . . liked having them, owning them. Breaking them, if he so chose. Girls were things. He also liked the hunt, as he saw it. Liked finding the perfect specimen—a particular sort of girl for a particular sort of buyer. Finding her, stalking her, kidnapping her. It was one of his passions, and he loved it.

So far, all contact with this new person had been via text. No phone calls, no direct meets.

That was good.

He wasn't happy about being here, and this ludicrous cabin had him irritated. He'd hidden it, during the few phone calls, even hidden it inside the cabin, in case it was bugged.

That was a worry, one Joss hadn't considered and should have—

But the place wasn't bugged.

Not yet . . .

That strange little buzz in his mind had him hunching his shoulders, almost like somebody had whispered that in his ear. But he knew better. It was just another facet of Jillian's gift. The cabin wasn't bugged, but it would be. Soon. Great. Just great. Now Joss also had to worry about getting Hennegan out of here before that happened. Wasn't that just awesome?

Okay, so he'd get ahold of Jones. Put his new friend in the trunk of a car.

Step into those size thirteen shoes and bring this entire house of cards crashing down. And heaven help anybody who got in his way.

Dru's face drifted through his mind, and he seized on it. Thinking about her was one definite way to chill his rage down.

And a hell of a lot more pleasant. Once this was done . . . then he'd go after her.

Spoken for? Damn right. He'd spoken for her another lifetime ago and that hold was still there. She still felt it.

He just had to prove it to her.

And he would.

After he got through this hell.

* * *

BUSINESS rarely bothered Patrick.

He enjoyed business pursuits of all kinds, and sometimes they came with necessary evils. He accepted them because, in order to excel, he had to handle those small details with the same care he'd apply to the big details.

In the end, it all added up to the big picture.

It mattered.

But in just that moment, he'd rather be doing something

other than seeing to business. Back with Ella, preferably. Or . . .
ideally . . . at his place, nearly thirty miles away. Private, lush . . .
and his. Lush, and his. That was what mattered. Just as Ella was
lush . . . and his. Elegant, yet possessing an earthy sensuality that
had stunned him rather pleasantly just a short while ago.

He could already imagine it happening again. He thought of
having her back at the estate, that elegant sexuality ready for him
whenever he wanted. He could see them sitting by the pool, her
clad in one of those lovely dresses of hers, her pretty legs neatly
crossed. He'd let her hold the cat. Demeter would like her, he
thought. He could feast on her with his eyes . . . and then have
that tiger she kept inside her come out to play.

His penis twitched at the memory. He wanted more.

But that wouldn't happen tonight.

If it did, she might get it in her head that she could control
him through sex. He wasn't a man who'd be controlled through
any means, and there would be no thinking otherwise.

Still, it had been very nice.

It would happen again.

Soon, this tedious business would be dealt with and his operation would resume functioning like a well-oiled machine. It was
his own fault things had gotten tripped up. He'd been focusing
on the wedding, thought he'd make it an . . . experience, and
while he'd been focusing on that, he hadn't watched his business
as well as he should have.

When a businessman didn't keep his eye on all aspects of his
business, there were problems. Patrick had a problem of epic proportions. His best asset had become his worst nightmare and at
the very worst time. Then he'd been forced to replace him, because
things were already in motion for the wedding and he simply
couldn't cancel.

That wasn't about to happen.

This new man was costing him more money, but he was supposed to be top of the line and smoother than glass.

Excellent.

Things would level out and then Patrick could focus on the things that mattered, once his business got back to functioning as it should. Life as normal would resume and he could direct his attention to his career, his other business interests . . . his new wife.

It wouldn't be long until he had his new wife living on his estate and he could bring out that inner slut whenever he so chose.

It was dark and quiet by the time he pulled through the gates.

The security guard came out and smiled as he recognized him. "Evening, Mr. Whitmore."

"Hello, Jake. Out to have a drink with a friend. Couldn't get away any sooner," he said, giving the guard a pleasant smile. Always best to be friendly and pleasant to the staff. Assholes tended to be remembered. Patrick tried to avoid that.

The guard smiled. "That wedding of yours is getting close. I imagine you've got your hands full." With a nod, he disappeared back inside and the gate swung open, letting Patrick pass through.

Yes, the wedding had his hands full. Although it was the party afterward that was the most pressing detail.

Tonight would help cover the rest of those concerns, though.

As long as this new player worked out.

As he pulled up in front of the cabin he'd set aside for his guest, he smiled. He wondered what the man thought of the accommodations. While they were adequate, they were no doubt lacking, compared to what the man was likely used to.

Patrick had his reasons for doing it, though. One, he could control things, to some extent, on these grounds. Observe who came and went. And he had people on his payroll who would see to it things would be . . . monitored, if he hired this man.

If.

He also liked making sure people understood their place in the scheme of things . . . it was wherever the hell he wished to place them.

The man came highly recommended, but that didn't mean much. The last man had come highly recommended as well. It hadn't stopped him from trying to fuck Patrick over.

He parked the car and climbed out, giving a casual look around. The Ford Explorer was a deep maroon, looked like a family car. Good choice. Not quite the "drug dealer" or "dirty cop" car that some of the pricier models were, but it would provide a good ride, and lots of room. Appeared to be well cared for, and he didn't see a rental tag sticker. Noting the license plate number, Patrick committed it to memory.

He'd run a check once he left. He doubted it was traceable back to anything, but he had to be certain. If the man couldn't handle this small thing, then he was useless.

THIRTEEN

NOTHING out of place so far.

He was pretty sure Chapman was chasing windmills on this one, but so far, she'd managed to point him in very odd directions that had yielded some disturbing results.

Too bad they'd yet to find any evidence.

Just coincidences.

Tucker Collins couldn't exactly see the local cops doing shit to Patrick Whitmore based on coincidences. The bastard had deep pockets, and he had more than a few high-society bastards on his payroll, too. Collins had learned that a long time ago.

Granted, he hadn't thought Whitmore would be doing anything this twisted. Drugs, sure.

But this . . . nah. He hadn't planned on anything quite this deep. Still, Chapman wasn't often wrong. And they were friends. He didn't have too many people he could say that about. He'd hold tight for a little while, see what he could see.

Then he'd—

A woman appeared in his line of vision.

And dayyum.

What a woman.

He snapped a picture of her, although he wasn't here to troll for babes. Chapman wanted him to watch for the mark, and that's what he'd do.

Although this woman . . . man. She was practically a piece of art, strutting down the road, a little purse hooked over her arm, her ass swinging with each step, long legs, a pair of fuck-me shoes, that short little skirt . . .

Just looking at her made him itch. He wanted to keep on looking, just enjoy that view for as long as he could.

But he was here to work the job. And the jobs Chapman called him for were always the weird kind. That meant he had to to keep his eyes open . . . and not on that gorgeous woman . . .

* * *

HER name was Nalini. At least, that was what she usually went by. It wasn't a name she gave out easily. Honestly, she preferred not to give it out at all, but there were certain people who did need to know her real name.

When she didn't need to give a real name, she had a handful of fakes she gave out that were close enough. Nala. Lini. Nali.

The names varied, along with her appearance.

Lately, she'd decided to let her hair go back to her natural pale blond, just a few shades darker than platinum. There was nothing normal about the style she'd gone for, though. As if the unusually pale locks weren't odd enough, she'd let her hair grow long, and it grew fast.

A while back, she'd had the odd urge to do the thick mess into dreadlocks. And that had been a nightmare. The initial process hadn't been too bad. One day, and several long, tedious hours with her ass stuck in a chair while a woman who must have excelled in torture back-combed, twisted, and teased Nalini's hair into submission.

But the time after it? That was the pain in the ass.

There had been days when she wanted to just cut them off. White women just weren't the ideal specimen for dreads, she knew.

But the effect was stunning, and she was either honest enough, or vain enough, to admit it. When she looked into the mirror, the woman looking back at her was stunningly exotic, the long, dense hair falling more than halfway down her back. Her eyes were large, dominating the clean, elegant oval of her face. They had a faint, upward tilted slant at the corners, a sharp, clean line echoed in her cheekbones, her jawline. Her mouth was full, and although she rarely bothered with much makeup, she had a fondness for deep, dark red lipstick. It was stunning against her pale skin, and she liked that a lot.

Before she slid out of her ridiculously priced cabin, she slicked a shade just a bit darker than blood over her lips, paused to study the effect, and smiled.

She was dressed to impress these days, trying to catch the eye of a particular man.

Not that he seemed to be paying much attention.

But he would. He'd notice sooner or later.

It was, after all, why Nalini was here.

Grabbing a little purse that echoed the snakeskin design of her skirt, she headed to the door. Her heels clacked on the tile, a sharp, decisive sound.

Maybe it would happen tonight.

But then again, if it didn't, it didn't matter.

She had reasons for being here, and in the end, her patience would pay off.

* * *

THE fucker took forever, Joss thought, brooding as he slumped on the couch.

He'd been out there for more than a few minutes, and Joss knew exactly why he was taking so long—the stream of his thoughts was unending. He could shut that door, but he needed to know what he was dealing with—shutting the door just wasn't an option.

Yeah, you check those plates, dumb ass, Joss thought sourly. He'd done the same himself and the car tracked back to Mr. Mike Sellers, nice, normal dude who did indeed have himself listed as a computer system tech, freelance. Contract labor. Sellers always paid his bills on time, paid his taxes on time, and had a modest monthly budget that he stuck to without fail.

There was nothing a quick surface look would tell him about Mike Sellers. Joss knew because Taylor had already done one.

Joss muttered to himself as he got up and headed back to the bar. He splashed some more whiskey into his glass and tossed it back. It was smoother than he was used to and, he had to admit, there just might be something to be said for paying an arm and a leg for the good shit.

Still, he would settle for a bottle of Jack Daniels and he planned on having one after this mess was said and done. Getting shit-faced drunk might dull some of the images in his mind, and as soon as humanly possible, he was going to get resynced so he could strip away this excessive power surge.

He didn't know how Jillian—

If this goes well—

The thoughts in the man's mind came to a halt. Joss stiffened as he felt the predatory surge of interest and he closed his eyes, focused, concentrated. The man had seen something—no, *somebody.*

A woman.

Walking down the long, winding road, swinging a little purse, swinging her ass, every move a physical seduction. She was almost even with the monster standing outside Joss's cabin, and something about her face was familiar . . . the hair was wrong. Long and blond, hanging in a thick fall down her back, but those eyes.

Yeah. Familiar.

She glanced over, like she'd just noticed the man watching her.

Joss hissed out a breath.

The slow curl of her lips, those wide, dark eyes.

Then she winked.

He growled and pushed out with that gift.

But all he could touch were the same minds he'd felt earlier. All those open, vulnerable minds. Not hers. Hers wasn't open, wasn't vulnerable.

As the woman continued walking, strutting with every step, Joss closed his eyes.

"What in the . . ."

Then he groaned.

He had the weirdest damn feeling that wink had been meant for him. As though she was aware of him, although that shouldn't be possible.

"Shit, isn't this job complicated enough?"

There was no time even to contemplate the complications, though, because his visitor decided he'd waited long enough. Joss felt him moving closer—literally felt it, like the guy's very brain waves grew in frequency or something. No. Like a radio was moving closer to him.

How in the hell did Jillian manage to function like this?

He shoved it out of his mind and did one last mental exercise to calm himself—blue seas, unfurling out before him, the sun sinking down to meet the horizon. At his back were mountains and there was nobody around . . .

The knock came. It was polite. Firm.

Joss felt it to the very essence of his soul, and with it, he felt the man's evil.

Wiping his emotions from his face, he shored up his shields. *Modify the fucking door . . . let me see what I need to see*, he thought. If Jillian's power was that strong, he should be able to control something of what he was taking in.

He didn't want a damned window into this man's soul.

Crossing the floor, he opened the door, ready to face the devil.

* * *

THE towering, broad man was a little rougher than Patrick would have thought. He'd been told the man was big. And he was. Possibly six and half feet. Dark hair and dark eyes, very intense eyes, Patrick thought. He'd catch attention . . . catch notice. With those dark eyes set under the thick slashes of his eyebrows, a hard, unsmiling face. Yes, if Patrick saw him on the street, he'd remember him. Remember him and go the other way.

He'd gotten where he was by avoiding trouble.

This man . . . he looked like trouble.

But still, he'd come highly recommended. Patrick couldn't say he *trusted* the men who'd offered the recommendations, but he could say he knew those men wouldn't willingly fuck him over. Not because they feared Patrick . . . they moved in the same waters and it was just bad form.

So he'd withhold judgment for now.

For the past twenty seconds, they'd just stood there, assessing one another, and it was past time to be done with that. Patrick lifted a brow and cocked his head, waiting for the man he knew only as Mike to invite him in.

"Hey."

That was it. The man continued to stand there, arms crossed

over that brawny chest so that the muscles of his biceps bulged out. Those piercing eyes studied Patrick's face as though he was copying it to memory. *I don't think this is what I'm in the market for*, Patrick thought.

Still, his deadline was looming close, and he wasn't going to be able to get the goods he needed on his own, not with everything else he had on his plate. He had a few others who managed to snag a choice piece every now and then, but he didn't want to rely on luck. Not now. He needed skill.

"Interested in a job?" he said mildly, putting the first part of the pass code out there.

The man's mouth tugged up a bit at the corner, just the faintest bit of a smile. "Jobs are always nice. Especially in the current economy."

"Having the right kind of work is nice, too. It doesn't matter what the economy is—if you're not the right man for the work, it just leads to trouble."

"Trouble is never good." He moved off to the side, the invitation to enter clear. Dark eyes glinted in challenge as he said the required response.

Well, that was all said and done.

"I assume you can meet my fee?"

Patrick inclined his head. "Of course." He really hated it when people put money out there so openly. "Shall we discuss this inside?"

* * *

THREE women.

All taken within the next two weeks.

One white, one mixed, one Hispanic. Very exacting details. Joss kept his hands linked together loosely between his knees as he sat on the couch, studying the neat little note cards in front of him. The blond fuck had laid them out in a nice, straight row as he explained the merchandise he needed to procure in a timely fashion.

Merchandise.

Like he was shopping for a new set of dishes.

Pretty women. Unharmed. Delivered in time to be prepared for their . . . big event.

"This is your only chance to get this job right, and your only chance to get in on a very lucrative project," the man said as Joss lifted one card and studied all the notes made. "Get it right, and I'll make you a rich man. Get it wrong . . ." He let the words trail off, smiling a little.

Joss figured he was supposed to be suitably threatened there. He grunted and read the final few details on the card. *Blond. Slender. Elegant. Porcelain complexion—no tanning bed beauties, please.* " 'Tanning bed beauties'?"

"My client has specific requests."

"I see that." He eyed the next card. Light-skinned biracial woman. *Light*-skinned. Sons of bitches. The third was to be a Latina, slightly plump with long black hair.

Tossing the cards down on the table, Joss said, "Three weeks is a very short amount of time for such a big job."

The answers were there . . . right there, on the surface of the man's brain, but even that light touch flooded Joss with thoughts and memories he just couldn't stand. He made himself do it anyway, keeping his face expressionless as he grabbed the information he needed. He was too rough—watched as the man went white, his eyes tightening around the corners, eyes clouding from the pain.

Patrick . . . his name was Patrick . . .

The second Joss pulled back, Patrick shook it off. He frowned, absently reaching up to rub his temple.

Pretending not to notice, Joss said, "So what happens if I don't succeed?"

"You don't want to know that." Patrick smoothed his tie down. "Succeed and your life will be much easier."

"I take it the last broker you had didn't do a smashing job."

"Perhaps he asked too many questions," Patrick said.

Joss snorted. "Well, I haven't accepted the job yet. And I need to understand the . . . situation, seeing as how I'm running on a very tight timetable. Knowledge is power, you know? And I can't do my job if I'm handicapped."

"You'll accept the job," Patrick said, his tone bored. "And you can do it in three weeks. You're a resourceful man, I've heard."

Resourceful.

Yeah. Joss was a resourceful man. He had a modern-day slaver tied up in one closet, and another one sitting in front of him, and he was doing his damnedest to figure out the best way to kill them both without getting caught, without having his boss find out . . . and even if he could do that, he still needed a few days to track down his lady before he got yanked off onto another assignment.

If he was a resourceful man, it should be a piece of cake.

* * *

ONCE Whitmore drove away, Tucker relaxed a little. Job done. He assumed.

Although what Chapman thought he would accomplish out here, he didn't know. But she was running this show. Out of curiosity more than anything else, he continued to study the cabin.

Instinct didn't let him go any closer. He knew *that* much without lowering his shields at all.

Trouble lay inside that cabin, and he wasn't getting paid to get in trouble. Shit, he wasn't getting paid to do *anything*. He was just helping Dru because he'd realized she was in over her head and she was one of the few people he called friend. He'd rather not lose her. That was a thought that left a weird little ache inside.

Lingering in the shadows, he continued to watch the cabin.

It was quiet.

Damn quiet.

Sighing, he settled down. He could head home, he knew. He'd done his part.

But he wasn't quite ready to do that yet.

* * *

DRU wished she hadn't destroyed the phone.

Lying in the bed, she wished she had a way to contact Tucker, but it would be tomorrow before she dared. If she hadn't destroyed . . .

Bugger all.

She was so tired, her mind frayed out and stretched thin. She wasn't thinking. She'd been shattered from everything that had happened that day, from the odd man she'd met, her reaction to him . . . both when he kissed her, and when she'd thought of him as Patrick was there. All of it left her not thinking well.

There had been no *reason* to dispose of the phone so hastily. None.

She could have gotten up for her run early, as she always did, and disposed of it then. But no. She'd panicked.

Had he learned anything?

She wished she had a skill that was a bit more useful, able to reach out and touch his mind. Tucker had a mind that was open to that, when he allowed it. He couldn't talk back, but if she was telepathic at all, all she would have to do was initiate the contact and they could have a nice little chat, right inside his head.

He'd spent quite a few years hiding from his abilities, a self-defense mechanism more than anything else. And he hid well. She felt nothing from him. Not a burn on her brain like what she'd felt earlier with . . . *him*. Not a spark of recognition that sometimes passed when she sensed another like her. With Tucker, she felt nothing.

But her gift didn't work that way. She had no way to contact him that wouldn't catch attention. Not until she could swipe another phone. She had a few more throwaways stashed, but she had to be careful not to use all of them, and getting one out now was just being silly.

She lay there, in the silence of the room, worrying, brooding.

It was a long, sleepless night. But she'd had a lot of those lately.

* * *

"RUN that by me again."

If Joss hadn't been so pissed off, he might have been amused at the tone he heard in Jones's voice.

"I have a body." He paused for a count of five and then added, "Relax. I didn't kill him. I want to, and if you don't get here soon, I just might let myself. He's in the trunk of a car that I'm stealing from him. I don't know what to do with him, but we can't exactly just let him start making all those free phone calls he's entitled to."

Joss believed in rights—he believed in rights even for the guilty—the very fucking guilty, in this case. But he also knew that if this guy went and lawyered up right now, he'd be making phone calls that would endanger their case . . . and lives.

That was a pickle, he supposed.

One he was glad Jones would have to juggle.

"I'm starting to think you enjoy this," Taylor muttered. "All of you. Complicating my life has become a pastime in this unit."

"Nah."

"If it's not a pastime, it sure as hell ought to be."

"Oh, it's a pastime. But you said *has become*. It's more like *always been*. We love seeing you get a little hot and sweaty and smoothing down those ties you like to wear. I told people that was the one sign you showed when you were getting pissed—you smooth your tie down. Dez used to make you do it three or four times a day."

Taylor didn't sound amused as he said, "I'm not smoothing my tie right now. I'm about ready to take it off in preparation to strangle you with it."

"Nah, you won't do that. Then you'd have to find somebody else to stick in here, and you can't exactly stick your lady in here, can you? Call me when you're ready to meet." Joss hung up and glanced around. He didn't see anybody, sense anybody.

It had been a fun thing, rolling the body in a blanket and then lugging it out to the car. If anybody had looked, *really* looked, they would have figured out what he was moving, but fortunately, nobody had seen.

He was ninety-nine percent certain that no cameras could have caught it, either. He had a few small gadgets on him, but he'd get more sophisticated ones after he hooked up with Jones. His scanner told him there was nothing in the area currently. More than likely, it was correct.

More than likely.

Now he just had to worry about getting out of here without being stopped. Get this bozo to Jones. Get back here. Get some rest. Figure out how he was supposed to pretend to kidnap three girls . . .

Think about *her* . . .

FOURTEEN

BACK to the warehouse.

That was where Joss found himself on his first full day working as a slaver. Broker. Whatever the PC term was for somebody who kidnapped women and girls and arranged for them to be sold to the highest bidder.

Ideally, he figured he could be out looking for his "mark" except there wasn't going to be a blind mark.

He already knew how this would play out.

All he had to do was wait for Jones to get in contact with him and then he'd lay things out.

First, though . . . back here. Back to where he'd had that crushing weight of grief.

Now that he had Dez's unique ability to gab with ghosts, he could find whoever was lingering here and maybe help them along.

Plenty of voices were screaming at him, but he ignored all of them, pushing through the cold weight of their presence to get back to the one spot where he'd felt all that grief. All that anguish.

And it was there . . .

Just there.

He could feel all the grief.

All that pain and anguish . . . bracing himself for her presence, he waited.

And he waited. But whoever he was waiting for, she never showed up.

* * *

"WE'RE going home today."

Jillian stared at Cullen, her blue eyes unreadable. But the pout on her face was unmistakable.

"I don't want to go home," she said, slumping in her chair and glaring at him over the breakfast table.

"Too bad," he replied, keeping his attention half focused on the closed door.

Taige hadn't come out of there all morning.

If she thought she could hide all day—

"She's not hiding."

Cullen jolted, caught off guard by Jillian's comment. Sighing, he passed a hand over his face, and then he leaned forward, bracing his elbows on the table. "Jilly, you know better than that. Thoughts are private."

"I know." She shrugged. "But I hardly ever hear yours and well . . ." She shrugged again. "Mom's not in the room. She's gone to talk to Taylor. She thinks he'll need her for the case." Something drifted through her eyes and her mouth turned down. "He's going to."

Cullen all but bit his tongue off to keep from swearing.

"Dad."

Looking up, he saw Jillian staring at him, her eyes somber. "Do you love me?"

"Jilly . . ." Unsure where that had come from, he shoved the chair back from the table and moved around to stand by her, kneeling down so that their faces were level. She looked so much like her mother, his first wife. Cullen's memories of her were dim—they hadn't really known each other, but he'd married her when they discovered she was pregnant. The marriage had been short-lived; she'd died during childbirth and Cullen had been on his own from day one.

Up until Taige came into their lives . . . into Jillian's life, *back* into his. He'd known Taige since he'd been a kid, just a few years older than Jillian was now. He'd known her then, loved her then. And because he'd been a short-sighted fool, he'd lost her. He pushed those dark thoughts aside and focused on his daughter . . . *their* daughter.

"Baby, you know I love you. You're everything."

"Would you try to change me?" She watched him with eyes that were far too old, far too wise, for a fourteen-year-old child.

This was boggy ground here, he realized. Blowing out a breath, he weighed his words carefully. Jillian might not be able to read him the way she could read others, but she'd know a lie. "Change who you are? Not in a million years. But if there was something I could do to make life easier on you? I'd almost sell my soul to do it."

"Mama's told you a hundred times over . . . some of us just aren't made for easy." She reached over and caught his hand, linked their fingers. "I'm not made for easy. Neither is Mama. Regretting and wishing she wouldn't do what she has to do hurts her, Dad. You can't keep doing this to her."

Old eyes. Old soul. "You're too young to be this smart," he said, sighing. "I'm supposed to be the one giving you advice. How did you get to be so smart?"

"That's easy. You gave me a good mom." Her nose wrinkled as she grinned at him. Then she bit her lip. "Dad . . . I want to go home. But Mom needs you here. Maybe Grandpa can come get me."

Cullen grimaced. He wasn't really quite ready to be away from his daughter. Not after how much she'd been hurting.

He knew his dad would take good care of her, but still.

"You think you'd be okay for a little while if I went to go talk to her?" he asked softly.

"I'm fourteen, you know." She rolled her eyes. "I'm not a baby."

* * *

TAIGE stared at a picture of a young woman.

If Taige had guessed right, the woman in the image was in her mid-twenties. Absolutely beautiful, with big, blue eyes, big breasts, tiny waist, round hips. She looked like a living Barbie doll. But there was something in her eyes that made her look . . . well, sweet.

Too sweet. Oddly innocent. It bothered her to think of somebody innocent and sweet caught in this mess. Well, it bothered her to think of anybody caught in this, but still . . . innocence wasn't exactly a common commodity in this world anymore.

"Who is she?" Taige asked, careful not to touch the picture.

"She was one of my prime's suspect's girlfriends," Taylor said without even bothering to look at the picture. "They broke up about eighteen months ago, and a few weeks later, she went on a trip to Europe. Disappeared. Hasn't been seen since. Naturally, he has nothing to do with her disappearance and is very distraught by it all."

"Girlfriend . . ."

"Rumors of an engagement were surfacing but not official."

"Hmmm." She bent closer to the picture, as though the girl could whisper to her, if she just got closer. If she kept the contact to a minimum, she could keep from going on a little psychic stroll, she thought. And there was one waiting to happen here. She could feel it. The edges of the gray hovered around her, just waiting to suck her up.

She just couldn't do it *yet*. She hadn't yet talked to Jones about hanging around to help out with the case. Over the past few years, she'd been cutting back on the work she did for him and she was torn now, torn between taking care of Jillian and staying here. The guilty ache in her heart demanded she take Jillian home, mother her, baby her, stroke her and soothe her and pat her . . . which would drive Jillian nuts.

The other part of her, the fighter, the psychic, *that* part of her was being tugged in the other direction. She was needed here. Taige didn't know why. Joss was the one most capable to handle this. The last thing she needed to do was plant her ass in the middle of a situation she wasn't equipped to handle and she knew it.

Sighing, she shifted her focus to another picture, using a pencil to draw it closer so she wouldn't have to touch. This was a girl, maybe twenty. Light-skinned black girl. Biracial, maybe, Taige thought, her skin the same coffee and cream as her own. Short hair, cut a little longer in the front. A pretty smile, just a little wicked. And all sorts of attitude and cockiness in her smile.

According to the info she had, her name was Daylin. She'd been missing for six months. Still officially listed as missing, but in her gut, Taige knew the girl was dead. And it was something awful . . . she could feel the horror lurking as the gray tried to wrap ever closer around her.

Carefully, she pushed it over to the *look-at-later* pile, again using a pencil so she wouldn't have to touch it. The ones she'd look at once she decided she had to get involved, she told herself. Although she already knew she was involved in this.

If you weren't supposed to be involved, you wouldn't feel like you need to be here. Talk to Jones. He'll let you know if he wants you in or not, a quiet voice in the back of her mind whispered.

Yeah, and that would go over well. She and her husband were already having a rough time. She'd slept in Jillian's room because she couldn't handle being around Cullen last night. But although she was mad at him, she didn't want to fuck up her marriage and Cullen had so much anger—

A knock at the door had her straightening in her chair.

"I'll get it," Dez said, rising from the couch. She slid Taige a grim look and added, "I'm not good for much else on this trip."

Taige didn't respond. Hunching her shoulders, she went back to staring at the picture she'd just pushed away. Her fingers trembled as she reached out, hovering just a breath away from the picture.

"You've been here for forty-five mintues, Taige," Taylor said quietly.

Looking up, she met the steel blue of his eyes.

"Is that your polite way of telling me to leave?" she asked. Vaguely, she heard the voices at the door.

He shook his head. "If I wanted you to leave, I would tell you to leave. But you've been here, avoiding a connection you know is there all this time . . . for some reason. And now you're going to do it, because of a knock at the door."

Curling her lip at him, she crossed her arms over her chest and leaned back.

As Cullen came through the doorway to the dining room, Taylor gave her a brief smile.

She barely resisted the urge to flip him off.

* * *

IT was a quick meet.

Joss could tell by the look on Jones's face that they weren't going to be chitchatting much. They hadn't chatted much the previous night either when Joss had dumped Hennegan's unresisting body into Jones's lap. No telling what Jones had done, but the man didn't look any worse for wear, although Joss knew he'd slept even less than Joss had.

"Here," Jones said, his voice terse as he passed on a black duffel. His voice made it clear he wasn't in the mood to talk.

That was fine with him. He had managed to mostly settle his new gift back into place, but he still needed some time to solidify those shields and get a grip. He'd done this too soon, and he knew it—now he was left trying to patch a busted flood wall.

Studying the black duffel, he hefted it, tested the weight. He had a rough idea what was inside it, although he'd take a better look once he didn't have so many people around him. "Gee, boss, you shouldn't have. I didn't bring you anything," he drawled.

Taylor gave him a withering stare. "How is your head?"

"Feels like it's about to split into a million pieces." Joss shrugged. "Dez, I can handle her talent. It's creepy sometimes. I can feel these whispers, even in my sleep if I'm not careful. But I can handle that one. The girl, though . . ." He snapped his mouth shut, staring off into nothing. He could still feel the echo of her terror, rooted deep inside him, and it was a raw, twisting ache. He could hear the echo of screams, and unlike Dez's ghosts, these women were still alive. He *knew* it—this unreal, uncanny insight that he couldn't even define. He could feel the echo of their pain, and the knowledge of what awaited them . . .

Now he just had to figure out how to save them. How to stop the monster behind this. Sometimes, this job really sucked.

"It was getting to be too much for her," he finally said, slanting a look at Jones. "You know that?"

Jones lifted a brow. "I suspected. Once I saw her. She was . . . fragile. Jillian's been through hell. Kids tends to be fairly resilient anyway, and she's even more so. But I suspected she was too close to an edge this time."

"Suspected?" Joss studied his friend's face. He knew Jones didn't categorize himself as psychic, but there was something there. Jones had a knack for finding people like Joss. Taige. Dez had sought the unit out, but most of the psychics had joined after Jones had ferreted them out. He also had a way of knowing who was the right one for the job, who needed to take a break. Who was walking a line. "Or knew?"

Taylor shrugged. "Semantics. She's a child who saw something nobody should have to see. It's no surprise it's hurting her."

"That's why you used her." The power of Jillian's gift was twisting through him, too much and too strong. Joss knew it would come in handy. But there were others who could get him through this. A telepath could have connected with Jillian and gotten the information Joss needed. An extra step, they both knew, but it would have left Joss a little less keyed up. Which wouldn't be a bad thing. "You're trying to find a way to let her exorcise this demon."

Taylor's lids drooped, shielding the unreadable blue of his eyes. "Save the armchair psychology for somebody else, Crawford. Her abilities will be useful, and she came to me. I didn't seek her out."

"Yeah, yeah." He nudged Jones in the shoulder. "You just don't want anybody to know you've got a heart inside there."

Once more, that withering stare returned. "Do you have any idea how you're going to go about making contact?"

As the job reared its ugly, ever-present head, Joss sighed.

"Now *that* . . . is already done. The rest of it will be hard." Turning around, he headed back to his car. Jones followed along behind him, the two of them doing another casual look around. There were people everywhere. The Waffle House was packed, people inside chowing down on a good old American breakfast. Eggs. Bacon. Waffles. His belly growled just thinking about it. Joss was going to head in there shortly and do what he could to clog his arteries. He'd invite Taylor, but Taylor wasn't going to be interested.

Resting the bag on the hood of the car, he glanced inside. At first look, all he saw was a neat jumble of electronics. It was too heavy for that to be all, though. Slipping Joss a quick look, he arched a brow.

Taylor leaned in and tapped the bottom.

Joss smiled.

"I need to think this through for a while before I talk it over," he said in reply to Taylor's question. "But I made contact last night. Give me some time to think everything through, okay?"

Under his breath, Taylor grumbled. Joss grinned.

There weren't a lot of people who could get by with that— *think it through*. Taylor was a control freak and wanted, almost *needed*, to be involved every step of the way.

"How much time?"

"A few hours, a day maybe." He sighed and shrugged, looking out across the parking lot. "Too much shit crammed into my head. Got to let it all settle and then see what pops up out of the madness. Once that happens, I'll know if I'm working this the right way."

Taylor reached up and pinched the bridge of his nose. "See what pops up? I don't like the *pop-up* approach, Crawford."

Joss waited a beat. "That's gotta suck for Dez. Spontaneity is the spice of life."

For a second Taylor just stared at him. Then, a faint smile came and went. "Go fuck yourself, Crawford." Passing a hand over his face, Taylor sighed. "This is going to be one of those cases, isn't it? The kind that has me scrambling to cover everybody's asses, my own included."

"Probably." Zipping the bag closed, he pointed out, "You're already scrambling. You cussed twice in one breath. That's not typical for you."

"Again, go fuck yourself." Taylor glanced at the restaurant. "Are you really going to eat in there?"

"Yep." Tugging the bag down, Joss patted his belly. "I finally hit a corner last night and got some peace in my head. Crashed and slept for eighteen hours and now I'm starving."

"We could find someplace a little less heart attack inducing." Taylor smoothed his tie down.

"We?" Joss cocked his head. "You're joining me?"

"Yes." Blowing out a breath, he said, "Taige and her husband are pissed off at each other. They've decided to have it out in my room, probably so they don't do it in front of Jilly. I tried to get Dez to come with me so she didn't get caught in the line of fire, but she wanted to stay. Her weird idea of entertainment."

"And you're chickening out . . . staying here."

This time, when Taylor smiled, it wasn't a faint smile. It was a full-blown, all-out grin. "Damn straight."

* * *

PART of Dez felt bad for loitering in the hotel room.

It was pretty damn clear those two needed to talk.

But when she got up and shot Taige a look, Taige had pinned her with a direct stare.

If you leave, I'm kicking your ass.

Dez rolled her eyes and mouthed, *Pussy.*

Taige just curled her lip and went back to gingerly poking through some of the files Taylor had left behind.

Okay. So Taige wasn't ready to talk to Cullen yet?

What was the deal there?

Sighing, she flopped back onto the couch and pulled her pillow to her chest, staring at the TV. She was stuck watching TV for the duration because she couldn't get involved in this case. As much as she wanted to help, this was too big for her and she'd just cause more problems than she'd solve.

Of course, she wouldn't mind if she had a ghost of her own whispering to her, but that just wasn't happening.

The silence in the room was so heavy, she practically came out of her skin when Cullen broke it.

"Taige, can we maybe go get a bite to eat?"

"I already ate, thanks." Nice. So nice and polite.

"A cup of coffee?"

From the corner of her eye, Dez saw Taige point to the coffeepot in the kitchen.

"Shit. Okay, screw subtle. I need to talk to you. Alone."

Dez groaned and shot Taige another look, lifting a brow. Taige shook her head. "Too bad, sweetheart," Taige replied. "I'm working."

He snorted and pushed at the pages she'd been messing with for the past little while. "You look like you're trying to keep busy, if you ask me."

"You're right. I'm keeping busy ignoring you for the time being," she said, leaning back and staring at him. "I don't want to talk to you right now. You don't get that. Fine. But I still don't want to talk to you . . . not yet."

A muscle jerked in his jaw.

Dez almost felt sorry for him.

"Fine." He headed for the door. Halfway there, he stopped

and turned back to face his wife. "I think I'm going to call my dad to come and get Jilly."

"You should just go home with her," Taige said quietly. "I think I'm going to be needed here."

Cullen closed the distance between them once more, curled his hand around the back of her neck. "I'm not leaving. Not with what's going on . . . not with this between us unresolved."

* * *

TAIGE waited until the door shut before she dropped her head onto the table.

"You can't ignore him forever."

"I don't plan on it. But I don't want to listen to him rail at me about how I put his precious baby in a bad situation, either," she said, her voice thick with anger. And hurt. It was still lodged in her chest, turning her heart to ashes.

"She's your baby, too."

"You can't tell by the way he's been acting." A sigh shuddered out of her, and she lifted her hands to her face. "Damn it, life would have been easier if we'd gone to New York the way Jillian wanted."

A few seconds later, there was a soft sound and she looked up, watched as Dez hauled a chair so they were sitting side by side. "Easier. Maybe. But if this is as big as Taylor thinks it is . . ."

They both looked at the table, then at the board placed by the window. It was covered with small images of deceased victims. The missing women they *thought* were connected to this . . . they'd need a good ten boards to even make a dent. "Do we even have a victim count yet?" Dez asked quietly.

"No." Taige shook her head.

"You picking up anything?"

Taige stared at one neat pile of images. It was growing. Every time she saw something that made her instincts scream, she'd made Taylor handle it. She couldn't get lost in the gray yet. Not yet. She didn't know why she was holding off, but she couldn't go yet.

"Yes," she said woodenly.

Dez followed her line of sight, and when she saw the stack of images, a soft hiss escaped her. "Shit."

"Yeah."

FIFTEEN

A hot meal.

A hard run through downtown.

And when he got back to the hotel, Joss deliberately sat in the lobby for an hour.

Surrounded by people, listening to them come and go.

Dimly, he was aware of their thoughts. The chaos. It was like rain pounding against an umbrella he carried, though. It didn't leave him overwhelmed this time. Finally.

It was an exhausting exercise and his head was still reeling, so he didn't feel at all bad about missing the evening powwow in Jones's room. He headed to his, showered, and crashed.

It was another night of deep, tormenting dreams.

He would have liked to fight, but this time . . . the dreams reached up and grabbed him. Pulled him under. Choking him . . .

* * *

CHOKING—

Fuck all, the pain choked him, but it didn't matter.

All that mattered was that he get up. Get on his feet and get her away from here. Struggling to roll over, he clawed at the grass, searching for something to hold as he clambered to his feet.

But there was nothing—

Then there was something.

A hand. Pressing on his chest.

Her hand. "Be still now, do you hear me? You must be still. Oh, look at . . . no. It will be fine."

Fine . . . No. He wouldn't be fine. Everything was getting black and gray, his vision fading as he tried to focus on her face. "Amelie. You must run now," he rasped, grabbing her wrist and trying to blink away the gray clouds that wanted to hide her face from him. "Run. Get away . . ."

"Hush. I need to stop the bleeding."

"It will not help. You must run—"

In his bed, he flung out a hand, closed into a tight, useless fist.

* * *

"You didn't really think I'd let you run."

Dru gasped for air as Patrick let her up, just once, for a gulp of air.

Then he was pushing her down again and the heavy, wet silk of her wedding dress was sucking her under.

The cold water pressed in around her, and it was deep, so much deeper than a bathtub full of water should be—she'd been taking a bath. That was all. Taking a bath, in her wedding dress . . . then he was there, trying to push her under.

His hand fisted in her hair, jerking her back up.

She blinked the bubbles and water out of her eyes, sputtering and gasping for air. And realized . . . they weren't in her bathroom anymore. They were on a bridge. The wet, heavy silk of her gown was gone, replaced by an equally heavy, equally ornate dress of all black.

"Mourn him, do you? Foolish cow. Think you can run away from me?"

Dru stared at the man in front of her. The angry glint in his eyes reminded her of Patrick, although he wasn't Patrick. The cool, angry words . . . they reminded her of him, as well. Even the way he made her skin crawl . . .

"Amelie, dearest. Did you really think I'd let you leave me?" he asked casually, just before he backhanded her.

Amelie . . .

She went flying. But before she could crash to the ground, big, gentle hands caught her and she sagged against a chest that seemed terribly, terribly familiar.

The black, ornate dress melted away.

As he pushed one big, capable hand into her hair, Dru stared up at him. "You again."

It was the guy from the park.

The one who'd kissed her.

The one who made her feel like . . . everything.

"He hit you before. I remember that," he murmured, studying her cheek before looking past her to stare at not-Patrick. "Does he still?"

She turned her head, followed his stare. He was watching the man who'd reminded her so disturbingly of her fiancé. "I . . . nobody has ever hit me before. Well, he has. But only him."

The man shook his head. "You're wrong there. He hit you before . . . when we were all different."

"That's nice and . . . unclear."

"Another life," he murmured. Cupping her cheek, he stroked his thumb along the sweep of her cheekbone. "I always remembered. But you've forgotten . . . haven't you?"

She stared up at his face. "If I ever knew you, I'd remember."

"Not if you weren't supposed to." He pressed against her lower lip. "He hit you before . . . and he killed me. After that, I don't know what became of you. But I think you do. If you'll let yourself remember."

Dru grimaced. "That's insane."

"So is kissing a man you've never met . . . but you did that. And you did a damn good job of it." He lowered his head, rubbed his lips over hers. "Wanna do it again?"

As she opened for him, that sane voice in her mind whispered, "This is just insane."

But the voice was quieter this time. Quieter . . . and she wasn't quite so sure of her sanity, either.

"It's not insane . . . this is the most rational either of us has ever been."

"Is it?" She stared up at him, some part of her insisting that this was crazy. All of it. But she couldn't. Because it felt right. Seemed so right. Far better than anything having to do with Patrick . . .

"Don't think about him," he ordered.

"Hard, that. Seeing as he's standing right . . ." Dru lifted her head, and then stopped in midsentence once she realized Patrick wasn't, in fact, standing there.

And they weren't there anymore.

They were in a bright, open room that seemed strangely familiar, although she knew she'd never seen it in her life. The walls had the most ornate wallpaper on them, pink vining flowers that climbed up to a high, airy ceiling. A lovely, four-poster bed that made her think of a time gone by.

"Do you remember this?" he murmured, turning his arms so that they stood facing the bed.

Dru blinked. "No. Why should I? I've never seen this place."

He sighed. "You have . . . in another life."

A laugh escaped her. "Another life. You must have knocked your head or something . . ."

"Look in the mirror, Dru. See us . . ."

She lifted her head and her breath froze in her lungs. He wasn't the same. But the eyes . . . she knew those eyes. He stood at her back, longish blond hair pulled back from his face, his clothes clean but roughly made. She, though, her hair was done up in ringlets and curls, swept up high off her face, displaying her neck, a fine necklace. The gown she wore was something she expected to see on the cover of a romance novel, the kind where the man had his shirt half open while the woman was bent back over his arm at an impossible angle.

Swallowing, Dru shook her head. "That's not me."

And then she clapped a hand over her mouth. For it wasn't her voice, either. Softer, huskier, slower.

"It is you . . . it was. Before he took you away from me. Don't let him take you away again." He dipped his head and kissed her neck. "This was us. I loved you from the minute I saw you. Do you remember?"

Tearing away from him, she stumbled over to the mirror, certain this was a trick. That red-gold hair . . . no, that wasn't her hair. And those certainly weren't her tits. She glanced down at her chest and grimaced. "I can't breathe."

"I can help you with that."

"I just bet," she muttered sourly, but when she went to turn around, he stopped her. Stiffly, she stood there while he went about stripping her out of a dress that left her baffled. The dress. A petticoat? Other bits and pieces of clothing she didn't recog-

nize. Finally, she stood there in long, lacy underwear, a chemise, and a corset. "I still can't breathe."

"I always loved seeing you like this." He dipped his head and kissed his way down her neck. "Your favorite thing to do was tease me . . ."

"You want me to believe we were lovers . . . in another life."

"No." He sighed.

She felt him tugging, and then abruptly, she could breathe as the laces at her waist eased up. "We weren't. I wanted to be. You were . . . uncertain. Scared. I guess I don't blame you. I wasn't the kind of husband you'd been looking for, and you didn't know how we'd make it. But I would have made things work. I just needed you to trust me."

The corset fell away and she looked down as big, rough hands closed around her waist.

Her breath gusted out of her as he pulled her against him. The room spun. And a soft bed was at her back. "We weren't lovers, but we will be," he whispered. "Do I stop now? Are we going to wait until we're finally together, or can we at least have this?"

Her breath hissed out of her as she realized their clothes were gone.

She hadn't taken them off. Neither had he.

And it wasn't that other face she saw above hers.

It was the man she'd met in the park.

A harsh, craggy face, too rough to be handsome, but so fucking sexy he made her hurt from want. Eyes so dark and soft, like molten chocolate, and she just wanted to gorge herself. A mouth that was just perfect.

Reaching up, she touched his lips. "This is insane."

"No . . . insane is what we've been doing for the past hundred years, being lost. Now we're together." He pushed his knee

between her thighs, pressed the muscle length against her. "Do we wait? Do we stay lost?"

Dru curled an arm around his neck and pulled him closer. She stroked one hand down his arm and lifted her leg, wrapped it around his waist. "Even if it's insane, I don't want to wait."

"It's not insane." He slanted his mouth over hers. "And we won't wait."

No . . . no, we won't, she thought. It seemed as though no sooner had that thought left her mind than they were on the bed, his long, muscled body pressed to hers. As his hands cupped her breasts, she closed her eyes. So strange . . . and so not. She could almost believe this actually had happened. That maybe this wasn't just a dream.

"You have no idea how long I've waited for this," he rasped, pushing a hand into her hair. "All my life, Dru. I've been waiting all my life . . ."

"I can almost believe that."

"Believe it." He pulled her into his arms, lifting her as though she weighed nothing.

He laid her on the bed, his hands practically shaking as he stroked them up her thighs. "I won't hurt you," he said gruffly. "I won't . . ."

Dru pushed up onto one elbow and hooked her hand around the back of his neck, tugged him close. Scraping her teeth along his lower lip, she whispered against his lips, "If you don't shut up already, I just might hurt you."

For a second, something flashed in his eyes. And she felt something from him. That burn on her brain, it seemed to flare, expand . . . hunger pulsing. "Shutting up, ma'am." He took her mouth with his.

The heavy, solid weight of him was so unlike anything she'd ever felt. Yet it felt so perfectly right . . . so right . . . The wide, muscled wall of his chest crushed against her breasts, harsh, ragged breaths escaping him. She could feel the hard, rigid length of his cock. His hands stroking over her.

And that hunger . . . it was like it surrounded her very being. Overwhelmed her. Warmed her.

She sucked in a desperate breath, only to lose it when he reached between them, teasing her with the head of his cock. Slow, torturous . . . ah, hell. Wrapping her legs around his hips, she arched up. "Weren't you the one whinging about waiting?"

"Whinging?" Laughter lurked in his voice as he scraped his teeth over her neck.

"Whinging . . . whining, whatever you Americans call it. Bitching . . . would you just fuck me already?" she demanded.

His body went tense. Rigid.

Dru caught her breath. She'd been behaving herself so long, being the demure little twit who'd never dare speak her mind, but she hadn't thought—

A groan rumbled out of him. So fast, he moved so fast, one hand coming up and cupping her face, spearing over her cheek, fingers splaying wide. "Open," he demanded against her lips. "Open your mouth."

And he didn't wait. He just pushed his tongue demandingly into her mouth, hungry and certain. At the same time, he thrust inside her. Deep, so deep, and she screamed, shocked, into his mouth. Wide and hot, burning, he pierced her, and even when he was buried inside her, it was like he couldn't get deep enough, rocking against her.

"More, damn it . . ." He groaned. "Give me more."

Trying to breathe, trying to keep from flying into a thousand pieces, she wrapped her arms around him, holding on to the wide shelf of his shoulders. Her heart skittered in her ribs as he lifted his head, just enough to stare into her eyes.

"Dru?"

She heard his unspoken question, dancing through her mind. Felt it in a way she couldn't explain. Reaching out to him on that same connection, she tugged him back to her.

Yes, she thought. She needed more.

A dream wasn't enough.

As he started to move against her, she sobbed against his lips. If this only happened in a dream, she just might wither away and die . . .

It will happen again, and for real, *he whispered into her mind.* I'll make damn sure of it.

But she couldn't think about that. Not with everything that swamped her in real life. Not with the sensation of him driving inside her, the swollen head of his cock scraping over every sensitized nerve ending. Not with the feel of his presence pulsing inside in a way she couldn't even begin to explain.

It will happen, baby girl . . . it will . . .

The need pulsed. Expanded. And as he gave her another one of those breath-stealing, soul-shattering kisses, she started to shake, a shuddering that echoed in her very core. Stretching out, bit by bit . . .

As he withdrew, she cried out, clenching down around him, desperate to keep him inside her, her nails biting into his shoulders. He snarled, shoved deeper, harder.

She felt his hand tangling in her hair, the other hooking under her shoulders to hold her steady as his hips slammed against her. And it was so damned good, so damned amazing . . .

And although it was nothing but a dream, she climaxed hard, so hard, it stole the very breath from her lungs and left her crying.

Before she could even process what was happening next, though . . . she started to fade.

She could even feel the edges of the dream unraveling. Felt it withering away . . .

"Stay with me," he rasped.

Dru struggled as the dream started to fade.

"Look at me."

Lost, fighting whatever it was that seemed to pull her away, she stared into those dark eyes. They anchored her, pulled her in. "Just look at me. Stay with me," *he said, his voice firm . . . and yet under it, she heard a desperate plea.*

"Shit," *he whispered.*

"What's happening?"

"We're both waking up." *He looked around.* "I can't hold this outside of dreams."

"What's your name?"

Just before he faded completely, he flashed her one quick smile. "It's Joss."

* * *

Joss . . .

She came awake with his name echoing through her mind, his taste lingering on her lips . . . her entire body was still shuddering with the aftereffects of the climax, and although she *knew* she hadn't had sex, it damn well felt like she had.

There were tears on her face. Her heart still raced.

And fear had her skin like ice. The fear only got worse when she licked her lips and thought she could taste the echo of his kiss.

"Don't let him take you . . ."

As his words circled through her mind, Dru swung her legs over the edge of the bed and sat there, her entire body trembling, shaking, her gut a tight, cold knot.

Deep inside, in her soul, she ached.

It felt like somebody had taken her heart and just shattered it, smashed it, and then sewn up the biggest pieces without bothering to make sure everything fit. She felt incomplete. She felt broken.

All from a dream.

"I'm losing my mind. Went nuts under the stress, that's all."

Except she didn't *feel* like she was going crazy.

That thought made her laugh. *Oh, right, like the typical crazy person* feels *off their rocker.* Sighing, she shoved her hair back and buried her face in her hands. She had to get a grip. Ever mindful of the cameras, she pretended to sit there, like she did every morning, tried to pretend she hadn't just had the very foundation of her entire world rocked. *Just stop thinking about it. Just don't think . . .*

It shouldn't be that hard.

But the dream, it was like it was stuck on instant replay, right there in her mind.

Another life . . . I always remembered. But you've forgotten . . . haven't you? Those dark eyes, locked on her face, so intent. So full of want, need, desire.

Love.

If I ever knew you, I'd remember, she'd told him. And yes. She knew that to be true. That man . . . *Joss* . . . he wasn't a man she'd forget. Wasn't a man she'd let go.

Unless he was taken from her.

He killed me . . . Remembering *that* was like a brutal, two-fisted punch to her heart, and she wanted to scream from it. Wanted to rage, to cry.

He hit you before . . . and he killed me. After that, I don't know what became of you. But I think you do. If you'll let yourself remember.

Let yourself remember . . .

Maybe I really am losing my mind.

There was a massive headache pounding behind her eyes, courtesy of the massive amounts of rum she'd taken in last night after Patrick had left. She'd feigned sleep until he locked the door and then she'd promptly made free with the liquor cabinet and tried to drown herself in a vat of rum, but it hadn't done any good.

Neither had the blistering shower she'd taken.

Now she was stuck with a brutal headache, a brutal hangover, and crystal-clear memories of what she'd done.

She'd had sex with that monster. Again.

Granted, if she hadn't had sex with him, he would have just raped her. Again. She'd much rather be in control than let him force her again, but in the end, she still felt dirty. Used.

Bruised.

It hadn't bothered her quite this much before. Oh, it had bothered her, but now . . .

What had changed?

Except she already knew.

Don't let him take you away again . . .

She met a man. She shared a stolen kiss.

And suddenly, the shadowy, insubstantial dreams that had haunted her weren't so shadowy or insubstantial.

Let yourself remember . . .

She was either losing her mind . . . or she would wish she was, if she *did* let herself remember, she suspected.

SIXTEEN

H E heard her say his name.
Even as he lay there, more awake than asleep, Joss heard her say his name.

And he wanted to hit something.

They'd connected in that dream—finally, a real connection, not just those remnants of a dream.

But did he have time to track her down today?

No.

He was meeting Jones in an hour.

There was already somebody out there, lurking and waiting for him to vacate the premises—Joss could feel her presence, a tired, cranky bitch who just wanted to plant the *"effin cameras and get her ass back to bed,"* as she thought it. *But no . . . she had to clean the fucking cabin, too, what in the hell did he think she was, a maid?*

Her thoughts, high-strung and erratic, had Joss groaning.

Rolling out of bed, he shuffled to the kitchen and got a cup of coffee. He'd hit the grocery store last night and gotten himself a fresh bag of coffee. He wasn't touching anything his good buddy Hennegan had used.

He'd set the coffeemaker to brew before he went to bed, so there was already coffee waiting and the scent of it did something to wake up his lethargic brain.

Coffee in hand, he headed to the bathroom. Shower. Coffee. He just might wake up in time to meet with Jones and explain just what in the hell he needed to do. Convince the boss he had to do it this way. And wait for the shit to hit the fan. Listen to Taylor inform him in that very polite way of his that it wouldn't happen.

And then Joss would tell him to fuck off, he had to do it this way, and then they could get down to business.

There were things he was meant to do . . . so those certain things could unfold as they needed to.

This sucked.

But first he had to wake up enough to face the damn day. Still clutching his coffee as if it were a lifesaver, he shuffled to the shower and turned it on. Hot. Enough hot water pounding down on him should clear the cobwebs from his brain. Between that and the coffee, he should be able to handle facing Jones.

One more swig from the cup, hot enough to burn his tongue, and then he all but fell in, standing under the brutally hot spray and groaning as it beat down on tense, tight muscles.

Just needed to get past the dream. Needed to wake up . . .

Needed . . .

Dru . . .

Groaning, he slammed his head back against the tile wall. He needed *not* to think of her just now. Because that was all it took. He'd woken up edgy and needy and now . . .

The heat from the shower wrapped around him, kissing his

skin almost like a woman's mouth. Almost, but not quite. That was fine. He'd close his eyes and pretend.

Pretend Dru was here. Wrapping his fist around his cock, he let himself slip back into the dream he was trying to forget and started to stroke. Thought of her lips. Her smooth, honey gold skin and that sleek, shiny hair.

His breath hitched in his lungs as he neared the head, imagined it was her hands on him. Or her mouth. Or her sweet, sweet pussy . . .

"*Fuck*," he snarled, jerking harder. Harder.

Hunger, almost painful, twisted in his gut, and he surged away from the wall, slamming a hand against the tile in front of him, head bowed, water pouring down. Her face . . . her eyes. *Her . . .*

He needed her here. With him.

Instead he was alone . . .

With a ragged, tortured groan, he came.

And even though he was there alone, with nothing but his thoughts, they were thoughts of *her* . . . and it was more satisfying than anything he could remember in a long, long time.

She was real. *Real.* Here. And he could find her.

As soon as this damn job was done and he could leave.

* * *

LEAVING was the last thing Dru needed to do. She dressed like she was going to work out in the fitness facilities provided. She did that often enough. Sometimes she even ran on the grounds.

So that wasn't so unusual.

She kept her pace steady, knowing she had a shadow.

But she kept going longer than her shadow could.

Running was her escape. Even when she knew she had to come back.

She'd done this more than a few times, and Patrick hadn't been particularly pleased, but neither had he said anything.

The dumbfuck following her was going to get his ass ripped for letting her evade him, but that was his own fault, and this time, she had a hard time feeling guilty that another was going to suffer over Patrick's anger with her. She'd seen this one through the flashes with Patrick, seen him enough to know that Patrick used him for his dirty work.

If he chose to work for a monster, then he needed to be prepared for what the monster would do.

And maybe build up his endurance.

He fell back after the second mile.

By the third mile, he was no longer in sight when she rounded the corner and she let loose, pounding the pavement and letting herself take off.

Her muscles were loose and easy by the fourth mile, and she breathed easier once she'd fallen onto the lesser known paths to leave the resort property. She hadn't spent so much time crawling over satellite feeds of all of this property for nothing. She knew it like the back of her hand.

Part of her wanted to just keep running. She could do it . . . throughout college, she'd done long-distance running and she still kept up with it. Her muscles would ache and burn if she did more than eight or ten miles, but she could do it, if she had to.

She could run, leave this place behind.

She had contacts. She hadn't come into this job blind—that would have been suicide.

She had her phone, cash, stowed on her. She never left her room without taking a few necessary items with her after all.

And in a secure location not too far from here, she had everything she needed to get back to *her* life. To who she was . . . She could go back to England, pick up the pieces of her business, and forget all about this.

The echos of the screams stopped her. The pain they'd suffered. The loss.

Slowing to a halt, she bent over and gave herself a minute to catch her breath.

Yes. She could run.

Yes. She could leave Patrick behind, disappear and return to life, pick up the pieces, and get back to her job. The only thing she really had to do was make a couple of phone calls. The few people who knew where she was, well, she'd rather they not worry that he'd done her in.

She could let them know. Maybe even send an anonymous tip to people who were better equipped to handle the monster that was Patrick Whitmore.

It would be so easy . . .

"But that's not who I am."

I'm doing exactly what I'm meant to do.

Besides . . . if she left, it might make it harder for a certain someone to find her when this was all done.

I'll find you again, Dru.

She might have told him it was best if he didn't, and she meant it. For now.

But sooner or later, she'd stop fighting to keep him out of her head.

With a faint smile curling her lips, she straightened back and started to move. This time, it was at a slower, steadier pace.

Her legs might be nothing more than noodles when she got back.

And she'd want to eat like a wolf, sleep like the dead.

Sounded like the ideal way to handle her beloved fiancé.

* * *

TAIGE and Cullen were circling around each other like a couple of angry wolves. Still. Frankly, Taylor was tired of it, but there wasn't anything he could do.

Cullen was in a sullen state, eyeing everybody else in the room like he wished they'd just get the hell out and leave him alone with his wife.

Taige was in a dark, angry mood that he couldn't do a damn thing about.

Taylor needed to get his ass to that grease pit that served as a restaurant—he was supposed to meet Crawford shortly.

The question was whether there would be bloodshed while he was gone.

Eyeing Taige and Cullen, he figured probably not. Taige might look like she wanted to pound her husband bloody, but Morgan just looked miserable.

His own fault, Taylor figured. After all this time, he should be able to read his wife better.

He couldn't blame the guy for being pissed at him, and Taylor wasn't going to lose any sleep over it. It was only going to get worse for the Morgans, too. Jillian had it in her—Taylor wouldn't seek her out, but she'd come looking for him again. It was just fact.

It would cause some bumps and bruises for them. Taylor didn't see any way around it, but damn if he wanted to hang around and deal with it. He didn't much want to leave Dez here, either, but he couldn't take her with him and she didn't seem to want to bail.

Unable to delay any longer, he gathered up the neat stacks of his files, tucked them inside his briefcase. "I have to go," he said, directing his words to Taige and Dez.

Taige jerked a shoulder. "Hope Crawford is holding up okay," she said, hunched over the table, determinedly ignoring her husband.

Cullen was giving Taylor that same, determined attention—or lack of it.

Shifting his attention to Dez, he found her watching him with that familiar amused glint in her eyes.

It figured she'd find something to be amused about in this, he thought.

Crossing over to her, he skimmed his fingers across her cheek, down her neck, paused briefly to touch the scar on her neck. A smile canted her lips and she swayed closer, pressed her lips to his. "I love you," she murmured. "You know that?"

"Yeah . . . I know that." It was his miracle. *She* was his miracle. He rubbed his mouth against hers, reminded himself they weren't alone, that he had a job to do, an agent out there with a gift inside his head that he wasn't fully acclimated to. "I love you, too."

Pulling back, he glanced toward the tense couple sitting at the table. "You should go downstairs. Have breakfast. Go shopping."

"No." Dez smiled. "If I have a yen to shop, I will. And I already had breakfast. Now, go . . . I'm sure I can handle it."

He grimaced. Her handling it wasn't the problem.

After another quick kiss, he headed for the door. He'd already lingered longer than he should have, but he had enough time to get there, he figured.

But then the elevator doors slid open and he saw who was waiting for him.

* * *

IT was cool out. Cool, damp, and the air smelled of rain.

Joss leaned back against the prick's car as he waited for Jones to show up. It was early, the sun drifting up from the horizon,

slow and steady, painting the world in soft colors of gold. The
pretty display was lost on Joss. He was eyeing each of the cars
narrowly as though they'd magically turn into the car he needed
to see.

Jones wasn't here yet.

Brooding, he crossed his arms over his chest and stared out
into the still, cool gray of the morning.

He was tired. His head ached like a bitch. He didn't want to
be out here doing this job, even though, logically, he knew this
was one of the most important jobs he'd ever done.

Somebody had died here. He could hear her whispering,
although there was nothing he could do for her. She was too old,
just a fragment, and she was so weak and faint.

He doubted she'd even hear him if he tried to reach out. She
kept whispering, *Stop the car, please, just stop and let me out—*

Then there was a scream, over and over, and he felt the echo
of her death. Over and over. The only glimpse he could get of her
was of a woman dressed in a skinny skirt, her hair done in a
sleek style that made him think of the forties. She'd been dead a
long, long time, and even when he lowered his shields, her presence didn't get any stronger. Dez might be able to help her, but
Joss didn't have the . . . compassion she had. That was what
made her so damned good at her job. She connected because of
her heart. Maybe when this was done, she could come back here
and help—he didn't know.

So he was stuck there, listening to the woman whisper and
scream as she relived her death.

It had happened three times, and he'd let it happen each time
as he tried to figure out if he could help her, but halfway through
the fourth, he'd figured out he was useless. Although she'd never
hear him, he'd muttered an apology and slammed his shields
back into place.

Now she'd scream, beg, and relive her death over and over . . . but he wouldn't hear it. Made him feel like a damn coward.

He'd tell Dez about the place, though. If the girl could be helped, Dez would know how.

As the echo of her scream tore through his memory, he groaned and shoved away from the SUV, starting to pace. Jones wasn't here yet. What the hell? The guy was usually early. Like thirty minutes early, or more. Taylor liked to get the lay of the land. It was a wise way to do things in their line of work, Joss knew. Of course, his natural inclination was to stumble in at the last minute, but he went against his natural inclinations and was early more often than not. Never hurt to take a look around. Scope out the area.

And in this case, listen to a ghost cry for thirty minutes.

His phone vibrated and he pulled it out, saw the message.

Running late. Unexpected complication. Be there ASAP.

Joss scowled and went to text him back.

But the tingle down his spine stopped him.

Slowly, he lifted his head. He couldn't see her. Not yet.

But with his heart thrumming in his chest and his heart racing, he knew what was going on.

Her . . .

It was her.

Shoving his phone into his pocket, he moved away from the car, lowering his shields just enough so that he could feel her.

There—

Just down the road.

Running.

Form-fitting black spandex clung to her hips and thighs, stopping just a few inches below that delectable ass. A short sleeveless T-shirt, wet with perspiration. A grim look on her face.

Hurt so good, my ass. How many bloody miles have I done now . . . I'm going to have to crawl . . .

The ramble of thoughts in her mind stopped him from sensing anything else.

Then he stepped into her path and the dazed, numb shock replaced her rambling thoughts as he closed the distance between them.

Seconds later, there was no dazed, numb shock.

Just dazed, delighted pleasure as he caught her face in his hands and took her mouth.

She tasted of salt and sweat and woman. *His* woman, Joss thought. He groaned against her lips as her hands came up, gripped his wrists, her short, neat nails biting into his skin.

Her mouth opened for him and he growled with satisfaction, tracing the opening with his tongue before swooping inside to taste more of her, to *take* more of her.

It was heaven. It was perfection.

Then it was over, as she tore away from him, her chest heaving, her face flushed.

"You again," she muttered. A look that might have been fear came and went in her eyes as she glanced around.

Bugger—what if they caught up? If they saw that . . .

He couldn't keep up with her thoughts—her shields were too solid, and once she'd shored them up, he could only follow fleeting glimpses.

There was enough, though, to let him know she was afraid.

Very afraid.

Who would follow you? he wanted to ask. *Why be so afraid?*

But now wasn't the time.

For either of them.

But he wasn't about to let her leave so soon. Advancing on her, he watched as she backed away one step. Then another. "I guess I shouldn't be pawing you in the middle of the sidewalk," he said, crooking a smile at her.

She arched a brow. "It would be nice."

"I'll do it there, then." He glanced over her shoulder, watched as she did the same. A blush crept up her cheeks as she eyed the motel. "You think I'm going to let you grab us a quicky motel? I don't even know your—"

She stopped abruptly, swallowed.

"My what?" he asked.

She paused, eyeing him nervously for a moment. "Your name. I don't even know your name."

Joss continued to walk forward, one slow step at a time, waiting until she backed up. A few more steps had them in the shadow of a big RV—exactly where he'd been planning. "Now that's not true, baby girl. You know my name just fine."

"No." She narrowed her eyes. "I don't."

But the echo in her mind said otherwise.

Grinning at her, Joss dipped down and nuzzled her neck. *"Liar . . ."*

As his lips cruised along her bare skin, she groaned and arched her head back. "This is insane. Completely insane."

"Yeah." He traced a path along her skin with his tongue, heat punching inside him at the taste of her. It was different. She was different. Stronger. Wiser. Sadder. And she didn't remember him, but he didn't care. That may change and it may not, but he didn't fucking *care*. She was here, she was with him, and some part of her *knew* him. He could tell, could feel it.

As she pressed closer to him, he slid a hand around her and curved it over her lower back, spread his fingers wide until he could feel the firm curve of her ass. Lifting his head, he said, "What's my name, Dru?"

She stared at him through her lashes, a dazed look in her eyes. Shaking her head, she leaned in, seeking out his mouth.

He wasn't about to argue with that. When she opened for

him, he tugged her closer. The feel of her, all soft and warm and female, was almost too much. Through the sturdy fabric of the sports bra she wore, he could feel the soft swells of her breasts, and he wanted to peel the material off her, lick away the sweat, then make her sweat again . . . as he brought her to climax a dozen times.

His cock ached, throbbed, and each light brush as she moved against him was the sweetest torment.

Fisting his hand in her tank top, he dragged it up, baring skin damp from her run. Higher, higher, until it caught under her arms. Leaning back, he stared down at her. The utilitarian black sports bra shouldn't have been so fucking sexy, but it was. She could have worn sackcloth and ashes and she'd still be beautiful to him.

In his mind's eye, an image from a time long past drifted—her standing before him, in white petticoats edged with lace, presenting him with her back and asking for his help in lacing up her corset.

Swearing, he dipped his knees and wrapped his arm around her hips, boosting her high. Her breasts were on level with his mouth and he nuzzled them, wishing he could strip her naked, take her here.

"Joss . . ." she gasped out.

* * *

THE look in his eyes should have infuriated her. It was amusement, mixed with triumph . . . and something else. But as he dipped his head and brushed his lips along the edge of her sports bra, all she could do was cradle the back of his neck and wish she could get even closer. "You do know my name," he murmured, pleased.

"We're out in public," she snapped, reaching for the icy, snotty tone she'd crafted and refined so long ago. Really, it should have worked.

All he did was shoot her a lazy, slow smile.

"Yeah. It's a good thing, too, or I'd have you naked and I'd already be so deep inside you . . ." He raked her skin with his teeth. "It's going to happen sooner or later anyway, duchess."

For a minute, she let herself believe him. Let herself believe it could happen. Believe it would.

But then reality came crashing down on her, and she made herself think about what was *really* going to happen sooner or later. In a matter of weeks, she'd be married to Patrick Whitmore if she didn't find the proof she needed *before* then. If she didn't find it, then she'd marry him and keep on looking until she found it.

Either she'd find it . . . and get away from him.

Or she'd end up dead when he discovered what she was up to.

In all likelihood, the second option was what would happen.

She dreamed too often of her death, death at the hands of a violent, angry man who hated her.

She *knew* how likely it was if he discovered what she was up to. There was no point in pretending otherwise, and no point in trying to think up other options. Every time she did that, she ended up having to talk herself out of running. She couldn't run away from this. Too many girls had already died, and if she didn't do something . . . who would?

Big, strong arms came around her, and a gentle hand stroked her back. She didn't even realize she'd collapsed against him, her head against his shoulder, gripping him tight and close as though she never wanted him to leave.

She didn't. This man she'd seen exactly twice.

Yet some part of her felt as though she *knew* him . . .

Joss.

The dream.

"What's wrong, duchess?"

She shivered as he whispered it, his lips pressed against her neck as he spoke.

"Whatever is wrong with you, calling me that?" she said, swallowing around the knot that had lodged in her throat. Easing away from him, she eyed him nervously before glancing around. Nobody could see them from here, unless of course Patrick had managed to stash his men in the hotel. Not likely, that.

"I dunno. Seems to suit you. The accent. The way you carry yourself . . . all smooth and elegant." He touched his finger to her lip. "What scares you?"

"I don't see how that could suit me," she said faintly, ignoring the last part of his question as she tugged her tank down.

"Why are you afraid?" he asked, putting himself in her way.

With a brittle smile, she shook her head. "I'm not afraid," she lied.

"Don't lie to me. You know as well as I do, it doesn't work. You're terrified, damn it. Why?"

Dru shook her head. "It doesn't do any good to talk about it. You can't help anyway. I must go."

Part of her questioned why she wasn't furious with him—this was a *stranger*. She didn't know him. But all she could think about was how much she wished she could stay. How much she longed to go back to him . . . lean against him, touch him. Taste him. *Take* him.

But when he reached for her, she evaded him.

"Meet me here tomorrow," he said flatly.

"No." She continued to back away, glancing around for signs that one of Patrick's men might have caught up with her. Nothing. There was a shiny black car in the parking lot of the Waffle House across the street, but it wasn't one of Patrick's. If it was, she'd know. She'd feel it somehow.

"Dru, talk to me."

She shot him another look. Then, *finally*, fury and frustration sparked inside her, and she glared at him as it bubbled over and spilled out. "Stop. Damn you, why couldn't you have come into my life a year ago? Two years ago? Why *now*? I can't have you now."

Without bothering to explain, she took off running.

She was torn between hoping he'd follow, and praying he wouldn't.

* * *

I can't have you now—

The utter heartbreak in her words was enough to gut him.

He went to take off after her, but a strange burning tingle down his spine stopped him. The chiming tone from his phone two seconds later had him swearing.

Now.

Of course, *now* Jones comes on the scene. Still staring at Dru's back, he pushed a thought toward her. He didn't know if it would work—he didn't know what her skill set was, but Jillian's was strong enough, he should be able to make a *corpse* hear him.

We're not done, Dru. And you'll damn well talk to me. I can help . . . whatever it is.

She stumbled a little.

Then kept on running.

Yeah. She heard him all right.

Blowing out a breath, he looked back at the Waffle House. Taylor Jones was standing by his car. Dez wasn't with him . . . but he wasn't alone.

Joss recognized the blonde from here.

He didn't know her name, but he didn't need to. He'd seen her before.

This was the woman Patrick had been checking out the night before.

And Joss knew her vaguely. He'd seen her around. He just couldn't remember where.

* * *

"Joss, have you met Nalini Cole? She's with the unit. Fairly new, though."

Joss slumped on the couch, eyeing the long, cool blonde narrowly.

"I've seen her around," he said, directing his words at Jones, but still keeping his eyes on Nalini. "Can't recall where just yet."

She laughed. It was a clear, bell-like sound. Almost angelic. It matched that pretty, pale hair, matched the clear, refined oval of her face.

But it didn't match those dark, sultry eyes.

Her face said *angel* and her voice seemed to echo it.

Her eyes, her body, the way she moved, the way she watched people . . . all of that screamed . . . *devil*. Or maybe trouble.

As she leaned forward, a smile curved her red-slicked mouth. "Now that's not entirely true, is it?" she asked. She posed prettily, the swells of her breasts on display as she continued to watch him.

"Well, I did see you . . . last night. Just not entirely with my eyes. Before that? Don't recall just where I saw you, and I don't have time to wade through the maze of information I've got crammed into my brain."

Cutting his gaze to Jones, he said, "What's going on, boss? I've got a bitch of a job to do, and we've got some serious logistics we need to hammer out."

Jones opened his mouth, but before he could say anything, Nalini said, "He wants a blonde, doesn't he?"

She toyed with her hair. It was done up in a series of tiny braids . . . no. Not braids, exactly.

"Dreadlocks," she offered. She gave him a serene smile. "They're called dreadlocks."

"Next time I'm grilled on the hairstyles of women, I'll keep that one in mind." He raked her over from head to toe and then shook his head. "You're all wrong."

"No. I'm perfect." She leaned back, abandoning the seductive pose, the sex kitten smile, and gave him a grim look. "And more . . . I was pulled here for just this. I knew the minute I saw that fuck last night why I was down here, but I've been having nightmares, bad fits, things that I can't even explain, and it's been going on for weeks. My . . . abilities don't normally work like this, but something has been pulling at me, guiding me. I headed down here over a month ago."

"A month . . ." He shot Jones a look. "I thought you said she was with the unit . . . unless she's been working this, too?"

"Freelance," Jones muttered. "Cole has commitment issues."

She snorted. "I also have issues of being wanted for crimes I didn't commit—you don't want that on your plate, sugar." She continued to stare at Joss. "I've been down here a month. I'll be sitting at a table, and I'll hear a scream. But there's nobody there. Then I'll feel a knife, and it's like I'm dying. Or I'll feel hands on my wrists, my ankles. And somebody's tearing into me, raping me. Over and over. But I'm alone in my hotel room. The worst . . ." She paused, her lashes falling to shield her eyes. "I was in the middle of a mall, walking around, and then I was on the ground. I couldn't move. I couldn't breathe. But I could see . . . I should have seen the roof of the mall over me, but I saw trees, blue sky. And then there was something big, and fast . . . and I felt pain like I've never felt before. It was over in a few minutes, but it seemed to last forever."

Leaning back in his seat, Joss studied her. "You are . . . what, precog?"

"Not so much." She sighed and pulled something out of her purse, laying it on the table between them. Joss leaned forward, eyeing the gold chain, the silly charm that hung from it. "I found this at a pawn shop up in Atlanta. It shouldn't have ever been sold . . . the guy who sold it screwed up. They aren't supposed to take stuff from the girls they grab, but this one does. He takes whatever jewelry he sees on them and pawns it. This . . . I saw it in a store and for some reason, I had to touch it."

"You've got psychometry," he said quietly.

"Yeah. It's the weaker gift and I thank God for that." Shaking her head, she scooped the necklace up and tucked it back into her bag. "If I had a stronger connection to what was going on, I think I'd go insane. It's hard enough sleeping right now."

Joss could completely understand that. "Booze helps."

"Jose Cuervo and I are practically best friends right now." Still holding his eyes, she leaned forward. "You're down here because you're after a slaver. I'm down here because I'm feeling those girls . . . those women he takes. I can help you. I'm *supposed* to help you."

Joss continued to stare at her, and then he sighed, skimmed a hand back over his hair. "He may like your face, your body, but I think your hair is going to piss him off. Can we fix it?"

She shrugged. "Dreads aren't like pigtails. They don't come out the way a braid does. Save me for the last. It's not like he gave you a lot of time. Save me for the last, and then put me in there. The only other option with my hair will be cutting the majority of it off . . . and he wanted *long* hair, right?" Nalini paused and shrugged. "My hair's the least of the problems in the long run. Even if you get me in there and he decides I don't suit, then I've been there and I can still help."

"Not if he decides to shoot you between the eyes for not being what he needs," Joss snapped.

"Not going to happen." She shook her head. "And I think you know it. I wouldn't be down here if I wasn't supposed to help somehow. I'm here. Use me."

Use me.

Joss rubbed his forehead. *Use me*, she says.

The big problem, that was exactly what he needed to do.

And she'd already managed to take care of what he'd thought was going to be his biggest problem . . . informing Jones about how he planned to go forward with this bitch of a job.

He slanted a look at Jones. "I assume you know what I'm planning to do."

Jones stared at him. "I figured that out after I hauled the bastard out of the trunk last night and saw the very vague resemblance. Are you certain you can pull this off?"

"No." Joss shrugged. "But the idea has been in my head almost from the get-go. The kid you pushed on me planted the idea in my skull, so I'm assuming that's how *she* foresaw it. Hopefully she didn't foresee me dying, but if she did, I don't want to know that."

I'm not going to die, he told himself. *I've got too many reasons to be here.*

"I still need two more girls. Biracial, and a Latina." He paused and then added slowly, "We need to use agents on this. Preferably from within our own unit . . . the quieter we keep this, the less chance there is of fucking it up."

"I've got an agent who would be perfect for the biracial woman you need. Her name is Vaughnne MacMeans." Jones sighed and smoothed down his tie. He caught Joss smirking at him and he dropped his hand. "And she's a telepath . . . her reach is pretty much limitless. I think you've worked with her a time or two."

Joss grunted.

Jones could work out the logistics. He needed to get back into position for now.

* * *

"WHERE have you been?"

At the sound of his voice, Dru had to lock her knees to keep from collapsing.

She laid her keycard on the table and looked up, smiled. "Patrick! What a wonderful surprise."

He continued to sit in the armchair, watching her. He'd been out of sight, hidden by the wall. Lying in wait, she thought. Like an alligator.

"Where have you been?" he asked again.

"I went running." She gestured to her clothing and smiled, shrugged. "I needed to burn off some energy."

"And our facilities here aren't adequate?"

Careful . . . careful . . . Dru smiled at him even as she desperately, selfishly prayed, *Please God . . . let him leave, business, he doesn't want to touch me right now, I don't care!* "Oh, it's not that. I just needed a good hard run and I can't always focus as well on the treadmill. I wanted to be outside."

She took off her trainers and then went to him, kneeling down on the floor at his feet, even though her tired legs practically screamed when she did so. A light touch told her this was a good move to make . . . he liked the subservience of it. She wondered what he'd do if she shot a hand up between his legs and ripped off his bloody balls.

Giving him a simpering smile, she said, "It's so lovely here,

Patrick. The sky is so blue. I watched the sunrise as I ran. I can't wait, though, to be away from all the people and the buildings. Someplace where there's a bit more privacy." She pressed her lips to his knee. "Just us."

Some of the anger dimmed and she caught a random, fleeting flash. It wasn't a thought so much as an image. He wanted that privacy, too. So he could have her play his little whore whenever he chose. It was a sheer struggle of will to keep her smile in place.

"The wedding is just a few weeks away," he said. He touched the tip of her nose. "I'd thought perhaps we could go to lunch, but you need to bathe. Perhaps you should do that."

She had another flash. He hadn't come up here to take her to lunch. He'd come up here to fuck her. He didn't like seeing her all hot and sweaty, though. Now he was turned off. Excellent.

A way to smack down his libido without really making him too angry.

"I'll do that. Lunch out would be wonderful." She rose and gave him another smile. "After that run, I'm positively famished."

"You'll have to order it in, Ella. I'm running behind now." He eyed her critically. "Make sure you eat enough. You have to put the weight back on, and running like that isn't going to help."

SEVENTEEN

Joss waited for her the next day.

She didn't come.

He wasn't surprised, but he sure as hell was disappointed.

Still, it wasn't his only reason for being at the Waffle House that day.

Jones had come through with the first "victim" . . . the telepath. They were meeting to discuss how things were going to happen. Of course, they were meeting after Joss had parked his stolen car at a gym, gone for a walk, climbed into a bus, and then made his way over here.

Sometime during the previous night, the SUV had been bugged. He'd discovered that almost right away.

Jones had indeed given him some more useful toys, but Joss could have found the bug on the car in the dark with his hands tied. Not to mention that it had all but vibrated and called his name, it was so toxic.

Would have been nice to see Dru that morning. Cleared his head. His mind. Even as it clouded it. But he had to remember what he was here for. Because if he didn't keep his focus on the job, he was fucked and so were a lot of other people. He'd been waiting for her for too long. He'd live through this—he'd *get* through this. He hadn't waited this long to find her only to screw himself over by getting lazy or crazy.

Still, as he headed across the road, he strengthened that mental connection, found himself lodged quite firmly in her mind.

Hello, duchess.

She was mostly still asleep and she welcomed him with a startled sigh, then a smile. *Joss* . . .

You didn't meet me.

He wished he could actually *be* wherever she was. Wondered if he could picture himself there . . . and then he remembered. He'd seen the place. In that figment of a dream.

Building it in his mind, he kept a sliver of his focus on his surroundings and tried to imagine himself right there, mentally, with her. Tried to slide right into her dreams.

She was slowly climbing into wakefulness and he couldn't join her in her dreams, but her shields were lower now and he found himself with a deeper connection than he'd had before. In her mind, able to feel her surprise. Her pleasure. And that deep, innate fear. He tried to look deeper for that, but already Dru was scrambling to jerk up her shields there, and he didn't want to cause the pain that he knew he'd cause with his inept fumbling if he pried.

She'd tell him. Sooner or later.

* * *

SHE'D dreamed of him.

And she came awake biting her lip to keep from calling out his name.

Even in her dreams she couldn't fully let her guard down, and it was that self-preservation alone that kept her from fucking herself over as he settled himself rather determinedly into her thoughts. Like he'd opened the door to her room, it seemed, and just walked right in, brash as you please.

What are you doing? she thought, rolling onto her stomach and pressing her face into the pillow.

Saying good morning. Do you sleep naked?

Dru groaned. *No.*

Damn. Why not? I'd like to think of you naked in bed. Then his thoughts darkened. *Is your limpdick fiancé with you?*

No, she thought, all but ready to cry. If only Patrick had a limp dick, her life would be easier.

Baby girl, what's wrong? Joss's voice inside her mind was like black velvet, stroking against the ache of her heart and soul. *Why are you so sad? If it's him, just leave him. Hell, just leave him anyway. You should be with me . . . and I think you already know that.*

Hysterically, she laughed. *If only life were so simple, Joss.*

He sighed. And it startled her that she could *feel* it. She could feel *him,* feel that he was outside somewhere. If she concentrated, she could feel the cool, damp air against his skin, almost as clearly as she felt his frustration, his want, his need . . . and something more.

Something that warmed her to her very core, even as it broke her heart.

Love.

This man who didn't even truly know her loved her.

I do know you, he murmured into her mind, and she shivered. She'd have to be careful. He picked up on way too much, even when she thought she had shielded herself good and tight. *I know what I need to know and everything I don't know . . . I want to spend the rest of my life learning it. Are you okay with that?*

Tears squeezed out from under her lashes. Yes. If she lived through this, yes, she'd be just fine with that.

Joss, I'm in a mess right now, she hedged. She suspected she couldn't give him an opening, though. He'd barrel through any perceived weakness and stay until she was safe . . .

Yeah. He sighed. *So am I. I've got a . . . complicated job. We'll have a lot to talk about, but you and I, we're going to be together. Do me a favor . . . imagine me kissing you good morning . . .*

* * *

Joss blew out a breath before he headed into the Waffle House.

His throat ached.

It hadn't been quite the kiss he'd been thinking it would be. It was bittersweet, heartrending.

And he was tempted to say screw everything, just so he could go to her. Rescue her.

But the last time he'd barreled in, he'd ended up dead.

Plus, he had people depending on him, and she was in some kind of mess herself. He needed to know more about it before he did a damn thing, because he'd learned a few things this time around.

Barreling in led to bad, bad shit.

He was going to know what was going on before he did a damn thing.

And he'd wrap up *this* mess first. He had to think with his head right now . . . not with his heart. Not with his dick.

As he slid into the booth next to the woman, Taylor barely glanced up from the menu. "I think you want to see me keel over dead from a heart attack. Look at this menu."

"Fuck off," Joss snapped.

Taylor lifted his head, cocked a brow.

He just stared back.

Next to him, the woman shifted and lifted her hands to her head. "This is going to be a lot of fun. Jones . . . he's not stable enough to be doing this."

Slanting her a look, Joss curled his lip. "No. I'm not. But unfortunately, I'm the only monkey in this circus who knows this particular act." He studied her face . . . Vaughnne. Yeah, they'd met a few times.

Critically, he looked her over, tried to see her the way Whitmore would see her. Cute. Heart-shaped face with creamy, light brown skin. A smattering of freckles across her nose . . . kind of unusual, he decided. Her hair was shoulder-length and crazy with curls. She looked like the girl next door. She'd be a striking contract next to Nalini. "Hi, Vaughnne. Long time, no see."

"Not long enough," she muttered. "Jones, who did you pair him with, the local psycho?"

"Shut up," Joss snapped.

"Touchy, touchy." She smirked at him.

"Vaughnne," Jones said, his voice flat. "Back off."

She opened her mouth, then closed it. "Whatever. I'm just here for the ride, right?"

"So I take it Taylor's filled you in."

"I didn't need to." Jones said when Vaughnne fell silent.

Joss slid him a narrow look.

Taylor lifted a cup of coffee to his lips and took a hefty drink. "She requested time off two months ago. Personal reasons. And she's been down here ever since. Yesterday, she showed up at my hotel and told me she wanted in on the operation."

"And how do you know about it?" Joss asked, studying Vaughnne's profile as she stared at the table.

Her answer was a sly little whisper in the back of his mind, and as she looked at him, a smug little grin tugged at the corners of her mouth.

I'm psychic, genius . . . how do you think?

The problem was . . . she was lying. About something.

She slanted a look up at him and her golden eyes narrowed. He felt a none-too-subtle shove and then her voice, loud as a cannon, echoing in his mind. *Stay out of my head, Crawford . . . or I'll turn your brain into a sieve.*

He snorted. "Like you could."

"You won't always have that talent inside you, hotshot," she murmured.

"Thank God for that." Then he shut up, because the waitress was heading their way, and damn it, he needed some caffeine.

* * *

SHE had a smile on her lips as she stepped out of the shower.

Granted, it had been weird to wake up with dreams of him in her mind, but really . . . was it that bad?

"You look happy, darling."

At the sound of Patrick's voice, Dru jerked up the shields in her mind.

At the same time, she fought to keep the smile on her face. "Patrick! Oh, you startled me!"

He sat on the edge of her bed, and nausea churned in her belly as she saw that he'd taken off his suit jacket. It was draped over the chair in the sitting area. And his shoes and socks.

Swallowing, she clutched the towel around her tighter. She couldn't keep doing this.

"Come here, Ella."

* * *

"BE ready at four."

Numb, Dru just lay there.

Once he was gone, she was going to crawl back into the shower. If she thought it might help, she'd soak herself in a vat of bleach.

She wouldn't be clean, though. She didn't know if she'd ever feel clean again.

"Ella, did you hear me?"

Swallowing, she made herself answer, "Of course, Patrick. Where are we dining tonight?"

He frowned at her. "You're rather tiresome today."

I already realized that, she thought dully. She ached inside. She'd tried to find . . . something . . . to take control so he wasn't using her the way he had that first time, but she . . . hell. She couldn't. All she had been able to do was think about Joss. The way he'd felt as he whispered inside her mind. The way she knew he loved her, even though he didn't really know her.

How can he love me?

And she'd worked on keeping up her shields, solid and thick, so Joss wouldn't realize what was happening, so he wouldn't pick up on anything. Not on the pain, not on the shame. None of it.

"I don't know what is wrong with you, but you need to snap out of it. There's a party tonight, at my house, for some business acquaintances. You'll be there, and you'll be there *not* looking like death," Patrick said. He came to stand at her side, and when she didn't sit up, he bent over her and pushed his hand into her hair, fisting it and pulling until she had to bite the inside of her cheek to keep from crying out. And still he pulled.

Her eyes watered from the pain but she refused to make a sound. He could rip her hair out by the roots before she'd give him that pleasure.

A cold chill raced down her spine and a face flashed through her mind.

Are you such a silly girl that you don't realize what I could do to you? I could kill you. As easy as that and not a soul would say a word . . .

Cold, cruel eyes. A face not like Patrick's, but the eyes . . . they were his.

Don't let him take you away from me . . .

She shoved the memories away and continued to stare at the man before her.

"I'll be ready at four," she said coolly. She'd get through this. Get through this. Get it done. See the damn job through and hope she just had a chance at what life seemed to be offering her.

His house. They were going to his house. She'd never found anything there before, but maybe . . . just maybe there would be something, or somebody—the final connection.

All she needed was the right connection.

* * *

ALL day, something had felt off.

Joss had tried a couple of times to reach out to Dru, but never once had he been able to. Not once. Distant and cool, she'd rebuffed him every time.

The one time she actually acknowledged him, she was . . . quiet. Sad and quiet. *I'm having a bit of a rough day. I need some time alone, Joss.*

Time alone. Okay. He could understand that. Even if he hated it. Even if it drove him crazy.

Wasn't like he didn't have something he needed to be focused on. Some*body* . . .

Two somebodies, actually. That fucker, Whitmore, and Vaughnne. Currently, he was texting Whitmore, and Vaughnne was sitting across from him, gorging on Thai food like she hadn't a care in the world.

I think I got lucky on the first shipment. Perfect piece.

As Joss sent the text, Vaughnne snagged a spring roll from the plate between them.

Until they knew how Whitmore wanted to go from here, they were playing it cool.

Joss was ready to wait a few hours, or even a day or two.

His own food sat in front of him, barely touched. Distracted, wishing he could talk to Dru, but knowing he needed to give her time, he pushed the rice on his plate around.

"You look thrilled to be here," Vaughnne said. "Hell, I'd almost think *you* were the one getting ready to play little slave girl."

Joss just grunted.

What was up with Dru?

"You know, you used to be a little more chatty than this."

Shooting Vaughnne a dark look, he said, "I'll get chatty when there's something to chat about."

"Fine. Grouchy." She lapsed into silence, focusing on her food.

By the time she'd finished clearing her plate and the rest of the spring rolls, Joss had a text from Whitmore.

You're fast. Is it secured?

No. Still in the process of taking possession, but it's prime. Do you have the facilities ready?

Yes. If you can take possession, we can put the piece into place today. I'll have my team meet you.

Good deal.

Joss looked up and met her gaze. "This could be a rough few weeks for you."

Vaughnne gave him a sharp-edged smile. "No problem. I've been spinning my wheels, waiting for this for a long time, Crawford."

There was something in her eyes, he thought. Yeah. Rage. A particular kind of rage.

"This is personal for you," he said quietly.

She just stared at him, her golden eyes blank. "It doesn't matter if it is or isn't. I can do my job. That's all that counts. Besides . . ." She shrugged and said, "I'm the best person to put in first. Jones is still trolling for a decent fit for the Latina. There are a couple, but one has a gift like Desiree's and that's a bad match. There's got to be ghosts like mad wherever this is. The other is an empath. Even with shielding, it would be too much."

"What about Nalini?"

"Ahhh . . ." Vaughnne smiled. "Our resident psycho. She's the closest thing to crazy we've got, you know. No, she can't go in until the last minute. The longer she's in, the closer she'll come to snapping. And she'll hurt people when she does . . . it may not be the bad guys, either."

Joss wanted to know more about that.

"No matter how we look at it, I'm the best match. If things go bad, I can call for help. Jones is going to be expecting me to check in on a regular basis and if even an hour goes by when he doesn't hear from me, I can expect the calvary, right?" But before he could respond, there was another text.

If all goes well, I'd like you to join me at my place for a party. You could bring a few pictures of the shipment. I'll go view it tomorrow myself, but I'd like to get an idea of just how well you work.

Joss grimaced. "He wants me to kidnap you, deliver you to

the hands of slavers, *and* go to a party. All in one day. This guy makes Jones look like a kitten."

"Yeah. Jones never made us go to parties." She ambled toward the escalator. "We should go. I don't know how long this little production is going to take. We should do a few run-throughs. I think Jones has a house now."

EIGHTEEN

ALL day, he hovered just outside her mind, never once trying to push inside, but just . . . letting her know he was
there.

Dru could feel the soft, patient warmth of his presence, but
she couldn't do it right now.

Couldn't risk it, not with the day she had laid out before her.

Soon, she'd have to do the stupid-ass party, but more important, she'd have a chance to work through Patrick's social set
again. It was there, that connection she needed. She knew it.

She'd find it somehow.

Everything inside her thrummed, hummed, burned. Ready
and waiting, aching, just under her skin.

She'd felt like this before, more than once.

Just before a job got really hot. And it was about damn time.
Which meant it was even more vital that she focus. With her

mind carefully, tightly contained, she spent most of the day exercising, then meditating. She took a few minutes to slip out one of the concealed phones, make a call. *Be ready—*

Before Tucker could ask anything else, she'd hung up. It was harder than normal to dispose of it and in the end, she'd retreated to the bathroom and dismantled it down to bits and pieces, flushing it over a period of thirty minutes. Let the fucker think she was in there getting sick, she didn't care.

A long, blistering shower, scrubbing away the very echo of Patrick's touch. Then a hot soak, to relax, easing the relatively minor aches. She wished she could wipe away the deeper pains as easily, but she couldn't.

A late lunch of soup and a sandwich, easy, simple food. Although she wasn't at all hungry, she knew she needed fuel. Needed it to get through this day, to keep her mind sharp.

If she could get her hands on it, she'd be chugging some Red Bull or Monster like a camel at an oasis after a few weeks in the desert, but it wasn't something kept in the small kitchen here and she wasn't about to leave the room. She needed all the isolation she could get right now, all the seconds she could eke out of the day to focus her mind. Focus everything.

Soon . . .

She stared at her reflection in the mirror as she carefully applied makeup. As she swept her hair back from her face into a sleek, sophisticated knot. Very soon.

It was the only reason to explain this sense of hyperawareness, she knew.

Something would happen tonight.

Finally . . . something would pop on this damned job.

Soon.

But not soon enough.

* * *

THIS day couldn't end soon enough.

Joss's head ached. His lip throbbed. Dru still wasn't talking to him. And this pussy was standing in his way. All Joss wanted to do was knock him *out* of the way and get this done, but somehow, he didn't think that would leave a good impression on his "boss."

"If you deliver damaged goods, the boss is going to have your ass," the pussy said, his weasel-like face twisted in a scowl, his dark, nervous eyes darting all over the place.

That was Joss's introduction to Whitmore's team.

"What makes you think I damaged her?" Joss drawled.

"What, you want me to think you hit your face on the door this morning?" The little fucker sneered at him.

Joss ran his tongue along the inside of his mouth, probing the cut Vaughnne had so kindly given him. Then he smiled. He was fully aware of just what sort of reaction that smile elicited. Getting bloodied didn't help much, it seemed.

What kind of psycho did they find us this time?

Inwardly, Joss smirked. *Oh, the worst kind.* He continued to smile, watched as a shadow moved across the man's face. Something about that face bothered him, but Joss couldn't quite place it. Didn't know what about him was so familiar.

Then the guy started to shift his hand to his waist.

I've got him going for the gun already. It wasn't a record, but it was pretty damn close.

Joss dropped his gaze to the hand inching closer to the weapon he carried, still smiling.

If he drew it, they could have problems. But Joss was close, the man was nervous, and Joss was going to bet he could stop the guy without relying on any firepower but his fists.

"You really want to have that talk with your boss and explain why I had to beat the shit out of you when you pulled your gun all because you didn't like my face?" Joss asked, keeping his voice polite and friendly.

He figured it might be the best approach after all, since he'd already made the guy dislike him on sight.

The bastard curled his lip and lowered his hand. "Like you could. Keep it together." He paused and then added, "Or maybe you shouldn't. I'd like to see you go the way of the last one."

Joss saw it play out through the man's mind. He didn't know what bothered him more . . . the spray of blood as his apparent predecessor became gator bait or the way this fucker had enjoyed it.

Fuck him. Joss wanted to beat that smile off his face, but it wasn't an option right now. Maybe not ever. The job. Focus on the job.

Shifting his attention away, he looked at the gate. "Am I going in or not?"

There was no question of whether he was in the right place.

They waved him in and he followed along behind the three-wheeler that had come up out of the dense, heavy growth of green. *Lots of places to hide shit here*, he thought.

Lots of places to hide those bodies . . .

A scream rang through his mind on the tail end of that thought.

Nobody else heard the scream. Nobody else heard the woman begging for help.

But he sensed Vaughnne's discomfort, heard her ragged intake of breath, sensed the disquiet of her mind behind her shields.

You okay?

I'm fine, she assured him, but her mental voice was hard and tight. *Shut it down. Dunno if any of these people are sensitives.*

Well, she didn't know that. But he had a pretty good feeling. They weren't. He would have already picked up on that. Besides, the rampant pain, fear, and death here wouldn't work very well for anybody who tried to linger in this place, he knew.

There were plenty of psychics, plenty of sensitives who weren't decent people, plenty who did ugly, awful things, and he knew that, too.

But the ghosts here . . . they'd drive somebody insane. And an insane person wouldn't last long in this place. Not working for Whitmore. He wanted them without morals, without compassion, but clear minded as hell.

Another ghost sobbed in the back of his mind, broken and desperate, and he edged up another layer to his shields. This place was . . . hell, he realized.

Hell on earth.

Goose bumps danced along his flesh, and even in the sweltering heat, he felt oddly cool. Behind those solid shields, he heard endless, broken sighs. Quiet sobs. And screams . . . broken, tortured wails.

The cries of the dead.

This wasn't the place Dez had been.

It was worse.

Joss didn't want to know how many people had died here.

It was going to be an experience trying to work in there, find what he needed to find, without dropping the shields so much that he went stark raving mad. He could cut himself away from the ghosts, and he knew he handled their presence, for the short term, better than Dez did. Not dealing wasn't good in the long run, but since he didn't have to have these gifts for the long haul, he wasn't worried about it.

A shrink would have a field day with him.

Reaching out to those voices, he did what he could to ease

them, although he doubted it would do much good. *I'll do what I can, I swear.*

He wasn't Dez . . . he didn't have her heart, or her compassion. But he'd find a way to help these troubled souls . . . because he was damned good at putting killers away. That's what the lost wanted. Justice. Peace.

Once he did that, it would be safe and he could step aside. Dez could come in and clean house. He'd take his vacation . . . and find his woman.

* * *

DRU stared at her reflection.

The cocktail dress was ivory silk, and it glowed against her skin. The one-shouldered design did a stunning job of highlighting her figure without making her look completely flat-chested. It had a jeweled clip on her left shoulder, and she suspected the sparklies there were real diamonds. Her monstrous fiancé just wouldn't go for anything so base as that.

She looked elegant. Classy.

His high-priced whore.

Bracing her hands on the ivory-and-gold marble, she stood there, eyeing her reflection. Preparing herself. Bracing herself. And if she was giving herself another mental pep talk, so what?

This was so much more than she'd been prepared for. So much more. So much worse. So damned ugly . . . and the ugliness had seeped inside her, stained her. Changed her.

Ruined me—

"No." Allowing herself to voice that one thing out loud, she closed her eyes and tried to view this objectively. If it was happening to somebody else . . . how would she feel if a friend was telling her this horrid, awful story?

She felt stained, yes. Changed, no doubt about it.

But she wasn't ruined . . . unless she let that happen. And if she managed to do what she'd set out to do . . . *stop* this? Stop *him*? Then it was all worth it . . . every bit of pain, of shame, was worth it, to stop the death, the misery. To stop a monster.

She'd see this through.

Then she'd get away.

You have to get away.

Don't let him take you away again . . .

The ghostly echo of the dream danced through her mind.

Odd that it was the very thing to give her strength. But it did. In her mind's eye, she saw him. Joss . . . his name was Joss, and somehow, they mattered to each other. She'd get through this, because she had to find him. Had to understand what they were, who they had been . . . who they were meant *to be*.

She'd get through this because the scum that was Patrick Whitmore didn't deserve to draw another breath.

Because those girls deserved freedom, and the dead deserved justice.

Resolved, she lifted her head and stared at her reflection. Pale green eyes glittered and color flooded her cheeks. She studied her reflection one more time. The makeup was understated. Elegant.

And wrong.

She needed to feel like *herself*. Not even time to start from scratch, but she could do something. Darken the eye shadow . . . yes, that helped. She removed the lip dye she'd chosen and went for a darker shade. The softer color she'd had on was definitely an *Ella* color, but it wasn't for Dru. Dru wore lush, rich colors. Like this vibrant red. A bit more color on her cheeks.

Instead of the perfume she'd bought for Ella, she used her own. She'd kept some of that stuff from her real life handy, although she hadn't let herself use it in months. So many months.

Straightening, she studied her reflection, and for the first time in all those months, she felt just a little bit more in control.

It would be coming to a head soon.

Very soon.

In the back of her mind, she felt a soft, warm brush . . . Joss's presence.

She yearned to let him in, but not yet. Not right now. Couldn't get rattled when she was due downstairs with Patrick.

The bloody party. She'd go to the bloody party. Mingle. Talk. Laugh and play the good little fiancée. And she'd find what she needed so she could end this.

One last lingering look in the mirror . . . her appearance was just a little off. The dress was right, she knew that. But the makeup, her demeanor . . . it was all Dru.

She was Dru. She'd come here to kick ass. She needed to remember that.

Turning away from the mirror, she moved to the door.

As she opened it, she could hear the soft play of music drifting upward. Her rooms were in the east wing, and as she moved through the house, the music grew louder, but not terribly so. Patrick wouldn't want people to have to shout to be heard over the music, after all.

At the top of the stairs, she paused, eyeing the man waiting for her. He wore a tux, stretched across his shoulders, fitted to perfection. He wore it well, she knew. Kind of like the way a king cobra wore his skin, she supposed. But that was insulting to the cobra.

Patrick turned his head, smiling at her as she started down the stairs. There was a flicker in his eyes.

She accepted the hand he held out, smiling at him as she felt a rush of . . . disgruntlement. Even as she inwardly laughed, she kept a pleasant smile on her face. Pleasant, working hard to keep it from turning smug. She couldn't break her cover now, but oh, how she wanted to.

"You look . . . lovely," he said, pausing as he studied her face.

"Thank you."

I should win an award for the acting job I've done here, she thought as he stroked one finger up her bare arm. "I knew this dress would suit you," he said softly.

"I'm glad it pleases you." As she met his gaze, she thought about turning around, grabbing his wrist, and snapping his fingers, one by one.

He studied her face. "Is something troubling you, Ella?"

Cocking her head, she held his gaze. "Of course not. Why do you ask?"

His flat blue eyes narrowed. "I don't know. You just seem . . . never mind."

One of those random flashes hit her. *Too aware* . . . That was the problem. She was too aware, and not the blissfully stupid, insipid twit he always saw when he looked at her. *Too bad*, she thought. She toned it back a little, but she'd be damned if she shoved herself back into that confining little box. It had been choking her . . . killing her.

Don't let him take you away from me again . . .

She could do this without letting him destroy her.

Mentally squaring her shoulders, she smiled her sweet, docile little smile. "Shall we go, Patrick?"

* * *

"You'll meet a number of business acquaintances here," Patrick informed her a few moments later. The guests were starting to arrive . . . the party was set to begin at seven. It was 6:58. If she knew a thing about the man at her side, not many guests would even *think* about arriving before the set time. "Naturally, I'll be with you much of the time, but occasionally, I won't be. Please keep in mind who you are."

What you are.

The flash she heard from him made her want to curl her lip, but Dru nodded soberly. "Of course, Patrick."

There was music playing in the background, understated and low. Servers were ready with drinks and far too much food. Patrick gestured to one of the servers, and a few seconds later, she had a glass of champagne in her hand. Wonderful . . . just wonderful. She hated the stuff.

"Hmm." She lifted it to her lips and took a sip. "Lovely, thank you."

She was saved from having to listen to him say anything else by the arrival of their first guests.

Show time, she thought.

Judging by how tight her skin felt, the way adrenaline crashed inside her . . . how utterly hyper she felt . . .

Soon . . . soon.

Her heart knocked against her ribs. Hard, heavy beats that nearly stole her breath. *Must get a grip on this, and soon*, she thought, staring into the pale, bubbling liquid in the flute she held.

It wasn't long before she was surrounded by people, too many of them. There were air kisses to be exchanged, hands to shake. One brave, half-drunk soul actually palmed her ass. Drunken idiot, but harmless. Hopefully Patrick hadn't seen that.

Random flashes from many of them, but few of them held the blackness she was looking for. Not an innocent lot of people, but nothing she *needed*. Some of them were cheating on their husbands, their wives. One appeared to be cheating his boss, but that wouldn't be her concern unless she was hired on for it and how likely was that?

Nearly an hour later, she had a horrid headache and pleaded the need to visit the ladies' room just to escape.

She didn't use the one made available to guests, though. She dashed upstairs, bypassing a few people who'd decided to venture up to the second floor—brave souls, those people. She wouldn't have gone anywhere in this house she wasn't given outright permission to. Actually, if she didn't need to be here, she wouldn't be.

Apparently Patrick was prepared for all eventualities and the other wings were guarded, including the one where her rooms were.

The ugly arse who stood in the middle of the hall was a man she was all too familiar with. His shoulders seemed big enough to blot out the sun, his dark eyes were set under a prominent brow ridge, and his nose looked like it had been broken a good four or five times.

"Hello, Mr. Morris," she said brightly, smiling at him.

He didn't smile back.

In fact, she thought he seemed pissed off. Guess he was still put off that she'd lost him on the run the other day. Well, he could get stuffed for all she cared. "I need to use the loo and I wanted a bit of privacy."

He just stared at her.

She smiled brighter. "The restroom. There are so many people down there."

Slowly, still watching her with those sullen, angry eyes, he stepped aside.

She moved past him, and although she tried to avoid contact, her arm brushed his as he shifted.

Flash, flash, flash.

Excitement . . . new girl coming . . . can't touch . . . fuck, what fun is that . . .

Stupid bitch—

An image of her, with him kneeling over her, his hands around her neck.

Followed by another image. *Him*, on the ground. Legs broken. Hands and arms broken. And that alligator.

She stumbled a bit, caught herself on one of the lovely antique tables in the hallway, a few feet away from her suite of rooms. Just before he would have touched her . . . deepened that connection. He couldn't touch her. Not ever. She thought it would drive her insane.

No. No, I won't let that happen.

She wouldn't get sick, damn it.

She'd find out who in the hell this new girl was.

Carefully, without looking back, she eased away from the table and carefully walked to her room. Opened the door and slipped inside. Without looking back at Morris, she shut the door.

That wanker.

Both of them. All of them.

As the flash pieced together, bit by bit, Dru set her shoulders.

She was done playing around.

Nobody else.

Nobody. Else.

NINETEEN

"H<small>MM</small>. I guess I should have mentioned it was black-tie."

Joss gave Patrick a narrow look and then glanced down at the khakis and polo he'd unearthed. He'd thrown a sport coat over it and wasn't overly surprised when he was checked for weapons at the door. He'd surrendered them, because they hadn't found most of his weapons. Whitmore's men weren't as good as they'd like to be.

Plus, Joss also had a very powerful weapon crammed inside his brain—his hijacked psychic skills.

"Well, I left the tux back in storage," he drawled, shrugging. "Don't worry. I can't stay. Work to do and all of that."

"But you did so well on this one. You can take the evening off." Patrick guided him over to the side, an inquisitive look on his face. "Perhaps you have images . . ."

Rage bristled Joss. "I can e-mail some if you want. I took a few."

"No."

You prick. Can't take the bait that easy, huh?

Shrugging, Joss tugged out his phone and pulled up the photo album. "I figured you'd want to see, so I snapped a few on my phone, but I'll be deleting them soon."

He displayed one of the pictures he'd taken of Vaughnne in the mall. "I met her at the food court. She's here on vacation. Was supposed to come with a friend, and the friend had to cancel. Nobody will be looking for her for the next ten days." He smiled and let some of the dark, ugly anger he felt seep into that smile, knowing the menace would show. "And better yet, she's in between jobs . . . needs to go for a training thing in a few weeks, but you know how that goes. If she doesn't show . . ."

"Perfect . . ." Patrick murmured. He swiped a finger across the phone, studying the next picture. "She looks like the girl next door. Family ties?"

"Estranged mother. They maybe talk at Christmas, if she can't get out of it. No boyfriend. Some friends she sees back home, but it doesn't sound like there's anybody who'd raise an alarm for a while when she doesn't come back."

Patrick nodded. "Was there a car?"

"Yep." Joss slid him a sidelong smile. "We took her car. It's en route to the Everglades. I traded a favor."

"A favor." Patrick studied him.

Joss lifted a hand. "Hey, I know my business, trust me. This sort of thing will go smoother if they are looking for her *elsewhere*. Her car will be there, along with maps and shit. Like she was going on a day hike."

"And nobody can place you with her?" Patrick continued to watch him, those flat blue eyes icy, dead as a shark's.

Joss sighed, shaking his head. "Look, do you think I started doing this line of work yesterday?" He deleted the pictures of

Vaughnne, tried not to think about how she was doing. The woman had promised she'd reach out to him if she was in imminent danger. He could keep a tenuous link established with her, although keeping up with everything was straining his brain to the breaking point already and he'd just gotten started.

Keeping his face blank, he met Patrick's stare dead on. "You hired me for a job, right?" Then he smirked and added, "Besides, if I get placed with her, it's my ass. Not yours, yeah?"

"Hmm. We should really talk about what happened the last time one of my men crossed me." Patrick smiled. "Not that you would. But you seem interested in being informed."

"Well, seeing as how my . . . livelihood is at stake, I figure being informed is the wise thing to do, don't you? Only stupid men and trusting fools operate in the dark." Joss paused. "I'm neither one."

"So I see." Patrick glanced past him, an odd light entering his eyes. "Hmm. Would you care to meet my fiancée, Mr. Sellers?"

Joss swallowed the automatic response that rose to his lips. There was either a bitch dumb enough or greedy enough to marry this shark . . . which was it? He was betting on greedy. Even the brainless had survival instincts and this man was dangerous.

Tucking his phone away, he stepped aside. "I'd be delighted."

He glanced around, eyeing the thick crowd. It wouldn't be that hard to lose himself in this mess, he figured. In the next twenty minutes or so, he could break away from Patrick. Work the crowd a little, although—

His spine heated.

His breath hitched without him even realizing it and his heart started to slam against his ribs.

Oh, *fuck*, no.

She couldn't be here.

But even as he thought it, he found himself remembering that godawful fear he'd felt coming from her. The way she'd looked at him . . . *You can't help me.*

If any group of people spelled bad news, it was the people that Patrick Whitmore ran with. But how had she gotten involved . . .

Patrick was slowing to a stop near a long, leggy brunette. She was facing away from them, but at his touch, she turned.

If Joss hadn't had years, years upon years, of schooling his every emotion, he would have lost it.

Just plain and simply lost it.

No.

Just . . . no.

I'm spoken for.

The soft sigh in her voice as she said, *Damn you, why couldn't you have come into my life a year ago? Two years ago? Why now? I can't have you now.*

Her eyes widened just a fraction, and he saw her lips part.

"Darling, this is a business associate of mine," Patrick said, sliding an arm around her waist. "Mike Sellers."

Something darted through her eyes. He almost heard the words forming in her mind.

Stepping forward, he caught her hand. "I'm charmed," Joss drawled. "Patrick, your fiancée is absolutely lovely."

"Isn't she?" Patrick stroked a hand down her arm, the way he might have stroked a beloved cat.

And all the while, Dru just stared at him, her pale green eyes locked on his face. Like she couldn't believe what she was seeing.

* * *

Joss . . .

Patrick said his name was Mike—

Oh, like that wanker would actually tell the utter truth if he knew it.

But Joss . . .

Swallowing, she extricated her hand from Joss's, although just then, she was almost desperate for his strength. "Business associates, are you? Have you worked together long then?"

No. Not his strength . . . not his. Not if he was working with Patrick. What had he said? His job. Complicated. The slimy, evil wanker.

"Just starting out, love," Patrick said. He patted her shoulder. "Nothing you'd be able to follow, though."

Of course not. I can't comprehend kidnapping—

Flash, flash, flash.

A delivery . . .

Images of a girl, the light, creamy brown of a woman of mixed heritage. Freckles sprinkled across her nose. A charming smile.

And . . . most gut-wrenching of all, Joss's voice . . . *I met her at the food court. She's here on vacation. Was supposed to come with a friend and the friend had to cancel. Nobody will be looking for her for the next ten days.* When he spoke, there was an ugly, menacing hate in his voice.

She stumbled and slammed a hand down, bracing it by the curving wall of the stairwell at her back as the memory burned itself into her brain, followed by another. And another.

First there was a picture of a girl smiling at the camera. Then another, bound, gagged . . . and glaring at the camera.

The girl next door . . .

Patrick picturing the girl in a formal. Fuck . . . bloody fuck. Dru knew that dress. It was the one he'd selected for her bridesmaids. Of course, she didn't have any. He'd said he'd see to it . . .

This wasn't happening.

A cruel hand gripped her arm, so at odds with Patrick's gentle voice as he inquired, "Ella, are you feeling unwell?"

Swallowing back the **bile that** churned in her throat, she said softly, "The champagne, Patrick. I think it's gone to my head. Perhaps I should lie down."

Moments later, one of the house servants was at her side to escort her up the stairs. Just before she reached the top, she looked back, found herself staring down at Joss.

He was one of them.

Damn him.

The betrayal, the deep, gut-wrenching sense of pain, all but blinded her.

Damn him straight to hell.

* * *

"It seems your little bimbo doesn't hold her liquor well," Joss drawled, reaching over to pluck up the glass Dru had been holding. He grinned sardonically at Patrick, ignoring the fury biting there.

Hell, he should stop pulling the guy's chain, but he'd never been good at the subservient role anyway, and right now, he was spoiling for a fight.

Dru was here.

Dru was going to marry this fucker.

And she *knew.*

He saw it in her eyes, felt it in her mind . . . she *knew* and she was going to marry Whitmore anyway.

Well, no. No, she wasn't, because Joss damn well wasn't going to let it happen. He'd turn kidnapper himself and find a way to have her fine ass deported. By the time she got done untangling the red tape he could wrap around her, Whitmore would be in jail and she could kiss whatever money she'd hoped to get from him gone, gone, gone . . .

He glanced up and caught her looking down at him. There

was ice in her gaze now, a cool disdain that left him feeling meaner than a snake. And he already felt pretty damn mean.

He smiled and toasted her with his glass.

Then, as Patrick looked up, he watched her face go void and blank, that inner spark in her eyes dying, all the life, the anger . . . it was as if a doll's face had replaced the woman who'd been looking at him a minute ago.

Hell.

What the fuck did he care?

Amelie . . .

It's Amelie. Dru.

He couldn't fool himself, not even out of pride.

"Please watch how you speak of my fiancée, Mr. Sellers. We'll do business together . . ." Patrick said, pulling Joss's attention back to him.

As the other man took a step toward him, Joss lowered his shields enough to catch some of those iced-down thoughts. "But if you cross a certain line . . ."

Joss smiled as one of Patrick's thoughts filled the silence in his head.

I need him for the next few weeks, but if he continues to be such an ass, he's not going to work out. A pity . . . he's certainly the fastest I've ever worked with. Although it could be luck . . .

Joss winked at him. "I cross plenty of lines, Whitmore. Afraid I can't help it. But here's the thing . . . you'll never work with anybody quite as good at my job as I am." A waiter circulated by and Joss swiped a canapé, popped it in his mouth, and then glanced around. "I'll let you go do your host thing. Thanks for the invite . . . boss."

Revising the plans, Joss lost himself in the crowd, waiting until he found the right moment before he dumped Dru's champagne and then pocketed the flute. Needed to get more information on her background, seeing as how she went by one name for Whitmore. Told Joss another.

Seeing as how she was engaged to a fucking human trafficker . . . rage boiled in his gut, low, ugly, seething. The walls of his control shivered.

Voices barreled inside his brain.

He's one of them . . .

He's one of them . . .

Hot in here.

Uppity bastard, always got to show . . .

How can I tell her I lost my job . . .

I wonder if I can get Saul to leave a few hours earlier on Friday . . .

And under it all, there were tortured, tragic moans. Loud and demanding. Louder than before, and with the moans came a bone-rattling cold.

Help me . . .

Get me out of here . . .

He's one of them . . .

Lost my job. Twenty-nine years . . .

"Hey . . . don't I know you?"

Snarling, Joss glanced around, half-desperate, and shoved through a nearby set of doors.

He found himself in a garden, but it was far from dark, far from quiet. Shouldering his way through the crowds, he fought to hold on to the threads of his sanity, to his control, but as rage spiraled tighter, spun even higher, it became harder and harder.

Pain snaked in, grabbed him by the throat. His shields shuddered more, and in his mind's eye, he could see hairline cracks forming in those solid, stone walls.

Bad. This was bad.

He was almost shaking from the cold now, and the howl of the ghosts was more like a banshee's wail than anything.

Finally, he broke free of the people.

Finally, he was alone.

He went to the ground, one hand fisting in the grass as he slammed up another stone wall in his mind. Stone. Encased in ice. He had to take a page out of Whitmore's book, it seemed, and ice it down a few notches. *Ice it down, Crawford . . . ice it down.*

The voices receded bit by bit as he built up the stone wall in his mind.

But still, the pain that gripped his chest, all but threatening to rip his heart out, that . . . that remained.

Just fucking had it ripped out—

The stone wall cracked.

"Not now . . . not now." His fingers sank into the dirt and he squeezed his eyes shut. Stone. By stone. Ice encasing each one.

The pain didn't recede, but the voices eventually did. They faded to a dull murmur by the time he had the wall halfway built. It glittered in his mind's eye like a cobbled road slicked with black ice.

But the louder voices remained.

Help me . . . help me . . .

The cold, shivery trail of a ghost's touch along his spine. He could see her shimmering just ahead of him, too. Almost fully formed, her eyes locked on his but barely aware. "I can't help you yet," he said, shaking his head. "I can't."

Help me . . . please help . . .

As he continued to build the wall in his mind, she faded away, still sobbing, begging for help.

He's one of them . . .

The whispers faded as he sank the last stone in place, and finally, he was alone in the peace of his own mind.

No ghosts.

No whispers.

Just the ache of a broken heart that somehow managed to keep beating inside his chest.

"How the fuck did this happen?"

* * *

"THIS isn't happening."

She'd kicked off the ridiculous four-inch heels she'd been wearing with her equally ridiculous dress as she suffered through that dull party, waiting, just *waiting* for the moment. It would happen, she knew it. *Something* would happen.

And then something did.

"This isn't happening . . ."

Her skin continued to prickle and burn, alternating between hot and cold chills. Her chest ached like somebody had ripped her open and carved her heart out using a rusty old shovel.

And still, all of that adrenaline crashed through her.

It wasn't over *him*, though.

Not him . . .

Traitor.

She wanted to scream it at him, at this man she didn't know, and how utterly absurd was that? She didn't know him. He didn't know her. He didn't owe her anything, yet it felt like he'd betrayed her.

Doesn't betraying mankind and decency and humanity count?

Except she dealt with people who did that sort of thing all the time, and none of it felt like this. Like a raw, personal betrayal.

"Oh, God . . ." Dru sank to the edge of the bed, one hand

pressed to her belly, the other covering her mouth and trying to hold back the sob. This wasn't happening. Couldn't be.

There was a knock.

She barely managed to wipe the emotions off her face before the door opened.

"Ella."

Patrick stood there. But he wasn't alone.

Rising, she automatically smoothed a hand down her dress. "Patrick . . ."

"Darling." He came over. "You should be resting."

"I know. I was going to change, but I . . . well." At least, she didn't have to fake feeling a bit off her stride. "I haven't quite worked up the energy just yet to get ready for bed."

He gestured. "This is a friend of mine, Dr. Lewis Badger. He offered to take a look at you."

Inwardly, Dru wanted to scream. Outwardly, she managed an embarrassed smile. "Oh, that's hardly necessary, is it? I just need to rest, I'm sure."

"He'll look at you nonetheless."

Judging by the look in his eyes, Dru knew there was no point in arguing. She gave the doctor a weak smile. "Shall I change?"

"No, you're fine." As Patrick moved past them, the doctor's eyes rested briefly on her breasts. She managed barely to resist a snarl, and when he looked back at her face, he had a strange expression in his eyes.

Gesturing back to the bed, he said, "Why don't you sit down?"

Her skin felt tighter. Hotter.

No. Not now—

As he reached into a briefcase she just now noticed, Dru fought to control the anger, the self-loathing burning inside her.

The sense of betrayal, too. She'd found a reason . . . to keep going, to keep fighting.

And now it was gone.

Damn him.

Damn Joss straight to hell. Joss. Mike. Whoever in the hell he was.

So caught up in her rage, she was barely aware of it at first as the doctor laid the stethoscope against her chest. "Breathe in for me."

She did so, staring straight ahead. Her heart felt raw. Ripped straight open. And now, instead of being able to deal with what had happened, she was sitting here, letting some stranger put his hands on her and ogle her—

Cool, dry hands touched her neck.

Flash, flash, flash.

Pretty girl, dressed all in red . . . long dark hair flowing down her back . . . . skinny, but he'd take care of that.

Hands wrapped around her neck. Feet drumming against the floor as he choked her.

Eyes bulging.

Flash, flash, flash.

She swayed, then flew back under the impact of a hand.

"What's wrong with you, Ella?"

Looking up at the doctor, she reached up, closed a hand around his wrist. He'd been there . . .

Flash, flash, flash.

A road, winding through brush and trees, shielding them. Patrick glancing over. "We can't take much time, I'm afraid. If we're gone too long, my . . . fiancée will notice . . ."

Flash, flash, flash.

A woman, dark blond, pretty hair, and pretty face, fawning over Patrick. Laughing in delight over a kitten. Stupid little bitch—

"*She won't wake up anytime soon, will she?*"

"*No.*" *The doctor smiled as he straightened over her body.* "*This will keep her out for quite a while.*"

Dru groaned as hands jerked her back.

". . . what is your problem . . ."

Dazed, she stared at Patrick's face, into coldly furious eyes. She barely even heard him barking at the doctor.

Sagging under the influx of information, she went boneless in Patrick's hands, despite her attempts to claw her way back into awareness. Terror followed her into the darkness.

Terror . . . and dark, ugly dreams.

*   *   *

Joss ignored the press against his shields.

No point in thinking about her now. He'd deal with her once he had more information.

Just leave already, he told himself.

That's what he needed to do.

Get some distance away from this hell. Get his head screwed back on straight so that when he came back out here, he was in fuck-'em-up shape. He could tear Patrick's enterprise apart and leave nothing but shreds in his wake, but he had to have his head together.

Yeah.

That was what he'd do.

Just get out.

Get his head together.

Start scraping together the remains of his heart and maybe get wasted. He'd done that a little too often lately, but hell, it was one way to silence the cacophony in his head, and now, it just might dull the pain in his chest.

Shouldering his way through the crowd, he focused on the front door. Some of the security types eyed him warily. He gave them a friendly smile back. It wasn't friendly enough, apparently. A few of them backed away. Two started talking to each other. One reached inside his coat.

Joss kept heading to the door.

And he was almost through.

Almost.

A sudden, gut-wrenching knowledge exploded through his mind, though.

He couldn't leave here without making sure that Whitmore didn't find something to . . . occupy himself with.

Images slammed into his mind.

And even though he wanted to tell himself he shouldn't *care*, he knew that was just shit.

Dru . . . Ella, whatever her name was, caught in Whitmore's hands, her face white, eyes glassy. Her body all but limp. Patrick looming over her. The intent to hurt all but etched on his features.

Another image slammed into him.

Dru sitting on the edge of the bed, Patrick a few feet away. She looked up at him, and when he said something, she responded— halfway through, the fucker backhanded her.

Hissing, he stopped in the middle of the hall.

What in the hell did he do?

* * *

GLARING down at Ella's limp body, Patrick opened and closed one fist. Over and over.

She'd humiliated herself.

Getting drunk like that.

Did she think he hadn't seen how she'd been eyeing his new broker?

Little slut.

Drinking, passing out.

Drunk little whore.

He'd seen how flushed she was when he'd come in here with the doctor. Glassy eyes. The pulse in her neck had been racing as well.

Not feeling well?

Stupid bitch, did she really think he'd buy something as lame as that?

She'd gone and gotten her ass drunk, all but thrown herself at one of his men, then she'd done it *again* when the doctor had come in here . . .

"You hid that whore's side of you well," Patrick said softly, kicking her in the side. He didn't put much behind the blow. He didn't want her harmed, not with the wedding so close.

Still, she moaned, curling up in a ball and trying to roll away. She didn't wake, though.

Disgusted, he turned away, his mind racing. What now? He had a very major event riding on this entire wedding. So much business, so much money. It would lead to more money as well, because he was bringing in potential customers. Blind bidders who didn't realize the women he'd brought in were already spoken for, but he'd promise that he could get more . . .

An idea sparked in his mind and he glanced down at Ella.

Badger had asked earlier, mostly in jest, if he could buy her away.

At the time, it had left him infuriated.

But . . . narrowing his eyes, he ran his thumb across his cheek. He'd selected Ella as his own because she was refined. Elegant.

Many of the bitches he brought weren't quite the same quality as she was. A few had been close, but Ella with the cool accent, her natural elegance . . .

Combine that with the inner slut she'd been showing lately, well, she could be quite the moneymaker.

Perhaps in a different manner, though.

He'd have to keep up appearances. People were expecting a wedding. He needed to go through with it—too much money was riding on it, and it had been such a challenge to arrange.

And she needed to see what happened when you fucked with him.

It was, all in all, a clever way to handle it, he thought.

He'd have to make a few calls, he decided. He could start on that—

His phone buzzed. Scowling, he reached for it and pulled it out. This was his private line. He had a cell phone that he used for work, a number he had to give out, but this number was the one he used for his more . . . private pursuits.

The caller's number was blocked. Narrowing his eyes, he tapped on the screen and watched as the image enlarged.

For just one second, his hands went icy and cold. For that very same second, his heart started to race and blood roared in his ears.

It was Grace.

A picture of her from before . . . they'd been dating. He could see himself, the back of his head, likely bent over his phone as he worked. Grace was facing him, bent over the table and smiling. The image was zoomed in, focused mostly on her.

She was the focus.

There was no doubt of that.

Rage tripped through him, but he stifled it. This was nothing. Probably her new keeper . . .

The next message came up.

She was a pretty girl. Why did you have to destroy her life?

He stared at the bar along the top. *Private number.*

"Who in the fuck are you?"

Two seconds later, another message came up.

I look forward to making your acquaintance, Mr. Whitmore.

TWENTY

THERE were times when she dreamed.

She understood dreams.

But this . . . this was more than that.

Dru felt lost in it.

Staring at the mirror before her, she didn't even recognize herself. Except for her eyes. She recognized her eyes. She went to lean forward, but it was awkward—the awful contraption of steel and cotton around her ribs didn't want to let her move the way she should. Scowling, she dropped her gaze to it, touched the boning of the corset, and smoothed a hand down her hip.

"Not my hips." Then, startled, she jerked her gaze up and stared once more at her reflection. "Not my voice."

It was a slow, almost lazy drawl, rich with the drawl she'd come to recognize as the Deep South. Lazy, soft, easy. The cadence was a little different than what she normally heard.

And her voice sounded nothing like her own. Not just the accent, but even the very sound was different.

Nothing seemed right. Like those tits. Those weren't *her* tits. She eyed the lush white breasts rising above the lacy bit of fabric she wore under the corset. A chemise, she thought it might be called. And pantaloons. Historical clothing wasn't her forte. Finding scum, deadbeat dads, runaways, that was what she did.

But why was she . . .

Behind her, a door opened and she turned, staring at the woman with wide eyes.

"Amelie, you're not even dressed."

"Mama . . ."

Mama?

"Darling, you must get dressed. We're off to the picnic today, you know. You'll be seeing Richard before he leaves on his trip. He expects an answer . . ." The woman paused, her eyes, pale green, hesitant. "Have you decided?"

"Richard." She closed her eyes and turned away. *Who was . . .*

Marrying Richard—

Cold, lifeless eyes.

Patrick's eyes.

Richard. Hard, cruel hands.

Another pair of eyes flashed through her mind. *You'll come away with me, won't you, Amelie?*

Dark, dark eyes . . . a weathered, laughing face.

And hands that touched her so gently.

Don't let him take you away . . .

* * *

JERKING upright in her bed, Dru caught her breath.

She was on the floor.

Still wearing her dress, although it was rucked up over her thighs.

If I ever knew you, I'd remember.

"Not *if you weren't supposed to . . . He hit you before . . . and he killed me. After that, I don't know what became of you. But I think you do. If you'll let yourself remember . . .*

Let yourself remember . . .

"Richard," she breathed out. "Patrick . . ."

But those weren't the names that mattered the most.

Whether his name was Mike Sellers now, or Joss whatever, once he'd been called Thom. Thom Brady. And she'd watched as Richard shot him. Watched as he died. Watched as Richard threw the man she loved into the lake. *Nobody will miss him, you know. Now come along. We have a wedding to plan.*

I will not marry you.

Oh, but you will. Because if you don't, I'll tell the sheriff I saw your *father shoot that man.*

They'll never believe you . . .

Yes, they will. He threatened Brady to stay away from you before, didn't he? Your father is already teetering on ruin. You can marry me . . . and save him, your family. Or refuse . . . and I'll ruin all of you.

Dru shivered, rolling to a sitting position with her back braced against the bed. *I get what I want, Amelie. You should remember that.*

Bile churned in her throat as she rested her head back against the bed.

"I do believe I've gone rather mad."

* * *

"YOU'RE not doing well."

Taylor sat across from him at a crowded Starbucks. It was a

little too noisy for the two of them, but they couldn't keep meeting at the same restaurant. Stupid doing it more than twice.

And Joss could use about fifty espressos, give or take. He was on his second. It hadn't touched the fatigue. *Not doing well. You think?*

He'd done something that had left him ill. He had left her there. Yeah, it was her choice, but he'd left her there. With that monster. She was *safe* . . . for now. Safe *enough*, was the knowledge as it had come to him, and that made him puke his guts up once he'd gotten far enough away from the estate.

He'd stood there, shaking, sick with fury . . . and a clear burning knowledge in his mind.

Yes, Dru knew what Whitmore was doing.

And she was trapped. He didn't want to know why or how she was in those circumstances, but somehow she felt trapped. He wasn't sure he could ever forgive her, though. People who danced with the devil ended up in bad situations, and that was what had happened here.

Still, leaving her there, trapped, had left him ill. He could have gone up those stairs, found Dru. Saved her. And others would have died. The women he was trying to save. He could hear their screams, even thinking about it . . . screams that haunted him.

Walking away, leaving Dru in Patrick's hands, was another thing that would haunt him. But with that clear, burning knowledge, he knew she'd live through this. Patrick didn't want her dead. That gift that was trying to drive Joss crazy showed him that she'd live through this.

Of course, when it was said and done, he didn't know how *he* would live with himself. The woman he'd lived his whole life waiting for . . . and she was living with a man like Whitmore.

Too aware of Jones's intense gaze, he focused on his coffee.

"Quit staring at me, damn it. I'm not a bug on a slide. My head is a mess, but I'll live through it. Any luck on my Latina girl?"

"Yeah." Taylor nodded shortly. "She's an amplifier, so this won't be too hard on her, although hopefully we can keep physical contact between her and Vaughnne to a minimum."

"An amplifier . . ." Joss sighed. Touching the cut inside his lip, he said, "The last thing I need is anything in my head amplified, Taylor. Do me a favor—tell her to wear long sleeves and keep her head locked down when we're working."

"Like I said . . . you're not doing well," Taylor repeated.

With a scowl, he said, "I'm doing what I have to do, right? Not like anybody else can do this damn job." Reaching into the bag at his side, he pulled out the wrapped glass he'd lifted from the party. "I need a favor. There are prints on this . . . probably several of them. A server's—most of them were male. But the prints I need are female. She's British. Hopefully, there's a fairly recent passport. I need info on her and I need it fast."

Taylor's gaze dropped to the bag and he took it, slid it over. "I have to give you a message. Jillian said she's been trying to get through to you and you're blocking her out."

"And that would really *stop* her?" Joss muttered, taking another swig from his coffee.

"No." Taylor shrugged. "She could probably plow through whatever shields you have and leave you a crying, whimpering mess, if she wanted. But I doubt she wants that." He paused, blew out a breath. "The kid wants you to stop the ice. I don't know what that means, but I assume you do. She says you're not going to feel things you need to feel if you keep up the ice."

Joss clenched his jaw. "Tell the kid I got this."

"Crawford . . . I don't think you do." Taylor's blue eyes searched Joss's face. "It's only been a few days and you look like hell. You've done harder jobs."

Curling his lip, Joss hunched over his caffeine. "Don't count on it."

"Joss—"

"You got any idea what that kid is capable of?" he demanded, shooting Taylor a narrow look. The fury bubbling inside him had to come out, and it was better to focus it on anything other than what was really hurting him.

Storming out of the coffee shop, he headed for the stolen car he had to use. Even the car hurt to use now. All the screams, they were like ice picks, in his ears, in his skin, in his soul. The ghosts were colder, hanging on more heavily than they ever had.

And Dru . . .

For fuck's sake . . . he felt his heart tremble. Shatter. How was this happening? After all this time, how was it even possible that it would happen this way? Finding her . . . like this . . .

Damn you, why couldn't you have come into my life a year ago? Two years ago? Why now? I can't have you now . . .

Dru . . .

He had to get away from her. Stumbling toward his car, he reached into his pocket. Dug out his keys. But a few feet away, he realized Jones was trailing along behind him. Veering off to the right, he circled around the restaurant. Once Jones caught up with him, he wheeled on him, the agony, the pressure, the pain spilling out of him.

"It's almost like she's got every gift I've ever had shoved in my head and it's cranked up to the max," he growled out, turning around to face Taylor. "And some shit I didn't even know was possible, I bet. The only thing I don't think she's got is this mirror thing I do. I bet she can even see some of Dez's ghosts."

"She sees their echoes," Taylor said quietly. "She saw them when she was just a kid. But they don't speak to her, not the way they do to Dez." Taylor studied him. "Do we need to pull you out? We know where they have Vaughnne. We can send word to her, let her prepare and—"

Joss swore. "No. One person on the inside isn't enough." He groaned, some of that knowledge flooding his head. Blood. So much of it. Screams. They'd break more bones, but there wouldn't be a slow, subtle enjoyment this time. They'd dispose of the bodies as quickly as possible, because they wanted all traces gone. And hell, if they pulled *him* out, who would take care of Dru?

"If we try to rush in, people are going to die. He's prepared for that. He can't get rid of the evidence, even though he thinks he can. There's too much of it, but we don't want anybody else dying."

Jones continued to watch him. "Can you hold it together?"

"No choice."

A heavy sigh came from Taylor. "If I'd known Jillian and Dez together would hit you this hard, I wouldn't have paired both of them on you. I just . . . shit. I knew there'd be ghosts, and it felt like it was the way to go. I miscalculated. I'm sorry, Joss."

Guilt churned inside him. It wasn't Jillian and Dez that had him so twisted up. It was Dru. Ella . . . *Amelie* . . .

A whisper of her voice drifted through his mind.

A name he hadn't heard . . . not from *her* . . . in far too long.

Thom . . .

Hissing out a breath, he spun away. In a clipped voice, he said, "Get word to me about the next plant." Then he took off, running for the car, before his head exploded. Once he was there, he leaned back against it, lifted shaking hands to his face.

Thom . . . *Now you remember*, he thought bitterly.

Now. When he discovers she's been shacking up with a guy who had his hands in some of the worst crimes known to man.

He could have accepted a lot of things.

But Joss didn't think he could live with that.

More . . . he just didn't want to.

Briefly, he opened his mind, just a little.

Stay out of my head, Dru. I don't want you now.

There was a faint pause. Followed by, *You sodding bastard. As if I'd let you near me. Stay the fuck out of my head, my dreams, my life.*

He curled his lip. *Sure thing, duchess.* He wouldn't be doing that. Unless she was actively engaged in what Whitmore was doing, he didn't want to see her going down with the others. He . . . hell, maybe he was getting soft, he didn't know. But he couldn't let her go down over this, not unless she was involved in it. But he could walk away. That much he could do.

I'll see you around your sugar daddy's place sometime, but don't worry, I'll keep my distance.

If you had half a brain, you'd keep your distance from him entirely, you wanker. Now stay out of my head.

He distinctly felt a snap fall between them. Like she'd shut a door. Curious, he pushed against it, but it was a pretty solid wall. Not as good as those who'd gone through the kind of training he'd had, but she wasn't green the way he'd been when Jones had found him.

Self-preservation, he figured. She'd have to develop decent shields to stay sane around Whitmore.

Groaning, he slammed his head back against the SUV.

Life was such a bitch. She could sucker-punch you right after you thought she was giving you one hell of a gift.

Traitorous, ugly bitch.

* * *

DRU ran harder.

Hitting the control on the treadmill in Patrick's private gym, she inched up to seven miles an hour, the muscles in her thighs screaming. She'd been pounding away at the miles for a good forty minutes and she'd thought she was done.

Then she'd heard *him* whispering into her mind.

I don't want you now . . .

Like she was the dirty one?

Sodding bastard.

If she could just get her—

"You look like you're feeling better."

Caught off guard, she stumbled and went flying backward.

Ending up on her ass at Patrick's feet, she sat there, panting, dazed from the pain, her chest aching from the exertion, her heart pounding.

And as Patrick crouched down, fear exploded inside her.

The monster in his eyes . . . it was thirsting for blood, she thought.

"Hello, Ella. As I said, you look to be feeling better."

Swallowing, she tried to calm the racing of her heart. Had to keep her calm here, now more than ever, even though she was oddly more terrified than she'd ever been. And she didn't even know why. "Yes. I guess I just needed some rest. Champagne and I never did get along very well, although I never thought a half a glass would do me in like that."

"A half a glass," he murmured. He reached out, caught her wrist, stroking his thumb along her skin.

Flash, flash, flash.

Slut, little whore . . .

She saw herself through his eyes, and whether it was her fear or the sheer power of his fury, the connection was clear, too clear. It flooded through her and she saw the events of last night the way he had perceived them—her drunk, throwing herself at his guests, flirting with Joss . . . Mike, whoever the bloody hell he was, even the doctor who hadn't been able to keep his eyes off her tits, before she passed out in a drunken slump.

Then she saw more . . . and it left her almost ill.

Whore me out, will you? She stared at him, shaking with a fury of her own, and this time, she failed to do the simplest thing . . . Dru didn't give him the meek, mild face he wanted to see every time he looked at her.

There was a flicker of surprise in his eyes, but it was gone almost as quickly as it had come. Then he tumbled her against him.

Dru sensed it coming and she moved with him, twisting her wrist and jerking away at the same time. She was on her feet and moving, her mind working furiously. She could get away from him; there was no doubt of that. The question was what to do about those who didn't have an escape net.

But then somebody moved out from behind one of the columns. Dru came to an abrupt stop, staring at him for a blink.

It gave Patrick the split second he needed to catch her. She struck back with her head, smashing it into his nose. She heard him howl with fury, and hot, savage satisfaction burned inside her. She'd wanted to bloody him for so long, so, so long . . .

"Help me, damn it," Patrick demanded.

Minton went to grab her.

Dru processed everything she could feel coming from Patrick—he had plans for her, big ones. They didn't involve her being harmed; that was good. She could do a lot of damage if they were trying to keep from leaving marks . . .

But then Minton had his hands on her and *flash, flash, flash.* She didn't even have time to process what he was going to do before it was happening. Seconds later she was flat against one of the decorative columns, face first, something thick and sturdy entrapping her.

"You really shouldn't have tried to cross me, Ella. Did you think I wouldn't find out what a little whore you were under the skin?"

Patrick stroked his fingers down her cheek, down her neck, over whatever it was Minton was using to bind her in place before coming to rest against her hips. "Know what happens to whores, Ella?"

* * *

TERROR. Blind.

Rage. All-consuming. It seemed to suck him in and he was lost, forever.

Run, have to run—

It was a scream inside him and everything was fear, determination and terror. But not his—even as lost to this fear as he was, he knew it wasn't his.

Dru!

He couldn't break free from it. Couldn't break away from that choking, consuming fear. It tore into him and destroyed him—

"Damn it, you son of bitch! Come out of it!"

Icy water doused him.

Choking, sputtering, Joss shoved against the hands holding him. Long seconds passed as he struggled against them. He was on . . . the floor of the hotel where he'd been staying with Jones. Soaking wet. And on the floor.

In the hotel? What the hell? He'd just been in Starbucks.

"I found you in the parking lot," Taylor said, kneeling down beside him, eyes grim. "You were out. Tasing you didn't help—we had to douse you with water. You've been out of it for almost thirty minutes. I had to have Morgan help me haul your ass up here."

Joss closed his eyes, trying to process those words, but even as he *tried*, something awful and sick swelled inside him. A scream, trapped inside his mind, while a sense of wrongness grew and grew. *Fear—terror—*

Sitting there, water puddling around him, he blocked everything out and focused.

"Joss, what in the hell is wrong?" Jones demanded.

Ice.

. . . stop the ice . . . you're not going to feel things you need to feel if you keep up the ice . . .

Slowly, he eased back on some of the shielding he'd built in his head.

And fury slammed into him.

Shoving upright, he snarled. "Phone. Need my fucking phone, *now . . .*"

Just the little glimpse . . . that was all he'd take, but still. Couldn't reach out to her. Couldn't take that grief again. But this wouldn't happen.

"You're being an ass," Nalini said as she pushed the phone into his hands. Then she looked at Taylor. "We need to move up the schedule. Fast."

Ignoring her, he did a quick check, made sure he was secured, and then pulled up another image. Sent it. Sent another. Then a message.

Ever had the feeling your house of cards is about to come toppling down?

* * *

PATRICK stroked a hand along Ella's ass, digging his fingers into her rump. "I should let my boy here take a turn at you. And I might . . . later on. Maybe I'll let all of them. When I'm done."

Blood lay heavy on his tongue. His nose throbbed, but he

didn't think it was broken. If the auction wasn't so close . . . fucking cunt. One more thing she'd suffer for. After.

Reaching down, he pulled a condom out of his pocket, put it between his teeth. Peering up, he made sure Minton had her secured. She struggled against the leather that held her, struggled hard, but it was useless. Minton was the best at restraining them in a way that would leave no marks.

Reaching for his zipper, he said, "This is the first of many, many lessons, Ella . . . remember it."

His phone chimed.

He ignored it.

It chimed again.

He dragged his zipper down.

It chimed a third time.

When it rang, he swore and grabbed it.

* * *

SHOVING the phone at Taige, Joss glared at her.

She fumbled and then picked it up, swearing in silence even as she caught his mental line.

You really should have covered your tracks better on the blonde, Joss prodded, his voice a ragged snarl in her mind.

Good thing about telepathy. Made this a lot easier.

Taige's eyes sparked fire as she said into the phone, "Hey there, slick. You should have covered your tracks better on the blonde."

The panic she saw in Joss's eyes gutted her.

The panic, the urgency.

Fortunately for him, she'd let herself take a few walks into the gray over the past forty-eight hours and she'd figured a few things out.

"Who in the fuck is this?"

"Now, now, Whitmore," Taige drawled, smiling a little. "You really should have paid your boys better . . . might have kept one of them from crossing sides."

Heavy, ragged panting. "Who. Is. This."

"Oh . . . now *that* is going to make me talk, that snarly mean growl. She was a pretty girl. Hell, maybe she still is, but how the hell do I know? Hard to talk to her, seeing as how she's kind of indisposed . . . over in Dubai. Gotta go . . . having a chat with somebody you know very, very well in just a few. Ta-ta!"

Disconnecting the phone, she hurled it at Joss. He didn't even seem to notice, covering his face with his hands, groaning.

"You crazy-ass idiot. Are you trying to screw this up or get yourself killed or what?"

"I've got to get out there."

Nalini was behind him. "I'm going, too."

"No. It's too soon for me to take another girl out there."

She snorted. "Hell, he's going to get suspicious no matter what, and that's why you need me out there." She smiled thinly. "Trust me . . . this is my specialty."

"No," Joss growled. The fear continued to grow, beating and growling inside him, a pacing, caged beast. "Damn it, he's going to begin his stupid 'protocol' to cover his ass, which means he's going to start getting rid of people."

"That's why you need me," Nalini said gently.

"Listen to her," Taylor said.

"Fuck you," Joss bit off. They didn't know—

"She's going," Taylor said, his voice icy. "And if you don't like it, I'll have your ass arrested before you leave the city limits. You're walking an edge, Crawford, and you're not going out there solo. Too much is riding on this. Lives on the line, have you forgotten that?"

Joss glared at him.

A hand touched his side.

A rush of calm flooded him and he looked over, found himself staring into Nalini's eyes. For a moment, just a brief moment, those large, dark, compelling eyes . . . all he could see. "We got this, Crawford. Just trust me," Nalini said, smiling at him.

With a terse nod, he headed out of the room.

* * *

As the door closed behind him, Taige started to swear. "If he figures out what she just did to him, he's going to blow a gasket."

"He's close to blowing anyway," Taylor muttered. "We need to get ready. I think this is going to hit boiling point sooner than we'd expected."

Sighing, Taige turned away and headed toward the bag she had stashed on the couch.

Cullen was over there, arms crossed over his chest, waiting quietly.

As she passed by him, she avoided looking at him. "I'm in this now," she said flatly. "Doesn't matter if you like it or not. I've heard their screaming. Women are suffering. Girls are dying. People need me. It's what I am."

His hand touched her arm.

Despite her decision not to look at him, she was unable to stop herself, swinging her head around and meeting the impossible blue of his eyes. Blue that stared at her with so much love. So much heat. So much need. He touched her cheek gently, slowly, tracing his finger down to stroke it over her lip. "I know, Taige. I know who you are . . . and although I hate how much you suffer for it, I wouldn't change who you are."

A knot rose in her throat. "Wouldn't you?"

"No." He eased in, pressed his lips to her forehead. "You do what you have to . . . and then come back to me. Come to me, so we can go back home to our baby."

* * *

AWARE of the quiet scene taking place behind him, but distancing himself from it, Taylor continued to check the information they'd managed to amass over the past few days. They hadn't been sitting around idly. No, thanks to Taige, they'd been rather busy, and she'd made connections that just didn't seem possible.

Including tracking down a man in Dubai. One who had a woman in his house who really shouldn't be there.

Whitmore's last girlfriend.

Other bits and pieces were coming through. Enough, Taylor knew, just barely to wrangle a warrant. Just barely. And he was going to put a rush on it.

His phone rang.

He almost ignored it. He didn't care about the fingerprints Crawford had wanted the other day. But something wouldn't let him ignore it totally.

Five minutes later, he hung up.

Without saying a word, he crossed over to his desk and flipped through his files. "Taige . . . did you by chance get a look in Crawford's mind?"

She looked up from the bag, her shoulder holster in hand. "Not much. He's gotten too good at shielding. Shielding. Denying. I caught random glimpses but . . ."

Picking up a picture, he flipped it around and showed it to her.

Taige stared at the picture.

And if her husband hadn't been standing right there, she would have hit the floor.

As it was, Cullen was caught off guard and he damn near ended up on his ass as he caught her limp form.

"You son of a bitch," he snarled, shooting Taylor a dark look.

Taylor looked at the image of the woman.

According to his files, her name was Ella Castille.

English-American citizen. Engaged to marry Patrick Whitmore.

According to the fingerprints . . . somebody else entirely.

And there was no way she could have managed a cover this complete on her own.

* * *

STRUGGLING against the leather, Dru braced herself. This was going to happen. She'd live through it. Then she was falling back on plan B. Escape. She'd contact Tucker. Regroup. Because she couldn't stop this hell if she got pulled into it herself.

But first, she had to live through it—

Retreat . . . blank out . . . is that what I do?

No. She'd damn well fight. She'd retreated, acquiesced, changed, sold herself enough. She'd fight . . . and she'd survive.

Snarling and fighting against the leather, she kicked backward as best as she could, connecting with his leg. It wasn't much, but every mark she left on him was a victory. He swore and punched her, right in the kidney. Pain lashed her but she ignored it, shoved it down, shoved it back. Kicked him again as she struggled against the leather and glared at Minton.

"You bloody monster," she snarled at him. "Sodding cock-sucking coward."

He grinned at her. "I'll show you sucking cock, cunt. When I get my turn in a few months."

"I'll bite it off," she promised, curling her lip at Minton. "I promise you, whatever you stick in my mouth, I'm going to bite it off. I don't care what happens to me because of it."

A flicker of something that might have been caution showed in his eyes.

It wasn't enough. She wanted to see him terrified.

A harsh jerk stripped her running shorts down to her ankles and Patrick came up behind her, kicked her legs farther apart. "Be nice to him, or when he gets his turn, he'll tear you apart. I've seen him do it."

"He'll be lucky if I don't carve his dick off and feed it to him like a sausage."

A chiming sound filled the room, oddly out of place. Patrick grunted, moving in closer. It came again . . . followed by the ringing of the phone.

It happened so abruptly, it caught her off guard, but Patrick moved away.

Seconds later, over the sound of her own panting, she heard him speak.

"Who the fuck is this?"

His next words were filled with . . . well, if Dru didn't know better, she might have thought it was fear.

Minutes passed.

The call ended and she braced herself. She'd caught her breath, she could fight longer. Harder—

"Let her go. We need to go to the city," Patrick said.

The leather holding her restrained fell away and she sagged, falling to the floor.

He touched her, and it was a shock as the *flash, flash, flash* came. He was scared. Damn scared. And pissed. *Somebody knew* . . . For a second, she was scared as well. But he didn't know about her.

Who the fuck knows—

Going to kill—

Terror flooded her and she thought of Tucker.

But then sanity hit, realigned, as the flash settled into her mind. Patrick had spoken with a woman. Dru was safe . . . or safe on that front, at least. He didn't know about her, about Tucker.

And he was leaving . . . she could get the hell out.

"You'll be staying here, Ella," Patrick said. "And don't think of leaving. I'll just find you . . . and you'll be sorry."

"I think I'm rather done with this engagement bit," she said.

"Oh, no." He knelt in front of her, stroked a finger down her cheek. "No, you're not. But go ahead. Try. Run. I'd enjoy it. I can't wait to break you, Ella. I really, really can't."

She spit in his face.

When he hit her, she moved with it, just at the last moment, enough to lessen the blow so she wasn't completely dazed.

As he left, she remained on the floor, pretending to cry.

Their time was up.

They had to move, and now, before he freaked and took actions to eliminate all evidence . . . which meant he'd kill his hostages.

TWENTY-ONE

THIS was a mess.

Taige struggled out of the lethargy of the gray to find Jones staring at her, Cullen glaring at Jones, Dez standing in the background glaring at the two men, and the air in the room thick enough to cut with a knife.

"Oh, hell." She rolled onto her side, cradled her aching head in her hands, and wished she hadn't given up drinking all those years ago. She could use a glass of wine just then.

A hand curved over the back of her neck, and she turned her head, found herself staring into eyes of the color of the sea.

"Here I was thinking it was Jillian who'd be hauled into this mess," Cullen said, sighing.

She stared at him, wishing she could make this easier on him. Poor guy. Saddled with two females who were going to worry him into the grave. Had to suck. Reaching up, she said, "You said you wouldn't change me . . . now is the time to show it."

Thick lashes fell, shielding his eyes. "I'd do anything to make this easier on you," he said hoarsely. "Some small selfish part of me thinks . . . *this isn't your problem.* You don't work for him anymore. *None* of this is your problem."

Then he looked at her, those blue eyes burning so hot.

"But looking back . . . neither was Jillian. She wasn't your problem, but you saved her, anyway."

"Suffering is everybody's problem," she said quietly. Slowly, not entirely trusting her queasy belly, she sat up. Her belly stayed settled. She hadn't been prepared for the strength of that vision. Hadn't been ready for the intensity of it, the power of it. It had damned near laid her low. "What's Joss's connection to this woman?"

A strange, tense silence fell.

Slanting a look at Jones, she found him eyeing her oddly. When he didn't answer her, she pushed. "Well?"

"To my knowledge, there is no connection. She's engaged to marry our prime suspect. She's one of the suspects, although I didn't share any information about her with Crawford. I wanted him focused on Whitmore, and only Whitmore, so he could find his own way through this mess."

Taige closed her eyes. Sighed. "A mess? This isn't a mess . . . it's a damned catastrophe." She plucked through some of the tangled threads in her mind. By now, Jones knew she wasn't a suspect, that woman, whoever she was. "Cullen, maybe you should head on back home. Get Jillian from your dad. I'm going to—"

"Jillian's fine. I'm sticking."

She cracked open one eye to stare at him.

He stared back. "I can keep my ass in a room and work. I'm useless here and I know it, but I'm not going back to Gulf Shores when you're about to plunge your neck into whatever mess . . . shit. I'm staying."

Taige groaned. She didn't have the energy to worry about him. "Jones . . . this woman, whoever she is, she's private. I don't know how long she's been working this, but she's been doing it a long time and she's willing to sacrifice everything. Whitmore has hurt her, more than once, and she takes it, because of the job. And if you think Crawford has no connection to her, you need to get your head examined."

A series of long, terse curses filled the room, and Taige was surprised enough to drop her hands and stare at the man.

Damn. That was more emotion than she thought he was capable of. "You okay there, Jones?"

He shot her a narrow look. "Do I need to pull him out?"

"You can't," she said honestly. "Even if you sent people after him, it wouldn't work. He's on a mission of his own now. Trying to pull him out would do more harm than good."

"*Fuck,*" he snarled, spinning away. Dez, silent until now, moved and went to him, laying a hand on his cheek.

He caught her wrist.

A long, tense moment passed. "She's private," Taylor finally said into the silence. "But she's got connections damn high up. Somebody with enough pull to help create one very, very solid identity."

"Shit."

Taige remembered the flash of echoes she'd caught from Joss. The images he'd shoved back behind walls so thick so he wouldn't have to look at them, think about them.

Living in denial might just cost him something very, very dear, she realized.

TWENTY-TWO

A vague sense of calm had settled over Joss. He was cool with it.

A quick stop by the room he still had here at the hotel—damn, this was turning into an expensive trip—and he had dry clothes on. Then, with Nalini walking along at his side, they were gone, out of the hotel and moving.

Every so often, she'd touch his arm.

He didn't think he wanted that, but every time she did it, whatever shiftless thoughts formed in his mind just faded away.

Job to get done, all that mattered.

"So, do we have a plan?" Nalini asked once they were outside of the city.

"I'm kind of thinking along the lines of: Get there. Get those women out. Burn the place to the ground."

"Nice idea . . ." She chuckled. Then she touched his arm again. "But we can't do that—you realize that, right?"

The splintering, massive burden in his mind was pushing him too hard, and that fragile calm danced away. "Don't see why not."

He wondered if Jillian could burn things. If she could, he could . . .

There was one of their people who had that ability. Just one that Joss knew about. Maybe Jillian had it, though . . . he wondered.

A hand closed over his wrist.

"Damn it, boy." Nalini sighed. "You're killing me. All you had to do was ease up on the ice, like the kid said."

A wave washed over him.

Blanketed him.

For a moment, he couldn't even see. If he could *think*, that might have bothered him, seeing as how he was still driving.

"Easy, Crawford . . . I got it . . . easy. Easy . . ."

* * *

As Crawford swung his head to glance her way, Nalini smiled.

He didn't smile back, but that didn't bother her.

She suspected he wasn't really the happy-go-lucky type.

And he was going to come after her if he figured out what she did. Her ability to control people through the power of touch wasn't a pleasant one, but it was useful.

She had to take in everything he was feeling, and *damn*, he was feeling a lot. Too much, really. Enough to leave her reeling as she laid her impression on him. Almost enough to make her vision fade out. She clung to consciousness by the skin of her teeth, channeled more into him, felt him resist . . . then, eventually break.

That's it, man . . . come on, I can help. I can help . . .

As he swayed under the weight of what she laid on him, she was left staggering under the burden of what he was carrying—all the stuff he'd acknowledged . . . and all the misery he'd been hiding from. It was enough to break her, if she let herself think about it.

But Nalini hadn't come this far to break.

None of them had.

Filtering all that ragged, rampant emotion out of herself, away from him, she breathed through it, focused, breathed . . . and she might have even prayed a little. As the worst of the grief finally passed, she found herself fighting tears at the depth of the pain building inside him.

Pain.

Anger.

Too much of everything, all because he wouldn't open his damned eyes.

She wanted to smack him. But it was going to have to wait. He was finally calm. Or calm enough. If she hit him, the impression would fade and then she'd have to start all over again.

He was steady, for now. That was all that mattered, all that could matter, as they hurtled down the highway into the coming twilight. He couldn't get through this thinking about everything that had him so burdened.

But even as they sped down the highway, that ever-present threat lurked in the back of her mind. Not much time . . . not much time at all.

* * *

GETTING a message to Tucker was as easy as she'd expected, even with a guard lurking outside her door.

The fool thought having her sent to her "rooms" would do much good.

Pissant.

He'd do well to be more paranoid, she thought.

The last time she'd been out here, Dru had managed to stash several throwaway phones and not a one of them had been found. Including the one she'd managed to tape to the back of the bathroom sink. It was out of sight, inside a plastic bag, and once she'd pulled it out, she plugged it in and let it charge just enough to send the text. As it was charging, she finished up everything else she needed to do.

Running gear—excellent clothes for tonight. The tights would be horribly hot, but it didn't matter. They were close-fitting, they let her move, and when paired with a long-sleeved black shirt, it would help her hide in the dark.

She twisted her hair into a tight braid, securing it with a band, and tucked it inside her shirt. A quick look at the phone told her it still needed a few more minutes. No surprise there.

That was fine. She needed a few minutes herself. Taking up position with her back against the door, she did the one thing that was crucial. Dangerous, possibly, but crucial. Her shields were faulty, weak, frail, and if she didn't do something about it, all it would take was the wrong touch from the wrong person at the wrong moment and she was done for.

Psychic shielding wasn't like putting on a jacket and taking it off. It took practice and patience and control. If she didn't bolster the shields when she felt them faltering, she was, plain and simply, fucked. With her back lodged against the door, she closed her eyes.

This was always the worst. When she meditated, she had to let her guard down to some extent. Leaving herself unaware. Exposed.

Lesser of two evils, Dru, she told herself. *Do this now . . . or have one of them touch you later and you know what will happen then.*

She could control the flashes, and break away when she had to, but if she faltered in her control, then she could lose herself. Not an option.

So . . . *do it now.*

Endless moments later, she emerged from the light trance, panting slightly, a light sweat on her skin. And the restlessness that had hovered just outside her awareness faded a little as her shields settled smoothly back into place. She could get through this. She *would* get through this.

All she had to do was get the hell out of this house.

That part might be tricky.

She didn't take much. The clothes hanging in the closet didn't matter. Her cash, she was definitely taking that. She didn't worry about the fake IDs or the credit cards he'd given her. One quick glance at the cell phone told her that it had maybe a quarter of a charge on the battery.

Good enough. She sent the message before she unplugged it and then wrapped up the cord, tossed it under the sink counter so it was out of sight.

There was one last thing she needed. It was stashed inside her makeup case.

A place Patrick just never would have thought to look.

The slim vial was actually hidden inside one of her tubes of lipstick. The syringe and needle were secreted inside what appeared to be a mascara wand. Having those suckers made had cost a pretty penny, but it had been worth it. As she drew up a dose, calculating it carefully, the phone in her pocket vibrated.

She pulled it out. Checked the message.

I'm here. Had a feeling it was coming. Ten minutes away.

Tucker and his feelings. Texting him back, she deleted both messages from the memory and slipped the phone back into the zipped pocket of her top. Then she studied the syringe.

She wasn't sure who was outside her door, but she had an idea. It wasn't Minton. Minton had left with Patrick earlier, his good little dog. So it was likely either Peretti or Rawlings. Both of them, miserable bastards. They weren't as big as Minton, thankfully. Wouldn't need to use as much.

It left just a little bit of the opioid mix, enough for another dose. She had one more needle, and that, she tucked inside her sports bra. Would have to use the same syringe, not very sanitary, but oh well.

The liquid inside that tube wasn't anything the U.S. government would approve of. Tucker had gotten it for her, slipped it into her hand. *For when you need a way out.* At first, she thought he meant killing herself.

But then she'd realized what he was talking about.

She couldn't take anything recognizable as a weapon into this.

But there might come a time when she had to get away, and this very illegal opioid compound would swing the odds just a little bit.

Fight her way out . . .

Get free of this place.

It was time. Tucking the vial into another zippered pocket of her shirt, she stared at the door. Took a deep breath.

An image of Joss's face flashed through her mind. Regret, anger, misery twisted her heart, but she shoved them all aside. They'd never really had a chance anyway. Not if he'd dismissed her as easily as that.

"Fuck him." He didn't matter. *Couldn't* matter. And if he was involved in this nightmare, then he'd have to pay as well. Swallowing the knot in her throat, she curled her hands into fists. Thought of all the nightmares. The screams. The memory flashes into Patrick's mind . . . how many women had suffered.

No more. It stopped now.

It was time to get this done, get the hell away from here, and burn as many bridges as she could while she did it. *Then get the hell away.*

The one thing she thought she could go after . . . it no longer existed.

She was going to finish the job she'd set out to do. She had the bits and pieces in her mind now, and *that* was what mattered.

Bits and pieces. Like bread crumbs, she supposed. Or stones . . . stones that made up the trail she needed to follow. It blazed hot and bright in her mind now.

So hot. Burning bright.

"You're so fucked," she whispered, thinking of Whitmore.

So very, very fucked.

Casting a quick look at the door, she headed over to the window and peeked outside. Men on the perimeter, inconspicuous and well dressed. They had a pattern, one she'd tried to learn before, but she'd never been out here long enough up until this trip. This time, she'd been out here for more than just a meal, or a dip in the pool. She'd managed to make better note of the areas they patrolled, their timing, all of it.

It wasn't going to give her a lot of time to make a break for it, but as long as she got out of the house, she figured she'd be okay.

Carefully, she lowered her shields . . . *careful, careful* . . . The last thing she wanted was a quick visit from her unwanted lover or whoever Joss was. She felt nothing, though. Just cold, empty silence.

Good, she thought, ignoring the hollow ache inside. That was what she wanted, right?

Turning away from the window, she made for the door, pressed her ear to it. It was quiet, but she wasn't fooled. Somebody was out there. Peretti, Rawlings . . . maybe one of the others she didn't see much at all.

Who didn't really matter, though.

As she backed away from the door, she looked around. Distraction . . . needed a distraction. Just inside the doorway there was a table with a crystal decanter. It was pretty, expensive as hell, and heavy. Filled with water every morning, it sat there, along with two glasses. She had the syringe in one hand, uncapped, ready.

Smiling, she picked up one of the glasses, moved a few feet

away from the door, and then turned, hurling it against the far wall, where her guard would have to come inside to see it.

As it hurtled through the air, she dropped in a slump, carefully, holding the needle.

The door opened.

She held her breath.

"What the—"

Everybody saw Ella, an elegant-looking woman, she knew. But docile. Easily manipulated. Easily controlled.

And this man was no different.

As he knelt by her, she watched from under her lashes, her gaze shielded. The needle ready. And as he went to reach for her, she moved.

He snarled, but the needle was already in his arm, and at that concentrated dose, all he needed was a little.

Within moments, she had two guns, a knife, another cell phone, and more. She took his body, and not sure what else to do with his limp, unconscious self, she shoved it under the bed.

There. Rawlings was down for the count. She looked around the room, searching for signs of what had happened. There weren't many. Broken glass. The needle. She carefully picked it up, dropped it in the water decanter, and slipped into the hall, glancing around, left then right, her senses on red alert.

Couldn't go out the front.

Nor the back door.

Careful . . .

Careful . . .

* * *

SOMETHING rode just under his skin as they closed in on the compound.

He didn't know what it was, but it had him edgy as hell.

Careful . . .

Careful . . .

Nalini went to touch his arm and he edged away. "Stop it already," he bit off, even as that whisper danced through his mind.

Careful . . . careful . . .

A soft brush against his shields. A sigh.

Without understanding why, he eased them down.

Jillian's voice was a soft, hesitant whisper. *You have to stop the ice . . . and tell that woman to leave you alone. It's not helping.*

And then, like a wisp of smoke on the wind, she was gone.

"Stop the ice." He should know what that meant.

Shooting Nalini a look, he saw something dancing through her eyes. Wariness. Secrets.

What. The. Fuck.

She reached out a hand.

He slammed on the brakes. "You touch me again, I'm going to knock your ass out," he warned, feeling the burn of power rising in his brain.

"How?" A ghost of a smile danced on her lips. "It's okay, Joss. Just . . ."

She reached out again.

He pressed, sending a warning slice to her mind, watched as she flinched.

"Ahhh . . ." She went pale, even paler than normal. "Nasty, nasty trick, Joss."

"Don't touch me again," he warned.

The burn got hotter. Heavier. But it hadn't quite managed to penetrate whatever was muzzing his brain.

She sighed. "I'd say I'm sorry, but you have to understand how fractured you are. If you don't get it under control, you're going to screw every last one of us. Including her."

Something flickered through his brain.

Her . . .

Her.

His heart pounded against his ribs.

Heavy. Slow.

Her . . .

* * *

As she was running across the grounds, she heard them coming behind her.

One of them was coming at an angle, and he was close . . . fast, too.

Damn—

She heard an odd, muffled pop.

There was a shout.

She didn't slow. Didn't stop. The dude closest to her was *fast* . . . streaking her way with a speed that rivaled her own. Patrick had put a decent runner on his guard dog goon squad.

She put more into it, the ground slapping against her feet.

Another odd little pop . . . and the runner was down, screaming in agony.

Gunshots, she realized.

Somebody was shooting. Focusing in the darkness ahead, she thought she saw him. The vivid red of his hair, the spiral of tattoos on his arms. Tucker. Thank God.

The next few moments were a buzzed blur. Adrenaline thrummed through her veins. Her heart was in her throat. Almost out of here . . . almost. Almost.

As she breached the lovely stone gates that surrounded the property, she snarled. Had to climb. Damn. The main gate was closed . . .

Pop, pop, pop . . .

And then a gloved pair of hands closed on her wrists. "I gotcha," Tucker drawled. The muscles in his arms bulged as he hauled her up, making the tattoos dance and shift.

She looked up into his familiar eyes, his hair tumbling into them. "I gotcha, girl," he drawled, smiling a little.

Breathe, gotta breathe.

Seconds later, they were on the ground and Tucker was next to her. As they tore off into the night, they were too aware of those who were pursuing them.

"They're coming after us," she said grimly. "They'll be on the road the second we are."

"No." Tucker's voice was tight, controlled.

Shooting him a look, she saw the strained look on his face. "Not just yet, they won't." He pointed to the roadside and they slowed just before they would have slammed into the car. "I can hold them for a few."

The look on his face was one of strain unlike anything she could ever recall seeing. "Tucker?"

He just shook his head. "Get in. We have to go," he said thinly. "The farther we are when I lose the hold, the better."

Well, then.

She'd known he had a knack for odd things . . . a strong knack, but *that* strong?

* * *

THE mantra of *careful, careful* had given way to *breathe, breathe.*

Gripping the steering wheel, Joss shot Nalini a dark look. "What in the fuck did you do to me?"

"Nothing much, big boy. Just kept your head intact a little while longer," she said, eyeing the gate ahead of them.

She'd slid into the backseat. By all looks and appearances, she was lying there, bound. Of course, one look at her eyes and one would know she wasn't helpless. "This isn't going to work if you

can't look a little more scared," he snapped. "Vaughnne managed a better job than you are."

She smiled at him. "Vaughnne can't do what I do. You just
open the back for them."

He swore.

This was going to go bad.

Very bad.

"I haven't even called in to let them know I'm bringing you."
Frustration rumbled through him.

And still that faint whisper. Getting louder now. Familiar
even. A woman's voice. He knew her . . . who the hell was she?

There. It's there. It was so close . . . all this time . . .

What was she talking about?

"Don't worry. They won't care once you open that door. If
they don't touch me, you pull me out and *make* them," Nalini
said.

"Touch you . . ."

Pieces fell into place.

That odd calm that had washed over him.

With a composure he didn't feel, he said, "You control people, don't you? They have to touch you, but when they do, you
can control them."

"Yes."

In the rearview mirror, he met her gaze.

"That's not all, is it?"

She shrugged. "I do it through impressions . . . I leave an
impression, and I take some of the bad shit away. I don't take
memories, but I can haze things up for a while. When you push,
anything I do goes away." With a sigh, she said, "You were hurtling two hundred miles per hour down the wrong road, with the
wrong thoughts. And you still had too much chaff in your head
from the mind-fuck Taylor did on you. We had to fix it."

"*We* didn't do anything. That's not much better than mind-rape." He stared at the road. If he looked at her again, he just might pull the car over and do something he'd regret.

"I know."

As he slowed to a stop just outside the gate, Nalini said softly, "There wasn't much choice. You were disintegrating and you know it. You're thinking better now. Keep it that way . . . and start looking deeper, you brainless moron."

Looking deeper . . .

He curled his lip at her, but there was no time to ask what she was talking about.

There were two men striding toward them.

And they didn't look happy.

TWENTY-THREE

WELL, they'd needed a distraction of sorts, Dru thought.
The appearance of the maroon SUV counted.

As the men opened the gate to admit the SUV, both Dru and
Tucker heard the raised voices. "How steady are you now?" she
asked quietly, studying the gates.

The whole bleeding fence was wired. They had to figure a
way around that.

"Steady enough," he said, and his voice was easier now,
that slow, lazy drawl more like what she was used to. "I'm
good. Granted, I'll crash and burn when this is done, but I'm
good."

"Can you hold the gate?"

He shot her a look. "Hold it?" Red brows ratcheted up as he
studied her face. "Why, so we can just walk in . . . yeah, that will
go over well."

"No. If you hold it so they can't shut it . . . distraction." Her eyes narrowed as she thought it through. "But we need more than that. They'll have cameras. Lights . . ."

He reached over, caught her hand, squeezed hers. Even through the leather gloves, she could feel the heat of his hand. "Relax. I can get the gates. And then some."

She slanted a look at him. "And then some?"

"Yep."

On an unspoken cue, they rose from their crouched position, staring at each other. "Just what is *then some*?"

He stared down at the ground, a thoughtful look on his lean features. "I never much told you how I work, I guess." As he lifted his head, his gray eyes met hers, dark and turbulent as a summer thunderstorm. "I fuck with electrical shit. Any sort of electrical . . . including what's inside your head. I can do it just enough to slow some people down." Then he flashed a wicked, vivid grin at her, one that made him look just a little bit devilish, just a little bit wild. "Or I can do it enough to fuck up that gate, every last lightbulb, every last camera in there. Whatever I want."

Dru stared. Then she shifted her attention to the gate. "What about his SUV? Any weapons they have?"

"The SUV, oh, yeah. Weapons, depends. Stun guns?" He gave her a wicked grin. "Other stuff . . . if it's anything advanced, yes. Basic firearms, no, but I still can fuck with the owner. That's all that matters."

Turning her head to the SUV, she smiled. "Do it."

* * *

IT was a release sometimes, Tucker knew. The best kind. And if he wasn't careful, the worst kind, especially when he used it on people. That was why he had to be careful. People could die if he slipped.

But cars, electrical gates, cameras, that was so safe . . . and so much fun.

As he pictured all of it in his mind, his breath started to come in harsh, edgy pants. It was a rush, raw and erotic, and that just proved to him how fucked up he was. Although he didn't need proof. He knew he was fucked up, had been all his life.

The gates . . . several different series of them. Cameras . . . those first, and he felt the little *pop, pop, pop* in his brain as they went down. Damn, that felt good. He took a few seconds, probing at the series of gates, wondering why they were running on a couple of different generators, then it clicked for him as he felt the prickly burn of life coming from somewhere deeper in the compound.

Alien life. Not human.

All energy felt different to him, and this wasn't a human. He couldn't quite understand it, but he pieced the picture together well enough. After all, Dru had been sharing intel with him in case something happened to her. Somebody had to go to the cops, and although he didn't know if he'd be believed . . . well, if something had happened to his girl, he wouldn't worry about the cops. He'd kill Whitmore himself.

The gators. He was pretty sure that alien life energy he sensed was the gators. So a second set of gates, running off a different generator, was to keep the gators confined.

Okay. Leaving that one alone . . . on to the lights, and whoa. *That* was a rush.

They exploded with a glorious burst that had people swearing so loud, he heard some of them from out there. Even the lights placed on the grounds went up in a blaze as he flooded them with a power surge. So damned good. Felt so good.

On to the next . . .

He felt the probe at his mind.

Somebody new. Unwelcome. Deftly, he averted it, sidestepping for just long enough to disable any of the weapons he could. Didn't work on all of them; most of the weapons used here were firearms, but there were a few stun guns and that was good. He took them out, and by the time he was done, he was cruising so high, he might as well have been in the stratosphere.

One more thing . . . the car. He killed the battery, killed it so dead they'd never be able to start it, and then, just for kicks, he screwed up the rest of the electrical system.

"Whoa." Pressing the heel of his hand to his right eye socket, he blew out a breath. "That's a rush."

"You okay?" Dru asked.

She reached out to touch him—he didn't see it, but he sensed it coming, and he stepped away. "Don't touch me just yet, darlin'. Dangerous until I blow some of this off."

That mental probe came back, and Tucker shut himself down just before it could connect.

Sweat was dripping off him as he swung around to Dru. In the gilded moonlight, she stood there silently, but not very patient, her eyes glittering, hands clenched.

"Is it done?"

He smiled.

"Taking that as a yes, then," she muttered. "Bloody dark now. Didn't think of that."

"Don't worry. I always think of that."

Swinging his pack off his back, he pulled out two sets of night-vision goggles.

As he slid his pair on, he was treated to the pleased smile curving Dru's lips.

"You, Tucker, are fast becoming my very favorite person in the entire world."

* * *

"You gotta leave."

Joss glared at the man in front of him, tried to restrain the edginess burning under his skin.

"I have the next delivery for him and you want me to leave?"

"We're having problems. Deliveries have to be postponed."

"Hmm." He started toward the back and gestured to the back of the SUV. "Come look at this."

Jerking open the door, he said a mental prayer that Nalini would at least *try* to look scared. Or something other than, *I'm going to eat your eyes the second I get my hands on you.*

One of the men peered inside.

Nalini lay there, a sex-kitten smile curving her lips.

"Ah . . ."

Closing a hand around Nalini's arm, he jerked her out and shoved her at the guard. Reflexively, the guard's hands closed around her.

His face went slack.

In the next second, he started to smile.

And the second after that, Joss felt the weirdest damn thing happening . . . it wasn't *inside* his head, but it was happening on a level that wasn't exactly physical. Almost the way his ears popped when he was on an airplane. *Pop, pop, pop.*

Seconds passed as he shook his head and tried to process it. The hair on his arms rose, stood on end.

The guard stumbled back against the SUV. "Hey, Bruce . . . gotta come help a minute," he called, his voice thick, rough. And he stared at Nalini like he'd never seen anything so amazing.

"Sanchez, we're not supposed to be doing anything but watching the gate," Bruce snarled. He came around the back of the

SUV, glowering. Took one look at Nalini and went to shove her back into the SUV.

Joss could barely process it. He was too aware . . . something. A mind. He realized. There was somebody out there. *Pop, pop, pop.* And then screaming . . . darkness.

All the lights around them exploded into darkness.

"What the . . ." Bruce began. But the rest of his words died as he laid hands on Nalini.

And she stole away his will.

"There we go, boys," she said, pleased. "Into the back, if you would."

Joss ignored them, turning his back, trusting her to deal with his. He focused on the woods around them, reaching out. He felt it, damn it. He'd find whoever it was—

But then that mind, cagey and adroit, deflected him, swatting him away with relative ease. "Oh, no, you don't."

When he went to try again, though, it was gone.

Whoever it was, Joss couldn't sense him again.

Him . . .

Swinging around, he stared at Nalini, who was in the process of cuffing the two guards. "What in the fuck is going on?"

She lifted a pale brow at him. "Are you asking me or just snarling to snarl?"

"I . . . shit."

Behind him, he heard the faintest sound. Heard the rustling of trees. He had his weapon in hand before he even turned, edging so that he had Nalini behind him.

"You know, it's nice in theory to have a man doing that, but I'm as capable as you are," she said coolly, moving out from behind him.

He never even noticed.

The moon shone down, casting its full light on a face that hit the very heart of him.

Her . . .

Her . . .

It all came rushing back.

The elation, the dizzying need, want, and love. The misery.

All of it, gone. Not for long. But it had been gone.

However Nalini had taken it away from him, he didn't know. She'd stripped it away, though. Thoughts of everything and everybody but finishing this job. Including his knowledge of Dru, replacing all of that edgy, troubled misery with false lassitude.

The last vestiges of that calm shattered into a million tiny little pieces, withering to dust, drifting away on the cool night wind.

Just like his heart.

Slanting a look at Nalini, he said quietly, "If you ever do that again, I'm going to hurt you. I don't care if you're a woman or not."

She reached out and cuffed him on the side of the head. "I told you . . . *look deeper.*"

Then she turned her head and the two of them stared at the other two, standing on the side of the road.

She held a gun, Joss thought numbly.

She held a fucking gun.

He'd been prepared to help her out of this, as long as she wasn't really *working* with Whitmore.

But she had a fucking gun.

Look deeper.

As she raised the gun on him, Joss figured there really wasn't much chance he could be misconstruing this.

But then she knocked the foundation of his world out from under him.

* * *

"IF you come over here," Dru said to the woman, although she kept her eyes focused on Joss, "we'll keep you safe. I've got a car. My friend will get you to it. Nobody will hurt you. And if that son of a bitch tries to stop you, I'll shoot his balls off."

The woman just smiled.

And that was when Dru realized she wasn't cuffed.

No cuffs . . .

And where were the guards? They'd lost sight of them as they came through the woods, trying to keep as quiet as possible, but there had been two guards.

"Tucker." She shifted.

He might not be able to read minds, and maybe she couldn't read thoughts, but he understood her well enough, turning so that he had his back at an angle to hers. She scanned the area, hating the goggles even as she was relieved to have them.

"If you're looking for the guards, you can find them in there," the woman said quietly.

She jabbed a finger to the trunk.

Dru glanced over. Then did a double take as her mind started to process. Two men. Bound. Two *guards*, men she knew. They'd taken turns trailing after her more than once. And they stared at the blond woman like they couldn't stop. It was *eerie*, the way they watched her. Like they adored her. Needed her. Worshipped her.

Setting her jaw, she swung her gaze back to Joss just as he moved forward.

"Stay back," Dru warned.

"Oh, for fuck's sake," the woman snapped. She turned to the truck. "This Mexican standoff is all very entertaining, but there isn't much time. The others will be rushing up here in no time, and I'm sure none of us want Whitmore's men moving into his cleanup protocol or whatever he calls it."

Cleanup protocol—something tugged in her mind. A tug . . . then a push. She fortified her shields, even as she eyed Joss. He'd told her to stay out of his mind, damn it. She didn't want in his mind, didn't want him in hers, even though she was starting to suspect there was something more complicated going on.

Still staring at Joss, Dru nudged Tucker with her shoulder. They needed to move. Needed to do . . . something. What should they do? Had to get in there. What was going on, though?

"Here, English. Catch."

"Cole," Joss said, his voice hard with warning.

Dru tore her eyes from Joss's face as something came flying through the night. She snatched it out of the air.

"Stuff it up your ass, Crawford," the woman said.

Dru tuned them out, eyeing the leather ID holder she held. Tucker shifted positions with her, automatically guarding her as she stood there, stunned, slammed by the images crashing into her. Just touching an *object* usually couldn't do this to her.

Hadn't been prepared—

The woman, disguised. Holding a gun on a man.

Another disguise, shoving somebody into a waiting car . . . sirens flashing.

The bottom of her stomach dropped out.

The pressure on her mind increased as she stared at the credentials in front of her. The woman looked different, hair was shorter, darker, but there was no mistaking her eyes, those cheekbones. Or the *FBI* written in clear, dark letters.

FBI.

Tucker darted a glance at what she held. Started to swear. "Chapman, you get me in the worst messes. The fucking *FBI*?"

Dragging her gaze up, she ignored the steadily increasing pressure on her mind as she threw the ID back at the woman. Then she turned on her heel.

FBI or not, she was going inside.

This had waited long enough.

* * *

As Dru spun on her heel and stalked off, Joss swore.

He hadn't gotten much more than fractured glances at her mind, but the images he'd gotten . . .

Look deeper.

Yeah. He'd looked deeper. Not deep enough, but he'd seen . . . well, he'd seen some things he hadn't expected.

He'd felt her misery—that sudden, gut-wrenching betrayal when she'd seen him at the party . . . *he's one of them* . . .

And he'd seen her escape from Whitmore's mansion. And an escape it had been, no doubt about it. If she'd planned an escape, then she hadn't been there to marry that fucking monster.

"She's been trying to stop him, hasn't she?" he asked grimly.

"Now you're starting to figure it out. I knew you could do it." Nalini smiled at him.

He decided he really, really didn't like her. Shooting a look at the two in the SUV, he focused on them. "How long will they stay moon-eyed?"

Nalini shrugged. "If I'm around, awhile. Once I'm gone? Not long."

"You won't be around." He focused. Pushed. One of them groaned, harsh and broken. The other just lapsed into unconsciousness, a fine line of blood trickling out of his nose.

"Get in," he growled, staring down the road, following the shadowy figures of Dru and her companion as they ran through the night.

"You're not helping matters any, you know," Nalini said as she slipped into the front seat.

"Shut up."

"I don't respond well to that," she said, shrugging. She stared out the window. "She's been working this for a long time. Months. Longer, I think."

Curling his lip, he asked, "And you know that how?"

"You might have a mad power crammed inside that hard skull of yours, and it might let you read minds—obviously, she's blocking you. But she can't block the flow of her energy—can't stop the pain and the misery. I read *that*. And the very heart of her is tied into this. She's ready to die to see this through."

Ready to die—fury punched through him. He'd lost her once . . . not again.

"You'll lose her again."

"Stop it," he growled. "Just fucking stop."

"Unless you stop feeling, I can't." Then she shrugged. "But since you're determined to screw this up, I'll be quiet."

He gave her a dirty look as he twisted the key.

Nothing happened.

Not a damn thing.

Nalini started to laugh. "Oh. Now *that* is cool."

Twisting his head to look at her, he lifted a brow and waited. When she didn't respond, he finally just asked, "What's cool?"

"Oh, come on now. You had to feel it—that weird little popping thing? It was the dude back there. He fucks with electricity, has to be. And he just shut down your car."

* * *

FBI.

But he'd taken another woman . . .

Shutting off that flow of thoughts, Dru skirted around

through the shadows, trying to avoid the people she could barely make out.

Every now and then, Tucker would grab her arm, jerk her to a stop. Then she'd feel that odd energy spark from him. Damn, he was handy to have around. She was panting, edgy by the time they hit the first building. Leaning against it, she sucked in a breath of air like she'd been running for hours instead of minutes.

Tucker rested a hand on the back of her neck. "We've knocked down about six of their men, not including the two guards," he said, leaning over to murmur in her ear. "There's another fifteen here, but I dunno who is a guard and who is just one of the victims."

She wasn't going to ask him how he had such an exact number. Apparently he had a number of tricks up his sleeve.

Nodding, she took another breath and then straightened, turned to look at the building.

"Joss took somebody in here," she said quietly. "I know he did. If he's federal . . . maybe it was a plant."

And both Joss and the woman had freaky-ass gifts.

Glancing at the low, squat building, she thought. Hard. Then she turned to Tucker. The first time they'd met, she'd known he was like her. Had felt it. Like Joss, he'd been a burn on her brain. Not as intense, nowhere near, but it had been there.

But he'd sensed it on an even deeper level. They'd been working the same case, hired by different parties, working toward a common goal. He'd realized she had a gift—had felt it, he later told her. So he'd sought her out.

"Can you tell if there's somebody like us in there?" she asked.

Tucker gave her a pained look.

"You're killing me, Chapman." He scrubbed his gloved hands over his face.

Then he looked at her, sighed.

"I can tell you that." Joss appeared out of the darkness at her back, the woman at his side.

The low, rasping sound of his voice was a stroke over her skin. One she didn't need. She sensed what he was going to do before he even did it, and she tried to twist away, but . . . too late.

His hand curled over the back of her neck.

Stunned by the shock of it, she tried to jerk away, but he held her too firmly, his other hand coming up to wrap around her upper body.

No. *Oh, no.* Just who in the hell did he think he was, touching her now, like he had a right to? She reached up, grabbing his arm.

Flash, flash, flash.

A woman. The woman she'd glimpsed in the picture he'd shown Patrick. But now she was in a room. Dru recognized the setup. A guy in a suit. A crime board. *You're sure this will work?* the suit asked.

Fuck, no. But do you have any better suggestions? Joss demanded.

The woman, the one Dru had thought Joss had kidnapped, smiled. *Stop looking so worried. It's going to be fun for me for a little while. After all, I get to hit you in that pretty face of yours . . .*

Groaning, Dru severed the connection.

But Joss still held her. "Let me go," she said hoarsely. She could feel that connection trying to reestablish itself and she had to get away.

"You're not barreling in there blind," he said flatly. "This is a federal investigation and—"

Snarling, she dropped and pivoted, trying to throw him off.

It didn't do much good, because he moved with her and now she was pinned against the building, with that big, heavy body pressed against her. "Stop it, Dru," he rasped against her ear. "It looks like you want this done as much as I do, but I'm not risking this getting fucked up."

"You want it done?" A hysterical laugh burning in her throat.

Memories of all the pain she'd taken. The abuse. The times she'd allowed Patrick to hit her, and she'd just *taken* it. All so she could be *here*. Right here . . . finding a way to stop him.

"You have no idea how badly I need this," she said, and the misery from all the past months tried to crush her. Her shields fractured. She felt bits and pieces of herself slipping out, and desperate, she clung to them. "Let me go, damn it. Just let me—"

"Not until you get ahold of yourself—"

From behind them, Tucker spoke up. "Actually . . ."

Joss went rigid.

From the corner of her eye, Dru saw Tucker, that fine line appearing between his brows. "You're going to let her go now, or I'm going to fuck you up in so many different ways," Tucker said, his voice lazy. Easy. But there was a storm in his eyes.

"Stay the—"

A strangled groan was all that escaped him after that and his body went rigid.

Dru wiggled her way out from his grip, moving to stand by Tucker, eyeing Joss narrowly. He was pale, eyes glittering like black ice in the night. And the woman, she was watching it all with the keen interest of a hawk watching her prey.

"Here's what we need to do," Tucker said easily. "I can't hold you forever without killing you. And I'd rather not do that. But if you put your hands on her again, that's what I'll do."

A growl escaped Joss.

Tucker arched his brows and slipped his hands into his pockets.

"This is a federal investigation now," the blonde said.

"Tough shit." Tucker shrugged. "There's information inside her head that you all probably don't have. And if you keep dicking around, people are going to die."

And then the next card was thrown.

A voice, clear and sharp, rang through their minds, so loud, it practically rattled their brains. *The guards just arrived. With guns. Big, ugly guns with silencers. That cleanup protocol apparently isn't a myth.*

Dru closed her eyes, not even wondering why in the hell some unknown woman was speaking into her mind. She turned, ready to run into the building.

But Tucker continued to stand there, holding Joss. "Are you done?"

* * *

WHATEVER it was freezing his brain, it was like a boa constrictor or something, and it loosened just enough that he was able to snarl out, "For now."

Then it was gone. Whatever weird energy that had been freezing him, pressing in on him and sucking out his ability to move, even *think*, it was just gone.

He could move, could think. Although he could barely breathe . . . flickers from Dru's mind danced through his own and he wanted to kill. So badly, it was a scream in his brain. He tightened his hand on his weapon, but the object of his wrath wasn't here.

It had to wait, though. Had to, because he hadn't been able to miss the urgency in Vaughnne's voice.

"Where are you, Vaughnne?" he asked.

Two of them, Dru and her companion, gave him startled looks. Nalini just checked her weapon.

Just start moving. I'll get you here the best I can.

Not very reassuring, that. But it would have to work. They were now on borrowed time.

The red-haired son of a bitch studied him and Nalini before tugging off his pack. A few seconds later, night-vision goggles hit his chest. When he looked back at him, the guy just smiled. "Me and lights don't always mesh well. I like to be prepared."

"Imagine that," Joss muttered as he put them on. Glaring at the other man, he asked, "You got a name?"

"Sure. Call me Tucker."

Tucker. *Asshole* suited him better, Joss figured.

Somehow said asshole ended up in front. Twice, they had to stop and Joss felt that power rip through the night, those little *pop, pop, pop*s . . . it seemed so innocuous, but it was like the force of a hurricane trapped inside one drop of rain.

Once, Tucker caught somebody—he moved so fast, Joss barely saw what he did as he jerked off one glove, then laid his hand on the guy's throat. Light flashed between them—the light had *glowed*. Just . . . emanated from Tucker's hand, flowed into the other man's neck. A second later, Tucker let him go and the man crashed to the ground like a fallen tree.

Joss didn't know if he was dead, but at the moment, he couldn't even let himself worry about it.

More people. Too many, milling in the darkness, panicking, shouting for flashlights, screaming about phones. Too many. Joss used his gun to club one of them over the back of his head. Nalini, with her devious little smile, laid her hands on the two closest to her, and they slid to the floor with a smile. He turned to check on Dru as the agent pulled a couple of cable ties from her belt.

Dru was nowhere to be found.

Vaughnne?

He felt the whisper of her thoughts in his mind. Distracted. Flooded with tension.

He reached for Dru mentally. Came up smack against her shields, felt her rebuff. And was just fine with it, because she was okay. Somewhere in the dark maw of this squalid hellhole.

TWENTY-FOUR

SHE followed her gut.

There was a miasma of fear and horror, and that was the path she followed.

Twice, she had to duck inside a doorway as she heard people coming. When she was slipping out of the doorway a second time, she crashed into a hard male chest. Immediately, she panicked and went to head-butt him, only to have Tucker jerk his head back out of range at the very last second.

"Ease up, sugar," he murmured, absently stroking a hand down her hair.

"Fuck me," she said, her voice harsh. Edgy.

"Oh, will you? What do you say, when this is over?" he teased.

"Ha, ha." As her heart continued to race, she let herself lean against him for a minute. Solid, sturdy, there. The one person she knew she could count on, thank God. Through the thin material of his T-shirt, she could feel the heat of him—the *burning* heat. "You're bloody burning hot."

He gave her a playful leer. "That's what all the pretty girls say."

"So damned insistent to get in here but you've got time to stand around flirting," Joss said, his voice not much more than a snarl as he came around the corner.

"Piss off," she said, turning to stare down the hall. Tucker laid his hand on her shoulder.

Joss went to say something and then he stopped, shook his head. "Five more ahead . . . they're hurting. Somebody's screaming."

Dru looked at him. "I don't hear screaming."

"Aw, *shit*."

* * *

HUDDLING up in the seat, Taige Morgan clamped her hands over her ears and whimpered as the scream echoed through her mind. Loud. Endless. No human could scream like this, not using their vocal chords, because at some point, they needed to breathe.

A hand curled over her shoulder, shaking her.

"Damn it, Taige, snap out of it," Taylor shouted.

She groaned. Tried to push her shields up, but that scream just carried on. And on.

"If you don't snap out of it, I'm going to use that damn Taser on you."

"Kiss ass," she gasped. And still the scream raged.

Shield. Had to.

One thin, shaky layer.

Then another.

Finally, by the time she was establishing a fourth, she had a little bit of peace in her mind, and she could almost hear herself thinking. Almost. "Who the hell did you put in there?"

"Vaughnne."

"I'm going to punch her," Taige said fervently. "I don't know her. I don't want to know her. But I'm going to hit her."

"If she's making noise, it's because there's trouble."

Taige groaned, her head still ringing. "There'd better be. Or I'll *make* trouble."

Uncurling from the ball she'd drawn herself into, she sat up and stared out the window as Taylor slowed down. "I don't like doing this with just us."

"No time," Taylor said, shaking his head. "Wasn't supposed to go down this fast, and we're running on a shoestring these days as it is. If I had more intel, I could bring in one of the regular units, but—"

"It's just us."

She reached down and pulled her ID from her bag. She rarely used the damn thing anymore. Somehow, though, she couldn't just walk away from the unit entirely. Some part of her understood there would be times she knew she was needed, she guessed. Slipping the cord around her neck, she adjusted her jacket, her weapons. "It's damn dark in there," she murmured.

"Yes. And that's the truck Crawford is using."

* * *

THE screaming was about to drive Joss out of his mind until he managed to ice it down.

Yeah, yeah, the ice wasn't good, but he'd already figured out what he needed to figure out, and if he kept hearing the screaming, he was going to go insane, and how much good would he be *then*?

And he needed to come through this sane, because there were about two hundred and fifty thousand questions he needed answered. Couldn't do that if he was in the hospital getting treated for a mental breakdown.

Even through his shields, though, he heard the echo of that scream.

Nalini seemed fine.

Dru was unperturbed.

The redheaded guy looked a little off, but what did he know?

Then they came to a door, and both Dru and her guy—what were they to each other?—moved off to one side, standing close enough to touch, while the man studied Joss and Nalini with dark, stormy eyes. He angled his chin toward the door. "Damned federal op, you go in first," he said. His gaze dropped, eyeing the vests both he and Nalini had put on before they left the SUV.

Abruptly, he was all too aware of Dru's *lack* of a vest. Even the guy's. Too vulnerable.

Bad idea, bad idea.

"You two need to leave," he whispered.

"Oh, hell, no. Tucker, you with me?" Dru said, not even looking at Joss.

Shit. Shit. Shit—

The fervency of that scream increased and he knew there was no time. None at all.

"We go in first," Joss said.

Tucker skimmed a hand back over his hair, sighing. "Now wasn't that what I just said." He snagged Dru's arm, tugging her over.

Joss looked at Nalini. "High or low?"

"Low."

They stared at each other. Joss took a deep breath and then shoved open the door.

And stepped into hell.

* * *

VAUGHNNE had held it as long as she could.

She hadn't been joking when she told Joss she could turn his brain into a sieve, but it wouldn't be a fun exercise.

She'd tried just piercing their minds, doing that to hold them at bay, but one of them had been a psychic null.

As he'd moved on her, her control had faltered and she'd slipped up. Two of them were on the ground, convulsing and bleeding from their ears. And she had the memory of how it had felt to break their brains in her mind.

Fuck—

But at least she had a gun now, one with a nightscope . . . score. There were no lights in here, save for a few small, high windows.

Holding it steady on the man she considered to blame, she smiled.

"Put it down and I won't kill you," he said.

Oh, yeah. Like that was going to make her feel all warm and fuzzy.

There were still two others in the room, and they were recovering from her mental attack. She launched another one, swaying a little from the toll it took. "How about *you* put it down and I won't kill you?" she said.

"You're outnumbered," he said, shrugging. Then he glanced behind him, although how much he'd be able to see in the dim light, she didn't know.

His partners were still incapacitated, but not for much longer.

Hurry it up, Crawford, she all but screamed to the man on the other side of the door.

The women had huddled in the corner. Not willingly. She had to use sharp mental jabs on each of them, but if they'd moved, they'd be in the way. No innocent bystanders. Now they were as out of the way as they could be. Good thing, too.

It was show time.

"Not for long." She smiled.

She made sure to sever the connections with anybody and everybody as she turned and lunged for the other women.

Get down, Vaughnne. Get the other women down, Crawford warned.

We're down and ready. DO IT. She held her breath . . . said a prayer.

The door swung open.

She heard a muffled curse, followed by shots.

Then silence.

Joss's familiar, surly voice sliced the hair. "Vaughnne?"

Vaughnne sighed. Closed her eyes. It was over. She thought.

In her mind, she saw a face.

Sugar, I'm sorry I didn't get here in time . . . rest in peace, Dayline.

A light appeared close by, too bright, paining her eyes. "Point that somewhere else, Crawford," she groaned. A headache slammed into her as Joss crouched at her side. His eyes, harsh and unblinking, were narrowed, watchful. She didn't care.

Her part was done.

She'd finished her job. What she'd set out to do.

End of—

Barely able to hold on to consciousness, she whispered, "Jones?"

"Getting ready to call," he said, his voice softer, a little gentler.

Vaughnne grimaced. Couldn't black out, not yet. What if it wasn't safe?

Sweeping out with her mind, she felt . . . yes. "He's coming. Close."

With a groan, she sank into the black depths of agony.

TWENTY-FIVE

"THAT sure as hell is a lot of federal-type-looking people," Tucker muttered.

"Yes." Dru stood off to the side, arms crossed over her chest, eyeing the busy hive of people in front of them with a worried gaze. Slanting a look at Tucker, she murmured, "You should leave, shouldn't you?"

He jerked a shoulder. "I'm fine."

"No, you're not." He'd always done his damnedest to avoid any sort of government type, and she'd pulled him into this. Unwittingly, yes, but she'd done it just the same. "Go on, Tuck. I can handle this."

"If you're going to go down for any of this, I'm going, too," he said, sighing.

Dru sighed. "I won't go down for anything, darling, I promise." She skimmed the crowd with a studied eye. There were more than a few dead bodies, and she knew by the blank look in

Tucker's eyes just how those bodies had come to be *dead*. "I think we're clear here, although they may try to jerk us around. If you're not here to jerk, you'll be fine. Just go lose yourself again." She leaned over, hugged him. The heat she'd felt from him earlier had dissipated, leaving his skin oddly cool. Chilled. "I know how to find you if I need you, mate."

"You do at that." He bent down, brushed his mouth against hers. "If you're certain . . ."

"Yes." *Flash, flash, flash* . . . fear, guilt. All wrapped up in leaving. Running, the way he saw it.

But Tucker had spent a good, long time in hiding. He wasn't going to come out easily. She knew that.

"You best go. They won't stay busy for long," she murmured as he drew back.

"Yeah." He glanced at her, and then back behind him.

A few people glanced their way. He gave her a wild, reckless grin. "I'll bust my way clear if I need to."

She smiled a little sadly.

"Have at it. And if you feel the need for another one of those distractions . . . be my guest."

No sooner had he slipped away than those FBI-looking types decided to amble in her direction. Slowly at first. Then faster. She wasn't too terribly surprised when the maroon SUV still sitting at the entrance to the gate started to smoke. The fire started a few seconds later.

She continued to stand there, arms crossed, staring at the ground, while the engine exploded into flames.

See you around, Tucker.

Part of her wanted to go with him.

But she was no longer on this job just to see the slave ring shut down.

She had to see Whitmore go down, too. Go down in a fiery, burning blaze of glory.

That was the only reason . . .

A rush of adrenaline burst through her. Her breath caught in her throat. Jerking her head up, she searched the grounds. The agents had set up field lights all over the place and she could see clearly. Too clearly, considering who was bearing down on her.

The badge hanging around his neck didn't do much to set her mind at ease.

So. He was FBI.

She remembered the power she'd glimpsed in his mind. Maybe she should have had a little more faith in him, but she'd operated on the information her mind had given her. She didn't *know* him.

She could still remember that lapse she'd had. The dream, how she'd unconsciously reached out to him.

And his response. So flat, and cold. *I don't want you anymore.*

Asshole. She couldn't see inside his head, but she knew he could have looked inside hers if he'd tried. He just hadn't bothered. So much for her being worth it. Tears threatened, but she shoved them back.

Not the time. Or the place. She'd break once she was out of this mess, in some place nice and private.

"Where is he?" he demanded, once he was close enough.

Of course, he didn't stop. Four feet wasn't close enough apparently. He kept coming until he was right in her space, just a few inches away, so that the warmth of his body reached out to tease hers.

"Who?" she asked. With a mean little smile, she rose up onto her toes and pressed her lips to his ear. "If you're asking about my dearest fiancé, I'm trying to break up with him. But it isn't going well. However, I can't tell you where he is."

"Not him," he growled. "And you know it. Where is your sidekick? Tucker whoever?"

"Tucker . . . my sidekick." She smiled a little. "Oh, he'd like that. Do I get to wear some sexy little vinyl suit? Can *he* wear vinyl, too? Black, I think. Or maybe dark gray. He'd look smashing in gray, especially with those eyes. Sleeveless, if we can, because I'm rather fond of his tats."

A snarl quivered on his lips. "Dru . . . don't push me. We need to talk to him. He's part of the investigation."

"No." She leaned back against the fence, studying her nails. "He's not. Anything *he* knows, I know. He was just here to help me if I got into a jam. Now he's gone and I've no idea where you can find him."

"Damn it, Dru!"

With a patience she really didn't feel, she sighed again. "Yelling at me just isn't going to help any, you know. Not at all." She turned away from the fury burning in his eyes, but before she could move, the exhaustion she felt slammed into her and she swayed.

His hands, big and hard, caught her shoulders.

Shrugging him away, she tried to pull free. "Let me go."

"Not likely."

You don't have a choice, she thought bitterly. She jerked away with a fury that surprised her, but her legs were clumsy, heavy, and she would have gone to the ground if he hadn't caught her a second time.

"Stop it," he growled. "You're exhausted, about ready to pass out. When was the last time you ate a damn thing? When was the last time you slept?"

She curled her lip, fighting the urge to say something really, really ugly. Fighting the urge to hit him, but if she did, that hard skull of his might break her hand. Bastard. Fucking bastard. "It hardly concerns you, does it? My personal business? Don't you have a job to see to, Agent Crawford?" she asked, keeping her voice as flat as she could.

A muscle jerked in his jaw. "Now that's where you're wrong. It concerns me in all kinds of ways." He raked her with a critical eye and then turned his head. "Kingsley!"

Somebody separated himself from the mess of people. "Yeah?"

"Get her a chair. And sit on her. If she tries to leave, cuff her."

Dru narrowed her eyes. "And exactly what right do you have?"

Although she knew they had all sorts of reasons to detain her. Jerking his chain wasn't going to do much good. Except . . . well, it made her feel better.

"I could start listing them, but we'd be here all morning, noon, and night," Joss drawled. "And I don't know about you, but I want to wrap it up here so we can focus on your *fiancé*."

A look of disgust crossed his face as he said it. One that cut her to the bone.

She turned away, wrapping her arms around her middle. She'd done what she had to do. There was information she could present them with, and would. Once she was able to get to it . . . of her own free will.

If that made her seem less in their eyes, that was their problem.

* * *

It was hours later when Taylor caught up with Joss.

"Go back to the hotel."

"Still got too much to do here," he said, shaking his head. In all honesty, part of him didn't want to leave because he wasn't sure what to do about Dru. Part of him was also hoping for two things . . . her cowardly little friend Tucker would come back. Or maybe Whitmore would appear.

Neither was going to happen, though. And he had to have

some kind of reason to keep up with Dru. He was terrified she'd disappear, like dust in the wind.

"Ms. Chapman isn't going to disappear," Taylor said. "She's spent too much time on this."

Slanting a look at a man he trusted more than just about anybody else, he studied Taylor's face. "Won't she?"

"Not until she sees this through. She stuck with it too long. She's . . . you've figured out the fact that she's been working this on her own, right?"

Rage, frustration, guilt twisted inside him as he looked away. "Yeah. I got that far on my own. Would have been nice if you could have gotten me that information a bit sooner."

"We had a lot going on," Taylor pointed out. "And if you'd . . . shit. Look, I don't know what the deal is here, but this isn't done for her. I know people. She's not done." Then he grimaced. "Although she's pretty much done in for now. She needs some rest, and I doubt she wants to go back to the place Whitmore had her at, even if it *was* safe to do—which it's not. Take her to the hotel. Have them put her in a room. I'll cover it."

Joss passed a hand over his mouth. Oh, he'd put her in a room all right.

His room.

They'd have this out.

"Ah, I don't have a car."

Taylor tossed his keys. "Take mine. Taige and I'll be here for a while, and we'll catch a ride back with somebody from the team when we're done."

Tossing the keys from one hand to the other, he hesitated a moment longer. "Vaughnne?"

"In the hospital, resting. Exhaustion, mostly. She overdid it this time, but she'll be fine. Nalini is with her." Somebody called his name, and he glanced back for a moment before looking at Joss. "Go. Now. Before I make it an order."

"I think you just did."

Weariness dragged at him as he and Taylor separated, the SAC heading back to the crime scene, Joss moving back to his woman. His woman.

This was killing him.

What in the hell was going on?

He'd just adjusted and reshaped his mind to what he *thought* was the reality, and now reality had just done a number on him and jump-kicked him right in the face.

Working it privately. On her own. Damn it, for how long? How could she have gotten so deep in a job like this? Did she have any idea how *dangerous* Whitmore was?

Those images flared to life, dancing through his mind.

So vivid and dark, twisted. Fear. Pain. Shame. They grabbed him by the throat, and for a moment, he was almost sick from them.

Up ahead, some thirty feet, she was sitting there, all but ready to fall asleep, and if he knew anything, it was nothing but will keeping her eyes open. Will, determination.

Rubbing the heel of his hand over his heart, he blew out a breath.

She knew, all right. All this time, she'd been doing this alone, and she knew how risky it was. But it hadn't stopped her.

He wouldn't let anything stop him, either.

They'd waited too long. Focusing on her, only her, he made himself move, closing the distance between them as he mentally rehearsed something, anything, to say to her.

Kingsley, the agent he'd put at her back, gave him a look. "You can go. I'm taking her to a hotel to get some rest."

Dru tipped her head back, studying him through her lashes. "And if I'm not interested?" she asked, biting off each word.

"I don't much care if you're interested," he replied. *Okay, that wasn't smooth*, he thought. But she needed to get some rest. Standing there, arms crossed, he waited.

She didn't move.

Bending over her, he whispered, "You're either going to get your sweet little ass out of that chair, or I'll just throw you over my shoulder. Trust me, duchess, nobody here will be surprised."

He almost wished she'd push him. He felt like if he could just get his hands on her, maybe he could figure out a way to undo what he'd done. Fix what he'd broken. There had to be a way. He'd fucked up, damn it, and he was just starting to realize how badly.

But after a long, cool look, she heaved out a sigh. A very aggravated, disgusted sigh that made it clear she'd rather go anywhere, be anywhere but with him. "If I must," she said, rising. The sleek black running tights she wore clung to her legs like a glove, and as she turned around, he wanted to jerk off his shirt, cover her with it to make sure nobody else was looking at her.

She paused and looked over her shoulder at him. "You are coming, correct? I'm not going to walk to this hotel?"

Sucking back the instinctive response, he moved to join her. It was a forty-minute drive to the Peabody. He could figure out what to say. He could find the *right* thing to say.

Level things out between them.

Then he'd get a little bit of sleep. Cuff her to the bed. Get his ass back out in the field and track down Whitmore, beat him bloody.

It sounded, all in all, like a fantastic plan.

He needed sleep, after all.

Figured if he cuffed her to the bed, she'd still be there when he got back. And Whitmore, well, that fucker needed to be beaten. He actually needed to die, but it would be hard to do that and not screw up the case. If the case wasn't already screwed.

* * *

"ALL of them," Patrick said.

Minton's eyes jerked off to the side and his throat worked. After two unsuccessful starts, he finally managed to say something. "Nobody can get close to the compound, sir. The place is surrounded by feds."

"And the cameras?"

"None of them are operational."

Patrick nodded, stroking a hand down Demeter's head. The cat purred and butted her head against Patrick's hand. Happy. Satisfied. All the little cat wanted was food and attention. And she was pleased. If only everybody else were that simple to satisfy.

Ella . . .

"And has anybody seen Ella?"

He cut a look to Rawlings, curled up in a ball on the floor, blood flowing from so many cuts and lacerations, his face bruised beyond recognition. His brother, a weasely, smarmy little bastard that Patrick had no use for, lay dead on the other side of the room. He'd thought Larry was perhaps the one who'd gone to the police. He was always looking for money, but he had an eye for girls and had managed to find Whitmore a few choice pieces by doing a tourist bit—ghost walks, fortune telling. Petty things, but it worked.

It hadn't been him. He'd killed Larry to make a point with the brother . . . and he still wasn't done. Rawlings had let Ella escape.

"No." Minton cleared his throat and darted a look to the door, like he really didn't want to be there. Patrick didn't imagine he did.

Too fucking bad. Already he had others scrambling to clean things up, cover things. He had time, he knew. Nobody could connect the compound to him. It was several miles away, not purchased in his name, but he needed to be cautious nonetheless.

Getting out of the country had to come first. Although he really, really wanted to take care of those loose ends.

Like Ella.

She'd gotten away.

That was one problem that needed to be addressed.

Reaching for his phone, he punched in a number. She was a loose end he couldn't afford, and he was going to make sure she didn't come back to bite him.

* * *

No words were coming.

That was a problem, Joss knew, because they needed to fuck-ing talk.

But no words, no brilliant explanation or clever twists, were coming.

And there, right up ahead, he saw the turn for International Drive. Meaning he was running out of time.

Clearing his throat, he glanced over at Dru as he slowed at the light. He'd just brazen his way through. He'd done that through just about every area of life; he could do it now, right?

A soft, sighing little sound escaped her.

He blinked, squinted, certain he was seeing things.

No. Ah, shit.

Somebody behind him laid on the horn. Joss responded the only way that was appropriate. He flipped him off as he checked the light, after one last glance at Dru.

Asleep.

How in the hell could she have fallen asleep?

But there she was. Making those soft, kittenish little sounds under her breath as she shifted on the seat, snuggling against the leather like she just couldn't find a comfortable enough position but damned if she'd let that stop her.

Sleeping. While he was sitting there, brooding and thinking so hard his head felt like it was about to come apart as he tried to figure out how to fix this.

Isn't this just fucking perfect . . .

He pulled up in front of the hotel and climbed out. As the valet came around, Joss tossed the keys at him. Taylor may or may not like having somebody else park his snazzy little car, but Joss sort of had his hands full. Or would in a second. It occurred to him then, as he opened the door and knelt by Dru, studying her wan face, if she didn't wake up, he didn't have to worry about getting her another room, right?

Gingerly, he slid one arm under her. She immediately rolled toward him, curling into him like she'd just been waiting for the chance. It hit him, square in the chest, like somebody had swung a lead weight at him. The warmth of her, the feel, the scent of her. All of it. *Finally . . .*

Turning his face into her hair, he squeezed his eyes closed. *Finally . . .*

Then, because he needed to have a chance to say it, even if she wasn't awake, he murmured, "I'm sorry, duchess. I'm so damn sorry."

She mumbled under her breath, the words thick and heavy, indistinct. Then, she shoved her face against his neck, as though she wanted to block out everything. Including him.

"Okay, sweet girl. You sleep." She apparently needed it. Hell, how long had it been since she'd rested? It was pretty clear she realized what a dangerous game she'd been involved in. She had to have known.

Hooking her bag on his elbow, he rose, cradling her against his chest. He took another second to kick the door shut and then he headed into the hotel, taking just enough time to look around. Although he suspected he'd feel it if there was a problem, he wasn't about to turn his back on years of training. Especially not now, with the precious burden he carried.

The walk to the elevator, then to the room, somehow seemed to both take hours, and end in just seconds. He was all too aware of his own exhaustion catching up with him, all too aware of the fact that he still didn't know what he'd say. All too aware of the fact that he needed to figure it out.

By the time he hit his hotel room, though, it was pretty clear she wasn't going to be waking up.

The room was quiet, clean as a whistle. The clothes he'd left behind several days earlier were exactly where he'd left them, although it was obvious the housekeeping staff had been in there in the meantime. He scowled at the neatly made bed, looked at Dru's face. Scowled at the bed again, and then sat near the foot, leaning upward to snag the comforter and sheets, dragging them down with one hand so he wouldn't have to let her go.

Not ever . . . you hear me, he thought, rubbing his cheek against her hair. *Not ever letting you go. Not if I have anything to do about it.*

A fine line formed between her eyes, and she made another one of those grumbling little sounds under her breath, turning her face into his chest.

Okay. They'd save all of that for later.

Rising, he laid her down on the bed, taking a few minutes to strip her shoes off, and then, because he wasn't about to risk it, he also searched her for weapons. She had a slim-fitting holster under the top she wore, with a gun. He took that, along with a knife that had been tucked into a sheath on the holster. Those, combined with a couple of weapons in her bag, he locked inside the in-room safe. She probably wouldn't leave without her weapons. But he wasn't going to take that chance.

He kept his cuffs with him, although he did lock his own weapon up in the safe. Barely any room left in there, he thought. A quick trip to the bathroom, then he brushed his teeth, washed his face. After that, the only other thing he bothered with was kicking off his shoes and shucking his shirt.

Joss didn't trust himself to do anything else; he kept his jeans on. Slipping into the bed beside her, he pushed up onto his elbow, staring down into her still face. There was little expression on it now. None of those odd little mutters, no sign that she dreamed. Nothing.

Just deep, deep sleep.

Again, he wondered how long it had been since she'd rested.

Maybe, just maybe, she'd sleep long enough for him to think his way out of this mess.

Although he wasn't going to bet on it.

With that in mind, he pulled the cuffs out of his back pocket. Cuffing her right hand to his left, he lay back. Closed his eyes. Sleep. He was going to sleep.

Nothing else . . .

He wasn't going to think about her sleek, warm body lying just inches away. They needed to talk. Needed to work through this mess.

And he wasn't going to touch her until they'd done that.

The bed shifted.

Joss caught his breath as the cuffs rattled. Then she moved, wiggling closer, her face pressed against his arm, her free hand on his belly. Another one of those soft, disgruntled little sighs.

Hell. It was going to be a very, very restless long—

He dropped straight into sleep, like a rock thrown into the bottom of a well.

*   *   *

HER clothes still hung in the closet.

Her makeup case rested by the sink.

Her scent still hung in the air.

And her engagement ring was on the floor. Like she'd just dropped it.

Discarded it.

Patrick stared at it, fury pulsing inside him. Women didn't *discard* him.

The little whore would pay for this.

The phone in his pocket vibrated and he reached for it. He no longer had the luxury to avoid calls. He was calling in favors, resorting to blackmail and bribes, just so he could be ready. So far, it didn't look like they had traced the compound back to him, but it was just a matter of time and he needed to finish clearing out before it happened.

He was almost completely packed.

He had his passport.

In just a few more hours, he'd be on a plane to Morocco. That was just his first stop. After that, he wasn't sure where he'd go. But he'd like to have some company. Ella. He'd like to have Ella.

The phone buzzed again and he answered with a terse, "Yes?"

"There's no sign of her at any of the airports. She hasn't rented a car. The bus terminals are harder to watch, but it doesn't appear she's taken that route, either."

"Look harder," Patrick said quietly.

"I'm doing what I can." There was a pause and then the man

on the other end asked, "Does she have any friends here? Anybody who could help her?"

Patrick frowned. There had been a man glimpsed on his property, but nobody had a physical description and none of the cameras were operational. There was no telling who it was. "She's been isolated since she came here. All phone calls were monitored. If she had friends, it's your job to find them."

"I'll keep searching. I think I'll do a deeper dig on personal details."

"Do whatever the fuck you want," Patrick bit off. "Just *find* her." He checked the time on his watch. "I'll be leaving in eight hours. If you find her before that, I'll double your fee. But you're to keep looking, regardless. I'll be in touch."

TWENTY-SIX

S HE dreamed.
    She knew she dreamed.

Sleep held her in its tight, captive fist, and she couldn't have broken free if she tried.

In the dream, she stood at a place so familiar, it almost hurt to see it. It was the first time it had ever been this clear, though.

The lake.

Swallowing around the knot in her throat, she stared out over the lake and remembered. Almost everything, it seemed. Bits and pieces drifting into her mind, settling into place as she stood on the shore.

It was like she stood on the edges of two places in time.

Two realities maybe.

In one reality, she saw the place as it was. She'd been here once. Following a dead-end lead. Two girls had been seen in this area . . . one had been the girl she'd been searching for . . . Sarah

Hale, the runaway she'd been hired to find. Or at least somebody resembling her. And then Daylin Crosby.

Dru had never found any sign of them, but this place had freaked her out. Oddly enough, this was where she'd met up with Tucker again. He'd been prowling around the lake and they'd all but bumped into each other.

"I don't want to be here." She turned away from the lake to stare at the warehouse. It was old and vacant, covered with so much graffiti, the walls were barely visible under it. Perched on the edge of the lake. It was a travesty to see, really.

Because in the other reality, this place had been lovely. She stood there, remembering. Because all of those dreams, all those echoes of memory . . . they'd been real.

It was hot. Oppressively so, and she hated it. But she couldn't make herself pull away from the dream. She could make herself stop it . . . if she had the will. She recognized that it was just a dream . . . a powerful one. And yes, there were bits and pieces of something that was *more*.

Yet it was simply a dream and she couldn't be held captive in this, not if she didn't allow it.

When he appeared behind her, she sighed and shoved her sticky, sweaty hair back from her face. "You know . . . since this is my dream, it seems that I should have a little bit of control. I don't want to see you. So you should just go *poof* . . . and disappear."

Big, muscled arms wrapped around her waist.

"Yeah? How is that theory working for you?"

Scowling, she twisted away from him, breaking his hold. Putting a few feet between them didn't help. Turning around to glare at him didn't help, either. It was just another strike to her already battered heart. She was relieved, though, to see that he looked like he should. Like Joss. That harsh, craggy face; short, dark hair; and those near-black eyes that stared at her like he could

see right through her. So if he looked like he should . . . she dared
a look down and saw her meager breasts, the long, familiar lines
of her body.

Good. Very good, indeed. She had enough on her mind without having to deal with the body of the woman she'd been.

Shooting him a dark look, she said tiredly, "Well, you haven't
gone *poof,* so clearly the theory isn't working at all."

Plucking her shirt away from her sweaty chest, she turned
back to the lake.

"Do you know this place?" she asked quietly.

"Vaguely." He moved once more to stand behind her. But this
time, he didn't touch her. "You're sad, Dru. Why are you sad?"

Why . . . oh, why, indeed . . .

Lifting a hand, she pointed to the loading dock, just a few
yards away. In the strange, shifting realities, she could see it as it
had been. Then, it had been green. Impossibly green. Until the
ground ran wet with blood. "He killed you there."

A harsh breath gusted out of him.

"Amelie . . ."

Dru shook her head. "Don't call me that name," she said.
"That's not who I am. Whoever she was, whoever I might have
been, that's not who I am now."

She turned her head and stared at him. "I thought you remembered all of this."

His eyes glittered as he stared at her.

"I remember *you,*" he rasped. "More than anything, I remember you. Everything else was just dust in the wind. Then it was all
gone."

"Dust in the wind," she murmured. "Apt, I suppose." She
eased around him, careful not to touch. The words he'd spoken
to her were still a broken, jagged wound on her heart and she just
couldn't handle it.

"You remember more."

"Just now." She continued toward that spot, the ache inside growing. Spreading. "He killed you. I don't remember what it was about. I guess it doesn't matter after all of this time . . . although . . ."

She stopped and spun to look at him, head cocked. "Do you know who he is?"

A muscle jerked in his jaw, throbbing.

"I guess you do," she murmured. Absently, she reached up, touched the back of her hand to her cheek. Remembered the few times he'd hit her. All the times he'd hurt her. Whether it was one of the rapes, or the way he had of grabbing her wrist and squeezing, just hard enough to make the bones grind together.

And how often she'd yearned to make him stop. She could have. So many times. In so many ways. She'd had reasons, she knew that. But now . . .

It was so much harder to take now.

"I always had trouble sleeping," she said, giving him her back and continuing on her walk to the place where he'd died. Where Thom had died. All those years ago. "Nightmares I couldn't remember. Awful dreams. Waking up with fits of choking. Or just crying. But none of it made sense. Then I came back here and I met him. The first time he touched me, I had this awful, horrid sensation . . . death."

"He can't hurt you now," Joss growled. "He can't hurt you ever again."

Dru smiled sadly. "Oh, I'm not worried about him *now*. If it hadn't been for the job, for what I had to do, he never would have hurt me to begin with. I was counting, you know. Every time he touched me. Every time he hurt me, scared me. Threatened me. All of it . . . and I promised myself I'd bloody him. He doesn't worry me *now*," she said, her voice savage. "But then . . ."

It hit her in a rush, breath stealing. The cold water. The heaviness of her dress. She'd never learned how to swim. The weight of her skirts, dragging her down. Choking on the water. And Thom . . . in her mind, she'd felt so guilty because even though she'd longed to be with him . . . had been ready to end her own life, even . . . yes. She remembered even that. The knife she'd tucked into her purse . . . no. Reticule. It had been called a reticule. She'd had it in her bag and was thinking about killing herself. Debating over it even as she tried to convince herself there were other options. Cousins . . . she'd had cousins up north . . . yes. More memories breaking free.

Then Richard—

Big hands, hard, strong . . . but so gentle closed over her shoulders, forcing her to turn. She found herself staring at the black T-shirt stretching over his wide chest. A nice chest, all in all. She wanted to lean against him and just rest. Close her eyes for a while and rest.

"What's going on, Dru? There's something in your eyes . . ."

"Memories," she whispered.

"Dru," he growled. He cupped her chin and some of his gentleness was lost under his frustration. As he pushed his hand into her hair, he moved in closer, crowding his body against hers. "Talk to me, damn it."

Talk to me . . .

How did she tell him this?

Sighing, she reached up and closed her hand over his wrist, thinking to tug him away. It would be easier, she thought. If she wasn't touching him. But instead, she found herself curling her fingers around him tighter . . . clinging to him. Closing her eyes, she leaned in and pressed her head to his chest. "It was here," she murmured again. "All those dreams, it all comes back to this place. I saw him kill you here. And I sat by your side, and watched. You told me to run, but I couldn't leave you . . . then, when I tried to stay away from him, he wouldn't let me."

She swallowed. "All those details are fuzzy, but he wouldn't let me go. I have memories of coming back here. Day after day. And then one day, he was here. He was angry . . . and then . . ."

A fist clamped around her throat and the words she tried to pushed out were trapped. Lodged there. Choking her. *Choking* . . .

"Dru!"

* * *

THE dream ended in a harsh, broken cry.

Jerking awake, Joss crouched over Dru and hauled her upright. Her eyes, still glazed with fear, stared into his.

Her mouth was slack, her breathing coming in harsh pants like she'd just gotten done running a marathon.

"Dru!"

She whimpered.

He went to touch her face and saw the cuffs. Growling, he used his free hand, cupping her cheek, leaning in and pressing his brow to hers. "Dru, what's wrong?"

She shook her head. "I . . . I can't . . ."

Odd bits and pieces of emotion splintered off her, and he eased his shields down, flinching as he realized just how faulty *her* shielding had become. "I can't, I can't, I can't . . ."

"Shhh . . ." he murmured, leaning in to kiss her.

And as their lips touched, another one of those splintered, broken emotions fell away. No. Not an emotion. Memory—

She was back at the lake, just as they'd been in the dream. Only it was Amelie . . . with another man. She wore a black dress, stood there with her hands folded in front of her, head bowed.

"I'm leaving, Richard."

"Leaving, are you?"

"Yes. Mama has family in Boston and I plan to spend the summer with them. I want to get away from this dreadful heat, visit with my cousins."

The man moved closer, dipped his head to murmur, "Amelie, dearest. Did you really think I'd let you leave me?" He struck her.

The woman's petite, delicate body went flying. She cried out, but when he approached her, she didn't cringe, didn't try to move away. She just lay there.

"I am leaving, Richard."

"Leaving . . . no. No, you aren't."

He bent over her and fisted a hand in her hair, jerked her upright. "I warned you what happens to those who defy me, Amelie, and you're no different. I'll ruin you. Your family. Everybody."

She laughed, the sound pained. "My father has already told me, you can't do what you seem to think. The sheriff has his people watching you already. And Papa was gone the week Thom disappeared, you stupid fool. So threaten me if you wish, but I am leaving."

He shoved her backward. "No. You are not."

And Amelie swung out her hands, struggling to catch her balance. Her slippered feet slid on the dock and then she plummeted. Straight down into the dark, cold, watery depths.

* * *

THERE wasn't enough whiskey in the world to get him through this, Joss figured.

So, for the first time since this had started, when the thought *I need a drink* rolled through his mind, he didn't bother.

Instead, as Dru cried, he held her against his chest and stared out the window, his gaze not tracking much of anything.

He'd killed her.

It was a hollow, empty ache in his gut, and it didn't matter that it was another life ago.

It felt like moments ago. Seconds ago. *Now.*

She'd died . . . and Joss hadn't been there to protect her.

Stroking his free hand up her back, he decided he'd rather be back in the predicament he'd been in before he'd gone to sleep. When he'd just been trying to figure out the right words to make her talk to him again. Yeah, when their main problem had been a cold-blooded slaver. Sure, there had been that weird little past-lives thing, but it had been something to put on the back burner.

Now it was a boiling, raging fire, one that threatened to suck him in and burn him alive.

As her sobs started to ease, he closed his eyes.

Long moments passed after she'd stopped crying, and still they didn't speak. He just didn't know what to say. But finally, after nearly thirty minutes of silence, the one thought that kept circling through his head came to his lips.

"I should have been there," he said quietly.

"And how could that happen? You were already dead," she pointed out, her voice weary. "Listen to me . . . this is insane."

"It's real. And you know it."

"Do I?"

"Yes." He turned his face into her hair, nuzzling her gently. "It's real. You know it. I know it. For whatever reasons, we were put back here to find each other again."

She snorted at that. "Well, I'll agree that it's *real.* I won't say I agree to anything else. At least I know what happened at the end of it all, though." She sat up, nudging him against the chest with her shoulder. "Why am I cuffed to you?"

"Ah . . ." Joss looked down, staring at their joined wrists. "I didn't want you waking before I did and trying to slip out. And that *isn't* the end of it all. We're not done, Dru. You have to know that."

"Do I?" She jerked on her hand. "Undo these now."

"No." Studying her face, he tried to decide. She seemed level, he decided. Or level enough. And they wouldn't have much more time before he had to leave. There was still work to be done, and as much as he wanted to say *fuck it*, Patrick Whitmore still ranked very high on his priority list.

She stood, her eyes all but shooting fire at him. He rose with her. So pretty, he thought. So pretty and so damned strong. He hadn't given her credit, he realized. Not enough now, and not then, either. She'd been ready to walk away. Not run in terror, but walk . . . after standing up to a monster. It had ended in a nightmare then.

This was their second chance, and they weren't going to lose it.

A sneer danced across her face, chasing away some of the shadows and brightening her eyes. "I said, undo the cuffs." Her voice was cool, icy, and oh so damn proper. She jerked against them.

The exact thing he'd been waiting for. He jerked back, spinning at the same time and moving in, taking her back down on the bed.

He caught his weight on his elbows and one knee, keeping the impact of his body from crushing her. "There," he murmured, lowering his head and nuzzling the curve of her neck. "This is right about where I've wanted to be for maybe a hundred years. And that's not even an exaggeration."

"Get off me, you stupid git," she snarled.

"Stupid git?" he echoed, lifting his head and staring down at her, amused. "How is it you can insult me and still sound so proper doing it?"

Narrowing her eyes, she said, "How proper does this sound? Get the fuck off of me, you sodding wanker."

"Hmmm. Sounds sexy as hell." He dipped his head to hers. Two seconds later, he jerked his head. "Ouch! Damn it, you mean little brat."

Licking his throbbing lip, he eyed her closely. She lay there, still. "Try to kiss me again, and I'll do more than bite you. I'm done with you, do you hear me, Crawford? Done."

He felt something drive into his heart . . . claws, maybe. Too jagged and rough to be a blade, and a knife couldn't shred him to pieces like this. "No." Shaking his head, he leaned in, pressed his forehead to hers. "It's not done. It can't be . . . don't you see? We never even started. How can we be done if we never even had a chance to start?"

Her body lay below his, a long, rigid line. "It would never work. You don't bother to look at anything but what you see with your eyes, even though you damn well have the ability. If you can't do that . . ." Something dark and tormented danced through her eyes. "I've got enough to deal with, just on my own. I don't need your crap, too."

"I'm sorry." He laid his hand on her neck, fingers spread wide so he could stroke his thumb along her lip, feel the graceful curve of her neck under his hand, the silk of her hair along his fingers. "It's not an excuse, but you need to understand . . ." He trailed off, tried to figure out the best way to explain the truly fucked-up mess that was his head. "The gifts that are in my head aren't . . . mine. And I'm little screwed up over them at the moment. Actually, I've been screwed up over that for a while now and it's . . . I can't think clearly. Nothing's clear. Except how I feel about you. And I know it can't be over, Dru." Dipping his head, he took a chance, a quick kiss, desperate as hell, pressed to her mouth. "It can't be over. It never started."

She twisted away from him, staring at the headboard. Very intently, it seemed. Probably so she wouldn't have to look at him. A soft shudder racked her and he groaned, feeling the rippling of her body under his. Killing him, damn it. Just killing him . . .

"Let me up," she whispered. And something in her tone got to him.

Rolling away, he lay next to her on the bed, eyes closed, hunger and heartache burning in him until he couldn't think.

"What . . . what exactly do you mean the gifts in your head aren't yours?" she asked.

He hesitated for a minute. "Are you going to talk to me? Tell me what's going on and why you're so determined to walk away?"

"What, it can't be because you acted like an *ass*?" she pointed out.

He lifted his head, craned it around to look at her. But she wasn't looking at him.

Unwilling to let her block him out so easy, he rolled onto his side, hovering over her. "I felt what you were feeling, Dru. Shock. Fear. And I heard you. You kept thinking, *He's one of them*. At first, I thought you were just afraid, but looking back, that's not what it was. You were *pissed*. You didn't think anything better of me than I was thinking, so don't go pulling this high-and-mighty routine. Somehow I don't think hypocrisy is your style. We both fucked up. We can deal with it and move on or make ourselves miserable. Which one are we going to do?"

She turned her head, glaring at him.

"*I* can't read minds," she snapped. "If I could . . ."

"It's common courtesy not to go barging in without permission." Lifting his hand, he laid it on her chest, felt the rapid beat of her heart against his hand. "And you're shying away from what the problem is. Are you going to talk to me or not?"

"I'm not in the mood for this shite, but fine, you bloody moron. I'll tell you, but then you'll have to leave me be. And you'll explain yourself first, you hear me?"

"Why are you so determined to leave?" he asked.

"Because once you hear what I have to say, you'll *want* to," she said, her voice thick and heavy. "Trust me."

"No." He shook his head.

"Yes." She jerked on the cuffs. "Undo these. I'm not talking to you like this, like I'm some sort of prisoner." Her eyes darkened. "I let myself be treated like a prisoner for too long. I've been investigating this for two years, but for more than twelve months, I've lived, slept, and breathed this case—I couldn't do a damn *thing* without him watching, and every move I made, I worried it would be my last. It's *done* now. *I* am done."

* * *

ONCE the cuff fell away, Dru sprang away from the bed, desperate to get away from him. Before she let herself lean on him.

The dream had left her shaken. She couldn't even explain how deeply it had rattled her. It felt like the very foundation of her world had been shattered, and she was still trying to find solid ground to stand on.

Joss seemed so very solid.

But it was an illusion—she knew that. He'd proven it already.

"Talk," she said, folding her arms across her chest and turning to stare at him.

He still sat on the edge of the bed, shirtless, hair mussed from sleep. With his head bowed, she let herself take a longer look at him and oh . . . what a lovely look. That body of his was absolutely delicious, she decided. Hard and strong and muscled. She'd always gone for a sleeker, leaner look, but there was just something so lovely about his strength. She wanted to climb on top of him and just spend hours learning that body. Hours she didn't have.

Fuck it all.

"I'm probably the most screwed-up kind of psychic you're ever going to meet," Joss said, his voice flat, his head still bent.

She pursed her lips. He was . . . strong. She knew that much. The burn he left on her brain was almost too much, almost too intense, but she didn't see what was so fucked up about it. "How so?"

"Well, right now . . . I can talk to the dead, I'm telepathic, there's some precognitive abilities, retrocognitive abilities, psychometry, and telekinesis. Plus, a very, very weird ability to manipulate matter in a way that I can't quite comprehend. All psychic abilities have a root in science . . . there's a way to explain them. But I can't explain this."

"You are what you are," Dru said, frowning as she studied him. This wasn't exactly what she'd expected. Joss had struck her as a little more self-assured. Self-*aware*, but he was bemoaning his abilities?

"No. I'm not *this*," he said, finally lifting his head. He held out a hand and the cuffs he held rose, hovering above his hand, held by a force she couldn't see. But she felt it.

It was almost like the charge she'd felt in the air when Tucker had been doing his thing, but not quite.

"This isn't my gift, you see," Joss said, smiling a little. "It's borrowed. I'm what you'd call a mirror. I pick up gifts. Or rather, I'm paired with whatever psychic I need to be paired with. We call it syncing. I'm synced with another psychic, given a particular gift set, and then sent to the job. Sometimes the person who has the gift we need just doesn't have the right . . . skills for the job. Or the right sex. The two psychics I was synced to were females. They couldn't have done this job."

Dru stared at him. About five seconds later, she realized her jaw was hanging open. Snapping it shut with an audible click, she shoved a hand through her hair, only to realize it was still in the braid from yesterday. Yanking it out, she snapped the band onto her wrist and started to finger-comb her hair. "You . . . so, you're basically just . . . what, like an SD card or something?"

He flashed a grin at her.

"Actually, that's exactly what I am. I take in data. I can take in any skill I need, take it in . . . *use* it, for however long I need to." Then he blew out a breath and scrubbed his hands over his face. "The problem, though, is this last sync was bad. The psychics, well, it's not their fault. Both of them have control and everything. It's complicated and confidential and I can't explain it all, but one of them . . ." He lowered his hands, curling them into fists. "She's got too much inside her. She can handle it. I was getting a handle on it. But I needed more time. Didn't have it. Between that, the dreams . . . all the ghosts . . ."

"Ghosts?" she echoed. Now there were ghosts in the mix.

"Hell." He shoved upright and started to pace, prowling the room like a caged, angry tiger. "I sound like a fucking pussy. Yes. Ghosts. The other psychic communicates with the dead, and this case is *crawling* with ghosts. I hear them everywhere. All they want to do is rest, and I can't . . . I couldn't help them do that until I did what I needed to do to help the others. But their voices were inside my head all the time. It was just too much, and all of it, you, the dreams, everything . . ." He trailed off, jerked his shoulder in a shrug. "I started to go a little crazy and I wasn't thinking well."

Then he turned, shot a glittering look her way. "I messed up. *I* was messed up, but that's no excuse. I screwed up and I'm sorry. I'm still fucked up, I'm still tired, but I'm not surrounded by death and ghosts and screams right now, and I'm also not torn in ten thousand different directions while I try and understand what's going on with you. This *isn't* done."

As he came toward her, still moving in that sleek, easy way, predatory, dangerous . . . deadly, but oh so fucking sexy, her breath caught in her throat. He shoved a hand into her hair, tangling as he tugged her head back. "I'm sorry," he whispered, his rough voice even rougher. His eyes searched her face. "I hurt you and I'm sorry, and I want to spend the next fifty years making it up to you. But I'm not ready to give up on *us* just because of a couple of mistakes we made while we were involved in a very, very bad situation. You can't tell me that's what you want, Dru. You weren't a coward in the last life . . . don't be one in this life."

It wasn't about being a coward. But he wasn't going to want her . . .

The shame, the misery, twisted inside her.

As he lowered his mouth to hers, she groaned and opened for him.

Maybe . . . maybe just once, she thought. Couldn't she have just once?

He slid a hand around her waist, pushed it under her shirt.

Damn it, yes.

He'd be angry. Maybe he'd hide it, maybe he wouldn't.

She didn't know, and just then, she didn't care. She'd been shoving everything she wanted, everything she needed, off to the side for too long. It was time she took something she needed. Something she wanted. For the first time since she'd started working this bloody job, she'd take what *she* deserved.

Pushing him back, she grabbed the hem of her shirt and jerked it off. The harsh intake of his breath echoed through the room. Staring at him, she stripped out of her sports bra. But as she reached for the waist of her running tights, he beat her to it.

Big, strong hands caught her around the waist, hauling her up against him.

"Dru, I already told you I was going a little crazy . . . are you trying to push me completely over?" he snarled against her lips as he stripped the clinging black tights away.

"Maybe." Tipping her head back, she stared at him. "Do you care?"

"No . . ." He spun around and put her back up against the wall. "I don't care at all."

She was ready for him to just unzip his jeans and take her. Ready for it to just end that fast. But he surprised her as he dipped his head, skimming his lips along her shoulder. Along the curve of her collarbone. When he went lower and caught the tight bud of her nipple in his mouth, Dru gasped.

Too much time had passed since anybody had done anything like this . . . Reaching up, she gripped his shoulders, sinking her nails into them.

Gentle, slow tugs with his lips, then his teeth. Teasing strokes with his tongue. Back and forth, and each stroke sent an arrow of pleasure darting down between her legs until she was rocking her hips restlessly, the ache there about ready to make *her* go crazy.

Her breath caught in her throat, lodged there as he went to his knees, trailing a line of burning kisses straight down her torso. When he reached her pubis, he pressed his mouth to her and Dru tensed, her entire body tightening. One hand stroked up the back of her thigh, possessiveness in every touch.

As he guided her legs farther apart, she stared down at him, watched his dark head, so intimately close.

The sight of it was so beautifully erotic, she felt herself cramping from need, aching for want of him. He nuzzled her curls, his breath ghosting over her clit. Not even a touch and it was too much. Then he flicked his tongue against her . . . and she shattered.

Too much need, too much sensation, and that light touch was all it took.

She heard a rough groan from him as she erupted with a cry and his hands came up, gripping her hips, holding her steady as he teasingly flicked his tongue over her, again, and again, pushing her higher . . . oh. Oh . . .

It ripped through her, brutal and fast and wicked. The heat of it, the intensity of it, all of it was too much. She shuddered her way back to earth, and if she'd had five seconds to think, she just might have been embarrassed.

But there was no time to think, or even breathe. Strong arms came around her waist, hauling her up. Too dazed, too breathless, she stared down into Joss's face as he carried her over to the bed. The soft, smooth sheets were cool against her back as he laid her down, her hips on the edge.

"Stay there." He bent over to kiss her, his voice a ragged growl in his throat.

Stay here . . . I can do that, Dru thought, her brain barely operating. Getting up. Moving . . . not going to happen.

That had been . . . wow. And he'd barely done anything.

* * *

HIS hands were fucking shaking.

As he tore into his duffle bag, he couldn't help noticing that small, significant detail.

Up until this case had started, he was pretty much unflappable. Women just didn't get to him like this. They didn't.

But Dru wasn't a woman . . . she was *his* woman. The only one. His everything. And she had him shaking. If he wasn't careful, she just might have him coming in his pants before he even had a chance to unzip them.

No. Finally spying the box of condoms, he ripped it open and pulled a couple out. He damn well wasn't going to lose it before he made love to her. Not after all this time. It might be over quicker than his first time, but damn it, he'd still make it good for both of them.

And who the hell cared if his hands were shaking?

Rising, he turned around and then stopped, dead short, a fist rising up to grab him, a fist right around his heart. The breath in his lungs dwindled away to nothing as he stared at her. Her lids were lowered, a soft flush on her cheeks, and a smile curved her lips upward.

That smile . . . it was the kind of smile that would elicit riots. Start wars and end them. And then she lifted her lashes and caught him watching her.

Feeling like a lovesick fool . . . feeling like exactly what he was . . . he was helpless to do anything but go to her as she lifted a hand.

So much they needed to talk through, so much they needed to figure out. And none of it mattered as long as she kept looking at him like that, because it meant she hadn't totally written him off, right?

Crossing to her, he threw the condoms on the bed next to her and knelt down, pressing his lips to the soft flesh just inside her left knee. "You're so damned beautiful . . . so damned amazing."

From under her lashes, she watched him, the smile fading, until nothing but naked longing remained on her face.

"Make love to me, Joss."

"Gladly." Skimming his lips up her thigh, along the satin of her skin, he took in her taste. Salty skin. Sweet woman. His woman. Slipping his hands under her hips, he dragged her to the very edge of the mattress and lowered his head, pressing his mouth against her.

She bucked against him, slamming her hands down on the mattress. "Joss," she hissed out, her voice a garbled little shriek.

"I love the taste of you," he whispered. "Love it."

She whimpered and reached down, cupping his head in her hands and holding him against her, moving her hips, rocking up to meet his mouth. "Oh . . . like that," she said, her voice a broken gasp when he stabbed her clit with his tongue.

When he pushed a finger inside her slick sheath, she keened out his name, her nails biting into his scalp. And then he twisted his wrist, adding a second finger, screwing them in . . . out. As she came a second time, his dick gave a violent, demanding jerk.

Inside her . . . *now*.

As she started to come back down, he stood up, tearing his pants open, shoving them down. The kiss of air on his painfully sensitive flesh was torture, and then she sat up, languid and slow, reaching out to curl her hand around him. "Is it my turn now?" she asked, her voice breathless, odd little tremors still wracking her body as she leaned in and pressed her lips to the head of his cock.

He wanted to tell her that it could be her turn whenever she damn well wanted, except then she opened her mouth and took him inside. She curled her tongue over him and every last muscle in his legs started to tremble, threatened to give out. Closing his hands around her head, he started to tug her back. But then she took him deeper. Pulled back and rolled her eyes to smile up at him. Did it a second time, a third . . .

With a ragged snarl, he fisted his hands in her hair and started to rock forward to meet her, fucking her mouth, easy and slow, while his legs trembled and his knees threatened to give out on him.

He was absolutely certain he'd never seen anything as erotic as this, not in his life. Dru's mouth, so pretty and soft, on his cock, one hand holding the base, the other gripping his thigh, her neat nails biting into his skin. So erotic. So perfect. So very his . . .

His . . .

The need to come spread through him, sizzling through his spine, tightening his balls. Fisting his hand in her hair, he tugged her back, shaking his head, feeling half-crazed when she tried to take him back in her mouth. "Not this way," he growled. "First time is inside you, damn it. In you."

A bit of a smile curved her pretty lips. "You didn't let my first time happen with you inside me."

"So I'm a chauvinistic bastard." He nudged her back on the bed, coming down on top of her, and then he had to stop, closing his eyes at the feel of her body against his. After all this time. *Finally.*

"Joss?"

Groaning, he turned his head to hers, blindly seeking out her mouth. He hooked an arm around her neck, needing her so much in that moment, so much he was all but stupid with it. Couldn't think, breathe, or speak without her. She was everywhere, inside his head, his heart, under his skin.

Finally . . .

His cock jerked against the soft curve of her belly, demanding. Insistent.

She whimpered low in her throat and rocked, like she couldn't wait to have him inside her.

Damn. He understood that feeling. Although it was like severing an arm in that moment, he tore his mouth from hers and shoved upright, fumbling on the bed for one of the rubbers. "A week," he rasped. "When this is done, you and I are gonna find someplace where we can be alone and do nothing but this for an entire week."

Her eyes, dark and serious, rested on his face.

His fingers felt too big, awkward, as he tried to tear the foil packet open.

"Let me," she murmured, easing upward and taking it from him.

Licking his lips, he watched as she discarded the foil, and started to roll the latex sheath down over him. Her slim fingers were strong and confident as she smoothed it down, her hand steady.

And when she looked back up at him, there was still something in her eyes . . . something almost haunted.

No. No time for that, not anymore. Nothing mattered now. They were together.

As she lay back down, he stretched his body out over hers . . . felt that amazing, gut-wrenching connection. Nothing would ever feel as right as this, her body against his, her eyes staring into his.

Except . . .

Something was off—

She was holding back. Those solid walls of hers were back in place, holding steady as he pushed his thigh between hers. He wanted to sink completely into her. Body to body, soul to soul . . .

"You're holding back from me," he muttered, settling in the cradle of her hips.

"Shhh," she whispered, pressing her lips to his jaw. One hand curved over the back of his neck, tugging him closer. She slid the other hand down over his chest, across his abdomen, and he shuddered, his muscles bunching and jumping under her touch. Her fist closed around him, stroked up. Down. "Make love to me, Joss . . . haven't we waited long enough?"

A hundred years . . . a lifetime.

Groaning, he caught her knee in one hand, dragging it up. As he did, he pressed against her, the head of his shaft seeking out her soft, wet heat. Her lashes fluttered down. Shoving his hand into her hair, he tugged her head back. "No," he snarled. "Look at me, damn it. I have to see you . . . see this."

Slowly, her lashes rose.

Her lips parted.

Catching one of her hands, he twined their fingers. Palm to palm. Skin to skin. As he slowly started to sink inside her, the slick, wet tissues of her sex closing around him, he sank lower, felt her heart pounding against his. Heart to heart.

"Mine," he muttered against her mouth. "Finally mine."

She opened for him, twining her legs around his hips, her tongue seeking out his as he stabbed it into her mouth. So hungry for her. So desperate.

Her pussy, wet, slick, and sweet as sin, gripped him, milking him as he pulled out, surged back in. She cried out against his mouth. He felt the pleasure splintering through her, despite the shields she tried to keep between them. It echoed through him, and he knew he'd been right . . . this wasn't going to last.

Working a hand between them, he flicked his thumb over the erect little bud of her clit. The hood was stiff, pressing against him, and when he pressed against her, her entire body quaked. "You like that."

She didn't answer in words, but he felt it as she moved against him, her slender, strong body a long arch under his. She tore her mouth away, sucking in one ragged breath after another.

He flicked her clit once. Twice. She tensed, the muscles of her sheath resisting him as he surged back in. Tight, so fucking tight he had to work just to get back in. A hot flush started low on her breasts and her breaths came in broken little pants.

Another teasing stroke and her eyes locked on his. Joss stared at her, and felt it shatter through her.

Echoing through him.

As she broke into a thousand pieces, he felt it . . . and he shattered right along with her.

TWENTY-SEVEN

"WHAT do you mean . . . she doesn't *exist*?"

Patrick eyed the organized chaos taking place in his house as he listened to the voice on the other end of the line.

"Mr. Whitmore, I've gone as deep on her as I can and it's a good front. A very good one. But you're dealing with a woman who faked her identity. I don't know how she managed to craft a false identity quite so thorough, but that's exactly what she's done."

Faked her identity . . .

Rage seethed through him.

Storming through the mansion, he made his way to Ella . . . no, not Ella. The whore. The *whore. Who* was she?

As he came into her room, he stood there, looking for something . . . anything.

There. By the sink was her makeup case. Lowering the phone, he bellowed for Lydia.

She emerged from the depths of the mansion only seconds later, her face remote, expressionless. "Get a plastic bag, gloves. I want Ella's makeup case bagged. I want it sent out."

She nodded and disappeared.

Something rubbed against his ankle. Looking down, he saw Demeter rubbing her head against him. Rage tripped through him. For a second, he thought about grabbing the little feline, snapping her neck. Instead, he sucked in a breath. Picked up his cat and stroked her back. It didn't soothe the enormity of his rage, but after a moment, he could think. Lifting the phone back to his ear, he said quietly, "Have you found out *who* she is?"

"No. The identity trail just stops. I'm not searching—"

"No," Patrick cut in. "You're not. Come out to the mansion. I have some of her personal belongings. Run her prints. Find out *who* she is. *Where* she is. And once you know . . . you let me know."

* * *

LYING there on the bed, curled around her, Joss was almost convinced that this was everything he'd ever need.

But when he leaned in to press his lips to her shoulder, those shields were still there. Still solid and cool and impenetrable. Sighing, he buried his face against her hair." Why are you still shutting me out?"

She stroked a hand down his arm. "It's easier that way, lover," she murmured.

"Easier. Easier how?"

One silent moment stretched out into another, and then finally, she rose.

Joss sat up, staring at her.

He'd wanted to make love to her again, but somehow, he didn't think that would be happening just yet. And soon, he had to figure out where Jones was, get his ass back on the job. But this first.

"You don't really want me to stop shutting you out, Joss," Dru said as she rose from the bed.

As she started to get dressed, he studied her. "And why is that?"

A bitter smirk twisted her lips. "Because once you've heard the entirety of what I've had to do since I started working this job, you . . ." Her voice hitched. She paused in the middle of putting her bra on, pressing her lips together. She lowered her head, her shining dark hair falling to shield her expression.

When she looked back at him, her expression was as remote, distant as the sun. "You won't want me anymore. I can tell you that."

"Nothing could make that happen," he rasped.

"Hmm." She tugged on her shirt. As she snagged her running tights from the ground, he stood up and went to her.

"Why don't we put that to the test?" he said quietly, taking the tights away and tossing them on the back of the nearby couch. He cupped her face in his hands. "Stop blocking me out. You're all I've ever wanted, and I've spent my entire life waiting for you . . . looking for you. Nothing is going to change that."

"Are you so certain?" she asked, her voice raw.

"Try me."

A bitter laugh escaped her. "You'll regret this, Joss. You really will. But I can't hide what I've done . . . what I am."

As her shields dropped, he fell into the very soul of her.

And his heart broke.

* * *

FLASH, *flash, flash.*

She felt it as her terror flooded him.

Her shame.

The pain. The times she let herself get hit. The first time Patrick had forced her. And the night she'd made the decision *not* to let him do it again, when she'd taken the choice into *her* hands . . . and away from him.

The shame of it tried to choke her, but she shoved it back. *What I did, I did for a reason.* She could all but hear herself screaming it inside her head. She might hate it, and she might wish it hadn't come to pass, but she'd done what was necessary.

Her heart pounded with each memory that flashed between them. It had never been this intense before. She wasn't just taking in *his* memories . . . that was what was supposed to happen. He was taking in hers, and she'd never had a dual exchange like this. She'd never felt anybody's reaction when she'd done this before.

And she didn't want to feel it—instinctively, she tried to jerk away. She couldn't feel his disgust, couldn't feel him pull away like she knew he was going to do. *No . . .*

But he wouldn't let her.

A raw, anguished cry left him.

They crashed to the ground. She felt the floor bite into her knees. Felt his hands grip her face, and she stared at him through a veil of tears, desperate to break the contact before . . . *no no no no . . .*

And then it was over and he was staring at her, his black eyes burning. She could almost see the flames in his eyes as he stared at her.

"How many times?" he snarled.

Trembling, she braced herself. So this was how it would end, she thought dully. This man she barely even knew . . . yet she *did* know him. The man she barely knew would shatter her, break her soul—even Patrick hadn't been able to do that.

In a flat voice, she said, "I did it as often as I had to."

For a second, he looked blank, but then he shook his head. "Fuck that . . . you did what you needed to keep him from hurting you. How many times did *he* hurt you?"

Her ragged, broken train of thoughts stuttered to a halt.

Her ragged, broken heart stuttered inside her chest.

Dru clutched at his wrists. "Wuh . . . what?"

"I'm going to kill him." Joss stared off over her shoulder. "I plan on doing it slow. I need to gut him. Slowly. That takes a long time to die and I need to hurt him. For every time he hurt you, I'm going to hurt him."

With an abrupt jerk, she twisted away from him and stumbled off, getting a few feet between them before she turned to face him. Her knees shook and wobbled.

"You don't get it," she sneered at him. Easier, she thought. Get some distance. Protect herself. "I fucked him, do you hear me? As often as I had to."

His eyes glittered as he stared back at her. Slowly, he closed the distance between them. She backed up, but the bed was behind her and she had nowhere to go. When his hand darted out and fisted in her shirt, she tried to twist away again, but he jerked her up against him. "I get that. I get it just fine. Maybe I don't like it and you can't much expect me to, but you did what you had to and I can damn well *accept* it. What I *can't* accept is the fact that he hurt you . . . now tell me," Joss growled, pressing his brow to hers. "Tell me how many times he hurt you, so I can go and kill him."

Trying to breathe around the aching swell in her chest, Dru shook her head. "No. You . . ." She licked her lips.

He cupped her cheek, his big hand gentle. "I waited a lifetime to find you again . . . and nothing is going to keep us apart this time. Not *him*." Then he tipped her head back, pressed a kiss to her lips. "Not him. Not you . . . not me."

* * *

SHE was staring at him like she didn't know what to think. What to say.

"A lifetime," he whispered, trying to think past the rage and heartbreak.

He'd known Whitmore had tried to hurt her. He'd sensed it a few times. But he hadn't realized . . . *My fault*, he had to admit that. He should have realized just how fucked up things were. He hadn't protected her.

But he could now.

He was going to find Whitmore—

Whitmore. His focus sharpened, and as if his thoughts were on a zip line, they zeroed in on that scumbag, and he found himself locked in on the man he wanted to kill, almost as much as he wanted to breathe.

Must leave. No time—Whitmore's thoughts, erratic and very unlike him. None of that cool condescension, none of that arrogant disdain. Just disjointed, edgy rage.

He stopped fighting it and let his thoughts flow.

Time, space, everything spiraled away as he found his thoughts lodged in a very nasty place . . . Patrick Whitmore's mind. And Patrick was in the middle of his slick mansion, pacing, swearing, furious, and completely pissed.

Surrounded by the flow of people, organized chaos as suitcases were carried out. Boxes neatly stacked.

Must get to the airport—

Sucking in a breath, Joss broke the contact.

"Aw, no. This isn't good. He's cleaning up and heading out," Joss muttered, his voice hoarse.

Dru blinked, looking confused.

"Whitmore. He's covering his ass and getting out of town."

"But . . ." She shook her head. "*How?* The compound?"

Joss swore. "Until we can connect it to him, we can't move on him. It's dicey territory, what we do. We can't exactly present a psychic as evidence for a warrant."

Dru looked down.

"I . . ." She licked her lips.

"I've got evidence," she said quietly. "It's not a lot. But it's evidence. Pictures of him with men that were out at the compound. A few pictures of him with some girls who are likely listed as missing now. It's going to be mostly circumstantial at best, but it will let you stop him from leaving for now."

"Evidence."

She nodded.

"Okay." He stared at her. "Just one last thing."

She looked away. "Yes?"

Hauling her against him, he slanted his mouth over hers, stole one kiss, hard and quick. "This isn't over . . . not what we have. Understand that."

She finally looked at him.

But this time, a faint, hesitant smile curved her lips. And that bleak look in her eyes was almost gone.

* * *

IMPATIENT, Joss barely managed to resist the urge to shift from one foot to the other. "Well?" he demanded as Taylor finished going through the photos and reports.

"It's enough." Then he grimaced. "For now, at least. Enough to detain him. Make him sweat." Then he added, "And keep him from leaving the country."

He flicked a look at Dru and inclined his head. "Well done, Ms. Chapman."

She didn't answer, just continued to stare out the window.

"We need to roll," Joss said. "I don't know how much time we have. Can we get the warrant rushed through?"

Taylor lifted a brow. "Is that a rhetorical question?"

Joss bared his teeth at him.

"I'm going with you."

Taylor slanted a look at Dru. "That's not—"

She crossed her arms over her chest. "You wouldn't have that evidence if it wasn't for me. And you know it. It's not like I'm a sodding civilian who's going to blunder into this and make things worse. But I've got a stake in this . . . more than you can even imagine."

Joss's phone rang.

When Whitmore's number flashed across the screen, he scowled. Then a tension knotted in his gut. Scenes played out in his head. Unlikely, awful scenes that he hated . . . hated . . . hated.

As he lifted a hand, silence fell through the room.

"Yes?" he said, his voice remote.

"Job is off," Whitmore said, his voice harsh and ugly. "But I've got a new one for you. You're so . . . resourceful, maybe you'd be good at this one, too."

Joss closed his eyes. Even he knew what Patrick was going to say.

In his mind's eye, spurred by that awful, amazing gift, he saw how everything would play out.

"What kind of job is this one?"

"You think you can find my fiancée?"

Joss slanted a look at Dru. Stared at her. "Misplaced her, huh?"

"One of these days, that mouth of yours, Sellers. It will catch up with you. Now do you want the job or not? One million, cash."

"Oh, yes. I want it. And it will be the easiest million I ever earned."

* * *

"THIS is a bad idea," Taylor muttered as both Joss and Dru finished suiting up with the thin, body-conforming armor. It was far less bulky than the typical armor, and when Dru pulled on a loose blouse she'd borrowed from Taige, one couldn't even tell.

"It's how it has to play out," Joss said, his voice remote.

"Does that mean I have to like it?"

Joss just grunted. Already his mind was focused on what lay ahead.

He needed a few minutes alone with Taylor. Just a few. Although the last thing he wanted to do was miss out on a single second with Dru. *Quit your bitching*, he thought sourly. He did what he had to. For the job. For her. Always for her.

As she started to smooth her hair into a braid, he caught Taylor's eyes, jerked his chin.

A few minutes later, they were out in the hallway.

"You're hiding something," Taylor said quietly.

Ignoring him, Joss said, "I want you to make sure she's protected if this doesn't go well."

Crossing his arms over his chest, Taylor glared at him. "What do you think is going to go badly?"

"Don't worry about it," Joss said. "Just make sure he can't get to her. He's trying to—I've already seen that. She's been working this thing alone, she has no resources, and I don't—"

"She's got resources," Taylor said, cutting in. Closing the distance between them, he studied Joss's face closely. "You need to tell me what's going on. I can't do my job if I'm in the dark, Crawford."

Joss just shook his head. "You'll make sure she's safe. Just tell me that. I need to know."

Blowing out a breath, Taylor said, "I'll make sure of it. But she's not on her own, Crawford. She had an escape plan. From day one."

"And you know this . . . how?"

Taylor stared at him.

Joss turned on his heel. There was no time to think through the many ways Jones could have gotten that information. The harder question would be . . . *why hadn't Jones figured this out sooner?*

"Damn it, Crawford, you need to tell me what's going on."

Shooting him a look over his shoulder, Joss lifted a brow. "Well, you always manage to figure things out on your own. I figure you'll do this one, too."

Then he headed back into the room.

He needed a few more minutes with Dru.

A few more minutes . . . a lifetime.

* * *

"CAN you read him?"

Taige glared at Jones as he closed a hand around her arm and jerked her away from Cullen.

"Do you mind?" she snapped.

But then she saw the look on the boss's face.

"What's wrong?" she asked quietly.

"Can you read Crawford or not?"

She didn't bother turning to look at him. "No. Not unless he decides to let me in, and I can tell you, he's not doing that."

Shit.

No time left to try and grill the bastard, either, Taylor knew.

Joss and Chapman were already heading out, and the rest of

the team was going to be behind them. Taylor wasn't going to be far behind them, not far at all. If he could find a way, he'd be riding in the damn SUV with them, but Whitmore was already about to run.

The evidence Chapman had given them, all circumstantial, was enough to hold the man. Taylor didn't want this man held. He wanted him dead. Very dead. Of course, he couldn't do that, so locked away for life would work.

Shoving his way closer to Crawford, he caught the man's dark gaze. *You're going to be careful, damn it.*

He didn't need to worry whether or not Joss heard him.

After all, he was just like Jillian right now . . . and all it took with this kind of psychic gift was *thinking loudly*.

Taylor was thinking damn loud.

Crawford gave him a sharp-edged smile.

But there wasn't time for anything else.

Damn it.

Damn it.

Damn it.

TWENTY-EIGHT

CLIMBING into the car Taylor had gotten him, Joss let the images roll through his mind one more time.

A lot of ways this could play out. But he needed to focus on the outcome *he* needed. Everything else was a distraction.

Dru was quiet.

She looked so fragile . . . like she'd snap or break.

The closer they got to Whitmore's mansion, the more strained the silence got.

The more haunted she looked.

He couldn't believe he had to take her back there.

Thirty minutes later, he pulled his phone out, dialed the number. He put it on the console, keeping it on speaker.

"I'm on my way."

There was a pause.

"Unless you've got my fiancée, I don't want to see you," Whitmore said coldly.

"Yeah, well, unless you've got my million, I have no reason to see you." He waited a beat and then asked, "Do you have it?"

A harsh breath was the only sound to betray Whitmore's surprise. But it was enough. "How?" he demanded. "How can you have her?"

"Hmmm. Well, let's just say, she found me. And you don't know her as well as you think. The dumb broad was playing both sides, you know that?" He glanced over at Dru, swallowed the bile rising in his throat. "I wasn't able to get much out of her, but I get the feeling some of your . . . competition was trying to get the inside scoop. She's been watching you a long, long time."

At that, Dru lowered her head, a faint smile curling her lips. *Not bad*, she mouthed.

Of course it wasn't bad. He had insider knowledge. Unable to keep his hands to himself, he reached over, curved his hand over her neck.

"And you know this how?"

"It was about all I managed to get out of her before she passed out." He stroked his thumb down her neck, staring at the highway, thinking of all the ways he'd liked to hurt Whitmore. Breaking his hands, to start. Those hands had hurt Dru. They had to be first.

"Would you stop it with the lazy-boy routine?" Whitmore bit off. "How did you *find* her so fast?"

"I already explained this . . . I didn't find her." Joss smiled. "She found me. Showed up while I was eating breakfast . . . and by the way, I've got to tell you, I'm pissed you decided to go and bug my car. I had to go and find a different set of wheels, but just so you know? No more bugs in my vehicles."

The SUV he'd been using would have been hauled away by now.

Had Whitmore seen footage from the compound, or had it all been shot to hell when the electrical blowout happened?

"Fuck the bugs and fuck your vehicle. I want to know about my fiancée," Whitmore snarled.

"Hey, *fuck you*, okay? Keep in mind, I didn't exactly ask to be made part of your merry little band of screwups, Those jackasses can't seem to do their job without screwing it up even worse, got it? Last night was a fuckup of epic proportions. What do they do, walk around with their hands on their dicks all night or what?"

Harsh, heavy panting breaths came over the phone now. "Last night." Whitmore's voice was ugly with its hate now. So very ugly. "What do you know about last night?"

"I know I came with another delivery, and your stupid men were too busy running around with dicks in hand to take the damn delivery."

"You . . ." More harsh breathing.

Joss smiled and stroked Dru's neck. *Temper is getting the best of you, boy*, he thought.

"You were at the compound last night."

"Well, not exactly. But your lazy-ass boys were too busy jacking off to let me in. I ended up leaving. Now my partner is dealing with the merchandise, you tell me the job is off, but hey, you want your fiancée . . . what the hell, are you *trying* to fuck up my life?"

And even though he wasn't there with Whitmore, he could feel the flickers of the man's rage. It streaked through Joss's vision, tainting everything with ugly streaks of red and black. Seconds ticked by. The erratic cadence of Whitmore's breathing calmed, and when he spoke, his voice was calm. Calm and smooth as glass.

"Whether or not I fuck up your life remains to be seen, Mr. Sellers. Why don't you tell me how you came to find my fiancée?"

"Again, she found me. Can you not hear?" He checked the

rearview mirror. He couldn't see Taylor's people. They wouldn't be around just yet. They'd be close. But not that close.

"She found you."

"What in the hell is your problem, Whitmore? Yeah, she found me. I was having breakfast and there she was, cool as a cucumber, she sits down and asks me, *How would you like to make more money than my fiancé could ever hope to pay?* I just stared at her for a minute, and then she goes on to tell me that she can pay me more than you can ever hope to."

"And here you are, on the phone with me. I wonder what you told her."

"Well, that's neither here nor there. The thing is, she wouldn't tell me who she's working with. You know how I like answers. She wouldn't give them to me. Then . . ." Joss blew out a breath. "Then she decides she's going to get all heavy with the threats. I don't much care for those. So I figured maybe I'd just . . ."

"You'd just maybe what?"

"She pissed me off. I brushed her off. Waited until she left, then I followed her. I was just going to teach her a thing or two, but I figured I'd make sure you were done with her. Was going to call you tonight, but then you called me . . . anyway, I had her with me when you called, but I wasn't at a place where I could explain that."

"You." Whitmore started to curse, long and low. "You've had her for *how* long?"

"Since a little after seven. Took a while to make sure I wouldn't have an audience."

"And you have her now?"

"What, you think I called just to talk about the weather? This isn't exactly how I'd like to be spending the day," Joss snapped. "You called about the job, remember?"

I'm going to kill you—

The thought came loud and clear.

It might have been Whitmore's, but Joss shared the sentiment. He wanted this bastard so very, very dead.

"Excellent. And who knows about this?"

Smiling, Joss said, "My partner."

"And who is this mysterious partner?"

Laughing, Joss said, "You think I'm telling *you* that? You're the one who kept telling me how some of your associates kept meeting this bad end. Don't worry. My partner will stay out of your way, as long as you stay out of his . . . and mine. Think of him as my insurance policy."

Insurance policy.

Boss.

General pain in the ass.

And occasional lifesaver.

*　*　*

"I don't have time for this." Whitmore spit out the words like they tasted bad.

Joss leaned back against the car and smiled as Whitmore came storming out of the house.

Images flooded his head the second he drove through the gates. Whitmore had his men stationed around the place. He wasn't going to try to kill Joss, not yet. But incapacitate, yeah. He'd do that.

Then take Dru.

Not happening.

Harder to do if Joss was out here.

Dru was still inside the car, slumped over, pretending to be unconscious.

He could hear the slow, steady sound of her breathing almost like it was his own. Feel the buzz of her thoughts, just behind the solid, sturdy weight of her shields.

And the cold, unearthly whispers of the dead.

They were everywhere.

As Whitmore came striding down the elegant walkway, Joss stared at him. The dead clung to him.

It was amazing the son of a bitch couldn't feel them.

But then again, if Whitmore could feel them, they would have already driven him insane.

Lifting a can of Coke to his mouth, Joss took a deep drink and then smiled at Whitmore over the rim. "You don't have time? You're ragging my ass about time but you're the one who called me about doing this damn job," he drawled. He emptied out the can, and because he knew it would piss Whitmore off, he crushed it with his hands and then tossed it on the carefully manicured lawn.

Whitmore's eyes cut to it, lips peeling back from his teeth in a sneer.

Before he could say a word, Joss held out his hands. "Exactly what in the fuck do you want me to do with her, if you're too fucking busy to take her off my hands?" Then he grinned. "Although if you don't want her, I'll take her. I'll have fun with her for a few days and then find somebody else who'll take her off my hands, trust me."

Two seconds later, there was a gun pointed at him.

Joss stared at it, lifting a brow. Wow. The guy was fast. Faster than he'd expected.

"You don't want to say anything else along those lines," Whitmore said, his voice all but soundless. "She's mine. Only mine."

Lifting his hands, Joss shrugged. "Hey, no problem there. I just want my money. I spent a hell of a lot of time on this job, left behind some profitable opportunities. I don't want to leave empty-handed."

"How about you leave *alive*?"

Whitmore took another step toward him.

Chaotic thoughts hurtled through the man's mind. *Follow him . . . get him the hell out of here, then have my people follow him and kill him. Ella . . . want her . . . have to . . .*

Blocking off that chaotic stream of thought, Joss scratched at his chin, pretending to think it over. "No. That's not good enough. You're going to pay me. Otherwise, I'll be sending a fucking treasure trove of information to so many different government branches, and I'm not just talking U.S."

Ugly, vile rage flashed through Whitmore's eyes, but his voice was cool as he said, "And how will you do that if you're dead?"

"It's more a matter of . . . *how will I stop it if I'm dead?*" Joss smiled. "You see, I don't know you well enough to trust you. You've been riding my ass from the get-go, pushing me nonstop, always with the same threats. You have to control every damn thing. I've worked with your type before. And they were always the ones who tried to fuck me over," Joss said, shrugging easily. "So I've always made sure to have an insurance policy. And not just my partner."

Shoving off the car, he closed the distance between them, close enough that the metal of the gun was pressing into his chest. "So . . . you want to kill me?" He craned his head, peering down at Whitmore's watch. "In exactly two hours and thirty two minutes, there's an e-mail that will go out. And it ties you into all sorts of shit you probably didn't realize I knew."

"You are rather full of it, aren't you?" Whitmore murmured.

"Am I?" Joss lifted a brow. "I wonder how your old girlfriend is enjoying Dubai."

Then he moved. Weapons got heavy after a while and this guy was getting twitchy. Joss knew how to push, when to push harder, and when to stop, but he'd rather not end up with a bullet in his skull. Hell, at this close range, he might not survive it if the son of a bitch pulled the trigger. Body armor wasn't infallible. In a matter of seconds, he had Whitmore's gun in his hand and Whitmore was exactly where Joss had wanted him since day one. Longer . . .

On the ground.

He leveled the weapon at Whitmore's head. "Tell your boys to fall back before I put a bullet in your brain."

"They'll kill you the second you shoot," Whitmore sneered.

"True. But you'll still be just as dead." Joss smiled. "I'm okay with dying if it means I take out a fucker who was about ready to screw me over . . . but are you ready to die?"

Whitmore went white. "Everybody, go inside the house."

A few hesitated.

Joss moved a step closer and applied pressure to the trigger.

"Get in the fucking house!" Whitmore bellowed.

As the rest of them scattered, Joss crouched down. "So, let's chat. You're going to pay me. You can have your fiancée. I'll get my money. We go our separate ways."

"And how do I know you won't share whatever . . . information . . . you claim to have?"

"You don't," Joss said, shrugging. "But here's the thing. You were planning on killing me the second I set foot in that house . . . weren't you?"

The flicker in Whitmore's eyes would have given him away even if Joss hadn't heard the answer echo through that discordant train of thought.

"See? I know when somebody's out to screw me over." Joss

shook his head. "You'll just have to trust that I won't do anything with it . . . and I'll trust that you'll stay the hell out of my
life after this. Deal?"

I'll see you dead . . .

Joss wasn't surprised by the thought tripping through Whitmore's mind. If he actually was the man Whitmore thought he
was, he might be a little worried.

"Deal?"

Whitmore got up, ignoring the gun Joss had all but jammed into
his face. Once he was on his feet, Joss did that, nudging the muzzle
against his cheek. "You pay me, and I go off on my merry way."

"Agreed," Whitmore said. "You'll bring my fiancée into the
house."

"No. You'll have one of your men come and get her. *After*
they bring my money out. A million is what you offered . . .
that's what you'll bring me."

"I don't have that on hand."

"Yes, you do." Joss pushed harder with the gun. "Now come
on. Tell me you can cough it up. Time is short and all, right?"
Then he smiled and leaned in. "Considering how edgy you are, I
imagine you want to be done with this in a hurry for a reason . . .
do you really have time to dick around with me?"

"You keep fucking with me," Whitmore said quietly, "you'll
go too far. Fine. I'll have the money brought out. One million, in
exchange for Ella. You'll leave and get the fuck out of my way.
And you won't share any information on me with anybody. Correct?"

"Right. All the information about your ex-girlfriend, her current situation in Dubai, your various illegal activities with slavery and shit. Mum's the word." Joss smiled widely and gestured
to the house. "Call one of your boys, Whitmore. Let's get this
show on the road."

Something glittered in Whitmore's eyes. Suspicion.

Doubt . . .

Pushed too hard.

* * *

DRU felt the mental jab against her shields.

Make a noise. Groan or something. Need him to focus on you, but don't get out of the car.

An award. After all of this, she deserved an award.

It wasn't that hard to groan. Hell, she was back in the one place she never wanted to return. So close to the monster she hated above all others . . .

The groan sounded feeble and weak to her own ears.

But Joss heard it.

"Hmmm. Sounds like she's waking up. If you're going to sit around with your thumb up your ass, I should probably dose her again."

"No."

A few seconds later, Joss's thoughts brushed her own. *He gives me the money and starts to take you into the house and it's done.*

Sounded so easy.

Jones and the rest are five minutes away.

She wondered if he was guessing at that or if he knew.

I know. Trust me . . .

Sighing, she tucked her chin against her chest.

Trust him. He made it sound so simple. So easy. And it was anything but. Blowing out a breath, she blocked out everything. Time to focus. Time to think. Everything was coming down to this . . .

All too soon, she heard the door open. Felt hands on her. *Flash, flash, flash.* Minton. The bastard. Worried . . . he was worried. Whitmore had killed more than a few people in the past few hours, and he was no longer certain he was indispensable. But he was still cocky, still determined. And still greedy. She felt the rush of it all through his touch, saw the memories. A body lying dead at his feet. *"You're certain he didn't say anything?"*

Minton shaking his head. *"As certain as I can be. He's a pussy. Would talk if you paid him or hurt him. I just hurt him."*

Hurt her—

The flash ended with that thought. That was what he wanted to do.

Hurt. *Her.*

"Are you awake, Ella?"

Lifting her head, she stared at Whitmore.

"Good . . ."

By the car, Joss stood there. Unconcerned. Like he wasn't bothered by a damn thing in life. If she didn't have the warm feel of his thoughts present in her brain, the burn of his anger, she just might have been a little disturbed by the very apparent lack of concern on his face.

"Let me go," she snarled, jerking against Minton's hands.

Whitmore came up to her.

She knew what he was planning. As he drew near, she sagged in Minton's grip, forcing him to adjust how he was holding her. When he did, she managed to smash her foot on his instep— under her booted foot, she heard the crunch of bone and it made her smile. His bellow was almost like a chorus of angel song, and when she drove her elbow back into his gut, she loved hearing the way his breath gusted out of him in shock.

She didn't get away, but she didn't intend to.

It was the need to fight.

Even as Minton dragged her toward the house, sucking in air, some of the bones in his foot broken, she continued to jerk against him. "Let me go, you twat." She shot Whitmore a glare. "You can't keep me here."

"Yes. I can." He gave Joss a narrow look. "We're done now, Sellers."

From the corner of her eye, she saw Joss continue to stand there.

She thought, maybe, she heard a car engine over the rush and roar of blood in her ears. Jerking against Minton, she twisted again, trying again to get away as he dragged her over the threshold. "*Let me go,*" she snarled.

"Not in a million . . ."

Minton's voice trailed off.

She saw him from the corner of her eye as he turned to look at her. But he was looking *past* her.

"What . . ."

"Let her go," Whitmore said, his voice soundless.

Minton didn't respond.

"Let her go *now.*"

She hit the floor so suddenly, the hard marble was biting into her knees. With a serene smile, she stared up at him. "Too late," she said softly.

Then, swinging out with her legs, she kicked his own out from under him, knocking him down before she scrambled outside.

Minton reached for her.

"Don't," Whitmore snapped.

As she scrambled upright, she watched from the corner of her eye and saw the black cars driving in through the gates. Five of them. Wow. She was kind of curious about the time.

Had it been five minutes?

She looked back at Whitmore, letting all the rage she felt show on her face. "I told myself I'd see this through, you know. No matter what. It was a promise I'd made myself."

Hatred flashed through his eyes. But as he rose to his feet, his face was calm, his voice cool. "I don't know what you're up to, but nothing will come of it, Ella. Nothing."

She smiled as she stood.

"Want to bet?"

TWENTY-NINE

As she walked away, Patrick stared at her.

Walking away . . .

To *him*.

No. Fucking *no*.

As the cars came to a halt, Whitmore walked quietly over to the elegant writing desk and pulled open a drawer. The baby Glock tucked inside fit neatly in the palm of his hand. He'd used it a few hours ago to kill Lydia. Now, he'd use it to kill Ella.

That fucker . . . his name wasn't Sellers. He knew that much. But his name didn't matter.

Minton glanced at the gun, then at him. "What are you going to—"

It was the last thing he ever said.

As he fell lifeless to the ground, Patrick positioned himself at the door.

All this time, he'd known Ella was the one for him. The only one. And now she was walking away—

Did you really think I'd let you leave—

"No," he murmured. "You won't leave."

"Drop the gun!"

The voices came bellowing at him from everywhere.

Oddly, he was aware of a strange sensation of cold, too. Very cold. Drifting along his spine, crowding into his mind.

You won't leave, he thought, pointing the gun at Ella. She turned, staring at him.

The big, rough-looking bastard was rushing for her.

All around him, lights started to flicker.

The voices in his mind raged louder.

"You can't have her," Patrick said.

He shifted the gun, pointed it at the son of a bitch responsible.

A blinding pain tore through his brain as he squeezed the trigger. It increased. Swearing, he screamed, "You can't have her!"

* * *

CROUCHED on top of the stone fence, hidden by the low-hanging branches, Tucker fought against the pull of his power. On a day like this, it was even harder than normal. Overcast, the thunderheads piling up overhead, and every now and then, lightning would flicker. He could feel it calling out to him . . . *play with me, Tucker . . . play with me . . .*

It was tempting, so tempting, and here he was, with no time *to* play, no time to toy with the lure of all that crazy, crazy power. So seductively sweet.

Once the rain hit, all that lovely, lovely energy would be gone. It was a high like nothing else, and even more powerful than normal because of how dry it had been . . . the air was charged, charged and ready for him. So tempting, too easy to give in to it completely, feeling along the line of life and giving in to the urge to play . . . his kind of playing could lead to death. He was already playing with death. Life.

He could feel all of them. Every person around him. All of their energy. All of their lives . . . they called to him like a siren's song.

But that wasn't where he needed to go. He couldn't pull their energy into him. He needed to shove it *out*.

Bit by bit. He bounced from one mind to another. The most powerful mind wasn't the one he needed to fuck with. No, the mind he gravitated toward screeched and twisted, black with ugliness. Automatically, Tucker wanted to pull away but he didn't.

He jabbed at the man's mind. Hard.

Felt him flinch. Not enough, not enough. Tucker had a way of knowing when he'd pushed hard enough, if he needed to go a little harder . . . and he needed to go a little harder.

"What are you doing?"

The woman's voice cut into the silence he'd wrapped around himself.

Hissing, he tore his attention away from the task at hand. If he had been anybody important, he wouldn't have been so careless.

As it was, he heard a harsh, panicked scream—male—coming from the big-ass mansion, one that ended too abruptly, and he didn't have to guess who it was. Snarling, he looked down, saw her standing on the ground just under the stone wall where he crouched.

It was the beautiful blonde he'd seen just days ago.

Back when this was supposed to just be a favor he was doing for Dru.

Now she had her head tipped back as she studied him, a curious look in her eyes, a smile on her lips.

She was so damned beautiful, Tucker thought, a little dazed.

So damned beautiful.

Something he hadn't felt in too long burned through his veins.

It wasn't the fiery burn of his gift. Wasn't the lure of electricity crackling through the wires or snapping inside the mind of some unsuspecting victim.

Lust. Plain and simple.

Tucker couldn't even remember the last time he'd felt lust.

It almost laid him low.

As she reached up to lay a hand on his ankle, he jerked his foot away.

"Don't," he said shortly.

He couldn't do contact unprepared. And he suspected if he did contact with her, it wouldn't matter if he was prepared or not, not considering the way his blood was already buzzing in his veins.

"What are you doing?" she asked again.

Drawing his leg up to his chest, he focused back on the house. That one mind, so loud and chaotic with its rage, had stumbled to a halt after Tucker had clumsily severed his link. "In the market to buy a house," he said flippantly. "Since I figure this one will be on the market soon, I'm taking a look-see."

She was quiet. Then, blowing out a sigh, she moved over and leaned against the stone wall, staring toward the house. "You know, it won't be long before he has agents and cops and shit crawling all over this place. If you don't want to get caught up in that, you might want to do your house hunting at a later time." She angled a look up at him, tucking those dense, exotic braids back and studying him with a queer little smile.

That smile said . . . *you're not fooling me.*

Tucker didn't like that smile.

"Jones can handle this," she said softly.

He continued to stare at the house. "I don't know who in the fuck *Jones* is." He had a friend in there. He didn't have many, but Drucella Chapman was one of them and she'd gone back to face a poisonous snake.

In the back of his mind, he felt it . . . that sluggish brain rousing, so black and ugly and awful.

Full of rage. Anger. The need to hurt.

A snarl peeled his lips back from his teeth. He shouldn't have thrown it off so soon.

Pressing the heel of one gloved hand against his temple, he stared at the house, focused, locked in on the brain.

* * *

Dru was almost to the car when she heard it.

Her brain didn't want to process it.

Her body already had.

A gunshot.

The hairs on her arms, the nape of her neck stood on end, and she didn't recall running, but she was.

The air was tight—charged the way it was right before a bad storm, and although it looked like rain, she suspected this was more. A lot more. A thunderstorm had never felt like this.

If lightning had struck in that very moment, she wouldn't have been surprised. Not surprised at all.

The car—so close—

And then, the only thing she was close to was the ground. And Joss. Trapped between him and the hard-packed earth.

He was still . . . so very still.

Time slowed to a crawl.

Everything merged together . . . voices . . . places. People. Dreams and reality.

Don't let him take you away again . . .

You must run . . .

As his weight crushed the breath out of her, shock froze her. For one very, very brief moment. She stared up at his face. "No."

He didn't move.

With a strength she didn't think she had, she shoved him off her, half wiggling, half pulling, until she worked free of him. And he didn't move. Crouched over him, her hair falling in a tangle, she cradled his head in her hands.

"Joss," she whispered. "Wake up."

Nothing . . . that harsh, unrelenting face, so still.

Their voices came to her through a hazed fog. "*. . . put the gun down . . .*"

Patrick's voice, barely sounding like him, as he shouted, "*You don't walk away . . .*"

"*Put down the gun and come out.*"

Blinking, Dru looked down. Joss's gun was still tucked inside his holster. Too big for her hands, but she didn't care. Slipping it free, she paused a minute to stroke his face. "I really wish you'd found me a couple of years ago," she whispered, her voice thick and broken.

As she lifted the heavy gun, she focused. She couldn't see Patrick. He was hiding behind the door, miserable twat. But she didn't need to see him.

The cold, ugly weight of his presence was like a stain on her soul.

"I promised I'd bloody you."

Then she squeezed the trigger.

A split second later somebody saw what she was doing.

But it was too late.

She'd already fired.

And before the gun was torn away from her, she saw what she needed to see . . . Patrick's body, half sprawled in the doorway. His face turned toward her. Eyes open, but empty. Lifeless.

The enormous ache in her heart ripped open and a sob tore out of her. Huddling over Joss's body, she hugged him. *Damn you . . you told me not to let him take me away. But what about you?*

Curling her fingers into his shirt, instinctively seeking out the warmth of his skin, she came across something else entirely. Before her mind could process that, though, hands gripped her arms.

"Ease back a minute, girl," a soft, familiar voice murmured in her ear.

"Let me go," she snarled, jerking away from Tucker. They were going to take him away. Panic settled inside her. They couldn't take him away, not yet, not yet—

But there they were, gathering around Joss's big, still body, and Tucker was hauling her away, and she didn't even have the strength to fight him. *No, no, no—*

"I will . . . in a minute. Come on, honey. Let them help him."

"Let me *go* . . . help . . ." She stopped and went slack in Tucker's arms as the blond guy jerked open Joss's shirt, revealing the black body armor.

"He had on body armor, honey," Tucker murmured, absently stroking her arm. "Calm down a minute. Breathe, just breathe. He's okay."

"But . . ." She shook her head. He was so still. Not moving. "No." Squeezing her eyes closed, she turned her head away, afraid to hope. Afraid to think.

"He's fine, Chapman. I can feel it—the shock of it just knocked him out, and he's going to hurt like a motherfuck, but he's fine."

* * *

He could feel her.

Her hands on his face.

Her thoughts, furious and full of grief, flooding his mind, battering his shields.

Damn you . . . you told me not to let him take me away. But what about you . . .

He'd like to tell her he wasn't going anywhere.

And he'd do it, too.

As soon as he could breathe.

Gone . . . She was gone. Everybody's voices and thoughts raged, and he lost hers in the thick of it. Lost himself in the pain of it, for just a minute, but then the pain, like a dragon, dragged him back into a state of semiawareness and he wanted to scream. Might have carved his chest open just to relieve the agony.

And still she wasn't there. Dru . . . he just wanted Dru . . .

He'd been shot before, and he was pretty sure it was less painful than taking a hit square in the chest with body armor.

Even unconscious, the pain was snaking into him, eating at him, firing away in his nerve endings . . .

Damn it, you can hear me. I know you can—

She was back.

Summoning what little strength he had, he flung out a hand.

And then she was there. Her hand in his. Tight, strong. Demanding.

Stay away. That was the one thought he could manage. *Stay the fuck away from Whitmore.*

He's dead, Dru told him. *Dead and done. And you . . . if you ever scare me like that again, I'll hurt you. You hear me?*

The pain pulled him back into its gaping maw. But it didn't matter. Dru was there. And she was safe.

And if he could ever manage to wake up . . .

THIRTY

Tucker watched from the sidelines as they loaded Crawford into an ambulance.

His head ached. Pounded like a son of a bitch.

All that power licking through the air wasn't helping, either.

Something soft butted against his ankle. Frowning, he looked down and saw a little fuzzball twining around his ankles. "Shoo." He nudged the cat gently with one booted foot.

As the skies ripped open and rain started to pound down, the cat gave a pitiful little *meow*.

Crouching down, Tucker sighed and stroked a gloved hand down her back. It was safe now. The rain dampened all the electrical currents in the air, and blissfully, some of the pain in his head receded. It had damn near split his brain in two, or at least it felt like it, what he'd done.

He'd seen Whitmore fire—felt the trajectory of the bullet

cleaving through the air. If it had been a sunny day, or if it had already been raining, it wouldn't have been possible. But with the storm so close, the air had been charged and he'd *felt* the bullet . . . felt it in a way he hadn't thought would even be possible. And he'd known what would happen.

"I tried to stop it altogether," he said to the cat.

She stared at him, looking rather regal despite her sopping wet fur.

"I wasn't able to. Bullets are a bitch."

She meowed in agreement.

Blowing out a breath, he reached for her and wasn't surprised when she let him pick her up. "You belonged to that fucker, huh?"

As she tucked her head against him, he felt the power train of a purr thrumming in her little body. "You need a decent home after that, I bet. I can't do much, but I'll feed you, at least. Let's blow this joint."

And before anybody could think to look for him, Tucker lost himself in the rain and the shadows, carrying a wet cat, who oddly wasn't too disturbed about being wet.

* * *

COLD—*so damned cold . . .*

Terror, for the longest time, gripped her. Death, something she'd longed for, was there. Just within her reach.

Horrid, really.

She'd come down here just to die.

In a shining burst of clarity, she realized she had only a few seconds . . . she could die.

Or she could try to live.

She knew what Thom would have wanted.

Clawing at the water, she struggled to the surface. But her clothes . . . they were so heavy, so, so heavy.

No, *she thought, as the darkness grew heavier and heavier . . .* I'm not going to die like this.

It was her clothing that would do her in. The dress. Had to do something—the water wasn't terribly deep and she couldn't swim, but he'd told her time and again nature would do much of the work for her—

That's my girl . . . his voice came to her on a whisper. Be strong. Be brave . . .

Her lungs screamed for air and she wanted so badly to breathe as she fumbled with them.

And then, she wasn't fumbling alone.

Panicked, she jerked away, but the hands that held her were strong. Unrelenting. And gentle as she was pulled to the surface.

"Be quiet," a man's voice whispered. Low and soft, smooth. And kind, she thought. Very kind. "Be quiet, or he might hear us and then we'll both die."

She looked up, found herself staring at a face that wasn't at all familiar to her. But it didn't matter. The hands hauling her out of the water were gentle. And his face was kind.

She would live.

Her heart might be broken.

But she would live.

* * *

DRU came awake, the burn of water in her lungs, choking . . .

And those memories in her head. Crystalline and bright, like it had just happened.

A face loomed in her mind.

The face . . . different.

Gray eyes, though. Gray eyes . . . she remembered those eyes.

Tucker. Damn it. Just how much more complicated would all of this get? How much more insane?

Yet . . . how insane was it really? Tucker, like Joss, in his own way, was a man she'd trusted from the very beginning. Although she couldn't remember anything more about him, just that brief, surreal flash, she didn't doubt it.

Sucking in a desperate breath, she clambered out of the chair, stumbled over to the window. Damn thing was sealed shut, though. Fucking hospitals. Had to breathe, had to.

Outside.

She'd go outside—

On unsteady legs, she made her way to the door and eased it open. She made it a few feet before she collapsed against the wall, covering her face with her hands as she slid down to the floor.

Enough, she thought. She'd seen enough. Dealt with enough. Now it was time to let her brain catch up to reality, she thought. Let everything settle into place.

"Hi."

Dru groaned at the woman's voice. "I'll get up in a minute," she mumbled, certain it was a nurse.

"Nah, you're fine. Matter of fact, I think I'll join you."

Startled, Dru jerked her head and looked over.

The woman's face . . . familiar.

"Shit," Dru whispered.

She smiled. "I look like my sister, don't I?"

Sister—

"My name is Vaughnne." She held out a hand.

Dru glanced down, not certain she was ready to touch.

"Ahhh . . ." A smiled curled Vaughnne's lips. "Sorry. Psychometric. You're touchy about being touched and all, right?"

"Pardon?"

"You pick up things through touch. Psychometric."

"Ah." Dru rubbed her head. "Sorry. Yes, I know what it means. I'm just . . . well, I'm not used to discussing it so openly."

Vaughnne stretched out her legs in front of her and sighed. "I'm telepathic. I was the one planted on the inside last night. And you . . ." She slid Dru a look. "One of the girls you tracked down here . . . it was my sister, Daylin."

"Daylin." Dru licked her lips, closing her eyes as the sound of that name brought an image to mind. Young. Arrogant . . . strong. She was one of the ones who'd fought Patrick, and tried to escape. He'd killed her for it, and killed her horribly. But that awful, horrible death had been one of those threads that had led Dru here. "I . . . I don't understand. If that girl had connections to the FBI, why . . ."

"Why . . . ?" Vaughnne shook her head. "Why, indeed?"

She blew out a breath and turned her ahead, staring at something neither of them could see. "My parents kicked me out of the house when I was fifteen . . . they wouldn't talk to me, wouldn't spit on me if I was on fire." Vaughnne said it without emotion, but her eyes were bitter and haunted. "If they'd called me . . . maybe I could have saved her."

Not knowing what else to say, Dru simply said, "I'm sorry."

Vaughnne nodded. "I never even knew she was in trouble," she whispered, her voice rough. "The job I do, all the shit I'm supposed to be capable of, and I couldn't save my own blood."

Dru said nothing. What could she say?

After a moment, Vaughnne blew out a breath and said, "I wanted to thank you. You went through hell, sticking with this the way you did. If you ever need a damn thing from me, I'm yours. I don't care what it is."

"I didn't do enough." Dru stared at the floor. She'd wanted to find them. Save them all. She'd failed.

"You did more than a million, ten million others would have done." Vaughnne paused and then said softly, "Maybe even more than I would have done for a total stranger. When you need me, call." She turned to leave.

A hundred, no, a thousand unasked questions buzzed into Dru's brain. "Wait!"

Vaughnne turned and looked back, one brow lifted.

"What's going to happen now?"

"What do you mean?" Vaughnne asked, looking puzzled.

"Just that . . . what happens? I killed Whitmore. I probably shouldn't have—he had to have information on how to track down the women he sold over the years. How . . ." The question faded away as the guilt rose inside her.

Sympathy glinted in Vaughnne's eyes. "Jones is probably already working that. He's got people around who can do things that make what you and I do look like parlor tricks." She shrugged and then winced, touching a hand to her head. "I've got a headache from hell. Look, I can't tell you *not* to worry about this . . . I know I'd be doing the same. But you did your part. More than. Jones can handle it from here. And he's good at it. He won't let this go, okay?"

Without another word, she disappeared.

Her chest tight, Dru stood up and slipped back into the room. Some of the misery, some of the guilt, shame, and horror inside her chest, melted away. It would linger, she knew. But it was a little easier to bear now.

Just inside the door, she stood there, watching Joss. He was so still, so quiet. His dark skin a few shades too pale against the white of the sheets. Face turned away, the stubble on his face thick, heavy.

Shit.

Her knees went all weak and wobbly and her heart skipped a

couple of beats before settling into a rhythm that almost resembled normal.

He was alive.

And he was *here*—

Joss . . .

Screw that damned dream.

Screw the misery that continued to linger in her chest.

Screw the regret and the shame.

Screw it all.

He was here.

She was here.

That was all that mattered.

Making her way over to him, she sat on the edge of the bed and laid her hand on his chest. Under her touch, he was warm, and she could feel the steady rise and fall of his breathing.

"You're here . . ."

Startled, she jerked her eyes up and saw him watching her from under slitted lashes.

With a weak smile, she murmured, "Of course I'm here. Where else would I be?"

He lifted a hand, covered hers.

"Tell me you're not going anywhere," he said, his voice broken, rough. "I think I'm stuck here for a day or two . . . my . . ." He closed his eyes, shook his head. "I think my head sort of went haywire and I . . . shit. If you leave, I'll have to crawl after you."

Dru was pretty sure her heart just about broke. "No." Bending down, she pressed her lips to his. "I think we've done enough chasing after each other."

"Enough chasing," he agreed. Catching the back of her neck, Joss held her close. A shudder wracked him. It hurt like hell, and he hoped he didn't break down and cry—never mind the fact that crying was for pussies. He just might have cried and been okay with it, but crying would *hurt*. His chest was on fire and every breath was agony. Crying wouldn't help, even if it was just a way to shed some of the emotion that swelled inside him . . . simply having her here.

She was here.

Finally.

Here.

Safe.

He swallowed the knot in his throat. "We start over. From here on out. Everything starts over."

She lifted her head, staring down at him.

"Is that what you want?"

"I have what I want." He closed his eyes. "You. Just you. Always you. Nothing else matters."

"Then there's no need for a do over . . . we accept everything that has happened . . . and go on from here." Her lips brushed his. "This is all terribly insane, you know. Terribly insane. You don't really know me."

"I do. I know what matters. I know I waited . . . all this time for you."

She eased backward and the look on her face made his bruised and battered heart ache even more. "I've remembered more. There are . . . pieces that keep trying to come together."

"And they don't matter. That life is done." He closed his eyes as the pain spread. "This life matters. Just this one. And now I have you . . . it's all I need."

This life . . .

Yeah. Dru studied his face, saw the pain he was trying to hide. Reaching for the call button, she pushed it despite the fact that he glared at her the entire time.

Ten minutes later, the drugs were cruising through Joss's system, thanks to the IV, and she sat down by him again, brushed his hair back from his face. "Is it . . . hard?" she asked. "Being in here? Is it too much with all the . . . um . . . however you want to call it, packed into your head?"

Joss smiled, and the grin was oddly . . . off. She decided that was the only way to describe it. Must have something to do with the painkillers. "No." He leaned his head back against the pillows, that smile still on his face. "The pain did a major reboot—shock and injury can do that. I'm a clean slate right now. Nothing and nobody in my head but me. And I kinda like it."

"Nothing, huh?"

"Nothing . . ." His lids drooped. "Except you. You're always there. Always have been. And now you're here, too."

"Yeah." She went to his side. Took his hand. "I'm here, too." Nothing was certain for her, except that. She was here . . . this was exactly where she wanted to be. Where she'd stay.